WAKE *of* VULTURES

THE SHADOW: BOOK ONE

Lila Bowen

www.orbitbooks.net

Copyright © 2015 by D. S. Dawson
Map illustration by Tim Paul

Orbit
Hachette Book Group
1290 Avenue of the Americas
New York, NY 10104
www.orbitbooks.net

Printed in the United States of America

RRD-C

First edition: October 2015

10 9 8 7 6 5 4 3 2 1

Orbit is an imprint of Hachette Book Group.
The Orbit name and logo are trademarks of Little, Brown Book Group Limited.

The Hachette Speakers Bureau provides a wide range of authors for speaking events. To find out more, go to www.hachettespeakersbureau.com or call (866) 376-6591.

The publisher is not responsible for websites (or their content) that are not owned by the publisher.

Library of Congress Cataloging-in-Publication Data

Bowen, Lila.
    Wake of vultures / Lila Bowen.—First edition.
        pages cm.—(The shadow ; book one)
    ISBN 978-0-316-26431-0 (hardback)—ISBN 978-0-316-26430-3 (ebook)—ISBN 978-1-4789-0620-9 (audio book (downloadable))
    1. Racially mixed people—Fiction.   I. Title.
    PS3602.O895625W35 2015
    813'.6—dc23
                                                            2015010160

This one goes out to #WeNeedDiverseBooks,
Gangstagrass, and everyone who bucks the binary.

MAP of
DURANGO
TERRITORY
of THE FEDERAL REPUBLIC of
AMERICA

According to the Newest and most exact Observations of
Timothy dePaul, Geographer

CHAPTER 1

Nettie Lonesome had two things in the world that were worth a sweet goddamn: her old boots and her one-eyed mule, Blue. Neither item actually belonged to her. But then again, nothing did. Not even the whisper-thin blanket she lay under, pretending to be asleep and wishing the black mare would get out of the water trough before things went south.

The last fourteen years of Nettie's life had passed in a shriveled corner of Durango territory under the leaking roof of this wind-chapped lean-to with Pap and Mam, not quite a slave and nowhere close to something like a daughter. Their faces, white and wobbling as new butter under a smear of prairie dirt, held no kindness. The boots and the mule had belonged to Pap, right up until the day he'd exhausted their use, a sentiment he threatened to apply to her every time she was just a little too slow with the porridge.

"Nettie! Girl, you take care of that wild filly, or I'll put one in her goddamn skull!"

Pap got in a lather when he'd been drinking, which was pretty much always. At least this time his anger was aimed at a critter instead of Nettie. When the witch-hearted black filly had first shown up on the farm, Pap had laid claim and pronounced her a fine chunk of flesh and a sign of the Creator's good graces. If Nettie broke her and sold her for a decent price, she'd be closer to paying back Pap for taking her in as a baby when nobody else had wanted her but the hungry, circling vultures. The value Pap placed on feeding and housing a half-Injun, half-black orphan girl always seemed to go up instead of down, no matter that Nettie did most of the work around the homestead these days. Maybe that was why she'd not been taught her sums: Then she'd know her own damn worth, to the penny.

But the dainty black mare outside wouldn't be roped, much less saddled and gentled, and Nettie had failed to sell her to the cowpokes at the Double TK Ranch next door. Her idol, Monty, was a top hand and always had a kind word. But even he had put a boot on Pap's poorly kept fence, laughed through his mustache, and hollered that a horse that couldn't be caught couldn't be sold. No matter how many times Pap drove the filly away with poorly thrown bottles, stones, and bullets, the critter crept back under cover of night to ruin the water by dancing a jig in the trough, which meant another blistering trip to the creek with a leaky bucket for Nettie.

Splash, splash. Whinny.

Could a horse laugh? Nettie figured this one could.

Pap, however, was a humorless bastard who didn't get a joke that didn't involve bruises.

"Unless you wanna go live in the flats, eatin' bugs, you'd best get on, girl."

Nettie rolled off her worn-out straw tick, hoping there weren't any scorpions or centipedes on the dusty dirt floor. By the moon's scant light she shook out Pap's old boots and shoved her bare feet into into the cracked leather.

Splash, splash.

The shotgun cocked loud enough to be heard across the border, and Nettie dove into Mam's old wool cloak and ran toward the stockyard with her long, thick braids slapping against her back. Mam said nothing, just rocked in her chair by the window, a bottle cradled in her arm like a baby's corpse. Grabbing the rawhide whip from its nail by the warped door, Nettie hurried past Pap on the porch and stumbled across the yard, around two mostly roofless barns, and toward the wet black shape taunting her in the moonlight against a backdrop of stars.

"Get on, mare. Go!"

A monster in a flapping jacket with a waving whip would send any horse with sense wheeling in the opposite direction, but this horse had apparently been dancing in the creek on the day sense was handed out. The mare stood in the water trough and stared at Nettie like she was a damn strange bird, her dark eyes blinking with moonlight and her lips pulled back over long, white teeth.

Nettie slowed. She wasn't one to quirt a horse, but if the mare kept causing a ruckus, Pap would shoot her without a second or even a first thought—and he wasn't so deep in his bottle that he was sure to miss. Getting smacked with rawhide had to be better than getting shot in the head, so Nettie doubled up her shouting and prepared herself for the heartache that would accompany the smack of a whip on unmarred hide. She didn't even own the horse, much less the right to beat it. Nettie had grown up trying to be the opposite of Pap, and hurting something that didn't come with claws and a stinger went against her grain.

"Shoo, fool, or I'll have to whip you," she said, creeping closer. The horse didn't budge, and for the millionth time, Nettie swung the whip around the horse's neck like a rope, all gentle-like. But, as ever, the mare tossed her head at exactly the right moment, and the braided leather snickered against the wooden water trough instead.

"Godamighty, why won't you move on? Ain't nobody wants you, if you won't be rode or bred. Dumb mare."

At that, the horse reared up with a wild scream, spraying water as she pawed the air. Before Nettie could leap back to avoid the splatter, the mare had wheeled and galloped into the night. The starlight showed her streaking across the prairie with a speed Nettie herself would've enjoyed, especially if it meant she could turn her back on Pap's dirt-poor farm and no-good cattle company forever. Doubling over to stare at her scuffed boots while she caught her breath, Nettie felt her hope disappear with hoofbeats in the night.

A low and painfully unfamiliar laugh trembled out of the barn's shadow, and Nettie cocked the whip back so that it was ready to strike.

"Who's that? Jed?"

But it wasn't Jed, the mule-kicked, sometimes stable boy, and she already knew it.

"Looks like that black mare's giving you a spot of trouble, darlin'. If you were smart, you'd set fire to her tail."

A figure peeled away from the barn, jerky-thin and slithery in a too-short coat with buttons that glinted like extra stars. The man's hat was pulled low, his brown hair overshaggy and his lily-white hand on his gun in a manner both unfriendly and relaxed that Nettie found insulting.

"You best run off, mister. Pap don't like strangers on his land, especially when he's only a bottle in. If it's horses you want, we ain't got none worth selling. If you want work and you're dumb and blind, best come back in the morning when he's slept off the mezcal."

"I wouldn't work for that good-for-nothing piss-pot even if I needed work."

The stranger switched sides with his toothpick and looked Nettie up and down like a horse he was thinking about stealing. Her fist tightened on the whip handle, her fingers going cold. She wouldn't defend Pap or his land or his sorry excuses for cattle, but she'd defend the only thing other than Blue that mostly belonged to her. Men had been pawing at her for two years now, and nobody'd yet come close to reaching her soft parts, not even Pap.

"Then you'd best move on, mister."

The feller spit his toothpick out on the ground and took a step forward, all quiet-like because he wore no spurs. And that was Nettie's first clue that he wasn't what he seemed.

"Naw, I'll stay. Pretty little thing like you to keep me company."

That was Nettie's second clue. Nobody called her pretty unless they wanted something. She looked around the yard, but all she saw were sand, chaparral, bone-dry cow patties, and the remains of a fence that Pap hadn't seen fit to fix. Mam was surely asleep, and Pap had gone inside, or maybe around back to piss. It was just the stranger and her. And the whip.

"Bullshit," she spit.

"Put down that whip before you hurt yourself, girl."

"Don't reckon I will."

The stranger stroked his pistol and started to circle her. Nettie shook the whip out behind her as she spun in place to face him and hunched over in a crouch. He stopped circling when the barn yawned behind her, barely a shell of a thing but darker than sin in the corners. And then he took a step forward, his silver pistol out and flashing starlight. Against her will, she took a step back. Inch by inch he drove her into the barn with slow, easy steps. Her feet rattled in the big boots, her fingers numb around the whip she had forgotten how to use.

"What is it you think you're gonna do to me, mister?"

It came out breathless, god damn her tongue.

His mouth turned up like a cat in the sun. "Something nice. Something somebody probably done to you already. Your master or pappy, maybe."

She pushed air out through her nose like a bull. "Ain't got a pappy. Or a master."

"Then I guess nobody'll mind, will they?"

That was pretty much it for Nettie Lonesome. She spun on her heel and ran into the barn, right where he'd been pushing her to go. But she didn't flop down on the hay or toss down the mangy blanket that had dried into folds in the broke-down, three-wheeled rig. No, she snatched the sickle from the wall and spun to face him under the hole in the roof. Starlight fell down on her ink-black braids and glinted off the parts of the curved blade that weren't rusted up.

"I reckon I'd mind," she said.

Nettie wasn't a little thing, at least not height-wise, and she'd figured that seeing a pissed-off woman with a weapon in each hand would be enough to drive off the curious feller and send him back to the whores at the Leaping Lizard, where he apparently belonged. But the stranger just laughed and cracked his knuckles like he was glad for a fight and would take his pleasure with his fists instead of his twig.

"You wanna play first? Go on, girl. Have your fun. You think you're facin' down a coydog, but you found a timber wolf."

As he stepped into the barn, the stranger went into shadow for just a second, and that was when Nettie struck. Her whip whistled for his feet and managed to catch one ankle, yanking

6

hard enough to pluck him off his feet and onto the back of his fancy jacket. A puff of dust went up as he thumped on the ground, but he just crossed his ankles and stared at her and laughed. Which pissed her off more. Dropping the whip handle, Nettie took the sickle in both hands and went for the stranger's legs, hoping that a good slash would keep him from chasing her but not get her sent to the hangman's noose. But her blade whistled over a patch of nothing. The man was gone, her whip with him.

Nettie stepped into the doorway to watch him run away, her heart thumping underneath the tight muslin binding she always wore over her chest. She squinted into the long, flat night, one hand on the hinge of what used to be a barn door, back before the church was willing to pay cash money for Pap's old lumber. But the stranger wasn't hightailing it across the prairie. Which meant...

"Looking for someone, darlin'?"

She spun, sickle in hand, and sliced into something that felt like a ham with the round part of the blade. Hot blood spattered over her, burning like lye.

"Goddammit, girl! What'd you do that for?"

She ripped the sickle out with a sick splash, but the man wasn't standing in the barn, much less falling to the floor. He was hanging upside-down from a cross-beam, cradling his arm. It made no goddamn sense, and Nettie couldn't stand a thing that made no sense, so she struck again while he was poking around his wound.

This time, she caught him in the neck. This time, he fell.

The stranger landed in the dirt and popped right back up into a crouch. The slice in his neck looked like the first carving in an undercooked roast, but the blood was slurry and smelled like rotten meat. And the stranger was sneering at her.

"Girl, you just made the biggest mistake of your short, useless life."

Then he sprang at her.

There was no way he should've been able to jump at her like that with those wounds, and she brought her hands straight up without thinking. Luckily, her fist still held the sickle, and the stranger took it right in the face, the point of the blade jerking into his eyeball with a moist squish. Nettie turned away and lost most of last night's meager dinner in a noisy splatter against the wall of the barn. When she spun back around, she was surprised to find that the fool hadn't fallen or died or done anything helpful to her cause. Without a word, he calmly pulled the blade out of his eye and wiped a dribble of black glop off his cheek.

His smile was a cold, dark thing that sent Nettie's feet toward Pap and the crooked house and anything but the stranger who wouldn't die, wouldn't scream, and wouldn't leave her alone. She'd never felt safe a day in her life, but now she recognized the chill hand of death, reaching for her. Her feet trembled in the too-big boots as she stumbled backward across the bumpy yard, tripping on stones and bits of trash. Turning her back on the demon man seemed intolerably stupid. She just had to get past the round pen, and then she'd be halfway to the house. Pap wouldn't be worth much by now, but he had a gun by his side. Maybe the stranger would give up if he saw a man instead of just a half-breed girl nobody cared about.

Nettie turned to run and tripped on a fallen chunk of fence, going down hard on hands and skinned knees. When she looked up, she saw butternut-brown pants stippled with blood and no-spur boots tapping.

"Pap!" she shouted. "Pap, help!"

She was gulping in a big breath to holler again when the

stranger's boot caught her right under the ribs and knocked it all back out. The force of the kick flipped her over onto her back, and she scrabbled away from the stranger and toward the ramshackle round pen of old, gray branches and junk roped together, just barely enough fence to trick a colt into staying put. They'd slaughtered a pig in here, once, and now Nettie knew how he felt.

As soon as her back fetched up against the pen, the stranger crouched in front of her, one eye closed and weeping black and the other brim-full with evil over the bloody slice in his neck. He looked like a dead man, a corpse groom, and Nettie was pretty sure she was in the hell Mam kept threatening her with.

"Ain't nobody coming. Ain't nobody cares about a girl like you. Ain't nobody gonna need to, not after what you done to me."

The stranger leaned down and made like he was going to kiss her with his mouth wide open, and Nettie did the only thing that came to mind. She grabbed up a stout twig from the wall of the pen and stabbed him in the chest as hard as she damn could.

She expected the stick to break against his shirt like the time she'd seen a buggy bash apart against the general store during a twister. But the twig sunk right in like a hot knife in butter. The stranger shuddered and fell on her, his mouth working as gloppy red-black liquid bubbled out. She didn't trust blood anymore, not after the first splat had burned her, and she wasn't much for being found under a corpse, so Nettie shoved him off hard and shot to her feet, blowing air as hard as a galloping horse.

The stranger was rolling around on the ground, plucking at his chest. Thick clouds blotted out the meager starlight, and she had nothing like the view she'd have tomorrow under the white-hot, unrelenting sun. But even a girl who'd never killed a man before knew when something was wrong. She kicked him over with the toe of her boot, tit for tat, and he was light as a tumbleweed when he landed on his back.

The twig jutted up out of a black splotch in his shirt, and the slice in his neck had curled over like gone meat. His bad eye was a swamp of black, but then, everything was black at midnight. His mouth was open, the lips drawing back over too-white teeth, several of which looked like they'd come out of a panther. He wasn't breathing, and Pap wasn't coming, and Nettie's finger reached out as if it had a mind of its own and flicked one big, shiny, curved tooth.

The goddamn thing fell back into the dead man's gaping throat. Nettie jumped away, skitty as the black filly, and her boot toe brushed the dead man's shoulder, and his entire body collapsed in on itself like a puffball, thousands of sparkly motes piling up in the place he'd occupied and spilling out through his empty clothes. Utterly bewildered, she knelt and brushed the pile with trembling fingers. It was sand. Nothing but sand. A soft wind came up just then and blew some of the stranger away, revealing one of those big, curved teeth where his head had been. It didn't make a goddamn lick of sense, but it could've gone far worse.

Still wary, she stood and shook out his clothes, noting that everything was in better than fine condition, except for his white shirt, which had a twig-sized hole in the breast, surrounded by a smear of black. She knew enough of laundering and sewing to make it nice enough, and the black blood on his pants looked, to her eye, manly and tough. Even the stranger's boots were of better quality than any that had ever set foot on Pap's land, snakeskin with fancy chasing. With her own, too-big boots, she smeared the sand back into the hard, dry ground as if the stranger had never existed. All that was left was the four big panther teeth, and she put those in her pocket and tried to forget about them.

After checking the yard for anything livelier than a scorpion, she rolled up the clothes around the boots and hid them in the old rig in the barn. Knowing Pap would pester her if she left signs of a scuffle, she wiped the black glop off the sickle and hung it up, along with the whip, out of Pap's drunken reach. She didn't need any more whip scars on her back than she already had.

Out by the round pen, the sand that had once been a devil of a stranger had all blown away. There was no sign of what had almost happened, just a few more deadwood twigs pulled from the lopsided fence. On good days, Nettie spent a fair bit of time doing the dangerous work of breaking colts or doctoring cattle in here for Pap, then picking up the twigs that got knocked off and roping them back in with whatever twine she could scavenge from the town. Wood wasn't cheap, and there wasn't much of it. But Nettie's hands were twitchy still, and so she picked up the black-splattered stick and wove it back into the fence, wishing she lived in a world where her life was worth more than a mule, more than boots, more than a stranger's cold smile in the barn. She'd had her first victory, but no one would ever believe her, and if they did, she wouldn't be cheered. She'd be hanged.

That stranger—he had been all kinds of wrong. And the way that he'd wanted to touch her—that felt wrong, too. Nettie couldn't recall being touched in kindness, not in all her years with Pap and Mam. Maybe that was why she understood horses. Mustangs were wild things captured by thoughtless men, roped and branded and beaten until their heads hung low, until it took spurs and whips to move them in rage and fear. But Nettie could feel the wildness inside their hearts, beating under skin that quivered under the flat of her palm. She didn't break a horse, she gentled it. And until someone touched her with that same kindness, she would continue to shy away, to bare her teeth and lower her head.

Someone, surely, had been kind to her once, long ago. She could feel it in her bones. But Pap said she'd been tossed out like trash, left on the prairie to die. Which she almost had, tonight. Again.

Pap and Mam were asleep on the porch, snoring loud as thunder. When Nettie crept past them and into the house, she had four shiny teeth in one fist, a wad of cash from the stranger's pocket, and more questions than there were stars.

CHAPTER

2

Nettie barely slept a wink that night. Every time her eyes blinked shut, she imagined the stranger pulling himself together, the sand shifting back into the shape of something like a man and slithering into the house past Pap sleeping on the porch. One eye dripping black, he'd rise up like a rattler, snatch his teeth from inside her boot, poke them back into his gums, and rip her throat out.

After the third time she jolted up with a fright, alone in the dark with a stick-knife in her fist, she figured to hell with it and just got on up. Despite the drenching Durango heat, she'd taken to dressing like a bandito's grandmother with one of Pap's old, faded shirts over her bound chest, baggy pants held up by a rope, and a moth-gnawed serape over that. The less the folks of Gloomy Bluebird could see she was a girl, the less trouble they gave her.

Mam and Pap had taken to sending her on all their errands into town, considering they owed so many debts. Nettie'd learned that if she kept her head down and sucked in her cheeks, folks usually took pity and gave her the tail end of a sack of cornmeal or their most pitiful, nonlaying chicken. At first, she'd been embarrassed. But then she'd overheard two of the old biddy church ladies whispering about how shameful it was for Pap to send his half-breed slave pup around to beg, and she realized that they counted her for less than a dog and Pap only slightly more than that.

Mam and Pap Lonesome were of old East stock, pale as salt fish and just as odorous, with matching hay-colored hair and blue eyes that seemed ever confused thanks to eyelashes and eyebrows as light as dandelion fuzz. The pair were shapeless and old enough to look like someone else's aunt. Nettie couldn't have been more different, with medium brown skin that could've been called liver chestnut, if she'd been a horse worth noticing. Her hair was thick and frizzy, a dead giveaway to anyone trying to puzzle out her breed. Half black and half Injun, or maybe Aztecan; any way you added it up, the end result was somehow less than the individual components. She was built tall and narrow like a half-starved antelope, with eyes as dark and thick as a storm-mad creek and high cheekbones framing a mouth that had little reason to smile. She was ugly, was all they'd told her. But she didn't find them beautiful, so what did it matter? The entire town was an eyesore.

It was widely agreed that Gloomy Bluebird was a stupid name for a town, especially considering Old Ollie Hampstead had shot the only bluebird they had back in 1822, right outside what passed as a general store. The damn thing had been stuffed and posed with little skill and now sat proudly on the storekeeper's counter as a reminder of what looking cheerful and bright would get you in a town as dusty as an old maid's britches. Nettie herself had seen a bluebird when she was just a little thing, hunting lizards out by the creek. When she'd run home to tell Mam, she'd been told to go fetch a switch for lying. Over time, she'd come to believe she must've seen a crow.

But crows didn't have red bellies, did they? At least the town lived up to the gloomy part.

The excitement of last night had burned off, and Nettie was feeling downright gloomy herself, like some part of her had blown away with the impossible, sparkling sand. A strange thing had happened, and she had no one to tell, no one she trusted enough to question. Being alone wasn't so bad when nothing ever changed, but now Nettie didn't trust herself, and she was generally the only person she could trust.

Although Pap handled most of her punishment, Mam had once thrashed her for lying about a bluebird, and then thrashed her again when she'd started her monthlies and ruined an old striped mattress and screamed that she was dying. How was she supposed to know that was what women did? Nettie didn't reckon much about the world, but she knew that what happened last night had changed things as much as her flux blood. The world was suddenly more dangerous, but she had no idea why or how to protect herself from it. Seemed like the best way to keep her skin was to get on with breakfast and not say a danged thing, to hide it like she hid everything else.

When she went to shake her boots for scorpions, it was four pointed teeth that fell out. Considering no crevice of the shack was safe from Mam's quick fingers, Nettie shoved them into the little leather bag she kept tied around her waist with what few precious things she'd found over the years. A glittery white arrowhead, hardly chipped. A shiny gold button with a bugle on it. A wolf claw, or something like it. A penny given to her once in the town when she'd been kicked in the leg by a frachetty horse. She'd kept a piece of dirt-dusted ribbon candy some town brat had dropped in the pouch for two weeks once, allowing herself one suck a day. The four teeth added a weight barely felt, but she stood a mite taller. Whatever that stranger had been, she'd won. And that felt pretty goddamn good.

Mam and Pap weren't up, of course. They gave the sun time to stretch and get cozy before they stopped snoring. It was almost peaceful, setting up the porridge in the pot and watching the skillet shimmer with fatback grease. She always loved snatching warm eggs from under the scrawny, sleepy hens; this brood was the result of Pap's once-a-year victory at the poker table. They'd definitely seen harder times, although Nettie didn't much get to enjoy the bounty herself. If Mam and Pap left any eggs on their plates, that was usually treat enough.

The sun came up so fast that if you weren't watching careful, you'd miss it. For just a second, it was a flat circle, hot-red and bleeding all over the soft, purple clouds. Nettie stared at it as long as she could, not blinking, then leaned over to turn the eggs, and when she looked again, the sun sat high and white, relentlessly beating down on the endless prairie. Sunset, at least, took its time, nice and lazy. She liked the colors of it, and the way that no one could own the sun. It couldn't be compelled, couldn't be roped. You could yell at it all day long, threaten and plead and cuss, and the sun would not budge a goddamn inch. It was what it was, and it took its damn time about it.

But Nettie had fewer choices, so she quickly bolted down her small share of the porridge. Not only because Mam and Pap would give her an earful if they woke up with her in the house, but also because she wanted to mosey over to the Double TK before the surlier of the cowboys were awake and taking out their hangovers on whoever happened by. The ranch next door was far richer than Pap's, considering they had more than a one-eyed mule, two nags for renting, a herd of cattle too thin for the butcher to carve, and one milk cow that barely squirted enough milk for weak porridge. Mam had sent her toddling over to the Double TK for the first time to have a knife sharpened when she was just five years old, and Monty had taken her on like a lost pup. The old cowpoke had told her, years later, that they'd figured her for a boy at first, as she'd been in britches and had a shorn head. But since she'd been mannerly and offered to help the wranglers by sweeping out the pen or tossing rocks at vultures, they'd generally tolerated her presence.

Over the years, she'd learned by watching Monty and had figured out better ways to work a colt than using Pap's whip. She was awful shy of the other cowpokes and never went near the ranch house or Boss Kimble, but Monty said he was right glad for her calm hand with the horses and general quietude. He was still thin and tough as leather, with a luxurious mustache, but she'd noticed that in the last couple of years, Monty had saved the wilder horses for her visits and chosen gentler mounts for himself, and that his mustache had gone to gray.

On her way to the Double TK, she stopped to feed the few critters Pap hadn't used up yet. Blue greeted her with his usual hollering, and she gave him a once-over and a fine scratch and fed him a precious handful of grain, plus a bite she'd held back from the porridge. He pressed his big, ugly mule nose over her shoulder, and she leaned into his skinny chest and breathed in his good horse smell. He didn't know he wasn't a horse, and he didn't know he was ugly. Pap's swayback mare, Fussy, took the grain and turned her tail, just as sour as her owner, and the aged nag they called Dusty refused to get up off the ground. The wild black mare was still gone and the water trough still clean, thank heavens. Nettie had already fed the cow and scattered the morning's corn for the chickens, but the poor things crowded around her with hopeful clucking. It was a sad joke, calling it a ranch.

Before heading off, Nettie snuck into the other barn to see if the stranger's clothes were still there. They were, rolled up tight on the old rig's seat beside his hat, which was rugged and new and featured cunning strings to keep it on a feller's head. For a reason she couldn't explain, she tried it on and found it a good fit. With the wide brim pulled down and her pigtails tucked up underneath, maybe people would notice her even less. If asked, she could just say she'd found the hat floating in the creek. By the time she'd walked past the fence and Pap's ranch was just a shimmer on the horizon, the hat felt like it was part of her body and always had been.

Slipping under the fence to the Double TK, Nettie felt instantly calmer, almost at peace. It was business as usual on Boss Kimble's land, just a passel of grown men doing men's work, and she liked the feeling of being part of the simple but effective machinery. She headed toward the colt pens, where Monty and Poke sat on the rail as Jar clung to a bronc's back, and poorly at that. Monty shouted easy encouragement while old Poke leaned out and hollered through cupped, stubby hands about how Jar rode like a one-legged frog. Which he did, a little, as the young cowpoke was fine on his feet but all knees and elbows in the saddle. As Nettie got closer, she admired the bronc crow-hopping around the round pen—a big, bone-white stallion. No way a proud, uptight feller like Jar could break a mustang like that, especially not with his saddle cinched so tight. She couldn't help smirking.

"I got a penny says he falls off within a minute," she called, feeling lucky and reckless in her fine new hat.

Monty and Poke turned with good-natured smiles. Poke pulled out his dented watch while Monty fetched up a penny out of his disreputable pants, which looked as though they'd been made out of the curtains in a whore's bedroom, all velvet with gold curlicues.

"I'll take that bet, Nat," Monty hollered.

He never called her Nettie or treated her like a girl, even though he knew well enough what she was. When she'd started her monthlies, Mam had tried to set her up in skirts, but she'd ripped the hated things into strips and used them to bind her growing chest instead. Mam had given up and wished her quietly to Hell, so long as she kept cooking and cleaning and breaking colts. Monty had called her Little Lady once around that time, and she'd whipped out her jackknife, all fierce and cold, and told him that she was no girl, and he'd nodded, all thoughtful, and started calling her Nat instead. It was one of the many reasons she all but worshipped him.

Just now, he was looking at her with his head cocked and a friendly grin. "Nice hat. Who'd you kill for it?"

Goose bumps rose on her arms, and she pulled the hat down lower. "Nobody you know. Found it in the creek." Hitching up her too-big britches, Nettie climbed to sit by Monty on the top rail of the round pen. She'd always admired the clean, white boards of the Double TK's fencing. Of course, you couldn't stab a stranger in the heart with one of their fence boards, but they sure looked nice.

"How long's he been working that white stallion?"

Monty rubbed the curled end of his gray mustache between two fingers. "Not long. Big fellow came in with the raid last night. Boss wants him broke right fast. Might keep him for himself, if he has a gentle gait. Otherwise, he'll be the nicest fancy in the territory."

Jar flew off said horse in a graceful arc and landed, spread-eagled, in the dust. He rolled to the side right as the big bronc's dish-sized hooves hammered the dirt where the boy's so-called handsome face had been just seconds ago. Before the bronc could stomp again, Jar had skittered back to the edge of the round pen and rolled under the boards to safety. Monty held up a shiny penny and winked at Nettie.

"You beat his time, Nat, and I'll double your winnings. Hell, I'll give you a nickel."

Nettie admired the big bronc trotting around the pen, always keeping a sharp, intelligent eye on the four folks watching him back. Jar climbed up next to Poke and mopped off his face with a hanky that had seen better days.

"Big white bastard. Boss deserves him," Jar said.

Nettie slipped off the fence, wriggled out of her serape, and stood to face the bronc, watching him watch her. Poor feller's saddle was too narrow for his withers, his girth was too tight, and his bridle pulled at his lips, giving him a meaner look than she liked.

"Gimme a rope, Poke."

Poke threw his lasso to her, and she caught it in midair. The bronc stomped a foot, but before he could decide what sort of gangly, dangerous critter she might be, she'd looped him around the neck with a gentle toss. He reared back, first off, but she held tight and gentle, like Monty had taught her. When he stepped back, she went with him. *You can't force a horse, but you can't let him force you, neither*, the old cowpoke always said. As she approached the stallion, calm and murmuring sweet words, she looped the slack from the rope and watched for him to lick a little. The wranglers on the fence whispered, and she heard the clank of coins as they placed their bets.

When she'd got up to the bronc's side, she reached to stroke his neck. His white skin shivered, and dust came away on her fingertips.

"Ho, big feller. We're gonna be friends."

The horse's ears flickered back and his eye stuck to her as she undid the cinch and knocked the saddle off his back, leaving a sweaty stain. The bronc bowed his head and danced in place as he shook and blew air. Nettie smiled and touched him all over. When she got to his face, she went straight for the throat-latch and then slipped the whole bridle off his ears. Once the reins were over his head, the horse stretched out his neck like he'd grown two sizes.

"Thought we taught you how to break a bronc, Nat. Nobody gets paid for settin' 'em free," Jar hollered, but Monty only snickered.

"Somebody else taught me you've got to loosen a creature up to get what you want," she whispered so only the bronc could hear.

A rope halter hung on the other side of the round pen, and she walked the bronc over there with Poke's lasso loose around his neck. He followed, not like he really wanted to, but like he was willing to see what her next idea might be. With fingers gentle as last night's rare breeze, she slipped the halter over the bronc's nose and ears and tossed down Poke's lariat. The horse let her pull his face close, and she blew into his twitching pink nostrils. Murmuring all along, she walked him a bit, turned him, got him to cross over his back hooves so she had control of his haunches. That was where all the power was—in the rump.

And when the horse had mostly got used to doing what she wanted, she slipped off her boots, grabbed a handful of mane and rein, kicked up off the fence boards, and launched herself onto the white bronc's broad, sweaty back.

Nettie had rarely been so high up, but she only had a second to enjoy the view, as the surprised bronc crow-hopped sideways. Still, it was nothing like the bucking he'd put Jar through, so she just tightened her knees and held on while he tried to puzzle out what was clinging to his back. The cowpokes took up hollering, trying to excite the horse into dumping her, but she clung tight and let the bronc wiggle out his worries. She knew the exact moment the fight drained out of him—when he realized she wasn't trying to fight him at all. She was just trying to go with him. His front hooves hit the ground, and he shook his head and craned his neck around to stare at her.

Patting his thick neck, Nettie murmured, "Good boy."

The horse blew air, and the wranglers on the fence clapped and hollered. She gave the stallion a squeeze and urged him into a walk. He'd be a fine horse with a little care, and not the kind a puffed-up feller like Jar was likely to give him. The bronc still looked like he wanted to take a chunk out of Jar's side as they passed the cowpokes seated on the fence. Poke's wide pumpkin face had cracked into a jack-o'-lantern grin, and Monty held up a nickel, a rare sight for Nettie Lonesome.

"Get him under saddle today, and I'll give you a quarter more."

Nettie just nodded and nudged the bronc into a trot. She'd never imagined such riches as a nickel, much less a whole quarter.

Until she remembered the roll of money she'd taken out of the stranger's sand-dusted pocket last night. The dollars were wound up tight like a cactus bud, so much largess that she couldn't really figure it and knew she'd get beaten if she tried to use any of the bills in town. A quarter she could maybe get away with, though. In between the hat and the quarter, she figured killing that stranger had been a blessing in disguise.

In a few hours, she had the big bronc under saddle and gentle as a kitten, and thirty cents in her little leather bag.

"It's 'cause Nat's so skinny," Jar grumbled, rubbing a bruise on his ass. "Ain't fair."

"You're just as skinny as Nat, Jar. But you're a helluva lot meaner." Monty hadn't seemed put out to give her the coins, not at all. Probably because the Boss offered his official hands a dollar for turning a demon bronc into a trustworthy mount. Not that Nettie minded; it was thirty cents more than she'd had yesterday. She could feel it thumping against her leg as she clucked the white stallion into a gentle canter that would make any so-called gentleman proud.

When the lunch bell rang, Monty jerked his chin at her. Stunned, she nearly swallowed a fly; in ten years as Monty's shadow, this was her first invitation to join the wranglers for grub at the ranch house. She tied up the bronc, loosened his saddle, and patted his neck before slipping on her serape and tucking her pigtails more tightly under her hat. Other than finding her real family, Nettie's greatest wish in life was to get hired on as a wrangler, but Pap had told her a thousand times that nobody would hire a girl to do such work, not even as a cook, and especially considering the color of her skin. Her worst nightmare was a life spent at Pap and Mam's beck and call, never finding freedom. Probably not until they were dead. Or she was. As it stood, lunch with the men of the Double TK was as high as she knew how to hope.

Nettie walked slightly behind Monty, Poke, and Jar, pulling her hat down low and hoping the boss wouldn't notice her until she'd got a full plate and managed to put it away. The food was bound to be better and more plentiful at the Double TK, and she'd even had the luck of tasting beef jerky here a few times over the years, when Monty had seen her looking rangier than usual and had tossed her a few strips like it was nothing.

Inside the ranch house, the men ate like it was a paying business. Golden squares of sunlight painted the long table and glinted off spoons and tin plates. The boards were straighter and nicer than the ones at Pap and Mam's house, the chinks between them filled neatly, and a little cross hung on a blacksmith's nail by the open door, not that anyone prayed. Nobody much talked while they chewed, and the cook handed her a bowl like everyone else's, with jackrabbit stew slopping over the side and a crust of cornbread to mop it up with. She nodded her thanks and sat down on the bench between Monty and Poke.

Half starved as she was, Nettie was the first one done with her food. When she put her bowl down on the table, more stew appeared in it. She kept her jaw from dropping, nodded her thanks, and shoveled in the rest. All the cowpokes around her did the same until the old cook was scraping his ladle across the bottom of the black kettle and shrugging his shoulders in response to the cowpokes' complaints and lazy threats. There were nine fellers kept on at the Double TK, although that number went up and down depending on the time of year, when they were running a herd, who had the trots, who'd gotten excitable with a pistol, and who'd gotten stomped to death in the round pen or broken a leg during a stampede. Wrangling was a dangerous life, but so was living with two drunks who thought you were a slave, Nettie figured. She'd lost her best blanket smothering the flames the one time a still-drunk Mam had tried to cook breakfast when Nettie and Pap were both in bed with the ague, and she hadn't had the poor sense to fall sick again.

"Who gentled that fancy white bastard?"

Boss Kimble strolled in like a damn giant, a hanky delicately tucked into his shirtfront as he ate what looked to be half a fried prairie chicken. The wranglers' eyes shifted uncomfortably around the table, each man wishing he could own up to the feat. But the person who had done it couldn't admit it, so

Nettie placed her empty bowl on the table, wiped her lip, and settled her hat more firmly over her eyes.

"New boy did," Monty said, poking a thumb at her. "Name's Nat Lonesome."

Nettie's head jerked up, but not so much that anyone could see her complete surprise. Monty kicked her under the table, and she nodded to Boss Kimble in acknowledgment.

"Where'd you come from, son?"

Monty cleared his throat. And Nettie didn't like to lie, so, keeping her voice low and husky, she told what wasn't *quite* a lie, because Pap had threatened to send her there in chains more than once.

"They tell me Tanasi, but I don't rightly remember." Another kick—a warning. "Boss."

The boss nodded, eyeing her up and down. "I reckon you're too young to ride steer."

"Young, maybe. But I can break a bronc stallion, Boss. Reckon I can handle some piddly ol' cows."

"I got two more likely fancies from the last raid. You break 'em as nice as you gentled up that white stallion, and we'll take you on. Pays a dollar a week, meals and board. Bring your own saddle. That suit you?"

Nettie shook her head and swallowed down her heart, which had jumped right up into her throat. Lord, she wanted to say yes. But even though she'd been told all her life she was worth nothing, she still knew she was worth more than the first offer.

"Heard you pay a dollar a bronc, Boss. Heard Lance Morgan pays a dollar fifty." She made like she was looking over her shoulder, out the glassless window, and down toward the Morgan Ranch on the other side of the river. She remembered what Monty had told her once: If you got nothing to lose, you might as well double your bet.

The boss grunted, his eyes narrowing at her from a tan web of wrinkles. "Cowpokes got loose lips at the saloon, I reckon. That's top-hand pay. For real sons of Durango."

She bristled, snorted like a bull. "This is Durango, Boss, and I reckon I'm as real as anybody."

"But you're brown. And more importantly, you're green, son. A quarter a bronc and two dollars a week is the best I can do."

God damn if it wasn't everything Nettie'd ever wanted in her useless, goddamn life.

But it wasn't enough.

"I 'spect that's awful low, Boss, but if you let me break a bronc to keep for myself, you got a deal."

Boss Kimble stared at her, and she knew that he couldn't catch anything but a glint of her mud-dark eyes under the hat. But still she felt like he saw straight through to her soul and out the other side.

He chewed his fat lip for a minute and spit a glob of chicken fat on the dirt floor. "We took over a hundred head last night, so I reckon that's fair. Montague, make sure he don't choose nothing too fancy from the second-tier pen. Nothing fancy, you hear?"

"Well, sure, Boss. Sounds right fair."

"Then why we jawin' around the table, boys? Get back to work. I ain't paying you to stare."

The benches scooted back, and the wranglers battered Nettie with shoulder punches and claps on the back. She absorbed it all and nodded at each man, unable to hide her grin. It was possible that Pap would report her to the sheriff as a runaway, but as the sheriff was as drunk and useless as Pap, they'd probably never get around to chasing her and wouldn't think to look at the ranch next door. Ain't nobody had money to post for a reward, anyway. Probably couldn't even describe her clear enough for a Wanted poster, considering nobody ever looked her in the face. Now that Nettie thought about it, she couldn't figure out why she'd never tried to get on at a ranch before, considering she had all the skills a wrangler needed, minus the drinking and whoring.

Once they were outside, she punched Monty in the arm. She didn't have the right words, and *thank you* wasn't something she'd had cause to say before. All that came out was "Hope I do good."

But the old cowpoke understood. He punched her back, but softly. "It's gonna be hard, but you'll do fine. Now let's go pick out your bronc."

Out in the second-string pen, Nettie began to realize that Pap had been feeding her lies all her life. The second-string horses were far nicer than anything Pap had ever sold or traded, but he'd always claimed his horses were the best and it was Nettie's fault they never sold for shit.

Most of the mustangs in Boss Kimble's herd were just young, green, short, or rangy. One, like her old mule, Blue, was missing an eye and seemed mighty pissed over it. A few horses had hoof cracks or other injuries that would either heal up or turn them into stew, if they couldn't keep up on the trail. But there was plenty of fine horseflesh hiding in the herd, and she and Monty settled on a kind-eyed, dust-colored appaloosa mare as long and skinny as Nettie herself, too ugly to catch a gentleman's fancy. The black-freckled mare took to the saddle easily and had a jouncy trot, but her breath and hooves were good and she had an intelligent sort of face. Nettie decided to call her Ragdoll in memory of a toy she'd once seen a rich little girl with blonde curls showing off in Gloomy Bluebird's general store. She didn't know what to do with a doll, but damned if she hadn't wanted one with a powerful yearning.

As Nettie tested the mare's canter and reining, Monty explained that most folks didn't want to buy an ugly horse with almost no tail or mane, but that the native tribes bred 'em that way on purpose, so they wouldn't get tangled up in the brush. Nettie didn't care about the horse's looks, as hair and beauty meant very little to her. What was the point of valuing something a body could never possess? To that end, she walked right into town that afternoon holding two long, black pigtail braids and traded them and a few faded bills from the stranger's wad for a used Aztecan saddle. And there was another lie exposed: The storekeep was more than happy to take Nettie's money despite her skin color. Whether it was the way her chin stuck out now that she wasn't begging or the pride she felt after a day of good work, the man didn't even try to cheat her.

As the sun set and the cowpokes headed for the saloon, Nettie snuck back over to Pap's land and into the old barn. He called to her from the porch, scratching himself in his drawers, but she didn't answer. He wouldn't bother getting out of his rocking chair to look for her until next morning's breakfast didn't make itself, considering his dinner came in a bottle. So long as she left Blue behind, maybe he wouldn't call the sheriff at all. Nettie was getting surly and hard to feed as she grew out of being a child. To a man like Pap, half-breed horses were worth more than half-breed people, even ugly mules with only one eye. He said she was nothing but trouble, so maybe her leaving would be a kindness.

Fetching the stranger's clothes from the old wagon, she rubbed out the black spot on the shirt as well as she could and patched the hole over the breast with the saddle-mending kit

Pap never used. The stranger's fine boots fit well enough once she put on his thick socks, and there was even a sheath built into the leather that held a fancy knife shinier than any blade she'd seen before. His pants were of sturdier stuff, if an inch too short and speckled with black blood. Her old clothes and the stranger's fancy jacket she left behind, gold buttons and all, to perplex Pap the next time he went to hide in the wagon bed when the storekeep came knocking with unpaid bills.

As the stars trickled out, she went to sleep on the porch outside of the Double TK ranch house, dressed in the dead man's clothes, his hat pulled over her eyes and her shorn head pillowed on her new saddle. When she woke briefly in the middle of the night, she was sure she saw a coyote watching her from the yard. "Git!" she hollered, half-asleep and dreamy. It shook its head and loped away.

CHAPTER

3

Nettie was finishing up with a sweet little sorrel when things started to head downhill.

The first sign of trouble was a wretched sort of wailing, like maybe a dog was dying in the worst possible way. She slipped off the sorrel and tied the mare to a post to go see what was wrong. Sitting a raw horse wasn't wise when trouble was afoot, and she wasn't about to get thrown in her first week as an official wrangler.

"What is that?" she said, walking up to Monty, who'd sort of taken up as her boss, which was fine with her.

He shook his head, his walrus mustache waggling sadly. "I don't rightly. But it ain't good."

They took off in the same direction the other available wranglers were headed, passing by Jar and Thomas, who were dragging each other out of a half-dug well to see what the fuss was about. A few of the cowpokes pulled out their pistols and cocked them, and Poke had his rifle in hand. The wail got louder as they got closer to the creek, and then a lumpy sort of critter crawled up from the arroyo.

Boss Kimble galloped up on his dapple gray mare and skidded to a stop in front of the thing, which was mostly a pile of dirty blankets.

"You're on Double TK land. You here for good or ill?" He cocked his shiny silver pistol, pointed it straight down, and waited.

The face that turned up toward him was gaunt, copper brown, and wet with tears.

"Pia Mupitsi," the woman said, then collapsed.

They sent Nettie to tend the woman. She wasn't sure if it was because they secretly knew she was a female and figured she'd be better at doctoring or because she was the newest wrangler or because she was closest to the woman's own color and might provide some comfort. In any case, instead of breaking broncs under the unforgiving summer sky, she found herself spooning watered-down stew into a woman who couldn't quit shaking. A woman who only said two words, again and again.

Pia Mupitsi.

Since nobody at the Double TK knew what that meant, including Nettie, the boss had sent Jar to town for Gray Hawk, the peculiar fellow who played the piano at the Leaping Lizard Saloon. Nobody knew what tribe he was from or if he spoke any languages or if he knew how to do anything but play the piano, drink, cheat at cards, and waste his money on whores. But everyone figured he was the best shot at identifying what had scared the woman bad enough to keep her crawling along through the brush. Her hands and knees were shredded, her torn feet weeping into rags she'd ripped from one of her blankets. Poor critter was parched and gaunt as a crow's skeleton, her cheekbones sunken and her lips curling inward. Every now and then, she'd wake from her fever dreams and reach for Nettie's chin and mutter something that always ended in *Pia Mupitsi*. Nettie couldn't stand the scratch of her

31

dry, dusty fingers and leaned away, just out of reach. Being touched made her skittish.

The woman was in the midst of a troubling dream when the door to the bunkhouse opened and Gray Hawk brought in his peculiar funk of weeds and spices. He wore a patched-up costume taken off a dandy who'd been gutshot over a pair of aces at the Lizard, which contrasted oddly with his long, smooth hair and heavy, dark brows. He'd been known, from time to time, to get too drunk and forget how to play piano and start dancing around town with a blanket, howling mournful songs that made folk feel right unsettled and strangely guilty. Nettie was a little scared of him, but she was more scared of whatever *Pia Mupitsi* was. She moved away from the bottom bunk and slid her hat down, just in case Gray Hawk had the keen eyes of his namesake.

"She say anything?" he asked, his voice deep and almost musical, like drumbeats.

"Mumbling. Mostly about *Pia Mupitsi*, whatever that means."

Gray Hawk put a flat palm against the woman's forehead, and her eyes startled open. She took his hand in hers and started yammering, and Gray Hawk nodded and looked over her shredded palms and spoke back in the same liquid language. Finally, the woman shuddered and fell back, insensible, and Gray Hawk pulled a leather pouch out of his candy-striped vest. As he fussed with his weeds, Nettie figured it was okay to ask him questions, considering he was about as low as she was on the totem pole.

"What is that stuff?" She nodded at the greenish-gray powder in his hands.

"Medicine." He spit into the pile, mixed it with a finger. "Go. Bring me a fat piece of aloe."

Considering she was a wrangler now, Nettie didn't have to

do what he said. But considering Gray Hawk was helping the woman, she figured she might as well. When she returned with an oozing green finger of aloe, he smudged that into his mixture, sang something that sounded like smoke, and smeared the spit-goop all over the woman's hands as he chanted. She sighed in her sleep, a tiny smile of relief fetching up at the cracked corners of her mouth.

"She has come very far." Gray Hawk placed the woman's arms at her sides, her ripped-up palms facing up so that the gunk would stick. They looked like pecked-over meat, which is what she would've been if the cowhands hadn't heard her hollering. If the woman had crawled up on Pap's land, she would've been nothing more than pig food.

"Why?"

Instead of answering Nettie's question, Gray Hawk gently began to unwrap the woman's feet, but the rags were dry and stuck together. Before he could ask, Nettie brought him the ewer of water. He took the rag she'd been using to bathe the woman's forehead and dabbed the bindings until they pulled away to reveal feet just as chewed and raw as her hands. Nettie almost wanted to throw up, but that would've been goddamn embarrassing on her first day as a hand.

"Why, I asked?"

"Pia Mupitsi."

As if that told her any damn thing. Gray Hawk mixed up more of his spit medicine and applied it to the woman's feet. It stuck on the pink soles of her copper-brown feet like a cow's cud. Nettie's feet had looked a little like that once, when she'd been between shoes and waiting for Pap's old boots, and she winced in fellow feeling. Gray Hawk had used up all the aloe, so Nettie ran out for more and placed it in easy reach. He stared up at her, his brows scrunched down.

"What are you?" he asked.

Nettie shrugged. "Cowhand."

Gray Hawk shook his head. "Maybe. Now." After he'd drunk some water from the dipper to make more spit and finished slapping his medicine on the woman's feet, he took up a pipe and packed it full and leaned back against the bunk to smoke.

"Pia Mupitsi is Big Cannibal Owl. Comanche monster. Lives in a cave in the mountains. When little girls and boys are bad, Mama says be good, be quiet, or Pia Mupitsi will come steal you away. Pia Mupitsi comes in the night, puts children on a spike and takes them away forever."

A sharp chill sliced down Nettie's back. She hadn't given it much thought, but that stranger she'd met and killed two nights ago had been more monster than man, which meant that an owl-monster with a spike wasn't too far off from believable. But she wasn't going to let anyone know she was frightened of an imaginary bird.

"You saying she's scared of a bogeyman?" Nettie spit on the dirt-daubed boards for extra emphasis.

He shrugged, and warm brown skin flashed through the unpatched bullet holes in his shirt. "Those were her words. Said Pia Mupitsi came to her village, stole all the children. Stole her child. All they found was a foot. Little baby foot. With toothmarks on what was left of the skin."

"Where's the rest of her village?"

"Beyond her. The foot was found in her cradleboard. They turned her out."

"That ain't fair. Was it her baby's foot?"

He looked at her, cold and stark and solemn over his frilly pink coat. "To the Comanche, nothing is more precious than children. It is a very grave thing, to hurt a child. She is lucky they did not stake her in an anthill."

"She don't look lucky."

"She said she ain't. Said she wishes she was dead. Wants to know where the Rangers are, so that they will hunt Pia Mupitsi and take back the children."

Nettie made a sound that was a bitter thing, the reverse of a laugh. "The Rangers won't help the Comanche. Might as well wish the sheriff was sober and giving out penny candy."

"I told her that. She don't care." He smeared the last of his medicine on the woman's bleeding elbows and placed a wet rag over her head before leaving. "It would probably be better if she died."

A weight lifted off Nettie's bound chest as soon as she was out of the bunkhouse and back to sweating under the sun, where she belonged. You could trust the heat, trust the sun's honest light. The things that happened at night flat out didn't have the guts to take place under the watchful sun.

Monty was working the next horse, exhausting the poor critter to hell with his spurs. He was a good hand, but Nettie liked her way better. She'd picked out the next mare and readied her loop as she headed into the corral, giving Monty a salute. Sun and horses and heat: That was what she knew. As she got acquainted with the bay and introduced her to the feel of a blanket, Nettie tried to forget the fear in the woman's eyes and the weirdly familiar smell of Gray Hawk's medicine. She tried to forget the dark imaginings of a shining gleam of silver, of a monster owl blotting out the moon, of falling through stars, of a man falling apart to sand and leaving nothing but teeth behind. It worked about as well as trying to forget that she'd been brought up as a slave in a drunkard's house and that Pap and Mam might, at any moment, wobble over to the Double TK and ask if anybody'd seen a no-good half-breed that needed another whipping.

Goddammit. Memories only made life harder. From time to time, she had a little flash, kind of like a dream, that she thought might've been her life before Pap and Mam. For just a moment, she was warm and weightless and free, held close, and it made her chest constrict painfully, like her heart was too big to be contained by her body. Those flashes of golden light always felt better than anything she'd known since. She looked into the sun until her vision went over white. And then she broke the bay with tears in her eyes.

And then a rangy grulla.

Then a slicked-up black.

And then the dinner bell was ringing and Monty was watching her, one foot on the fence.

"Nearly a two-dollar day," he said with a grin. "Not bad, Nat."

She grinned back. It was good, being ribbed like a man. "Well, it ain't as good as that nickel I made yesterday, but I got a bit done."

They washed the sweat and red dust off their arms and the backs of their necks at the well, the cool water drying almost the second it plopped in the sand around their boots. Nettie couldn't help being glad she'd chopped off her pigtails. It was mighty easy to keep her hair clean now that she just had to run water through it with a hand and shake it off like a dog did. Felt goddamn good to have her hat on top of a wet mop, and she forgot to hide her eyes and her happiness as she walked into the ranch house.

"Where you from?" one of the wranglers asked, a seasonal fellow called Sil.

She shoved her hat down and turned away. "Tanasi I said. What of it?"

"Just bein' friendly."

But Nettie didn't want that kind of friendly, so she hurried to a different part of the table and sat with Monty and Poke. Dinner was ham and beans and cornbread, which suited her fine, especially considering as how she hadn't cooked a lick of it herself. Living with the wranglers was about her idea of heaven, outside of her unsettled time in the bunk with Gray Hawk and the constant worry that Pap would come sniffing around for her. She finished her supper first again and gladly took another scoop of beans and a cool slice of ham. The ranch boys didn't talk much while they ate, just listened to the music of spoons scraping on metal and the burps that burbled up at the end. When Monty rubbed his spare belly and pushed away from the table, she followed him out the door, but not so close that it looked like she was tagging along.

"Come on down to the saloon, Nat. Friday night means we'll get a show. And I do believe I owe you a drink."

"I don't drink."

He lowered his head, gave her the gimlet eye. "You will if you want to fit in with the wranglers. Man passes you a jug, you drink and give your thanks."

Nettie nodded. There were about a million ways to start a fight with a cowpoke, and she wanted to learn as many of them as possible so she could avoid them. Up until the night she'd stabbed the stranger, she'd never been in a fight, but she sure as shit knew the feel of fists and boot toes and would do her level best to avoid them in the future.

The whole ranch was headed to the saloon, seemed like.

Hobnailed boot heels kicked up clouds of dust to blot out the starlight, and good-natured joshing started up, with men shouting dares and slurs at each other like little boys. Nettie lingered in the back of the pack, staying behind Monty and doing her best to go unnoticed. It worked until Jar pushed through the double doors into the Leaping Lizard, spilling warm light into the street, along with smells Nettie had never known but recognized instantly. Perfume, wine, and fine cigars mixed with the more familiar scents of chewing tobacco and moonshine. She only hoped that whatever rotgut Monty planned to toast her with tasted better than the bull piss she'd sipped once from Pap's jug, trying to understand why he drank so much of the damn stuff. Best she could figure was he wanted to scrape off the lining of his stomach on a daily basis with the liquid equivalent of a sharpened spoon.

Although she'd spent all of her life in Gloomy Bluebird, Nettie had never set foot into the Leaping Lizard—or any building in the town proper, outside of the general store. Not even the church. It had been made clear from early on that she could beg at doorsteps but wasn't welcome beyond.

The saloon was a peculiar mix of cheapness and fancy, with warped boards that let in chunks of night sky next to rich red drapes over the stage, the fabric as deep and soft as a horse's winter coat. A crooked staircase wobbled up to a narrow balcony with three plain wood doors. And as the wranglers pulled out chairs and stools at the splintering tables and long, rickety bar, those doors opened, and out came women like Nettie had never seen in her life. Her mouth plopped right damn open with surprise.

The men saw them, too, and the commotion that started up was about the same as the cowboys gave a good bronc riding. Whistles, catcalls, stamping. Sil took out his pistol and looked like he was thinking about shooting it, but the barkeep knocked it to the ground with his elbow as he came around with a bottle of spirits.

A loud whistle from the balcony split the shouts, and all eyeballs turned upward to gape.

"Don't go off half-cocked, boys. Just keep your pistols in your pants until you pay."

The woman who spoke from the top of the stairs was probably the prettiest person Nettie had ever seen, with creamy white skin and long, blonde hair and lips as red as the cherries on Mam's prized teacup. Even if Nettie'd only seen a hundred people in her entire life, she still knew that wherever this lady went, whatever she was wearing, men would go as weak-kneed as a sick cow and fall at her feet, tongues lolling.

"That's Dulcey," Monty whispered reverently, and as if hearing her name on his lips, the woman smiled and struck a pose.

Gray Hawk was back at the piano, a shot glass by his music book. He took up a song that sounded like horses galloping, and Dulcey and her girls hurried down the steps with a rustle of skirts and stomping of heels that made the thin wood banisters quake. There were only three doors, and there were only three girls, but they sang and danced and shook the boards like a goddamn army.

One had skin as white as Dulcey's and hair the fire-hot color of the sunset, and the other was small and fine and Aztecan, with hair so black it was almost blue piled high and curling down over soft shoulders. Each woman had a flower over her ear, and Nettie couldn't even begin to contemplate how anyone could find such a bloom within a hundred miles of Gloomy Bluebird.

Every cowpoke whooped and stared at the girls with the single-minded intensity of a stallion with an itch. But Nettie watched them like she watched snakes or coyotes, like they were a strange function of nature she couldn't quite figure out, and they might reveal their secret magic if she just watched long enough. At home, Mam was an unfortunate, doughy woman with a face like bad milk and hair that always seemed to be straggling somewhere else. Her dresses were sad, faded things bought secondhand when the last one couldn't be patched anymore. Nettie had decided long ago that there wasn't a damn useful thing about being female and had started studying the cowpokes' bow-legged swagger instead.

But, law, these women were a different sort of creature altogether, dressed in colors Nettie had never even seen before. Bright red and brilliant blue and a queer, hot green, shimmering under the oil lamps and glimmering with shaking black fringe to show forbidden, slender calves. When the redheaded lady stopped by their table and ran a satin-gloved finger under Jar's chin, Nettie nearly swallowed her own goddamn tongue. Something peculiar stirred in her belly, and she looked from Jar to the redhead, confused. She knew boys liked girls and girls liked boys...or they were supposed to. She thought Jar was an idiot and the lady was probably of loose moral fiber, but still she felt a powerful pull toward each of them, which didn't make a lick of damn sense.

That was another reason she preferred horses: Horses were simple.

When the song drew to a thunderous close, each of the women chose a table, and the cowpokes shoved aside to make room. Dulcey sat on Jar's lap, and as he was the youngest and best-looking wrangler at the table, no one saw fit to challenge him.

"Shall we play cards, boys?"

Dulcey's voice was like warm honey, and Nettie was just as

captivated as the men were. All the cowpokes fawned over her, complimenting her hair and eyes and figure, and Nettie just kept her hat down. When they started betting, she reckoned she could toss in about three of her pennies and be fine. Pap had taught her to play poker long ago, when the winter got long and cold and he wanted to feel like he was winning something. That meant she'd learned how to lose gracefully without the other players knowing about it. And it also meant she knew how to win.

So she figured she'd try and do that.

With two pair, Nettie won the first hand, easy. But then again, all the men were focusing elsewhere, namely in their sloppy-filled glasses and the crack in Dulcey's bosom every time she leaned over to select a card.

"Goddamn pup," one of the older hands muttered, throwing down his cards as Nettie scooped up the kitty.

Next round, she only bet one penny, and she made sure she lost it.

"What's the matter, sugar? You don't like whisky?"

Dulcey pulled at Nettie's chin, forcing her to look up, and Nettie fell off her stool. That fine, beautiful woman had eyes that matched her lips, eyes the color of blood. And they were filled with amusement and concern as she held out a gloved hand.

"Looks like whisky don't like you. Come back up and have another sip."

When Dulcey smiled, Nettie saw the last goddamn thing she ever wanted to see again.

Fangs.

CHAPTER

4

Nettie butt-scooted away and stood to bolt out the saloon doors.

"Nat?" Monty asked, but she just waved him off.

"'Bout to piss myself," she called.

Outside, she realized she already had pissed herself, just the tiniest bit. That beautiful woman couldn't be...whatever that stranger had been last night. Surely the cowpokes would've noticed. In the dark of the barn and the yard, Nettie hadn't seen the stranger's eyes, but then again, she hadn't noticed the teeth first thing, either. Dulcey seemed kind enough, but maybe that was just because they were in a fancy saloon with a dozen well-armed horny-toad men.

It wasn't until she felt a glove on her shoulder that Nettie realized running off alone into the night might've been the dumbest thing she'd ever done.

"What's got you riled?"

It was the Aztecan woman, her voice just as musical and Texan-twangy as Dulcey's and also just as amused. Sweat trickled between Nettie's shoulder blades, but she felt cold as ice.

"Nothing. Had to piss."

A dark chuckle. "Now that is a lie. I'm betting you don't piss unless you're good and alone. So they won't see what you ain't got. Now let me look at you."

The woman spun her around with strong hands and pulled her a few feet away, into the light spilling out the saloon's fancy glass window. Rude as you please, she knocked off Nettie's hat and grabbed onto her face in one hand to gaze up at her as if judging a balky mule at the auction.

And like a mule, Nettie spooked and went stiff all over.

Because what did she see?

The beautiful Aztecan whore had red eyes and fangs.

Goddammit. Another one. What was wrong with this town?

With a gasp, Nettie tried to yank her face away, but the woman was too strong. Nettie's fingers ached for the knife in her boot, but she couldn't just pull it out in the street on a whore. And even if she did, if this woman was the same thing the stranger had been, only a stick in her heart would finally fetch her up as sand, and no sticks were currently handy, unless she could start a bar fight and break a chair. If a critter could take a sickle in the eye and still live, Nettie didn't want to stick around long enough to need a sickle. The woman pried Nettie's lips apart and looked at her teeth like she was calculating a mare's age.

"Sixteen," Nettie said, yanking her face away.

"And still pure, I think. Don't know how you managed that out here. Might be pretty, if you had proper hair and smiled more."

"I had hair yesterday." Nettie took a step back and pointed at the woman's complicated updo and the curls cascading over her shoulder. "Reckon you're wearing it now."

The whore laughed like chimes and patted her head. "Then I owe you thanks. Much better than the old rat I was wearing before this. I keep thinking this little town will boom, but so far, it's just fizzled."

The woman shrugged and pushed up her bosoms and turned to go back inside, but Nettie's mouth opened up without her brain's permission and said, "What are you?"

The woman spun around, back as straight as a branding iron.

"I'm a whore, honey. But you can call me Rita." The kindness was gone from her red eyes, replaced by two things Nettie knew well: rage and indignation.

"That's not what I meant, ma'am. What about..." Nettie pointed at her own eyes before grabbing her hat off the street and stuffing it back over the cattywampus whirls of what was left of her hair.

Rita's head cocked to the side with a slow click.

"You asking what I think you're asking?"

"If you ain't going to kill me, I reckon so."

"And if I am going to kill you?"

Nettie pulled the knife from her boot.

"Then I reckon I'll make as much noise as I can before I turn you into a pile of sand."

They stared at each other, and a coyote yipped a laugh somewhere far off, and then the saloon doors exploded outward with Poke waving a jug of whisky.

"You takin' a shine to Rita, Nat? Can't say I blame you. Prettiest little strawberry this side of the border. Seeing as how it's your first offic-ielle week as a cowpoke, this one's on me."

Damn, but Poke was a sweet drunk, and damn if it wasn't the worst thing he could've done, just then.

Rita caught the silver dollar Poke tossed in the air and snatched up Nettie's wrist in an iron grip.

"We're gonna get along fine, Poke. I'll save a taste for you after, shall I?"

Poke tipped the jug up, letting the golden liquid wet his beard as he guzzled. "You'd best, girl. You know how I get after a good game of cards. Nothing settles me down like your mouth. Go easy on 'er, Nat."

Before Nettie could argue, Rita was dragging her down a dark alley and up the back stairs of the saloon.

"I don't want no poke," she said, yanking away as she suddenly realized where the old wrangler's nickname had likely come from.

"And I don't plan to give you one. I'll give you something better, if you'll just go easy." Nettie gave a powerful yank, and Rita slapped her hard upside the head. In a quieter voice, she whispered, "Carita, if I wanted you dead, you'd be dead. Now hurry."

The whore dragged Nettie up the rickety stairs, every step taking the girl one foot closer to death and away from a life that matched her wildest dreams. It just figured she'd get killed by a panther-toothed whore the week she finally got to be a ranch hand. Why had she agreed to come to this stupid saloon? And why hadn't Rita tried to hurt her worse, since it was so obviously easy? All Nettie could reckon was that whatever the tiny woman wanted, it wasn't going to leave much blood in the bed, as that would likely make a man like Poke downright uncomfortable.

The balcony out back was a lot less fancy than the one inside the saloon, but it had the same three doors. Rita dragged her in the one on the end, and Nettie's heart stuttered as the door slammed and locked. The room was over-warm and coated in red, thanks to an embroidered shawl draped around the lamp.

The furnishings tried hard to be pretty and failed, like most things in Gloomy Bluebird. The bed sagged, the armoire was spineless, and the coverlet still held a man-sized indentation stippled with sweat. Nettie paused on the threshold, gagging on the perfume overpowering the stale scent of rutstink on the air, but Rita gave a final yank and all but threw her on the bed.

Nettie scrunched away from the feather-leaky pillows and glared her defiance.

"How do you know?" Rita rounded on her, eyes burning red and teeth bared. Away from the saloon, her accent changed completely. All sweetness had fled.

"What's to know? You got cat teeth and red eyes and I killed a man like that. He tried to force me, out on Pap's farm."

Rita crossed her arms and nodded, eyes narrowed under black swooping brows.

"That's how, then. Once you kill one, you always know. You will always see. More's the pity for you."

"What the hell is that supposed to mean?"

Rita paced the room in her cracked maroon boots, flailing her arms and talking almost too quick for Nettie to catch her drift. "We are monsters, to you. You kill one, you start to see us everywhere. We hide among the people, taking what we need to survive. We are harmless enough here, in the saloon. But you don't want to go out alone at night, I promise you. A chupacabra will come along, suck you dry to bones, and crack them open for the marrow."

Nettie snorted. "A goatsucker? I ain't scared of no goatsucker."

Rita's smile curled like burned paper. "Then you haven't met one."

"Then that ain't..." Nettie pointed to Rita's face "...what you are? And that feller?"

Rita drew herself up tall. "I? Am a vampire."

"That supposed to mean something?"

Throwing up her hands and rolling her eyes, Rita said, "Have you never heard of a vampire, carita?"

"No."

"Ay-yi-yi. Vampire sleep all day and come out at night to drink blood. We are monsters."

But the way she said it was proud, which confused Nettie all the more.

"Why'd you want to be a monster, anyway?"

Rita sat down on the other side of the bed in a puddle of skirts, smoothing them down like arroyos in the rain. "Papa sold me off when I was young to a traveling man. That man used me hard, lost me in a game of dice. The saloon that won sent me upstairs with the girls. It was a nest of vampires, and they turned me that night. Since then, no man can strike me or give me the pox. I never get drunk. I cannot get pregnant and die in childbirth. I drink from the men, and they leave, thinking they have been pleasured, that they have bought me." She leaned back on an elegant elbow. "But they are offering themselves to me. I drink their strength. For a woman, it is the ultimate revenge."

Nettie shook her head, trying to take it in. "So all three of y'all are...?"

Rita nodded. "*Sí.* If this is the life you lead, it's better this way. Far better. Men are cruel."

"Then that feller that came after me was a whore, too?"

Rita flicked her fingers. "Men come and go. But women run this town. He could have been any outsider, a wrangler or a traveling man. Outsiders respect our territory and avoid our streets. But if they wish to eat the leavings of dirty farmers, that is their business."

"Jesus Damn Bullnuts." Nettie listened to the rhythmic rustlings of the corn-shuck mattress in the room next door as she tried to make sense of what Rita had revealed. Growing up on a farm, she'd had an eyeful of what critters did when they felt the itch, and she'd thought she had a pretty good idea of how whores made their coin, but now she felt sick to her stomach, thinking maybe one of the cowpokes was getting sucked dry in an entirely different way on the other side of that wall.

"Does it hurt 'em much?"

Rita shrugged a bare shoulder. "No. They like it. And we mostly suck out the liquor, which means they can buy more whisky and drink longer. The only problem is that they get very sleepy."

Nettie had just about come to terms with the whole damn thing when Rita was suddenly right up in her face, their noses almost touching. "Do you want me to make you a vampire, *carita*? Then the cowpokes cannot harm you."

Nettie jerked her head back. "Oh, hell no. Outside of Pap, the only man ever came close to harming me was one of you all, and I killed him for it. If I had to sleep all day, I couldn't be a wrangler." Nettie turned away, trying to hide the fact that she was working hard to keep from upchucking her beans at the thought of living off blood. "Thanks just the same."

Rita was somehow already at the back door, holding it open, her face a cold and inhuman mask. "Then go. Tell your friends that it was wonderful. And tell no one what I've told you."

Damn glad to leave the hot, red room, Nettie skittered out the door. But Rita stopped her with a small, hard hand on the shoulder of the dead man's shirt. Her cherry-red lips just brushed Nettie's neck, where the big blue vein was, and Nettie's heart stuttered stupidly.

"And if you do tell anyone, know that I will hunt you down and kill you in the night," Rita whispered.

Nettie gulped and nodded.

"I got nobody to tell."

Rita's door closed with a bang, and Nettie held a hand to her neck and tried to remember how to breathe.

"She break you in good, Nat?"

Jar was leaning against the crooked railing two doors down, smoking a cigarette. His eyes drooped, sleepy-like, but he was smiling.

"Oh, yeah. Lord, Jar, I can hardly walk."

Jar just nodded knowingly and stared off into space. "It takes a man like that, every time. You'll sleep good tonight, I reckon, but you might have trouble waking up come morning."

Walking over, spurs jingling, Jar clapped a hand on Nettie's shoulder.

"Best get on back downstairs. More liquor to drink. More cards to play. And we're on the trail with a herd, heading north in two days. Best be ready to ride."

Nettie's grin was as big as the sky.

Finally, she'd escape Pap and Mam and hit the trail as a wrangler. With any luck, they wouldn't notice she was gone until she was farther than either of them had ever been from the broke-down homestead. Maybe she'd stay with Boss Kimble, or end up on a ranch up north, where the mountains were so big they poked holes in the clouds. The only thing that stuck in her craw was what Rita had told her about monsters. Said she'd be seeing the goddamn things everywhere, now. Vampire whores and goatsuckers that would come after a human. Sure as hell explained why so many folks just up and disappeared. And maybe why that broken woman in the bunkhouse had been willing to crawl a hundred miles just to mumble about some cannibal bird. Maybe there really was a baby-stealing monster with a spike out there, waiting.

Nettie looked out over the prairie as she followed Jar down the saloon stairs, the wood swaying with each step. Gloomy Bluebird was barely a pile of goat squat on the long, wide land of Durango, a giant child's game of mumblety-peg in the rocky dirt. The stars poked out hard, the moon a quarter disk almost ripe for rustling cattle. A coyote wailed, and a horse snorted in its sleep. Before, those'd been normal noises, night music. Now, she could only wonder what the hell else was lurking in the desert.

Back in the saloon, Nettie took an empty seat and slurped down the swill that Monty slid across the table. The hot heat of the rotgut pooled in her belly, smoothing out the worries caused by a vampire whore and a weeping woman with shredded feet. A flicker of red caught her eye, and she watched Rita crook a finger at Poke from her door on the balcony. With a loud whoop, the skunk-drunk cowpoke wobbled his way up the stairs and disappeared inside.

Nettie lost two hands of poker and ten cents waiting to make sure Poke came out alive.

First thing he did was ask to borrow a dollar from Monty so he could go back for more.

With Nettie trailing behind, her knife in her hand, Poke and Monty hobbled back from the saloon on jelly legs, singing songs about fine women. They were happy as pigs in slop, arms around each other's necks, swaying back and forth. Nettie lagged in their wake trying to keep the liquor in her belly, as a cowpoke who couldn't hold his drink was likely to suffer a horrible nickname for the rest of his life and possibly be driven from the territory, which was what she figured had happened to a feller she'd only known as Urp Longly, who hadn't been seen in two years. As the least drunk and most wary of the ranch hands, Nettie nervously scanned the prairie, stark in blacks and whites under the grinning moon, waiting for a gleam of red and the reflection of moonlight on sharp, wet teeth. All she saw was a dead armadillo and, far off, a coyote. Critter yipped once and ran away before they got close enough to hit it with a rifle, drunk or sober. Smart things, coyotes.

And as Rita had said, the next day, the wranglers were sleepier than usual.

"Damn hangover," Monty said.

"Ayup. Girl drained me dry," Poke agreed with a grin, tipping his hat further over his eyes to shut out the sun.

Jar just grinned and rubbed two tiny red dots on his neck, muttering, "Mm. Love bites."

Nettie just got up for breakfast and went for the first bronc in the pen as usual. In the early morning after everyone else was asleep, she'd upended a stomach full of cornbread and liquor over the porch rail and had felt better almost immediately, more alert than seemed possible. The Injun woman had watched her from a tangle of blankets on a rocking chair on the porch and nodded her head.

"Best keep the sickness out," she'd said in a quiet voice. "Don't let them claw into you."

But when Nettie blinked, the rocking chair was gone, the woman just a huddled lump of blankets on the boards. Far beyond, green animal eyes glowed for just a second, and she imagined the whisper of a single word traveling over the prairie.

"Fool."

Nettie wiped her mouth on the dead vamp's sleeve. Liquor was more trouble than it was worth.

Over the next few days, Nettie did her best to fit in with the wranglers of the Double TK, which involved eating, farting, joshing, and breaking as many fancy broncs as possible, preferably while Boss Kimble was watching. Her proudest moment happened between dippers at the well when a gentleman in a pressed linen suit put the big white stallion through his paces under the boss's watchful eye before handing over a fat wallet. No wonder the boss didn't mind paying her a quarter a bronc; he'd made at least fifty damn dollars on the white.

As of today, she'd broken seven broncs. That was two more than Jar had done, and one of his had been chosen badly and nipped a chunk out of his arm after tossing him ass over kettle into the dirt. Sitting across the table at dinner, he couldn't stop worrying it with black-rimmed fingernails. It was likely to get inflamed, if he kept at it, but a man's business was his own, so she kept eating. The stew went down fast, chunks of goat mixed in with the beans and a few wild onions. She'd already settled in for seconds when Boss Kimble walked into the room and cleared his throat. All the wranglers went silent, the only sound a clatter of bowls on the table and hurried swallowing.

"Headin' across the border at moonrise. Scout says there's about two hundred head of cattle waiting over the river, Juan de Blanco's boys being lazier than usual after stealin' 'em from Lance Morgan. We'll swim 'em over, brand hides until we fall down, and set off quick as a lick to sell the herd up north. You all know your business. Best bring your pistols."

And then he took a double helping of stew and left to eat in the saddle while looking over the horseflesh in his pens. Nettie knew a crew's mounts were the difference between a successful cattle raid, drive, and sale and a bunch of dead cowpokes, but it hadn't really occurred to her until just now that the horses she'd been breaking would be among the ones they'd rope along in case their regular mounts got busted up. She knew which horse she'd pick, if Ragdoll stepped in a prairie dog hole or got shot up by de Blanco's banditos. And for just a minute there, her heart ached for sweet, dependable Blue.

Sure, the one-eyed mule was ugly as sin and slow as cold molasses, but you couldn't sit on a creature for that many years and not come to care for it. Considering a mule was half horse, half donkey, odd-looking, generally disrespected, and confused on the gender front, Nettie had a lot of fellow feeling for old Blue. She could only hope Pap wouldn't get too desperate and eat the damn critter when his bacon ran out. Or accidentally shoot the poor thing, if he went aiming for the pesky black mare again. At least that bit of trouble hadn't followed Nettie to the Double TK. It was almost like she'd shucked her old life as easy as a kernel of corn slipping the hull and finding fertile ground in which to sprout.

Of course, the best corn got eaten, transplanted in a bird's belly and shat out in more pleasant places, but Nettie figured it didn't hurt the corn much.

After Boss Kimble's announcement, Nettie was so excited she could barely eat her stew, which meant she actually had to taste it, which was a bad move. Something in the brew had clearly gone south, and she ended up on the back porch of the ranch kitchen, staring at something squirmy on her plate because her only other choice was to watch Sil piss onto a scorpion.

"You're scared, ain't you?" he said, spitting tobacco onto the wet tangle of black pinchers with grim finality.

"I ain't scared. The stew's gone bad." She spit a wad of meat on top of the scorpion to prove her point. As the scorpion died shortly after that, she felt justified.

"Grub's always been bad. But your belly's turned, sure enough. Ain't you ever been on a raid before, boy?"

She shook her head, pulled her hat down lower so he couldn't see her face. Her hip felt too light, considering she was the only wrangler of the company who didn't have a pistol. Without touching the stranger's money and rousing suspicion, she'd managed to break enough broncs and win enough hands of poker to buy a notched Bowie knife and leather sheath off the cook, but the damn thing was about as sharp as a hammer, despite the careful whetting she'd given it. Still, she liked the way it felt, strapped to her belt, and had grown comfortable enough yanking it out dramatically and brandishing it at splintered posts and one deeply confused armadillo. If they ran into trouble tonight, she'd just have to lay low on her horse and ride like hell.

"Don't influence the boy, Sil. Lord knows you still yark before every gunfight." Monty came up and pissed on top of what was left of the scorpion, and Nettie's eyes shot sideways as she tried not to see her friend's unmentionables. "Reckon I'll keep Nat with me so he don't pick up your bad habits."

"Hope he don't get you killed." What teeth Sil had curled up in his smile. "Lost three boys last time we went into de Blanco's territory. One feller got trampled, one disappeared, and another showed up nailed to the wall of the church a week later." Sil spit a wad of tobacco at Nettie's boot, and she stepped back without thinking. "Or at least, his skin showed up. Ol' de Blanco don't take kindly to being stole from."

"So why're we stealing from him?" Nettie asked.

Sil laughed. "We're just stealing back what he already stole from the fine folks of Durango. If that old Aztecan bandito hasn't got the sense to brand his damn cattle, that's what he deserves. Lord knows de Blanco stole 'em from Lance Morgan, and Lance probably stole 'em from some city fool from out east or some other Aztecan vaquero. Every damn cow in this territory's been stolen and sold and stolen again. That's why Boss is having us brand 'em for the Double TK. If a man values something, he'd best leave his mark on it."

Nettie thought of the scars on her back and down her arms and legs. For something she'd been long told had no value, she carried a lot of brands.

Maybe tonight, while Boss Kimble and his men stole the herd, she'd just gallop away from Durango forever.

CHAPTER
5

The moon was high, and Ragdoll was dancing between Nettie's knees. The little mare was skittier than usual as she pranced alongside Nut, the light sorrel Monty favored.

"You nervous?" he asked.

Accustomed as she was to ignoring questions from Pap and Mam, Nettie's instinct was to shrug and keep on riding. But she figured that if a feller like Monty had put up with her this long and got her the job she'd always wanted, she owed it to him to be honest. "Just a bit."

"Don't be. You're doing fine. Boss is right pleased—told me so himself. Does life on the ranch suit you?"

"Lord yes, Monty."

After a moment of thought, he said, "Other fellers giving you trouble?" And she heard a certain sort of concern in it and knew it meant more than it sounded like. If she'd thought of herself as a girl, if she'd dressed like a girl and let the cowpokes know that underneath her wraps, she had the same parts as the whores, they probably would've given her trouble. But she hadn't let that happen. She wouldn't. So they hadn't.

"Not after I punched Jar in the arm for joshing me too hard." She grinned to let him know it was truth.

Monty chuckled. "His bit arm?"

She just nodded and rode on, chin up.

"You don't miss...?" Monty trailed off and spit a stream of tobacco juice. He'd never asked her much about her life. He'd never had to.

"Nothing to miss," she muttered, and he nodded along, sympathetic-like.

"Just keep close and stay on your horse. Once we get the herd running, get behind 'em and holler hard as you're fit. That's all you got to do," Monty said for the fifty-first time, and Nettie gulped and nodded.

"You ain't worried about de Blanco?"

Monty twitched his graying mustache and wagged his long face. "Hell, no. We been trading horses and cows back and forth over this river for thirty years. Sil's just messing with you 'cause you're new. He bet some of the old hands that you'd yark your supper and fall off your horse. It's a long life in Gloomy Bluebird, and bettin' on the new kid dyin's more interesting than bettin' on which way a horse'll switch its crap." He looked her up and down and tugged on the faded red bandanna that was always tied around his neck. "Did you forget your kerch, Nat? Dust is likely to choke you to death. Best head back on up to the bunkhouse and fetch it afore we take off."

Nettie blushed hot and fumbled with the sweat-crusted collar of her shirt. "Oh, I reckon I'll make it all right..."

"Don't be a fool, now. You can't go on a raid without a bandanna. Run on back to the bunkhouse and grab one of mine off my bunk, if you need to borrow one until yours are clean." He grinned. "Better yet, you stay on your hoss during the raid so I don't lose the nickel I bet Sil, and we'll just consider it yours."

Nettie nodded until her cheeks felt cool again, spun her mare, and loped toward the bunkhouse. There was so damned much she didn't know about being a wrangler, and she was lucky to have an experienced hand like Monty around to help her out. But the rangy old cowpoke had always been kindly to her, ten years and more, for no reason she could name. Kindness was a thing as foreign and far-off as snow in .a Durango summer, as far as she understood it, and she wondered if the warmth and gratitude she felt for Monty was something akin to love.

Ragdoll skidded to a stop by the porch, and Nettie leaped off onto wobbly legs and ran inside. The only lamp was on the floor beside the Injun woman. She slept on the porch at night, but during the day, they let her stay inside on a pallet so the sun wouldn't bake her. Poor critter was still in a fever, sweating through her clothes and moaning under her breath in whatever language it was she spoke. Whenever a wrangler came into the bunkhouse, he'd dip a little water into her mouth from a pot kept by the door. Nobody liked having her there much, but nobody wanted to be the one to find her dead and have to bury her body in the rock-solid crust of the desert, neither. Nettie reckoned she'd been left inside tonight so a coyote wouldn't drag her off while the men were off raiding.

Nettie would've been silent if not for the stranger's boots, which had high heels that echoed on the boards. The woman's head jerked to stare, her eyes wide and dark and wet, reflecting the lamp turned low.

"Half-breed," she said, voice hard, before chuckling to herself. "More than half-breed. You are many things, and none of them have a name."

All the hairs on Nettie's neck rose up as she chose a mostly clean bandanna from the pile on Monty's prime-placed bunk.

Her sweat-slippy fingers found the grip of her knife. The woman had never spoken in any language but her own outside of Nettie's nightmares, and her voice was deeper than it should have been.

"You talkin' to me, woman?"

"Come here, child."

Although she lay on the floor in a tangle of moldering horse blankets, the woman's form seemed to rise up with the flap of dark wings around her battered face. Nettie's feet wanted to run, but something in her chest felt a tug, as if the fractured creature had lassoed her ribs and was pulling her forward, a step at a time, until she stood at the figure's bloodstained feet.

"Come down here."

The floor fell out from under Nettie's boots, and her knees slammed into the boards. With the suddenness of a hawk's dive, broken fingers caught the front of Nettie's shirt and yanked her face close to one drenched in sweat and tears and filled with a fervent fire.

"Pia Mupitsi," the woman said, a long hiss.

"The Big Cannibal Owl," Nettie whispered in response.

The woman nodded once. "You will hunt it."

Nettie struggled back and away, but the woman's hand was an iron vise around her shirt. "I ain't, begging your pardon. I'm a wrangler of the Double TK Ranch, and I'm headed out on a cattle drive."

The woman shook her head gravely. "Maybe not tonight, half-breed. Maybe tomorrow. But you will hunt it. And you will destroy it."

"Or what?"

The corners of the woman's mouth pulled back, showing a skull's rattling teeth. "Or I haunt you. I'll dog every step of your short, violent life until you die. You'll never know peace. Just as I will never know peace until my child is avenged."

"And what if I still say no?"

The mouth opened, a sucking cave, and Nettie couldn't pull away.

"The new moon brings death. Hunt Pia Mupitsi, or the blood of the next massacre will be on your hands."

"Next massacre?"

"Cannibal Owl needs to stock the pantry. New moon's the best time to fill the basket with children born in springtime. That's when Pia Mupitsi came to your village, little one."

Nettie's heart jerked. "Did you just say . . . my village?"

Outside, far across the prairie, the cowpokes unleashed a big, echoing whoop, and Nettie tumbled backward. When she looked again, the woman was small and dark and wet with sweat, drawn into herself again, her eyes crusted closed and her parched lips muttering. When Nettie leaned close, she heard the same two words rattle, again and again.

"Pia Mupitsi. Pia Mupitsi. Pia Mupitsi."

"What did you say? What about my village? What do you know, woman?"

But the crooked, broken figure on the ground gave only mutterings.

"Pia Mupitsi. Pia Mupitsi."

The spell was broken, or Nettie's imagination had run off again, or she was so skitty about the raid that she was hearing what her heart had always wished for. No way the dying woman could know what she'd claimed, could identify Nettie's kin. Death rattles couldn't hold truth. Just more questions. Just madness.

Nettie stood and tied the bandanna around her neck.

"You ain't doggin' nobody, Injun," she muttered. She dribbled some water from the bucket over the woman's lips, though, before she hopped on Ragdoll and took off.

Just in case.

The raid went off without a hitch. Nettie stayed on her horse, did her part, and didn't choke to death on the thick dust, thanks to Monty's bandanna. Two hours' ride down south, a swim across the silt-sticky river, a yipping, yowling, pounding gallop to hustle up two hundred head of cattle and a few dozen horses while a handful of drunk vaqueros randomly shot into the herd and cussed up a storm in Aztecan. Another swim, two more hours of riding, and they were home again, driving the cattle into pens and setting up the fires and branding irons with jaw-cracking yawns.

"That was almost too easy," Monty said, as they processed the sweaty beasts, keeping the cattle from doing anything too stupid with shouts and cracks of their whips.

"Seems to me too easy ain't much of a problem," Nettie answered, still full of piss and vinegar and pleased beyond punch that she'd managed to hop off Ragdoll in the middle of a tussle to grab the pistol off a dead vaquero and claim it for her own.

Far as Nettie could see, not a damn thing had gone wrong. The farther she'd gotten from the Injun woman, the better she had felt. In the heat of the raid, she'd forgotten all about Pia Mupitsi, about the whispered possibility that some time, long ago, she'd had a village, a people. The Double TK were her people now. She was a real wrangler, by crow, and she couldn't wait to see just how good her new gun could shoot.

Monty shook his head and rolled the corner of his gray mustache between his fingertips. "Should've been more vaqueros watchin' the herd. Best I can figure is the good ones were raiding across the river, maybe crossed right by us on our way back. While we were over here, stealing cattle, they were over in Durango, stealing some more cattle of their own. The fellers I saw didn't look like de Blanco's men, is all. And it's a right small herd."

"I still ain't seeing the problem."

Monty sighed. "Guess there ain't no point in making a problem where there ain't one. You did fine, Nat. But there's something unsettled tonight. Something about the way the moon's sitting, all distrustful-like."

Nettie looked up at the quarter moon, the Rustler's Moon. For a half second, maybe, it reminded her of the Injun woman's eyes, when they'd gone all wide and wet and promised to haunt her. But she shook off that fancy. The moon was just a slender, shiny thing, far off, and there was nothing to fear from its darkness except maybe tripping on a rock on the way to the outhouse. Surely the Cannibal Owl wasn't waiting for a day on the calendar to do dark deeds. The moon was the moon, and the crazy Injun woman was the crazy Injun woman, and folks who'd had only a one-eyed mule last week and now had a mustang mare, a Bowie knife, and a gun had no cause at all to complain. She picked up a cherry-hot branding iron and went to join the fray. For Nettie Lonesome, now Nat Lonesome, all was well.

At least until the company returned to the bunkhouse and found the Injun woman drowned in the middle of the floor, a puddle spread around her like wings, and the whole scene ten miles from a body of water big enough to dip in more than her toes.

CHAPTER 6

Of course, that wasn't the end of it. Most folks don't die that easy.

It happened the next night, just like the Injun woman had promised. Something in the air told Boss Kimble not to raid, to let the cattle sit a spell, send out a scout, and go out the next night to build up the herd. Still exhausted from the long night of riding and a longer day of branding, the cowpokes fell into their bunks without even glancing toward the town and the fine flesh of the Leaping Lizard.

The skin prickled all over Nettie's neck as she tossed and turned on her bunk. There was something rustling outside like a fox snuffling in a henhouse. But when she got up to look, there was nothing to see. Unable to swallow down the dry grit coating her tongue, she took a dipper of water from the ewer; when it held the tang of salt, she stepped outside to spit it over the rail and into the dust. There, out on the porch, lit by a tiny slice of moon, she finally saw it: a dark figure on horseback where no figure had any right to be, standing on the Injun woman's shallow grave. Watching.

The horse looked familiar. But surely her mind was playing tricks.

The troublesome black filly couldn't be caught, much less calmly ridden.

Without a sound, the shadow raised an arm, pointed a finger. Nettie swallowed hard and put a hand to her new gun. The black horse reared and spun and galloped away. When it was long gone, Nettie crept out, barefoot in the dirt. The hoof prints where the figure had stood in fresh-turned earth were filled with saltwater.

Nettie didn't sleep that night. And she didn't tell anyone what she'd seen.

Haunted cowpokes were probably as unlucky as women, when it came to rustling cattle.

The next morning, they found two half-eaten cows in a corner of the corral. All the other cattle were crowded together on the opposite side like old women hiding from a rat. As the newest of the wranglers, it fell to Nettie to do the dirty work and drag the carcasses out to salvage what they could of the meat.

"I reckon I don't want to eat a bite of this beef," she said to Chuck, the next most junior feller. They both had their bandannas pulled over their noses, as the meat had somehow managed to go bad in just a few hours. The edge of it was eaten away, all rusty-looking and none too appetizing. Dragging the carcass half a mile by horseback didn't help its attraction. She unhooked her rope from the cow's horns and looped it up on her hip, staying alert just in case whatever had killed the cows was still nearby and hungry.

"Ain't yours to reckon." Chuck had an unearned sort of bravado around Nettie, even though he was a year younger than her, mainly because he was taller and had managed to sprout a few whiskers. "Boss said to save what we could, and I don't aim to let him down."

Chuck's knife was no sharper than hers, but she wasn't willing to test her new blade on rancid meat, so she let him chop into it while she held the cast iron cook pot ready. The cow was a cavern of crusty entrails, the eyes all bugged out and the ribs and legs holding it open like a monster's maw. Chuck hacked into what was left of the flank, and a chunk of meat slithered off. When it slapped into his palm, he screamed and dropped it.

"It's just meat, you goose," Nettie said with a sniff.

"Goose yourself. Meat ain't supposed to burn, is it?" He held up his hand to show raw, red skin before sucking on the wound with an audible slurp.

"Huh." Nettie used a mesquite twig to lift the sand-sugared slip of beef out of the dirt. She dropped it in the pot, and it sizzled. When she flicked it back out, a chunk of metal had been eaten away, the seasoned iron as raw and red as Chuck's hand.

"Reckon that would eat through a man's innards, don't you?"

Chuck nodded and clutched his hand open and closed. "That I do, Nat."

Nettie stood and looked back to the ranch. Everyone else was going about the usual business, nobody paying the time of day to two green hands and a couple of cattle carcasses.

"Tell you what, Chuck. If you'll drag 'em out farther over that hill, I'll hunt up enough meat so nobody'll notice we left 'em for the crows."

Chuck stared at her through narrowed, close-set eyes, his burned hand clutched to his chest. "You just got a gun yesterday and you ain't ever shot it. How do you expect to kill anything?"

She shrugged. "I have my ways."

He chewed his lip for a minute, considering. "I'm gonna trust you, Nat. Best not let me down."

When Chuck stood and spit in his good hand, Nettie spit in hers to shake. They nodded at each other as men, and she hopped on Ragdoll and took off for the far corner where the Double TK backed up to Pap's land. He was too lazy to ride his fences, much less fix them, and she'd been hoping for years that someone would teach the old bastard a lesson. Sure enough, she found a few rangy, unbranded cows grazing on the wrong side of the fence, which meant, according to the law, that they were wild. For just a second, she let her fingers tickle the trigger on her new revolver, but in the end, she just found a big rock and took down the least noticeable of the beasts. By the time she'd wrapped her rope around Ragdoll's saddle horn and dragged the stolen cow back to the cook pot, Chuck had done his part with the rancid carcasses. All that was left were wet drag marks and a sweaty cowpoke with his hand wrapped in a dirty bandanna.

Together, wordlessly, they cut up the fresh beef. Chuck didn't have to ask where it had come from; its pathetic keep and lack of the TK brand told him well enough where it *didn't* come from, and that was all that mattered. By the time they'd butchered it and cut the meat up into small enough chunks to conceivably connect them with the chewed-up beeves, it was well into afternoon, and Nettie was sorely missing the feel of a fresh mustang twitching under her and a new quarter tickling her palm.

"Reckon I'll try to break a bronc before supper and practice with my pistol." She stood and wiped bloody fingers down her only britches. "You coming?"

Chuck looked up and flinched away from the bright sun, holding a hand to shield his eyes. She let the hat hide her face in shadow, should he stare a little too closely once the sun blindness had cleared. But Chuck looked downright feverish. His forehead shone with dirty sweat, and his eyes were red, and his hands shook as he shoved his knife's blade into the dirt to clean it.

"Sun took me hard." He wiped the blade off on his pants and fumbled it into its sheath at his belt. "Need me some water. Maybe rest in the shade."

Nettie nodded and dragged the cook pot toward the back door of the ranch house, where the old cook sat, whittling a spoon.

"Two beeves. Should be more meat," he muttered.

Nettie tossed the pot down with a clank. "Then go pick at the bones your own self."

She didn't ask Chuck what he'd done with the other carcasses. She didn't want to know.

That night, as they saddled up for the next raid over the border, Nettie couldn't help scanning the horizon. She didn't see a shadowy figure on a wet-black mare, but what she did see was Chuck riding his paint horse, Rain. The boy was all slumped over and jiggly, like maybe he was working on a good case of the trots. Nettie loped over, but he didn't look up.

"All right there, Chuck?"

He wagged his head sorrowfully, his hat fallen down his back and his eyes wet and red. "Reckon not. Feels like I ate a hive of bees, and they're right vengeful."

"What's the last thing you did eat?"

With a sad little shrug, he said, "I don't rightly recall. Will you ride with me? If I fall off, maybe you can tie me back on before the other hands notice?"

Nettie hadn't heard Chuck act anything but cocky as a banty rooster, so she just nodded and took up beside him at the tail end of the cowpokes heading out. As they hit up a hard trot, Chuck looked like he might wiggle right off Rain's rump, but as soon as the moon rose, he stiffened up with a renewed vigor that made Nettie think maybe he'd shaken off the sick.

"Feeling better?" She kept her voice low and husky, as the moon in the bright sky made her feel more exposed than usual.

Chuck put a hand to his forehead and then to his heart as if checking to see if he was alive. "Reckon I do. Feel like I could eat a whole damn side of beef, just now. Don't know what came over me for a while there. Moon feels mighty good, don't it?"

When Nettie looked up, her hat slipped down her back, and she hurried to stick it back in place. But Chuck looked at her, curious-like.

"What are you, Nat?"

Nettie grunted. "Wrangler. Bronc breaker."

"No, dumbass. Like, what are you made of?"

She settled her hat harder and kicked her horse to a slow lope. "Blood and bone and vittles, same as you, I guess," she hollered into the wind.

He kicked Rain to keep up, and the pony snorted in protest. "But what color are you?"

"Brown."

"Damned if you ain't thick-headed. I mean . . . who are your people?"

Her eyes slid sideways as they cantered, side by side, across the empty prairie toward Azteca. "Why's it matter, Chuck? I'll tie you to your damned pony if you fall off. Why's it matter where I come from?"

Chuck slowed his horse back down to a trot, and Nettie

did him the kindness of joining him. With his wet eyes on the moon, the boy said, "Just been thinkin' a lot today. I don't remember my mama too much, as she died of fever when I was little. Pappy was a farmer, but everything he did turned to shit. Older brother took to wrangling, and as soon as I could walk away from the plow, I followed him. But damned if I know who my people are. Sure enough I don't feel like Charles Ridgeway Jr. So I figured I'd see if maybe you felt that way, too. You feel at home on the prairie?"

"Being sick makes you right philosophical," Nettie grumbled, but he was looking at her all desperate-like, so she watched the horizon between Ragdoll's ears and told him a little truth. "Don't know who my people are. Some kind of red and some kind of black, I guess. I ain't white, and that's all that seems to matter to folks. All Pap and Mam ever said was I was lucky they took me in and taught me anything. I must've been right small when it happened. Sometimes, I think I recall the jog of a horse, watching backward over a spotted rump. I like to think maybe I was somebody's papoose. Just wish I knew what I did to get handed down off that horse." Immediately feeling like she'd said too much, she added, "Goddamn moon. It's too bright by half for a not-half-full thing. Let's catch up to the rest of the hands before they holler at us. I don't want to be chopping up beef tomorrow when I could be breaking broncs, that's for damn sure."

She whooped and kicked Ragdoll into a dead run, and after a few beats, Chuck followed her. For a time, they raced side by side, and Nettie lay low on her mare's neck and let her hat fall back in the wind, and it felt like flying, and flying felt good. As the run fell off to a lopsided canter, a shape turned off the pack of cowpokes up ahead and came back toward them, and she recognized Monty on his sorrel. She pulled Ragdoll into a trot, and Monty turned his far more polished gelding on a hoof and rode up beside her.

"Best hurry up, boys. River's just over that ridge."

As he said it, the last of the other wranglers disappeared into an arroyo, and Nettie caught her breath from the run to gather courage before crossing the river. Ragdoll had thus far proven to be a strong and fearless swimmer, but Nettie was always a mite scared of dark, running water and what might lie beneath the current. She'd once heard Pap tell of a boy he knew who chanced to cross a high river after a storm, and his horse swam right into a ball of water moccasins, and they bit the boy until he swole up to twice his size and died.

"You got any water?"

Chuck's voice was ragged, and Nettie pulled her hat back on and tightened the strings before she reached for her water skin. The boy's hand shook as she gave it to him, their horses at a slow walk side by side, and something about his moist, bulging eyes and dry, stretched-looking lips worried her.

"Monty," she said real low, inclining her head at Chuck as he gulped her water.

"You drunk, boy? Maybe hungover?" Monty asked, and Chuck handed back Nettie's empty water skin, a rudeness she would not have expected from him.

"Ain't been drinkin'."

"You fevered?"

"The opposite. Feel cold as ice, like I'm about to die of thirst. You got any water, Monty?"

Monty watched him a second, then said, stern and soft, "Get off your horse, son."

The night went quiet as the three horses stopped. Chuck slid off his mare like a boneless snake, and Nut pricked his ears and danced around a little as Monty dismounted and walked the sorrel around Nettie. The old cowpoke put the back of his hand against Chuck's forehead, saying, "I don't need no green wrangler mucking up this run, Charles. If you're sick, best turn around and head back to the bunkhouse to sleep it off."

Monty slapped Chuck's cheek lightly and looked up at Nettie as he patted Ragdoll's neck. "What about you, Nat? You've been working with Chuck, ain't you? You feeling poorly?"

"No, sir. Fit as a fiddle."

There was a peculiar bit of a pause as they both realized Chuck wasn't getting back on his horse to head home or to bravely defy his illness and gallop for the ridge. He was just standing there with his back to them, breathing funny.

"Chuck?"

The boy spun, fast as lightning, and jumped straight for Monty's throat.

CHAPTER

7

Monty gave a gurgling holler and stumbled back, holding Chuck away by his shoulders. The boy had gone plum crazy, growling and biting again and again for Monty's neck. Nettie could barely tell what was going on, what with the horse dancing nervously under her and the darkness of the prairie cut clean with stark moonlight and the fact that there was no reason at all for Chuck to go after a good man like Monty. Unless maybe he had the rabies? But then he wouldn't have asked for water. Not knowing what else to do, Nettie tried to grab for Rain's reins, but the fool horse ran off, and Nettie almost got dumped on her rump by Ragdoll's crow-hopping.

On the ground, the two men struggled and grunted. Chuck had managed to rip a hunk out of Monty's neck, and blood spilled all down his shirt, black as a cat in the moonlight. When Chuck jumped again and knocked Monty onto his back, Nettie'd had enough. She pulled out her whip and cracked the damn thing around Chuck's leg, yanking him off his feet and pulling him a few yards away so Monty would have a chance of escape. His well-trained sorrel gelding stood but a few paces away, whuffling and confused. Like any cowboy worth his salt, Monty hopped up, grabbed for his gun, and staggered toward his horse.

About that time, Chuck freed himself from the rawhide whip and yanked it out of Nettie's hand with a right unfriendly growl, almost tugging her flat out of the saddle. Luckily, her mare jumped away, and she managed to keep her seat. But Chuck kept on coming at her, hunched over like a buffalo with gut problems. Nettie spun her horse in a circle, keeping her distance. The mare was more jittery than usual, and for good damn reason. But still Nettie didn't go for her gun.

Because this was a feller who'd been kind to her, and that was a rare thing.

"What's got into you, Chuck? Are you hurtin' bad?"

Chuck shook his head like he was trying to rid himself of a pesky fly.

"So thirsty, goddammit. So goddamned thirsty." When he growled, it wasn't a noise Nettie had heard before out of animal or human.

Nettie yanked on the reins and kicked her mare, praying the raw critter had enough sense to back up instead of rearing and possibly smacking Chuck upside his fool head with a hoof. Surely whatever pained him could be fixed by a sawbones, or maybe Gray Hawk back in town? But Chuck didn't want help right now. He was stalking her. And when he jumped, she wasn't ready.

Her friend's hands dug into her leg as his teeth clunked into the leather of her boot. Nettie screamed, and her mare reared, and in that very moment, Monty pulled his pistol and shot. The night tore in half with a bullet's crack, and Chuck shrieked like a damned banshee and spun to figure out who'd shot him.

Monty hadn't made it to horseback. Poor feller just stood in front of his confused sorrel, one hand holding a bandanna to his torn-up neck as he pointed a shaking repeating pistol at the second greenest cowpoke of the Double TK Ranch.

"Ain't polite to bite your friends, Chuck," Monty said, voice thready, as Chuck twisted forward and backward trying to make sense of the hole in his back that never came out his front.

Finally, whatever'd taken Chuck over decided that revenge for being shot was worth more than Nettie's blood, and he jumped for Monty before the injured wrangler could pull the trigger again. Nettie had no choice but to draw.

A second shot rent the moonlight, and Nettie was grateful she'd practiced with her pistol all day or the kickback would've busted up her nose for sure. A startled little gulp drew her attention past Chuck's falling body to Monty's face. There was a hole in the middle of his forehead, and he fell on his face looking most surprised.

Jumping Jesus on a jackrabbit.

She'd shot Monty.

Monty.

Dismounting in a damn hurry, Nettie checked that Chuck was good and dying, which he was. Her bullet had torn straight through his throat, which was possibly why it had possessed enough gumption to bury itself in Monty's skull. She skittered around Chuck's still body just in time to flip Monty over and hear his whisper.

"What the hell just happened?"

Monty's eyes were trained on Chuck's face.

But it wasn't Chuck's face.

The skin was ragged and pulling away to reveal a layer of green-gray scales underneath. The eyes bulged over-large, yellow with black vertical pupils, all Chuck's haughtiness and decency fled. His lips had thinned, black and dry and shriveled around too-long teeth, the most prominent of which looked like viper fangs. Chuck's nose was pushed back into his face, his nostrils now slits. He looked like nothing so much as a snake in man form, and one that had died godalmighty pissed, at that. The blood from the bullet hole was dripping down his neck into the dirt, and Nettie watched it fall on a grasshopper. The critter got busy dancing to death like it was on a hot frying pan.

"I don't rightly know," Nettie whispered. "I'm so sorry, Monty."

"Not your fault, Nat. Best you run, now. Go on."

And then Monty died in her arms.

After saying something a little like a prayer over the cowpokes' bodies and closing Monty's eyes, Nettie took what she could, her hands heavy and gentle with guilt. Just a few days ago, she had a one-eyed mule and a too-big pair of cheap boots. Now she had an ugly mare, three pistols, three Bowie knives, and a borrowed bandanna that she couldn't even bury with Monty because she needed it to gallop away. Not to mention that she also had the vampire's wad of cash, more money than she knew what to do with and that she couldn't use in any town without somebody suspecting she was an escaped slave who'd stolen it. She left all the fellers' other personal items on the bodies and didn't bother ponying either horse, as hanging for horse thievery wasn't to her taste. She did take Monty's water skin, though, considering Chuck had emptied hers before turning on his friends.

When Nettie heard gunshots far off, she mounted her horse and rode away. Not toward the river, and not toward Gloomy Bluebird. Just away. Nobody would ever understand what had happened here, why a kind-hearted and hard-working fifteen-year old boy named Chuck had turned into a snake and attacked his boss and friend and been shot by the only feller lower than him in the ranks. And as a half-breed, a green cowpoke, a girl pretending to be a boy, and the only witness, she'd likely be hanged for murder just to simplify things.

With his last breath, Monty had told her to run. He would understand. And she would do her level best to avenge him, if she ever saw another...whatever the blue hellfire Chuck had become.

As she galloped across the prairie and into new territory, something far ahead caught her eye, up on a tableland. It was the Injun woman, or the ghost of her, mounted on the spooky black filly that always shone wet in the moonlight. The woman raised her arm and pointed to the west.

Nettie turned her horse in that direction and kicked her mare harder, running like all the world was chasing her tail.

The night went on and on as Ragdoll carried Nettie Lonesome into the unknown. The dead run skipped off into a long lope, and eventually that jittered down into a hard trot. Sometime around sunup, the mare gave a last jounce and fell to a dull walk, her head hanging low.

They hadn't passed a stream all night, and Nettie had brought no food, considering she'd planned on nothing more than a quick raid over the river with the rest of the hands to guide her. Best she could do was let the mare lap up some water from Monty's skin, but Nettie knew well enough that the luke-warm dribble would barely make it down the critter's throat. With the sun crawling up the horizon, the hard red disk promising a white-hot afternoon, she let her reins drop and gave the mare her head. If anyone could find water in the desert, it was a thirsty mustang pony.

Ragdoll twitched her tail and swung her head from side to side, dusty nostrils going wide and ears pricking as she chose a path. Judging by the sun, she was headed north. Nettie didn't know where the Injun woman had meant to send her, but she figured she couldn't get there if she and her horse died of thirst in the wasteland. North had to be good enough, at least until they found a way to survive the long stretch of nothing. There wasn't even enough shade to hide a fly out here. If somebody'd put a knife to her neck, she would have guessed they were somewhere north of Gloomy Bluebird, somewhere near the Durango-Azteca border. Near didn't mean shit when you were looking death in the eye.

Nettie's belly was grumbling something terrible, but she knew well enough that eating jerky on a dry stomach would only bring on a worse sort of pain. She allowed herself a sip of Monty's water, and she would've sworn she could taste the man on the leather, a lingering flavor of tobacco and kindness that made her eyes wet with tears she couldn't afford to waste.

The mare was headed toward a patch of green, but Nettie figured it was just mesquite, which didn't do anybody any good. Damn plants drunk up all the water, but you couldn't get the water back out of the tree. Stupid horse. But maybe there was a little creek or something that they could sip from, maybe get them as far as the closest city. If she didn't show too much coin, or maybe if she traded Chuck's gun, they could get a little food and water and find another ranch to wrangle at. Of course, considering that nobody at the Double TK would know what had actually happened, she might soon find a Wanted poster for a half-breed boy named Nat riding an ugly spotted pony the color of a prairie dog. Although it pained her mightily, the best thing to do would be to trade Ragdoll for a plain sorrel, trade the dead man's clothes for used, trade her name for a new one, and head up north or west. Maybe farther south into Azteca, to where they hadn't yet passed laws against folks that weren't white enough.

Then again, the Injun woman had pointed her straight west. But she couldn't find the Injun woman's Cannibal Owl if she got hanged in some two-horse town. And she didn't want to get hanged before she found out who her real people were, especially considering she'd just lost the old man closest to something like family. There was a hole in her heart, and she had to keep it beating to fill it back up.

But first: They had to live through today and find a town big enough to offer a spare set of boy's clothes and a sound horse. In a place as wide and wild as Durango territory, that was no small feat.

"Is it water, Rags?"

The pony was stepping higher, her nostrils flaring. If it wasn't water, it was something good. Nettie pulled her hat down against the sun's first slaps of heat and prayed to whatever was watching over her that water was hiding in the thicket.

Of course, the only thing currently watching over her was a particularly large, circling buzzard that wasn't accepting prayers.

It was waiting for her to stop praying.

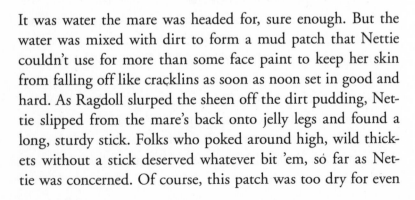

It was water the mare was headed for, sure enough. But the water was mixed with dirt to form a mud patch that Nettie couldn't use for more than some face paint to keep her skin from falling off like cracklins as soon as noon set in good and hard. As Ragdoll slurped the sheen off the dirt pudding, Nettie slipped from the mare's back onto jelly legs and found a long, sturdy stick. Folks who poked around high, wild thickets without a stick deserved whatever bit 'em, so far as Nettie was concerned. Of course, this patch was too dry for even the skinniest little rattler. The only breathing thing she could find was the buzzard that kept spiraling hopefully overhead. When she launched a rock straight up with her best throw, the thing screeched something that sounded a little like "Bitch," and Nettie decided she'd best sip from the water skin before the tumbleweeds started talking back.

Having lapped up what she could, Ragdoll walked over to nuzzle Nettie in the shoulder.

"I ain't got no grain," she muttered. The mare blew muddy air into her face, to which Nettie could only respond, "Rude. Why's everybody got to be so damn rude?"

When Ragdoll started delicately cropping the barest fuzz of grass, Nettie loosened the saddle and hobbled the horse and settled down with her back to a boulder in a scant sketch of shade. The sun was up, and the ground was starting to shudder with heat, and the mare needed to suck up every bit of life she could from the tiny dot of green in the great brown prairie. They'd set off again in the afternoon, when it was almost bearable.

"Keep watch for me, girl."

In response, Ragdoll tried to shake the saddle off and failed. Her bottlebrush tail twitched in frustration. Nettie sipped the warm, Monty-tasting water from the skin, pulled her hat down over her eyes, and placed her pistol on the ground, one hand flat over the sunshine-hot steel. Watching your friends die was damn near exhausting.

Way up high, the buzzard laughed.

Nettie fell into an uneasy sleep. The horse stepped closer, her cracked gray hoof almost brushing the girl's fingertips where they lay over the gun.

The buzzard landed, oily black wings held wide.

The horse blew air out her nose and lowered her head.

The buzzard crept closer, hopping sideways and in no way trying to hide.

She wasn't actually a buzzard. She was a vulture.

But she was more than that, too.

Nettie dreamed of biscuits and red-eye gravy, giant pits of creamy grease that smelled delicious but sucked at her boots and then at her bare feet as she tried to escape. Slurped down into the bacon-speckled ooze, she hollered and hollered and hollered, but no one answered.

The horse stepped gently over her prone form, hooves spread wide and planted firm. She snorted a warning and bared her long, yellow teeth.

The vulture laughed.

"You're a bitch, too," the bird growled.

CHAPTER

8

The mare screamed, and Nettie startled awake and sat up, smacking her head on Ragdoll's knee. Her heart just about ate itself when she realized just how close her soft parts were to a thousand pounds of angry horse. Luckily, the horse wasn't angry at her.

Unluckily, the critter that the horse was facing off with was also angry and probably even more dangerous.

It was a buzzard. Well, most folks called 'em buzzards for convenience, but Nettie knew well enough it was a vulture. Monty had explained once that buzzards were actually swift brown things, more like hawks, while vultures were the big, bald-headed scavengers that wheeled high up, searching for dead things to eat. There were black vultures and turkey vultures, and this one, with its bald, pink head, was a turkey vulture.

But then again, it wasn't.

The critter swallowing up the sun with its six-foot wingspan was mostly a vulture as Nettie knew one, but the eyes were human and the flight feathers were shiny and sharp as razors, and Nettie reckoned that no bird had any use for the floppy breasts that dangled their long, red nipples as the bird hopped closer and stabbed at Nettie's fingers with a blood-speckled beak.

"Holy crow!" Nettie snatched the gun away before the all-kinds-of-wrong buzzard pecked a hole in her hand.

"Not a crow," the bird hissed with an old woman's voice. "Bitch."

Ragdoll's teeth snapped where the bird's neck had been seconds before, and Nettie scrambled back from under the horse and crouched, pointing her gun under the mare's speckled belly. The vulture squawked and hopped back, dugs swinging, and Nettie was forced away as Ragdoll spun and shoved her aside with the full power of her rump. Still sleep-addled and not sure if she was fighting horse meat or a tar pit of gravy, Nettie did what her instincts told her to do: She shoved the horse aside and shot the dadblamed buzzard in the tits.

Feathers exploded, but the bird just knotted in on itself, threw back its bald, ugly head, and laughed with the sound of hot piss splashing over sharp rocks.

"Bullets, girl?" With a powerful retch, the bird vomited up a flattened chunk of metal. "Damn things tickle."

Mind spinning and heart yammering, Nettie kept her shaking pistol pointed at the buzzard while she took inventory of the other weapons on her person. Two more guns in her saddle bag, apparently useless against the bird. Her lariat, which the critter would probably just bite in half. Three Bowie knives, none too sharp, but she reckoned those were useless unless she could get within stabbing distance of a creature that didn't much care to be stabbed and came equipped with plenty of razor-sharp parts of its own.

"Any ideas, Ragdoll?" she muttered, and the horse just backed up a few steps and squealed.

From far away, she was sure she heard someone whisper, "Run, idjit," and she figured that was pretty good advice.

Peeking around the mare's left side, Nettie shot the buzzard again, and as the bird laughed and yarked, she whipped out her knife, sliced Ragdoll's hobble, swung into the loose saddle, yanked the horse's head left, and kicked with all her might. Seemed like a lot of steps for two seconds' worth of work and a cloud of dust, but the mare was ready and more than glad to oblige.

The buzzard spit out the bullet and screeched in rage, her wings beating the air as Nettie lay low and begged the mare to hurry. Considering neither of them were paying much attention to steering and it was all Nettie could do to keep the loosened saddle upright, they barreled blindly through the mesquite bushes. Nettie got a hand up over her eyes as the finger-length thorns reached for her and caught in her shirt. Her cheeks and arms burned with fresh scratches as they burst out the other side of the thicket and streaked across the bare brown prairie. Whatever water and grass Ragdoll had found gave her enough power to get them a good ways away from the bird's dark shadow, but Nettie could feel the nasty critter hovering over-head and chuckling to herself as she rode the wind. Their only hope was to find another green patch and some sort of cover, if not a town or other gathering of normal, heavily armed people who didn't take kindly to being cussed at by turkey vultures.

The day burned on in a haze of eternal bleakness. At some point, the saddle fell sideways, and Nettie rolled off the mare's neck on unsteady legs to tighten it. Trying to climb back up was a lot like being drunk, and she had to find a rock to use as a mounting block. Ragdoll took it in stride, more patient and gentle than a new-broke horse had any right to be. For a while, Nettie barely held the reins in one loose hand, and the mare obliged by zigzagging from thicket to creek to the occasional patch of shade thrown from a butte or boulder. Every now and then, a black shadow would flicker over them, a harsh laugh drifting down from the blue-white sky. All the vulture had to do was wait.

It wasn't until the horse had slowed to a sloppy walk and the sun was sizzling as it set that Nettie realized she'd taken a mesquite thorn in the arm. The damn thing had settled in good and deep through the dead stranger's shirt. In between the red heat of the scratches on her face and hands, the acid in her empty belly, the dryness in her throat, and the ache in her rump from two days of hard riding, Nettie somehow hadn't noticed a mesquite spine the size of tall man's finger sticking straight up out of her bicep. Apparently dying alone in the desert made folks right stupid.

Nettie dropped the reins over her saddle horn and felt around the thorn with fingers thick with blisters and calluses. As she yanked the mesquite chunk out and tossed it to the dirt, the buzzard laughed high overhead and let her wide shadow fall over the girl and the horse.

"Soon enough, girl. Soon enough," she called.

"Gettin' damn sick of listening to that bird talk," Nettie grumbled.

"Ain't we all," the desert muttered back.

Swallowing was hard, and staying awake was harder. The water skin was empty. Nettie's tongue felt like a Gila monster's tail fallen off after a scare and flopping around, useless. A hard pain in her belly and a hot, wet burn told her her flux had arrived, but for once, she didn't care, didn't even stop to tie on her rags. All the pain melted together in a pool of damp warmth that only made her mouth more dry. It felt like her life was bleeding out of her, staining her saddle with shame and leaving her empty as the cloudless sky. And she didn't care at all.

The sway of the mare's walk was a long ripple, a swallow, the rhythm of a boat at sea that lured Nettie into an uneasy sleep as the sun flattened into a flaming crown and began to sink beneath the black horizon like a penny in a bucket of water. The next time she blinked, stars exploded against the indigo, the moon a fat, white fang. Her belly was a stone, her thighs aching and chafed with dried blood and piss. Then it was noon again, the sun punishing and cruel. Rain fell, and her mouth was open to the heavens, her blood washed away to soak into the sand. A shadow covered her like a blanket, thick with stars. Ragdoll drank from a stream, but by the time Nettie looked at the ground, it was sand again, and the sun was laughing at her. Dark and light, hot and cold, wet and dry, pain and emptiness. Time meant nothing, direction even less. Her feet lost the stirrups and danced like broken puppets in the air below the short mare's mud-stained belly.

A bird's sharp scream woke Nettie in a panic, and she opened her eyes on a sunset unlike anything she'd ever seen before. Two buttes almost kissed dead ahead, a narrow path between them. The sky was black above, melting to blue and lavender and red, so bright and beautiful in the rocky frame that it made Nettie Lonesome want to cry. A shape filled the space between the buttes, a pitch-black vulture with wings outspread, larger than life and blotting out the dying light. But Nettie wasn't scared—not this time. She closed her eyes and opened her arms wide and felt the kiss of feathers on her face as she offered herself to the monster, ready to end this hellish forever of dying in the desert. Just as sharp claws and a putrid beak should've ripped into her chest, she felt a white-hot heat suffuse her, as if she'd swallowed the sun. But death didn't come. When she opened her eyes again, she saw stars and a steady, patient half moon. The vulture was gone.

Nothing changed for what felt like forever, and then the mare let out a little gasp and stumbled along faster. Nettie jerked awake and clutched at air, tumbling sideways off her horse and landing in a boneless heap on the last thing she would have expected: mud. Dang, but it felt good, seeping into her clothes and skin. Her grasping hands found marsh grass, sharp cat-tails topped with velvet. Somewhere nearby, the mare gulped and gulped and gulped and blew out with a splash, so Nettie dragged herself forward with the sharp spines of the water plants until her cracked and swollen lips touched real water.

If this was a dream, it beat hell out of biscuits and gravy.

Nettie drank a little water, threw it up full of dirt, and drank down some more. She began to think she just might live long enough to see to the thorn wound's damage by light of day when Ragdoll whinnied a challenge and splashed around her to stand, legs splayed, between Nettie and a dark shape falling from the sky.

"You carrion yet, girl?" the buzzard taunted.

"You wish, buzzard."

"Vulture. Harpy. Hungry."

"Don't matter. To me, you're just something that needs to die."

But behind the bold words, Nettie had gone ice-cold to her toes. She was half soaked in the creek, which meant her gun was wet, which meant she couldn't even distract the bird by wasting bullets. With a full-body shiver, she wrapped numb fingers around her Bowie knife and pulled it out of its sheath, struggling to her feet with the horse blocking her view of the vulture waiting on the moonlit bank. She didn't know much about vultures, save that they were generally agreeable birds that fed on carrion killed by braver creatures. Up until today, she'd never seen one closer than a stone's throw, and she'd certainly never heard one holler in human language and stare at her with bright blue eyes. Downright unsettling, even before it started calling her ugly names.

Nettie had never considered a foe that couldn't be taken down by a pistol, especially not at point-blank range. The vulture-thing was fast and had better weapons, but Nettie had one thing the bird surely didn't: a reckless fury backed by the desire to not be eaten. Make that two things: Nettie also had a bull-headed horse determined to serve as a barrier between her rider and the things that had set their mind to killing her.

As if on cue, the buzzard hopped forward and aimed a peck at Ragdoll's hoof, barely missing the tender coronet above the hard horn. In response, the mare reared and attempted to stomp the ugly thing's bald head, but the bird just giggled and jogged back, enjoying the game.

The creek was barely a dribble, not even enough for Nettie to get her head underwater, had she wanted to do so. But she did see plenty of stones on the bank, so she scooted back away from the horse and the bird until her wet rump fetched up on the opposite side. The first rock she found was the size of a hen's egg, and she flung it at the bird with all her might.

Instead, she hit her horse.

The poor mare squealed as the stone thwacked off her rear leg, and in the way of horses, her fear took over her good sense and sent her galloping away into the night.

Now, instead of a wall of horse and a saddlebag containing two dry guns, two dry knives, and a whip, Nettie had a wet gun, one knife, and a deep sense of regret. And the vulture had a clear shot at a mostly helpless girl just starting to feel sorry for herself and to wonder what it felt like when all the organs got yanked out through a person's belly button.

As the buzzard-woman clambered forward on tufted talons, Nettie grabbed another rock and flung it into the bird's wing. The creature cackled and flapped into the air, her feathers unruffled. The next rock went wide, and the third one clocked the bird in the tit, which didn't do a damn bit of good. Even though she knew it was foolish, Nettie pulled out her pistol and tried a shot, but the powder was too wet to do a damn thing. As the vulture landed in the middle of the creek with a splash, Nettie held her Bowie knife out in front of her, the foot-long blade still not long enough and not nearly as sharp as it should've been.

"Keep laughing, bird." She waggled the knife with false bravado.

"Last laugh's the best laugh," the vulture answered, somehow managing to smile when all it had was a rotten beak. "I'ma peck out your eyeballs first."

Nettie managed to stand, her boots full of water and her pants stuck to her legs. "Come over here and say that again, Ugly."

With a hellacious squawk, the vulture flapped her wings and slowly rose into the air.

"Don't! Call! Me! Ugly!" she screamed with each wingbeat, and Nettie took a deep breath and prepared to stab for the fluffy-soft feathers of the buzzard's belly.

"Shouldn't have called her that."

The man's voice, bemused and deep and coming from somewhere behind her, startled the hell out of poor Nettie, and she glanced back instead of leaping forward with her knife. Behind her on the bank stood a tall, wiry native man wearing only a few strips of leather in pertinent places, a peculiar sight that stole her attention away from the buzzard. As if they'd planned it that way all along, the bird attacked, barreling into Nettie claw-first and knocking the bedraggled girl to the mushy ground, the razor-sharp, gut-splattered beak aiming straight for one wide brown eye.

CHAPTER 9

The vulture's beak snapped shut close enough for Nettie to see the moonlight shining on tiny hairs caught in dried blood crusted to the black. Hard claws dug through her shirt's fabric to prick Nettie's skin as the bird sat on her in grim triumph, her long tits pressing up against Nettie's chest in a right uncomfortable fashion.

"I'll teach you ugly, girl."

The claws tightened, and the bright blue, all-too-human eyeballs peered into Nettie's as carrion breath washed over her.

"What are you?" Nettie managed to whisper.

The buzzard-thing opened her mouth to answer, and an arrow thunked straight down her gullet, the white feathers quivering by Nettie's cheek. Black oil sputtered out of the critter's mouth along with an enraged scream and a river of vomited filth. Bones, buttons, and a tiny human finger spilled into Nettie's lap. She sat up right quick and knocked the dying buzzard-woman off her body. The clumpy black blood burned, just like the stranger's had.

"She's a harpy." The man knelt beside Nettie, barely brushing her shoulder as he yanked the arrow out of the bird's head with a sick suck and kicked the writhing carcass away.

Nettie sat up, fingers shaking as she wiped the black gunk off her neck with the ruined sleeve of her shirt.

"Harpies ain't real."

"They ain't? Huh." He stood, towering over Nettie as he slung his bow over his shoulder and stuck the arrow back in his quiver. "Could've fooled me."

The way he was standing, Nettie got a right eyeful of the feller's rump, which was just as muscled and warm brown as every other bit of him. His hair brushed his shoulders, ink black and straight where Nettie's had once been wavy. His face was fine-featured, with sharp planes and high cheekbones and an intelligent, thoughtful look to it. He was probably twenty to her sixteen but carried himself like he was forty and the president of a goddamn bank. The way he'd said *ain't* implied he thought it was the punch line to a bad joke instead of a real word. And his accent was strangely low and musical, like he was half-swallowing the sounds before they could escape and was too polite to burp. He made her feel right unsettled. But then again, so did the dead bird lying on its back with blue eyes open and tits flopped into the dirt. Nettie pulled down her hat and looked away.

"It's probably the mesquite thorns, is all. Ran through a patch last night. You shot a buzzard, I reckon, and I'm mesquite-poisoned and sick with putrefaction and whatever the hell else a sun'll do to a feller."

The man barked a laugh. "You're not a feller. And that is no buzzard. But you will start seeing even more particularities, if we do not see to your injury."

She hunched her shoulders. "What injury?"

He looked her up and down, his nose quivering. "Shoulder. The thorn was stuck deep. The wound is hot and hard and red, so there's probably still a chunk in there. You didn't notice?"

It was downright uncomfortable, having a strange man claim to know what was under her clothes. Nettie twitched her shoulder and ran a hand down the neck of her shirt. Goddamned if he wasn't right. The place where she'd pulled the thorn out earlier was rock-hard and hotter than the sun. And there was no way he should've known that.

"I didn't know Injuns could see through shirts."

"Injuns can't. I can't. But I have my ways. You need doctoring before something else decides you're carrion. We've got to get you to the Rangers before you get yourself killed."

Nettie shook her head. "Ain't none of that made a lick of sense."

The man nodded. "It will soon, whether you like it or not. But for now, we have work to do." He knelt and swiftly, gently pulled her Bowie knife from her hand. She was too tired, hurt, and confused to argue, although she had a good hissy fit in her head; it didn't do to touch another feller's knife if he was there to take it back and stab you.

Crouching before the dead bird, the man closed his eyes, as formal as a preacher. He bowed, said something in a strange language, paused dramatically, and stabbed Nettie's knife down into the bird's chest, right between her dugs. The wings raised up, flapping, the eyes blind and the mouth shrieking, but only for a single breath. The man's back was to Nettie, but she could tell by the movement of his elbow and the thick stench of death and gore that he was butchering the critter. Soon he turned and presented her with a wet, purple thing cradled in both hands and shining with black like ink.

"What the sweet goddamn—"

"Take it."

Nettie jerked her head back and scooted away on her britches.

"I don't want that nasty chunk of gristle!"

He shook his head, stretched his arms out farther.

"If you wish to finish with this business and continue your quest for the Cannibal Owl, you must destroy it."

"I don't—I can't—How do you—?" Nettie swallowed a mouthful of dust as the world wavered around her, the air thick with heat that pressed in from every direction on a night that should've been cool. "You don't make any more goddamn sense than she did."

"You're not ready. And that's too bad for you. But it changes nothing."

Quick as a sidewinder, he grabbed her wrist and slapped the meat into her palm with a sick splat. It gave a trembling thump, all thoughtful-like, and she struggled to swallow down bile. The man took her other hand, forceful but gentle, and wrapped her fingers around the hilt of her own knife, which glimmered with the black muck that passed for the buzzard's blood.

"Now stab the harpy's heart to destroy her, and I will help you find what you seek."

Nettie looked up at him, her hat tumbling down her back and a rare breeze stirring her shorn hair. "And what, exactly, do I seek, you crazy-ass Injun?"

He guided her knife with the softness one shows a child, pushing the blade deep into the heart but not so deep as to cut her bare palm, underneath. The harpy dissolved into silvery sand and collapsed into the desert floor. The heart in Nettie's hand gave one last, sick thump and followed suit, the smooth grains pouring through her fingers and into her lap.

"You seek what we all seek, Nettie Lonesome." His eyes met hers, black to black. "Freedom and revenge."

The man paused meaningfully, and Nettie's eyes slid left

and right as if waiting for a crack of lightning and a fleet of goddamn unicorns.

"Mister, what the hot, sweet hell is that supposed to mean?"

He sighed, and as his shoulders lowered, the mask of solemnity slid off him like a shed lizard skin. He grinned, just a boy. A little older than her, a little redder than her, a lot more nekkid and amused than her. "It means I need to doctor you before you die of stupidity. Can you stand?"

Nettie dusted her hands off on her thighs and took to her feet with less grace and toughness than she would've liked. The ground in these parts had a tendency to wobble, that was for sure. The feller, on the other hand, rose smoothly. He seemed taller than Nettie, even though he wasn't. When he held out a hand as if to steady her, she swatted it away.

"I don't need help," she snapped.

In response, he poked her swollen bicep, hard, and the pain that thudded down her nerves and into her fingertips made her eyes roll back.

"I think you do."

She almost fell over, and he caught her with a dry hand on her good shoulder. Help wasn't a thing she'd ever really been offered before, outside of a few kind words from Monty. She was just about to shove the feller away when she was overcome with the most peculiar feeling. It was as if the stars had swollen up to blot out the night, and she was the only waking thing in a thousand miles, a furious sun in a world of heat that would be ripped down to bones by wind and sand before she saw another living creature ever again. A shadow flashed over her, and when she crouched and cried out, fearing another harpy, it hit home that she could take the nekkid man's assistance or crumble away into bones and sand beside the bitch bird's silvery remains.

But she planted her feet and stuck out her chin, because accepting help was going to be her own goddamn idea.

"Maybe if you got some water."

He inclined his head just the tiniest bit, the corner of his mouth curling up. "I do not. But there's a place where the creek pools, very close by. Your horse is waiting there, but I warn you: Her feelings are very hurt."

Nettie sighed deeply and cleaned her black-stained knife on her now-ruined pants. "Well, lead on, mister. You don't seem to know what pants are, but you know where I'm hurt and how my horse is feeling, so I suspect you can at least find water."

He shifted the bow on his shoulder. "You are an unkind woman."

For once, she didn't argue the point.

"Yeah, well, it's an unkind life."

Pulling her hat low, Nettie started walking in the direction he was facing, where just the haziest smudge of green tinged with moonlight suggested the presence of water. The man took his place behind her, close enough to catch her if she fell, which she found insulting as hell. But then she tripped on a scrubby bush, and he did catch her, and that unkind girl did him the great kindness of going unconscious.

When Nettie blinked again, firelight blinked back. Her initial response to existence in general was to panic and shoot something full of holes, but she felt too poorly. She could barely move, as a matter of fact, and her whole goddamn body ached like she'd been tossed in a gunnysack, thrown into a gulch, and beaten with old boots. Plus, her pistol was gone.

"I know you're awake. And I have your gun. I'll give it back once you decide you don't want to shoot me. In any case, it's still too wet to do any damage."

Nettie sat up and rubbed the sandy sleep out of her eyes. "You a mind reader?"

He grinned at her from the other side of a small fire, white teeth shining in the night as he roasted something on a stick. "Not quite. But your hand went to your hip before your eyes were open." He held out the stick to her, bringing her face to face with a skinned and greasy rabbit. "They call me Coyote Dan."

She stared at him. "That what *you* call yourself?"

He inclined his head. If they'd been keeping score, she'd won a point. "Names are just skins to wear for a while. Dan'll do."

"What's your friend's name, Dan?"

When she didn't make a grab for the steaming meat, he shrugged and held it back over the fire. "His name is Dinner. But I agree. He's not done yet."

A soft snort in the shadows alerted Nettie to the fact that Ragdoll might not have forgiven her but was willing to consider it. Standing on numb feet, she surveyed the camp. Aw, hell. It wasn't a camp at all. Just Coyote Dan, a fire, one dead rabbit, and one huffy mustang mare. At least there was enough bristly grass around to keep the horse busy.

"Sorry, Rags. My aim's bad."

The horse snorted and swung her rump around. But when Nettie staggered over to her to check that Coyote Dan had loosened the mare's cinch a bit, which he had, Ragdoll pressed her neck over the girl's shoulder and breathed out in a horse-type sigh that said they were both fools, or possibly that harpies were no-good varmints.

"You got any—"

"—water? You can help yourself at the creek. I've already filled both your skins."

And dang if they weren't dangling from her saddle like fat little babies. She flicked one just to watch it swing before heading in the direction Coyote Dan was pointing with his half-cooked dinner. Calling the dirty rivulet a creek was generous, but dang if it didn't feel good to have a wet tongue. The water ran down her chin and tickled the hot little marks where the buzzard's talons had pricked into her chest. Lord and crow, if her skin didn't itch all over like it was a size too small. Her britches were crusted to her body with dried flux blood and mud and piss, and she sat right down in the creek to wash away her shame. And that place on her shoulder... might as well have been a rock snatched right out of the fire. If she really focused, she could feel some foreign fleck of mesquite poison caught beneath her skin, angry and fighting to get out.

With nothing but the blue light of moon and stars, she couldn't see much, but she unbuttoned her shirt anyway and slid the collar down over her shoulder, her back to Coyote Dan and his fire. He'd been good to her so far, but life had taught her that showing weakness was the fastest way to being made even weaker. Her horse probably wouldn't even try to save her this time, if the man went for her.

The lump on her upper arm was swollen and hard. When she pressed on it, liquid oozed out, smelling sweet and dead.

"Aw, hell."

She'd watched an old man die on Pap's porch once, thanks to a wound that looked and smelled about the same. Of course, that feller had been dumb enough to get his leg caught in a trap, but the size of the injury didn't matter when it went bad. Gray Hawk had muttered something about the old fool being too stupid to let him cut off his foot, which Nettie figured meant she was either going to lose her arm or die with a fever hot enough to boil meat. Unless maybe she could squeeze out all the evil...

Nope.

She nearly fainted from the pain, although the burp of white ooze was gratifying.

"Dinner is ready."

She glared at him over her shoulder.

"You sure you want to waste a perfectly good rabbit on a dead cowpoke?"

At that, he really did laugh, so hard that he rocked back, his bare feet lifting off the ground. "You're not going to die today. But maybe don't eat too much, just in case."

When had she last eaten—yesterday's supper? No. She counted back the turns of moon and sun. Four days ago. It had to be. And she hadn't eaten much then, as they were getting ready to rustle over the river and the beans had been off. Skitty as a cat, she redid her shirt and approached the fire. She sat opposite her supposed savior, the flames keeping watch between them. Coyote Dan, he said they called him. Probably a name white men had given him, as nobody in their right mind would claim to be like the sneaky little desert dogs. He held out the stick, the rabbit's crisped, dead-black eyes staring at her. With a shrug, she grabbed a bit of bone and yanked off a haunch, the grease sizzling into the fire. Maybe it was just a jackrabbit, but danged if it wasn't the best thing she'd ever eaten, and pretty soon she was sucking on her fingers and trying to figure out the best way to ask for more without seeming rude as a coyote herself.

Something sailed out of the air, landing just between her boots. A rabbit skeleton missing one leg, picked clean.

"Next time, take what you want," Coyote Dan said in that preacher-type way he had, and Nettie picked up the carcass and flung it right back at him, where it splattered against his bare chest. He caught it as it fell and stared into its skull as if waiting for it to apologize.

"I know I look like a banker in my fine duds, Dan, but I wasn't born to a life of plenty. Now what exactly are you expecting in return for helping me and feeding me a quarter of a measly ol' rabbit? Because I won't be your wife, your whore, or your slave."

Coyote Dan wagged his head, slick hair swinging. "I don't need any of those things. Hasn't anyone ever helped you because it was the right thing to do?"

Unwanted tears stung her eyes. "Top hand named Monty was kind to me. I watched him die a few nights ago. So as you can see, helping me ain't exactly good for a man's health. What do you want?"

Without a word, he popped the skull off the rabbit and threw it back in what was becoming the dumbest game of toss she'd ever seen played. Instead of catching it, she batted it to the ground with her left arm. The right one was starting to swell up beyond the thorn wound, but she wasn't about to tell him that.

"Look at the skull. What do you see?"

Nettie looked sideways.

"Rabbit skull, nibbled down."

"Look closer. Look at the teeth."

She almost didn't. But the fact that this strange feller kept his bow close at hand convinced her that she might as well humor him. Leaning over, she inspected the picked-over bone, digging out the tiny, tender cheeks to pop in her mouth. And saw...

"Jiminy crow. Its teeth ain't right."

He nodded. "Fangs. That rabbit smelled you, came here to take a bite. Instead, you ate it for dinner. Do you know why?"

"You gonna tell me, preacher?"

He smirked off the insult.

"Because you and I...we can see things."

Nettie straightened back up and let a hand settle, all casual-like, on her gun.

"Yep. I sure can see a lot of things, Coyote Dan. And one such thing is that you're crazy as a bedbug."

Dan laughed again. It was getting downright uncomfortable, the way he did that. But when he looked up at her across the fire, his eyes were clear and sane and as dark as the inside of a cave.

"Tell me, Nettie Lonesome. What was the first monster you killed? The first creature that turned to sand and blew away? Because whatever it is, that's where you can lay your blame."

A shiver skittered down Nettie's back. "Did you just say monster?"

"I did." He grinned. "Once you kill one of us, your eyes are open to all of us."

CHAPTER

10

Nettie's eyes narrowed. How quick could she draw? How fast could he nock an arrow to fly into her mouth, silencing her like the buzzard-woman? And how long might a bullet hold him back, if he really was one of... them?

With her gun arm full of pus, she was at his mercy, of which he'd definitely shown a bucketful. So maybe she'd hear him out. At the very least, Coyote Dan believed the hogwash he was spouting.

And he didn't have red eyes or fangs.

So she gave him the truth to see how he'd swallow it.

"Man found me out by the barn. Tried to make me go inside, and I took offense."

"Did you shoot him?"

She shook her head. "Didn't have a gun yet. Put a sickle in his eye, but he just laughed. Ended up stabbing him in the heart with a chunk of wood."

"And then?"

She leaned back and sat her hat on the ground, feeling a sheen of sweat break over her forehead. He already knew her name and her gender and had her weak and on her back; what more was there to hide?

"I reckon you already know. He turned into sand. Blew away. I kept his clothes and boots." She shot her gore-stained cuffs as she'd seen the mayor do once downtown.

"And what did you see, after that night?"

Nettie gazed up into the stars. "Blood-drinking whores. A boy I liked turned into a killer lizard with fangs. That buzzard with the dugs." Ragdoll whuffed in the dark, and Nettie added, "And the Injun woman on a wet black horse, pointing me west." Suddenly, it was all too funny, and she flopped back on the ground, half-laughing and half-crying. "Am I going crazy, Coyote Dan?"

He rose smoothly and hurried around the fire to her side. With gentle hands, he rolled her onto her back.

"Not crazy. Fevered. Infected with mesquite poison, suffering dehydration, and thick with filth from a harpy's claws. You need medicine, Nettie Lonesome. Do you trust me?"

Her head rolled side to side as she tried to squint him from two men back into one. What was trust when you were dying in the desert with nothing but a stranger by your side? The fire burned up her arm, the wound sickly pulsing like the harpy's heart she'd held in her hand. His face was so warm, so urgent, lit by the orange flames, and when she blinked, she would've sworn his eyes glimmered green. She blinked again, and all she saw was concern turning the corner into worry.

"Might as well, I reckon." She swallowed around a lump of rabbit in her throat. "Ain't got much choice, far as I can see."

"Your confidence honors me." His eyes said it was a joke even if his mouth didn't, so she felt obliged to smile, just a little. "I must tend to your wound. I can cut open your shirt, or you can withdraw your arm. The choice is yours."

Nettie unbuttoned her shirt with shaking fingers and yanked her swollen, hot arm out of the sleeve, grateful for what little coolness the night afforded. Let the feller look; she kept her chest bound up tight in a strip of muslin for a dozen reasons. And his leather flap sometimes showed what little a man kept to himself, so they might as well be even.

"Listen carefully," Dan said. "I'm going to do things you won't understand, things that will confuse you and might hurt you, although I'll do my best to ease your pain. If you fight me or stop me, you'll most likely die or at least lose the arm. It will take you much longer than a monster to fall away to dust, but it will happen."

She tried to shrug her assent, but it hurt too much.

"Fine," she muttered. "Might as well try to keep from dust awhile longer."

Slowly, as if she were a wild bronc just brought to the corral, he unbuckled her gun belt and placed her pistol far out of reach. Her Bowie knife followed. As she watched the firelight glint on the blade, she realized that she was just about where she'd been last week: crippled by outside forces, without weapons, at the mercy of a man she didn't trust, and pretty much ready to die.

With a slight bow, Dan began singing in another language, a pulsing beat that drew her into the starlight. He moved around, in and out of shadow, cutting and pounding things and visiting the creek, giving Ragdoll a pat on the rump as he passed. Something pressed against her lips, his arm strong behind her shoulders as he helped her to drink. Oh, Lord, it was bitter, bitter as hell, but she drank it down so long as he urged it, the water skin's mouth clacking against her teeth. Soon the stars spun around in a whirl, thrumming with his song and, later, singing back to him. There was dancing, a dozen shapes hopping around the fire and throwing shadows against a canyon that she was danged sure didn't exist.

The harpy's beak ripped into her arm, but when her head whipped around, teeth bared, it was just her Bowie knife, heated cherry-red and pressing gently into the apple-sized lump on her shoulder. She shuddered as it burst, the worst and best thing she'd ever felt in her life as the evil drained out of her body to drip, a mix of black and white and red, onto the sand. Strong thumbs pressed, pushed, massaged, forced, expelled, probed, and then, holy crow, entered the knife's cut.

That was when she almost forgot. That was when she almost bit him and ended it.

If he hadn't growled at her, just then, showing fangs, she would've ruined everything.

Instead, she had the good grace to pass out while he cleaned the wound, packed it, and wrapped it gently in a stained bandanna he'd found in her saddlebag.

"I think maybe you'll live," he whispered into her ear, so sadly revealed by rough-shorn hair. "But first you must sleep. And dream. And then you've got a lot to learn."

In the darkness of her mind, Nettie felt exposed, watched over by some bigger, outside force that was waiting. And weighing.

"You journeyed for four days without eating or drinking. You received a vision. What did you see?" The disembodied voice was stern but gentle.

Nettie opened her eyes, straight up, and stared into the sun. She saw nothing.

"Answer me, Nettie Lonesome."

She swallowed, her throat a desert. "I saw a bird's shadow against the sunset, wings spread to blot out the stars."

"You saw a shadow."

"Yes."

"You are the Shadow."

"No, I saw—"

"—the shadow."

"So?"

She felt a tug at her waist but was unable to move. The leather pouch fell back against her hip, somehow heavier than it had been before. Everything was white light, hot and burning and fierce. "Your vision quest has shown you the truth. You are a man now."

Blind and confused, still she smiled at the rightness of it. "You're goddamn right I am."

The voice laughed and whispered, "Sleep, then, warrior. Find peace."

Nettie slept, dark and deep, not bothering to toss or turn on the cold, hard ground. She woke with the sun, her stained shirt painted pink and orange and her mouth tasting of leather. Her saddle blanket was carefully tucked over her, and her first notion was that horsehair on one's lips was probably the reason folks up and moved to big cities. Blowing out hard, she sat up, noting that her arm was back in her sleeve, her collar rebuttoned, and her hat somewhere else entirely. And her arm hurt in an entirely different way than it had, but the pain was already fading. Monty's bandanna was wrapped around a wound that stung and gave off an herbal-type smell but at least didn't feel like an egg about to hatch a devil.

Coyote Dan was nowhere to be seen, but half a roasted rabbit carcass sat on a flat stone, close enough for her to smell. Eyes all shifty for the man who'd doctored her, or possibly for some new creature that might attack, she gobbled down the food so quick she barely tasted it and burped rabbit breath behind a fist. Her filled water skin was beside her, and she drank so much that she felt like a water skin herself, round and full in the belly. Kind of funny, how she was eating better, half-dead and on the run across the prairie, than she had under Pap's barely-a-roof.

Knee-deep in the grass, Ragdoll whinnied in welcome, and Nettie followed the mare's line of sight to a shape wavering as it neared her. Her gun was back in its holster, and she checked that it was loaded. The Bowie knife had also been returned, far cleaner than it had been when she'd last seen it, and sharper, too. A weapon in each hand, she climbed onto a boulder and sat, legs aggressively spread and boots less than firm on the ground, to wait out the approaching horseman.

The horse clopped closer, but all she could see was a shadow wearing a wide hat. Ragdoll whinnied again, more insistent this time, and Nettie couldn't figure if the mare was just happy to see another horse or if maybe she recognized the pair. Holy crow—what if the Double TK cowpokes had come after her? Her belly flopped around, clenching in fear. She was weak and alone, as it was. But surely one feller wouldn't chase her down on his own, even if there was a bounty on her for killing Monty and Chuck.

She cocked the pistol, just in case.

The horseman laughed, an easy and familiar sound that carried over the prairie. "Are you going to shoot me, Nettie Lonesome? You must be feeling better, then."

All the fight and worry bled out of her, replaced by slight annoyance. She shoved her gun and knife back into place. Not only did she find this particular feller's attitude off-putting, but she hated owing anybody anything, and now that she was clear-headed and mostly alive again, she realized just how much she owed the the man who'd doctored her.

At least he'd finally put on some damn clothes.

"Well, shit, Coyote Dan. I still could shoot you, if you like."

He dismounted and walked his gelding to Ragdoll to introduce them. "I don't think so. You can barely stand. Too much trouble to pull the trigger. Besides, I come bearing gifts." She could see him better now, and he looked entirely different in a cowpoke's get-up. He wore butternut britches, a red plaid shirt, and a wide-brim hat with his hair braided back as hers had once been. But he wasn't wearing boots, and he hadn't been using the stirrups in his Aztecan saddle, which struck her as the most peculiar of his peculiarities thus far. Something about his voice plucked at her, reminding her that she'd had and forgotten a dream that seemed more important than most.

"How do you feel?"

Nettie twitched her head back and forth, ran a hand thoughtfully down her arm and chest. "Better, I reckon. What'd you do to my arm?"

Dan unlaced his saddle bags and carried them over a shoulder before dropping them, clanking, by Nettie's feet. "I used Inde magic."

"Bullshit, Dan."

His face lit up in a grin, all white teeth and good humor. "You caught me. I used white-man medicine. Just removed the piece of thorn, bled the wound, rinsed it with boiling water, applied a salve, and burned it closed with the blade of your knife."

"Why don't it hurt more, then?"

A grin. "I told you. Inde magic."

She flapped a callused hand at him. "Sell that manure somewhere else, boy."

His grin didn't waver as he kicked the saddlebags with a

dusty bare foot. "Perhaps I spent a few years working with a sawbones in the city. Don't you want to know what's in the bags?"

Nettie spit in the dust, glad to have enough spit to do so. "More Inde magic, I reckon."

But she was curious, so she waited a few minutes just to vex him before unbuckling the flap to peer inside. It was mostly clothes—a clean plaid shirt; a pair of britches; tall, thick socks; and a passel of bandannas. The clanking she'd heard was spurs and bullets, all garbled up in the bottom. The other bag was full of grain packed down under jerky.

Looking up and blinking against the sun, she speared Dan with narrowed eyes. "You steal this?"

He shook his head at her like maybe she was soft-headed. "Of course."

"Where from?"

Coyote Dan shrugged and grinned. "A cattle outfit north-west of here. We're a bit far from Gloomy Bluebird, you know."

Nettie was holding up the shirt against her own to compare sizes, but she dropped it when she heard that, her hand falling on her gun.

"How'd you know about Gloomy Bluebird? Did Pap send you after me?"

Dan sat next to her, legs crossed, and handed her a strip of jerky. "There's no bounty on you. Boss Kimble thinks you were beset by vaqueros, and your owner is too drunk to care who cooks for his breakfast. He sold your mule, I'm sorry to say."

"He ain't my owner." Nettie spit again, this time with more feeling.

Dan quirked an eyebrow. "Not anymore, he isn't. Now eat."

Nettie threw the uneaten jerky at the man's face, and he

caught it and took a large, ripping bite. "Look, Dan. You been good to me, so I ain't shot you. Yet. But you got a smart mouth for some stranger that found me in the middle of the desert. So how do you know so much, and what the hell do you want from me?"

"It's not so much what I want as what I consider my duty. There are things you need to know."

"No shit, Dan. Let's start with how you know every god-damn thing about me."

Dan didn't act a bit mannerly, for all that he was dressed in cowpoke clothes and talked like a preacher. He placed his hat on the ground, leaned back against a rock, and chewed his jerky for a few minutes as if searching for the right words in the beef fat.

"So far, if I count correctly, you've met a vampire, a chupaca-bra, and a harpy. Is that right?"

"A bunch of vampires," she muttered. "Whole whorehouse of the damn things."

Coyote Dan nodded. "So you've met three kinds of danger-ous creatures. Three individuals who wished to cause you harm and, as you put it, 'a whole whorehouse' of creatures who did not wish you ill but could've killed you on the spot, yes?"

Nettie's eyes were almost permanently slitted in suspicion, at this point. "I reckon."

"And now you've met me. Do you think I'm a bad creature?"

Breakfast rose in Nettie's throat. Coyote Dan was a...thing? A monster? He'd admitted as much last night, but she'd been too weak and mad with fever to challenge it. It was clear he wasn't a vampire, a harpy, or what Chuck had become—a chu-pacabra, supposedly. So what the heck was he? The way he sat across from her, back straight and face open and hands empty of weapons, made him seem trustworthy. And he could've easily killed her a hundred times over since shooting the harpy off her. But he hadn't. He'd helped her, again and again.

But that didn't necessarily mean she trusted him.

"You don't seem bad," she finally said. "But I reckon most bad things don't think they're bad."

He nodded. "That's wise. Many monsters will hide what they are, especially when they suspect you might see the truth. Truth requires trust. So my question, Nettie Lonesome, is this: Can I trust you? Because I can smell that you still do not trust me."

Lord, Nettie felt like she was standing on a cliff and staring down, about to take a step into nothing. But what was her other choice? Admit that she was scared to know whatever Coyote Dan wanted to tell her? Considering he'd all but admitted he was a "bad creature," she wasn't much in the mood to arouse his anger. And she now owed him even more, considering he'd confirmed that no one back home was currently hunting her.

"I don't trust easy, but I sure as hell won't shoot you unless you try to kill me first," she finally said.

"Is that a promise?"

Nettie spit in her hand and held it out, and Dan spit in his hand, and the wet globs merged against her dry palm.

But Dan didn't say anything, didn't explain. He just stood up and walked away.

"Where are you going now?"

He glanced over his shoulder and grinned. "You'll see. Just remember that you promised not to shoot unless I tried to kill you. Unless you want to be haunted by two angry Injuns, you'd best keep that promise."

Filled with doubt, Nettie placed her gun on the ground and kicked it away.

Dan walked past the horses and around a big boulder. Nettie

wiped her spit-gloppy hand off on her pants, turned away from the direction Dan had gone, and was just about to change out her shirt for the new, unstained one from the saddlebag when she heard a familiar yip.

Turning around, she found a coyote staring at her with intelligent green eyes. Her hand went to where her gun usually sat on her hip, but the holster was empty, her gun five steps away. Heart ratcheting up, she called out, "Dan? There's a coyote out here staring at me. Must be rabid. Can I pick up my gun now?"

He didn't answer, but the coyote sat back on its haunches and opened its mouth wide in a yawn that showed sharp white teeth devoid of froth. As Nettie's hand crept to her knife, the critter shook its head back and forth as if scolding her. When she left the knife alone, the coyote's mouth split open in a grin, tongue spilling out as if laughing.

"Dan?"

The coyote yipped.

"Not you, feller. I got a friend out here. He's got good aim, too. You'd better git."

It yipped again, turned around, and ran off. As if it understood her. Maybe it was Dan's pet?

The second the coyote turned around, Nettie went for her gun, but by the time she'd snatched it out of the dirt and aimed, the dang thing had darted behind a boulder. She'd never seen a friendly coyote, and the critters weren't often out during daylight, but it hadn't seemed mad. It had appeared . . . right clever. Pap had put down a mad dog once, and the thing had acted like it was trying to fight out of its own skin, its eyes insane and rolling and its mouth dripping red foam.

"Don't shoot me, Nettie. I'm not mad."

Dan appeared, buttoning up his shirt and deeply amused.

"I ain't worried about you, Dan. There was a coyote out here acting peculiar. Did you pass it?"

In response, Dan let out a familiar yip and tied his bandanna back on around his neck.

Nettie's mouth dropped open wide enough to admit a buffalo.

"I didn't pass the coyote, Nettie Lonesome. I *am* the coyote."

CHAPTER 11

"What the Sam Hill business do you got being a coyote, Dan?"

Nettie wasn't particularly surprised, which surprised her. Considering what had happened in the last week, she was ready to believe just about anything, provided it didn't attack her. He'd said from the start his name was Coyote Dan. After the fact, she felt a bit stupid for not having figured out that the meaning was literal. He'd showed up nearly nekkid. He'd known about the lady-buzzard, known how to kill it. He'd counted himself among the monsters. Of course he was one of... them.

"I could ask you what business you have being a runaway slave girl who thinks she's a boy."

Her cheeks flaring hot, Nettie bared her noncoyote but still threatening teeth. "I ain't no runaway slave girl."

Dan's head cocked, and he finished straightening his cowpoke clothes and sat down across from her, too far away for her to strike him, if the urge took her.

"There's no shame in being what you are."

She pointed her knife at him. "I'm the only one who gets to say what I am."

"But once you accept what you are and what you want to be,

you'll be closer to your goal. You were a slave, Nettie. Why do you deny it? Did Pap and Mam show you any love?"

"Plenty of folks don't show their kids love. Preacher used to beat his kids in the street while reading from his Good Book."

Dan sighed. "You performed every piece of work on that sad little farm. They barely fed you. They didn't pay you. They didn't school you. They dressed you in rags, passed on their old shoes. There was no talk of you marrying or taking a trade. Perhaps they didn't hold papers, but you were a slave as sure as any woman in chains in Tanasi."

A dark rage bubbled up in Nettie's belly, and before her brain could put a foot down, she dropped the knife and launched herself at Coyote Dan, aiming to strangle him silent. The feller halfway let her, holding her gently but firmly away as if she were a kitten caught by the neck scruff as it clawed the air.

"I. Ain't. Nobody's. Slave!"

Dan didn't say anything, which was what finally sucked the fight out of the girl. She flopped over onto her back on the hard ground and stared up into the white-fire sun, hoping that Dan wouldn't see her tears. Of course, considering he'd been able to sniff out her wound, he could probably smell her tears just as easily.

"You're nobody's slave now, and now is all that matters."

She breathed in deep, considering. It was true. And yet the truth of it washed the first sixteen years of her life with a shameful pain that she'd pushed deep down into a dark hole in her soul, one where she never had to look at the ugliness that was human nature. Pap and Mam said they'd adopted her, that she owed them for taking her in when nobody else wanted a little nut-brown baby with a loud yowl. Nobody ever said *slave* or even *servant*. But they'd definitely said *whip* and *switch* and *Come out now, girl, or I'll beat you blind*. And they had sure enough followed up on that threat, plenty of times. She carried the scars on her back to prove it.

"Never again," she muttered. Then she sat up. "Wait. Answer the original question. What the hell are you?"

He shrugged, easy in his skin. "Shapeshifter. Skinwalker. There are many names, many bands, many kinds. When I wish it, I walk on four legs."

Nettie stared at the bottoms of his feet, dusted tan with prairie dirt. They were one big callus and made her twitch her toes, just thinking about what it must feel like to step on the various pokey things of the desert without thick boots.

"Does it hurt?"

Dan cocked his head, and she saw the mischievous look of his coyote self shining through his human face. "When I was a child, it didn't. But then, when I first became a man, it hurt terribly. Because I fought it and tried to deny it, to push it down. Now that I've claimed it and accepted it, it's natural. It flows like the river over rocks. You have to let it take you. You have to embrace it."

A shadow flickered overhead, and Nettie stared up at the circling vulture. When she flinched and went for her gun, Dan shook his head.

"That's not a harpy. Just a regular vulture. Don't waste your bullets."

Nettie shaded her eyes and stared up, squinting for details. "How can you tell?"

"The fact that it's circling instead of descending and laughing. And there's a tremor in the air when a monster is near. Like throwing a pebble in a pond, it ripples outward and laps against the skin of one who knows. You've simply grown accustomed to mine, but you'll learn to feel it. Every creature has its own particular feeling."

Nettie glared knives at him.

"And why can I feel it? You saying I'm one of...them? Of you?"

Dan threw back his head and laughed. "You're not one of us. You're human, all human, tempered with long suffering and brief mortality like a blade forged in fire and ice. And yet... you're not."

Standing up, Nettie stared down at him. Her patience was a slim thing at the best of times, and just now, it was spiderweb thin. "Excuse me for bearing bad news, but you sure got a way of sayin' a whole lot of nothing. Now if you'll kindly point me toward the nearest ranch that could use a wrangler, I'll leave you to your coyotin', or whatever you call it." She turned to face west and added, "With thanks for the doctoring. Hope I can pay you back one day."

"You don't want to leave now. There's more to tell. I've told you what you're not, but aren't you curious about what you are?"

Nettie snorted. "I know what I am, and that's leaving."

She checked Ragdoll's saddle, tightening the cinch and running hands down the mare's legs to check for hot spots or thorns or stones in her hooves. The horse bumped her, and she absentmindedly scratched her neck and muttered, "Sorry 'bout that rock I tossed, sugar."

Coyote Dan stood and brought her the saddlebags. "You should change. That shirt looks like you murdered somebody in it. And monsters can smell the blood of their kind. They know when you've killed before, when you can sense them. The best way to avoid notice is to pretend you can't see them and stay far away." He gave her a peculiar look. "At least, that's how it's always been before."

"Fine," Nettie snapped. "I'll change. But I'm leaving after that."

"*We* are leaving after that."

"I didn't say you could come along."

"You have no choice. I won't have your death on my conscience. Nor will I take up your task."

Giving Ragdoll's saddle a final cinch that made the mare gasp, Nettie snatched the saddlebags from Dan's hand and took off for the same big rock he'd disappeared behind before supposedly becoming a coyote. Lord, if she found a pet coyote tied up back there with a rabbit carcass in its smiling jaws, she would finally follow her gut instinct and shoot Coyote Dan for a liar. But all she found on the other side of the rock was more endless prairie and a scuffle in the loose dirt where human footprints mixed with coyote prints. The coyote prints, she noticed, only went in one direction, and it was right to where the coyote had laughed at her.

"Goddammit," Nettie muttered, dumping out the saddlebags.

She checked that Dan was still with the horses before shucking her old shirt and unwinding the strip of sheeting she used to bind up her chest. There was a very similar piece in the saddlebag, which almost got her dander up again until she remembered that he'd doctored her arm and the buzzard claw wounds on her upper chest. So he'd seen her binding but not touched it, which she could allow. Once she was tight and comfortably tucked above, she unrolled the pants and took stock of her current situation. At least her godforsaken courses were done for another month, bled out over four days lost in the desert. No point in ruining another perfectly good pair of pants. No wonder women couldn't get anywhere in life, considering they spent a week out of every month in pain and inconveniently gushing blood.

"Dan, could you toss me a water skin?"

She poked her head around the rock, and he lobbed one right to her like he'd been waiting for her to ask. Catching it hurt like a bitch, but she felt much better after its application.

The new britches still smelled like the herbs they'd last been boiled in to wash, and they were a damn sight better fit than her old pair. The shirt was meant for a slender man, too, plaid with plenty of tail to tuck. Right thoughtful of Dan, stealing from a tall, thin feller. The new bandanna felt cool around her neck, and she kept Monty's old one on her upper arm. Not because Dan wanted it there. Because it was Monty's and she liked the feel of it.

Switching out her sweat-hard socks for the nicer pair in the saddlebags, she immediately felt like a new person in a new skin. She wasn't Nettie anymore, and she couldn't be Nat— they might be looking for him. Ned, maybe? Pat? Or something entirely new? She'd never put too much thought into being a girl, didn't really feel like a girl or identify with the little girls she'd seen in skirts around town. Being a boy just felt… natural. There were plenty of benefits to looking and acting like a feller, including never having a man look at her like Pap had, just once, when he found her bathing in the creek in her ratty white nightgown. Being a woman in Nettie's world meant being a whore or being a wife, which was no better than a slave to her taste. Either way, she'd just be taking a feller's orders for the rest of her life. Now that she'd tasted freedom, she'd die first. A feller would have to earn her allegiance, by crow.

But now she had to put actual thought into being a boy without Monty around to hand her the name.

"Matt Lonesome. Newt Loner. Pat Friendly? Goddammit." Slapping her hat back on and tilting it down, she put a boy's swagger into her walk, stuffed her old rags in the saddlebag, and rounded the rock to face Coyote Dan, man to man. If there was one thing she didn't need, showing up on a new ranch to start her life over again, it was a dirty-footed Injun feller who laughed too loud and turned into a coyote when he took the notion.

Dan sat his horse, a plain but rangy sorrel with agreeable eyes and forgettable markings. His feet hung bare beside the stirrups, his bow was slung casually over his shoulder, and he held his reins more loosely than Nettie considered wise. Beside him, Ragdoll was packed and ready. The fire was smothered, all evidence of their camp erased. There was nothing left to do but mount up and hope Dan got thrown off his horse and broke his neck.

It was past noon, and the sun was awful high, but Dan set out flat east, whatever that meant. She kicked Ragdoll ahead, but the damn mare did her best to lag behind, following Dan's sorrel gelding with stupid contentment.

"Just like a woman," Nettie muttered, giving the mare a kick that made her pin her ears.

Dan clucked his gelding into a trot that Ragdoll gladly joined. "Not all women are weak, you know."

"I ain't never met one that wasn't."

He gave her his coyote smirk. "And how many women have you actually known?"

Nettie grunted. "Besides them vampire whores, just Mam, I reckon. Went begging in town, when I had no choice. Saw nothing in skirts I wanted to be."

"Don't blame what's between a creature's legs. Blame what's in its heart."

She spit in the dirt. "You got anything to say that ain't crap?"

"I have plenty to say, but you have to want to hear it."

"I'm trying, Dan, but all I hear is jabber."

In response, he clucked his horse to a canter. Ragdoll followed, the little ninny.

Nettie had to admit Dan had a helluva seat on a horse, riding the lope easy as pie despite his lack of stirrups or rein control. With the afternoon's cruel heat, they couldn't keep up the pace much longer, which meant he had to know where they were headed and that easy water lay in that direction. She didn't like him, but she recognized that he knew the land here better than she did.

As they galloped across the prairie, Nettie's worries fell away. For so long, she'd ridden her old mule at a snail's pace, barely able to entice the bag of bones into a jaunty trot. She'd broken more than a few broncs, but that was always in a round pen made of rough twigs or clean white boards, barely far enough for a few good skips of a canter. And she'd rustled cattle with the wranglers, but she'd been scared to the point of yarking, too anxious to enjoy it. She'd always dreamed of the freedom of a flat-out run, a loose lope across the wideness of the world. As if sensing her exhilaration, Dan glanced back at her, grinned, and whooped loud enough to hop his horse into a race that Ragdoll took up easily with a little shake of her neck. Before she could stop herself, Nettie had whooped, too, and her hat was in her hand, slapping the mare's rump to bring them neck and neck with Dan's gelding.

Holy crow, but she'd never felt so free. Like nothing could stop her. Like she could run forever on the endless plain. Like she could fly. Like the word *stop* suddenly held no meaning, and walls were just something to knock down. She inhaled the wind and breathed out fire, sucked in life and spit out the bones. The horse ran hot and sleek beneath her, muscle and bone, perfect and pure. The ground was just something to pass by, the sky something to aim for. And when she looked over, Dan's grin echoed the one she felt on her own face.

God damn. She didn't know a heart could feel so light.

And then it fell off. Run to canter, canter to lope, lope to trot, trot to a bouncy walk.

The horses were breathing hard, and so was Nettie, as if she herself had been running.

"Like flying," she muttered, half to herself.

"I imagine so. I have a friend who shifts to a hawk. He can't fly if he's thinking human thoughts. Goes into a roll and falls like a bag of rocks. He has to let go completely to stay in the air."

Nettie's eyes went shifty.

"You're gonna start jabberin' again, ain't you?"

"I must. For your own good."

"Pap used to say that before he beat me."

"There are things in the world worse than Pap."

Nettie shrugged and swigged down some water from her full skin. "Go on, then. Give me all your damn jabber. I don't know why a cowpoke needs to know anything aside from breaking broncs and eating beans, but go right ahead."

Dan rode in silence for a moment, eyes straight ahead and jaw working.

"This is what you know now: The world is filled with monsters hiding in human skins. Just like people, some are bad, and some are good. Many contain the seeds of both. Many change their alignment with the winds. Do you understand?"

Nettie nodded.

"You've killed these creatures, and you'll kill more. There's only one way: Puncture the heart. Shoot it with a bullet or an arrow. Stab it with a knife. Crush it with a rock or throw it in a fire. Do that, and the monster dissolves to sand. Until that happens, the creature might fall or take a wound, depending on its nature. But it won't truly die. Given time, it will heal almost any wound."

"That don't sound good."

"If the creature is good, then it's a blessing. I'm awfully hard to kill. But if the creature wants you dead and holds a grudge, it's very, very bad. An immortal thing can hunt you forever."

"Like the woman on the black horse?"

He shook his head. "No, she's something different. A ghost. The water horse took pity on her, and now they travel together until her revenge is final. You are their instrument of redemption."

Nettie pulled Ragdoll to a stop so suddenly that the mare squealed and almost sat down.

"Water horse? Instrument? Redemption?" She spit in the dirt. "Bullshit."

Dan circled his gelding around to face her.

"That woman lost her child to a monster. A bad one, the only thing the mighty Comanche fear. She swore a blood oath for revenge, and she passed it on to you before the water horse drowned her. It was a mercy." He nickered and nudged his horse back on track. "Do you not wonder why she chose you?"

Ragdoll followed Dan's sorrel before Nettie had decided to go. Whether it was because the danged critter liked Coyote Dan or his horse, Nettie couldn't say. She kicked her mare until they rode side by side, so at least she would feel like they were on equal footing.

"What the Sam Hill is a water horse?"

He chuckled. "The wet black mare. She took a liking to you. Must've recognized that you were special. They're mischievous creatures with peculiar whims, known for luring men to ride and then drowning them. Perhaps you led her to the woman, or perhaps she knew what was coming. But they'll trail you now, forever, those two, until justice is served."

Nettie snorted. "Injun woman told me I had until the new moon. Or else the Cannibal Owl's gonna reap again. And I'll never know the truth about where I came from."

Dan looked up as if counting the days in his head. "My village was struck on a new moon. Every village in our part of the territory lost children that night. You'd best hurry, then."

"Look, son. All I want is to get me another job breaking broncs, rustling cattle, and trailing as far away from Gloomy Bluebird as I rightly can. As much as I'd like to know where I came from, I ain't special, and I don't want revenge. And from what I hear, the Injuns wouldn't want someone like me around, anyway."

Dan's head whipped around to face her, mouth open in shock. "Why do you say that?"

Nettie pointed at the face Pap had called a thousand ugly words. "Ain't nobody wants a stupid, useless half breed."

Dan's eyes went all sorrowful and angry at the same time. "You poor creature. Those are a white man's lies. The Injuns, as you call them, value children above all else. Any tribe would've taken you in, had they found you. They would've raised you as their own, valued you. They would've loved you." His hand twitched like he might try to touch her, and her lips twitched like she'd bite off a knuckle if he tried.

"That...can't be true."

Nettie licked dry lips and felt her stomach wobble as the world spun around her. She could accept that she was surrounded by monsters all the time; raised the way she had been, monsters were a regular part of life. And she had almost gotten used to the taste of the word *slave* in her heart, mainly because *free* had a much stronger flavor. But she had always been unwelcome, unwanted. Always. Even some of the fellers at the Double TK had refused to sit beside her or speak to her. And to know that somewhere, somebody might've been glad to have her around but she'd stayed with Pap and Mam instead, thinking it was the best and only life available to her... well, that was the last straw.

Leaning over, she threw up all over her left boot and Dan's right foot.

And... another coyote?

Nettie pulled her horse to a stop and watched as the honey-brown critter spit out a bundle of leather and wood, shook itself, bent its head, and trembled. As Nettie stared, the coyote curled over, sort of rippled inside its skin, and unfolded. Seconds later, a tall Injun girl stood, nekkid as the day she was born and beautiful as the morning, her black hair sweeping to her waist. She had Dan's same high cheekbones, fiercely straight nose, and intelligent dark eyes, but her lips were wide and plush. She pointed up at Nettie but spoke directly to Coyote Dan.

"You call this ragged... thing... revenge?" Giving Nettie the briefest of stares, she snorted and bent for her bundle, brushing off flecks of chewed eggs. "Then truly, brother, we are doomed."

CHAPTER 12

Nettie wiped her mouth on her bandanna and straightened her spine. She wasn't about to take shit off a coyote.

"Name's Nettie Lonesome," she said, tipping her hat. "You need to borrow a saddle blanket before the cactus wrens try to settle on them things?"

The girl looked down at her bouncy bosom and quirked an eyebrow. "Please. I have standards. And horse hair is so very itchy." She unrolled the package she'd been carrying and tied on a brief leather skirt and a narrow apron over her chest. The last two things in the roll were a loop of leather and a knife, both of which she stuck through the waist of her skirt. "Is this less offensive to you, slave girl?"

"Winifred, don't—"

But Coyote Dan's worry was spot on, as Nettie leaped off her horse's back and punched the girl in the face. For a prissy-looking thing, the half-nekkid coyote girl gave as good as she got, growling and struggling to pin down Nettie's shoulders as they tussled in the dust. Dan watched for a moment before hopping off his horse, grabbing the coyote girl by the hair, and yanking her backward. Nettie got in one good kick to the girl's shin and stood, dusting off clothes that had seen the last of cleanliness the moment they'd found her hands.

"I ain't nobody's slave. Reckon I don't care to be nobody's revenge, neither."

The girl stood primly despite the red prairie dirt dusting her skin and the tumbleweed puppies caught in her straight hair.

"Unless you know how to put a ghost to rest, you haven't much choice. What you are now is living on borrowed time." She looked to Dan, who simply glared at her, arms crossed. "You're taking her to the Rangers, yes?"

"Yes. And we don't need your help, Winifred. You know what will happen if you get involved." He gave her a significant look before turning his back, mounting his horse, and kicking the sorrel into a walk.

Nettie hopped on Ragdoll and followed.

"What the hell does she mean, you're taking me to the Rangers?"

The girl sighed deeply behind them, but Nettie didn't look back. Her hand hurt, which surprised her, as she'd never punched anyone and hadn't expected it to cause her any pain. And yet it felt damn good, to actually punish rudeness, an extravagance she'd never known with Pap and Mam. The girl was making a fuss of her belongings, and in a few moments, the coyote was once again trotting beside them with a leather-wrapped bundle held tenderly in its teeth, although it did have the good sense to stay on Dan's side instead of getting anywhere near Nettie and her pointy boot tips.

"The Durango Rangers?" Nettie prompted, and Dan shot a dirty glare at the coyote before answering.

"The Rangers are not what they seem. Many believe them to be heartless white men who fight the native tribes and the

Aztecans, that they are thieves and murderers who kill and pillage and destroy. But that's because few can see what the Rangers truly hunt. Chupacabra, werewolves, harpies, minotaurs, vampire covens gone wrong. Horrible things. Things like the Cannibal Owl you now hunt. The Rangers have much to teach you. They see the monsters, too."

Nettie thought back to everything she'd ever heard of the Rangers. By the time the news reached Gloomy Bluebird, it wasn't news anymore so much as ancient history passed down by blind idiots. An entire tribe of Comanche murdered, their village destroyed. A vaquero's ranch just over the border turned into a pyre, the men nothing but ashes. Thousands of buffalo slaughtered, their bones left to rot in the sun.

She had always hated the Rangers because they killed people who looked like her. But what would she see now, if she looked at those smoking corpses? Fangs and inhuman skeletons? Or just piles of sand?

Scanning the desert all around her, she was suddenly overcome by a body-wide shiver that struck at her very heart.

Where had all this sand come from in the first place?

"You saying the Rangers are friendly fellers? That they'll take me in?"

"I never said they were friendly, but they won't have a choice. You can't hunt the Cannibal Owl alone. If they're not already aware of this creature, they must be made aware. And once they know what you've seen, it will become their duty to train you. They're bound to defend those who have seen the truth, because so often those people become victims of monsters themselves. Monsters don't like to be stared at."

Nettie realized she was staring and looked down. "Sorry, Dan. It's just..."

The horses clopped along. The coyote sneezed. Dan waited.

"It's just that I forget that you're a monster."

Dan and the coyote beside him both snorted at the same time. "There aren't enough words in the world to describe everything as it wishes to be known. For now, *monster* will have to do. It's better than *savage*, at least."

"So why are you good and some things are bad?"

Dan took a long drink from his water skin. A trickle leaked down from his lips. "Why is one snake deadly and another harmless? What is the difference between quicksand and mud? How is Pap different from any other man?"

Nettie's nose wrinkled up. "Are... are you asking me?"

"You are asking yourself."

"I don't know. I figure a critter's born what it is."

Dan nodded patiently. "And then what happens?"

"It... lives."

"Or dies. And if it lives, what does it do?"

Nettie's head hurt from all the thinking. She'd never been to school or learned her letters, never had anybody try to teach her more than how to cook eggs or skin a rabbit or sweep the floor so they wouldn't have to do it anymore themselves. Most of the things she knew, she knew by watching. That was how she'd learned bronc breaking. Just watching what the fellers did differently who stayed on compared to those who fell off and broke something important, and then figuring out how to improve on that technique.

"Shit, Dan. I don't know. I never went to school."

Dan grinned. "There it is, Nettie. Learning. A creature learns. If a man beats you, you learn to hate him. If your mother tells you to hate dogs, or if a dog bites you, you learn to hate dogs. If you eat a berry and vomit, you don't eat that kind of berry again."

Nettie closed her eyes to sort through it all. "So you're

saying... you were born a monster, but your folks taught you to be good?"

"To rise above it, yes. To accept it. And master it."

"That's why you're helping me?"

He waited so long to answer that Nettie got the fidgets and drank from her water skin just so she'd have a reason to stop and piss if he kept it up forever. She was getting right hungry, and lunch would not have been unwelcome, especially considering she'd upchucked most of her breakfast onto that mouthy coyote.

"My sister and I are twins, born under a blood moon. Our mother said she was visited in the night by Coyote himself and that we were his gift. Skinwalkers are rare and celebrated in our tribe, although some bands number only the two-natured. We were raised to be special, taught by our shaman to serve the people. When our tribe was attacked, we fought and took many wounds. Our mother could not be saved. When no hope was left, the shaman urged us to transform and run away to the white men. Winifred went to a mission school, learned proper language and rules and religion."

Nettie's disgust rose in her throat at the thought of wearing hoop skirts and sitting still all day when one could turn into a coyote and run wild and lawless under the sky. "Why'd your shaman tell her to do that?"

Dan had gone all solemn now, no trace of his grin. "For revenge."

"She stayed with the white folks as revenge against another tribe?"

The grin came back. "The white man has all the best weapons, and not all of them are guns."

"And what'd you do?"

Nettie couldn't imagine Coyote Dan in a schoolhouse,

tying a cravat, carrying a white man's water in a bucket. But he talked like a white man, and the firm set of his jaw told her that wherever he'd been, he hadn't much cared for it.

"I went to the Rangers as a scout. They have an outpost near here, one of many."

"Why'd you go to the Rangers?"

His head turned to her, slow as an owl and twice as judgmental. "Same reason. Revenge. Better weapons."

She was just about to ask him how hunting monsters with the Rangers could help anybody get revenge when the coyote yipped and Dan yanked his horse to a stop.

A ripple went through Nettie's stomach, and she let out a little burp. "We stopping for supper? I'm either starving or about to upchuck again."

Dan unhooked his bow and knocked an arrow while Nettie fidgeted around what felt like a ball of worms in her belly.

"That's the ripple I told you about. Many monsters approach us. If you live through meeting them, there's dried meat in the saddle bags."

Nettie exchanged the creek-soaked gun in her holster for a dry one from the saddlebag, swallowing down the collywobbles. She scanned the flat, brown land up ahead, but all she could see was more of the same nothingness broken up by scraggly gray bushes, a couple of stuck-up mesquite trees, and the usual shimmery ripples the sun made bouncing off the hard earth. When the shimmers shimmered a little darker, she focused on the same place Dan was watching. His arm didn't waver, and his arrow didn't shake a bit. The coyote dropped her packet and trotted back and forth nervously, watching the same spot, her hackles up as she growled.

The dark splotch inched closer until Nettie figured it had to be some sort of low-to-the-ground animal. Not buffalo. Not men or anything that might pretend to be men. Not harpies. But...wait...

"Law, Dan. Is it pigs?"

"Not pigs. Javelina. Skinwalkers. An entire tribe." He paused meaningfully and squinted. "No. Not an entire tribe. They're missing the most important part." Shaking his head, he lowered his bow and laid it across his saddle, a grim set to his mouth.

The coyote sat back on her haunches and howled, all haunted-like. Nettie swallowed down the lump in her throat, trying to keep it in her belly where it belonged. Something definitely wasn't right, and she felt edgy and vulnerable, out on the prairie.

Up ahead, the crowd of brown, hairy pigs stopped as one. Several in the back of the herd pulled sledges loaded with bundles of leather and wood. A big feller trotted ahead, his tusks poking up like little swords. When he was just close enough for Nettie to see a queer intelligence in his black eyes, the hog bent over, snoot to the ground, and rippled like a sack of kittens. Soon, a tall, thick-built Injun man stood, nekkid but for dust, and walked toward the horses with grim determination, his hands in fists at his sides.

"Greetings, friend," Coyote Dan called, holding his hands up to show they were empty.

Nettie shoved her gun back in its holster as a show of good faith but kept her hand on it as a show of not quite trusting a pig. The coyote, Winifred, trotted behind the horses and sat back, head cocked.

"Greetings," the man answered, his voice deep and heavily accented, as if he swallowed his words slowly and found them bitter.

"You are far from home," Dan said, and he didn't sound

stuck-up and preachy, not one bit. Nettie couldn't help wondering just how many masks Dan wore, when he pleased.

"We hunt." The man stood tall and straight, his arms corded with muscle and his chest scarred from battle. Try as she might, Nettie couldn't stop herself from glancing at his business and wondering if it was hairy when he was a pig. The man caught her looking, and the corner of his mouth quirked up just the tiniest bit, making her flush red.

"Pigs don't hunt," she blurted out, and Dan cussed under his breath.

"We are Javelina. Not pigs. Javelina have tusk. Cut you, neck to belly." He sneered and looked her up and down, and she felt like he saw straight through her, through her stolen clothes, her chest wrap, all the way to her shriveled black heart. He gestured at her with his chin and looked to Dan. "What is that?"

The coyote yipped a laugh, and Dan sighed deeply. "One who has killed but remains a fool in many ways."

"I ain't no fool," Nettie muttered, slipping her hat down to hide her blush.

"What do you hunt?" Dan asked, ignoring her.

The man glanced back at his tribe. "Children stolen. We hunt thief."

Nettie opened her mouth, but Dan interrupted her. "Did you see it?"

The man shook his head slowly. "Came at night. Silent. New mother woke at dawn, found blankets empty. Baby stolen from breast." He shook his head, and Nettie was surprised to see tears gleaming in his eyes. "Evil monster. We end it. Take back children."

"How do you hunt it? Scent?"

"The mothers know. It lives in mountains. High up." He

pointed west, toward the Aspero mountains, and Dan followed his gesture and nodded knowingly.

"Good hunting," he said, and he turned his horse slightly north to edge around the nervous cluster of Javelina.

Nettie muttered, "Yeah, good luck," and nudged Ragdoll to follow him. The coyote stayed on the far side of the horses, snatching up her bundle and jogging along, keeping her head down and easy.

The man stared across the plains as if he could see all the way to the tallest mountain. Grunting, he put a hand to his heart before doubling over, trembling, and sprouting a back full of wiry brown hair. He shook his stubby head and squealed, and the passel of hogs hurried to join him and trot off toward the treacherous mountains on the far west edge of Durango, their sledges leaving long lines in the dirt. They were headed in exactly the same direction the Injun woman had commanded Nettie to go with her pointing finger and insistence on showing up every night as a grisly reminder.

"So why ain't we headed that way?" Nettie asked, voice low.

Dan kept his horse walking. "Don't look back. Let them go. You need the Rangers to hunt this creature. The Javelina will fail."

"How do you know?"

He pointed down to the coyote—his sister, Winifred, and what a strange, oh-so-lily-white name it was for a brown girl currently walking on four black paws. "Coyotes are lone creatures. But in groups, there is always a hierarchy. You know what that means?"

"Nope."

"In a herd, every horse knows his place. The stallion, the lead mare—and it goes down from there. Every day, they test each other for strength and courage. A new animal appears, they don't accept it until they know where it will stand. That's a hierarchy: a ladder from top to bottom, each creature in the system a rung, everyone knows where they stand. Yes?"

"I guess." The thought that Nettie had been the lowest on a crappy, broken ladder at Pap's homestead surfaced in her mind, bobbed briefly, and was shoved back under. With horses, she understood it.

"Animals are like that, people are like that, and monsters are like that. The Javelina think they're brave and strong, and they are, but they've never faced werewolves or bearfolk. They don't know Pia Mupitsi. They think that because a creature thieves in darkness, it must be a coward, easy to vanquish. And they are very, very wrong. But they must do this, and so we let them."

"So where do y'all stand on this ladder?"

She didn't call them coyote folk. It just seemed rude now.

"We're in a strange place. We're not powerful hunters, but neither are we a food animal. We're somewhere in between. Scavengers fill a unique niche, to put it in the sawbone's terms. The bear sits where he wants, but the smaller animal never sits."

"And what's the coyote do?"

Dan grinned. "The coyote watches. And waits. And learns."

"But I'm not a bear or a coyote. So why're you helping me?"

"Ah. Finally, you ask a good question. My sister and I want revenge for our mother and our tribe. When we came back the next day to lay their souls to rest, we found everyone accounted for... except the children. We have searched for years, but no tribe claims to have taken them. Since then, many children have been stolen, and now I think Pia Mupitsi took them. Whatever this monster truly is, we can't rest until it's dead."

Nettie pulled the gun out of her holster and spun the barrel, watching the bullets flash and remembering how the metal looked when the harpy had spit one out, laughing. And the harpy was just a bird, really. "And you think I'm gonna do it for you? Hunt this thing? Why don't you do it your own damn self? I saw your aim. You're faster than me. Bullets don't work. What good am I gonna do that you can't do better? I'm just a damn cowpoke, and a green one at that." She hated saying it, but it seemed a fine enough reason for not chasing her own death around like the Javelina did.

Dan shook his head, shielded his eyes with a hand, and squinted across the prairie. Nettie couldn't tell if that meant he didn't know the answer himself or if he was just being an ass.

"What do you know of legends?"

The voice was close by, and Nettie's head whipped around. It was Winifred, suddenly walking by her side, tall and graceful in her scant leathers. The older girl's attitude was grave, her voice daring Nettie to laugh.

"I ain't religious, if that's what you mean."

"Religion and legend aren't always the same thing. The Comanche follow no gods. But there are legends, like Pia Mupitsi. Among our kind—monsters, as my brother calls us—it's said that a shadow will rise to fight evil. But 'Shadow' is said as a name, as an unstoppable force. The Shadow moves among us but cannot be found, cannot be sensed. It can see us, find us, track us. And destroy us. The Shadow is a hunter. A weapon. A new kind of monster."

She looked at Nettie with slender eyebrows raised, a heavy significance falling between them.

"And you're saying you think that's me?" Nettie rocked back, laughing and surprising Ragdoll into a snort and twitch. "Coyote girl, I ain't nothin'. A vampire almost killed me, then a lizard feller nearly killed me, and then your brother barely stopped a harpy from killing me. Hell, even a chunk of mesquite nearly killed me. I ain't a hunter. I'm barely a wrangler. I ain't a new kind of monster." She spit at the girl's feet and shook her head. "I ain't your Shadow."

"Listen to yourself. *Almost. Nearly. Barely.* You're still alive. When you should be dead."

Nettie shrugged. "Most people in Durango rightly fit that bill."

Winifred grabbed Ragdoll's reins and jerked the mare to a dancing stop. "Do you know what your problem is, Nettie?"

Nettie tried to yank the reins back, but the other girl's fist didn't budge. "Besides you laying hands on my horse, Winifred Coyote?"

Stroking Ragdoll's neck to calm her, the girl looked full-on into Nettie's eyes for the first time. Nettie expected pride and anger, but she found pleading and earnestness, which made her downright uncomfortable. "Your first problem is that you're a fool. Just because you've been told your entire life that you're nothing does not mean you are nothing. The wolf doesn't care what the sheep think."

"Nice words for somebody who has family and can turn into what's pretty much a small wolf. People look at me, they figure I'm nothing. How am I supposed to prove 'em wrong? Maybe you haven't noticed, but my skin's darker than yours. Most folks don't take kindly to that around here unless it's out back digging a well."

Winifred shook her head sadly. "You're not part of that world anymore. You're part of our world, and there are plenty colors of skin that contain monsters and saviors alike. Forget the people who raised you. This is your destiny. Tell her."

Dan gave her a solemn nod. "Your vision quest confirms it. You are the Shadow, and you're the only one who can end the Cannibal Owl and save our children. *All* the children."

Nettie bit her lip until she tasted blood. "You think a fever dream is truth?"

He'd stopped his horse just a bit ahead of hers as his sister spouted off her foolishness. Now he turned to face her. "That's why I saved you, Nettie. To help you find your destiny."

"But if you can't feel me, if I'm not a monster and I don't have a ripple, how'd you find me?"

He grinned. "It makes sense if you're the Shadow. A monster wouldn't sense you, nor would a Ranger or another person who had killed monsters. You're hidden from everyone, everything. I was following the water horse after she killed my sawbones friend. I wanted to kill the mare and end her games, but something held me back. She seemed focused, like something called her. They're peculiar, sensitive creatures that rarely stray this far from the sea. She was strangely attracted to you, even before you killed your first monster. And yet she never touched you, never let you get close enough to ride. Clever things, water horses. Now that she carries the lost mother, she's not a threat. But I was watching you after that, curious to see what made you different. I was in Gloomy Bluebird for weeks. I watched you kill the vampire as if you knew his heart was waiting for your stake. And you did not disappoint. Did you know that you speak Comanche when you sleep?"

"This is bullshit."

With a harsher kick than she meant to give, she yanked the reins free of Winifred's hold, the mare lurching forward in a buck and galloping on past Dan. Nettie needed space to think through all their jawing, but suddenly, the prairie wasn't big enough to hold all her feelings. A flap of the reins and an angry kick sent her horse into a dead run, hooves flying across the sand.

The thing was, Nettie had been raised to think she was

nothing—they weren't wrong about that. But she'd also held, somewhere deep down in her heart, that she was special. That she was more than an unloved child, an unpaid servant, a dark splotch in their dirty white life. She'd figured maybe the homestead would catch fire and she'd drag out the drunk old coots and suddenly find out what a hug felt like. Or maybe she'd be in town, begging for cornmeal, and save the mayor's wife from a runaway wagon, get a medal. She'd reckoned that one day, for some reason as yet unknown, someone would actually look at her instead of through her.

And now two people were, and it was downright unsettling.

They thought she was somebody that mattered. Someone special. A hunter. A legend.

The Shadow.

That sounded awful ominous, like a thundercloud waiting to strike a body dead. And yet...something about it felt like home. The dream vision was all but printed inside her damn skull. The Shadow. So she was supposed to, what? Spin around until something twisted her guts like she was gonna upchuck, then kill it? How was she supposed to know if the monster was good or evil? What if it was a good monster having a bad day? Was there a polite way to ask a mostly nekkid person what sort of critter they turned into? And what happened if she decided Coyote Dan and his sister were crazy as a bag of cats, turned her mare around, settled with a ranch up north, and fiercely ignored everything that made her insides wobble?

She reined to a halt, glared into the sun, and scanned the prairie while lightning was still bursting across her eyes. Against the blinding white, she saw an inkblot shade on horseback, pointing west, where the Javelina had gone. Blinking ferociously, she forced the image away, but it lingered against the black of her eyelids. Would that fool Injun woman haunt her forever, endlessly pointing from the back of a wet black mare?

That would be reason enough to kill the Cannibal Owl, whatever it was. Just to be free. Nettie didn't care to be pointed at so damn much by somebody who didn't have the good sense to stay dead. And underneath the weight of all the stolen children, Nettie remembered what the Injun woman had said: Nettie had had a tribe, once, and the Cannibal Owl knew the truth of it. Dan said she spoke Comanche in her sleep, but that didn't tell her how she'd come to have black blood. The goddamn monster might be the only creature alive who knew where Nettie'd come from.

With another savage yank on her reins that she immediately regretted, Nettie trotted back to where Dan and Winifred squatted around a fresh little brush fire, farther behind than she'd have guessed. She'd run the mare longer than she'd meant to, been gone longer than was smart, and Ragdoll sighed in relief when Nettie pulled her cinch loose and hobbled her. A long, thick snake was skewered over the coals, its head sitting on the ground and judging her with an alien sort of distaste. She dismounted and kicked the snake head away.

"If I kill this owl thing, can I go back to just being a normal cowpoke?"

It came out all breathless, as if she'd been running instead of her mare. Dan's and Winifred's eyes met and narrowed.

"It's possible," Dan said slowly.

"But unlikely," Winifred finished.

"What the Sam Hill does that mean?"

Dan stood, picked up a stick, and walked to where the rattlesnake's head had landed. When he returned with the grisly thing impaled on the twig like a puppet, he picked up a chunk of petrified wood and shoved it into the jaws. The snake's head snapped down, fangs leaking milky venom. A shiver ran up Nettie's arms as she thought about how much of her life she'd spent turning over boots and stirring up the bottles in the lean-to, making sure she never found out exactly how hard a rattler could strike.

"A creature is what it is. Even death can't change that. If you kill the Cannibal Owl, you won't stop being the Shadow."

Nettie squatted down. The rattlesnake seemed to watch her, its mouth still working to pierce the rock-hard wood. It reminded her of Chuck, damn its scaly skin.

"So you're saying"—she poked the snake's snoot with her own stick, positive that its eyes rolled back in annoyance—"that if I don't kill the owl, I'll be haunted for the rest of my life. And if I do kill it, I'll feel like I've got to kill whatever monster starts acting up after that?"

Dan squatted beside her, elbows easy on his thighs.

"As I see it, you have two choices, the same choice as every animal. Hunt or be hunted. What will you choose?"

CHAPTER
13

Nettie picked up the stick and used it to fling the rattler head as far as she could. The dang thing soared into the white-blue sky and landed beyond her vision. She imagined it spitting out the chunk of wood and cussing at her.

"Shit, Dan. I choose lunch."

He grinned. "I thought you might."

They passed a few minutes in expectant silence, waiting for the snake to finish cooking. Winifred started to say something a few times, but a hiss and head shake from Dan stopped her. They ate before the meat was fully done, and Nettie was more than happy to suck down half-roasted rattler and feel the burn down her throat. It was better than the lump that had been living there, reminding her with every breath that she was going to have to do something she didn't much care to do.

At one point, she poked the long skin with her toe and said, "Why don't more people eat snake? It tastes like chewy chicken, don't cost nothing, and doesn't shit all over the yard."

Dan licked his fingers. "Our people consider them unclean. But when I lived with the sawbones, I studied his books and specimens. There is nothing unclean about a healthy animal, no matter what a shaman says. Outside of monsters, meat is meat. Science is a powerful teacher. And hunger is a cruel mistress."

"I still refuse to eat fish," Winifred added. "But snake grows on me."

When she'd finished the last of her share and felt a little more settled, Nettie checked the ground around her for scorpions and centipedes and settled down with her legs stretched out and her back against a rock.

"Fine. So let's say I'd rather hunt. What kind of critter is the Cannibal Owl?"

Winifred snorted, and Dan finished his last bite of snake and tossed the bones in the fire.

"No one knows. No one has seen it. The night that our tribe was attacked, there were werewolves and harpies first, before Pia Mupitsi came. Too many ripples to pick apart a single thread. There are endless kinds of creatures in the world, with new ones born all the time, half-breeds and mongrels."

Nettie bristled. "Like me."

Winifred shrugged. "Settle down. It's not an insult. Nothing is pure. What happens if a skinwalker and a werewolf mate in human form? What happens if a human gets a skinwalker with child? Whatever is born is something new, something unique. Nothing is pure. Everything is a half-breed."

"But nobody calls a white man that."

"No one pokes the biggest, dumbest bull in the herd, but no one follows him, either," Winifred shot back.

Dan just snorted.

Nettie stood and dusted off her pants. Much as she didn't like it when Winifred was right, her world had definitely changed. Now she was a wrangler, she'd killed three monsters, and she had something like a destiny dogging her every step. And she couldn't seem to hold her head low anymore. Her chin stubbornly stuck up and out and wouldn't see a bit of reason regarding turning south in spirit or body.

Whatever part of her that had feared Pap? That part was dead.

She had bigger things to fight.

"Hellfire, Dan." She looked far across the prairie. First west. Then north. "I figure you'd better take me to the Rangers so I can get this destiny thing finished and get back to breaking horses."

As the sun staggered down, bloody and beaten, to collapse on the horizon, Nettie could sense that they were very near their destination. Must've been something in the way Winifred's coyote ears flicked back and Dan finally picked up his reins instead of steering the sorrel with his knees. The stark black teeth of a small ranch not unlike the Double TK nibbled at the low clouds as if waiting to devour the night instead of it being the other way around. They hadn't stopped for dinner, and Nettie's stomach grumbled over the clopping of the horses' hooves. The snake was just a greasy memory of a burp. They were just about done in, with nothing but a little creek to slurp from that afternoon, which meant it was a bad time for jerky. Nettie was spent, too. At least until she felt the wobble.

Her stomach turned over right about the same time the horses pricked their ears and sped up to a gangly trot, their necks stretching out as if they could get to the hay faster that way. With a soft yip, the coyote turned and slunk toward a low butte near a mesquite thicket. Her eyes gave one acid-green flash in the gloaming and winked out. As far as Nettie was concerned, a pretty woman like that probably had no business among the Rangers, especially if she was draped in nothing but some scanty bits of leather wet with a day's worth of dog drool. And speaking of which...

"You gonna tell me how to act, Coyote Dan?"

He snorted. "What's the point? You are what you are, even if you're lacking manners. You're what's needed. If they don't like it, there are other Ranger outposts. But this captain is a good man, so try not to make him angry, even though you'll want to." His horse whinnied, and the bugle was answered by half a herd milling behind a rickety fence. "It's just your nature," he added. "Stubborn thing. No wonder you favored that old mule."

Someone carried a tin light out onto the porch of a long ranch house. Spurs jingled against the wood as two dozen men stepped through the door and spread out along the railing, cradling rifles or putting hands on the butts of pistols as they talked in low, threatening voices. They all looked like normal men, but someone... wasn't. At least, that's what the lump in Nettie's belly and the prickle on the back of her neck were telling her.

"One of them's a... thing," Nettie whispered, and Dan nodded.

"I already knew. But don't you forget."

A throat cleared, and one shape detached and hopped off the porch onto the dirt, a sheathed cavalry sword hung over his shoulders like an oxen's yoke and a sombrero-type hat shading his eyes. He was an older man made up of gristle and bristles, gray and wiry with heavy muttonchops. But his leather vest was well fit and nicely kept, his tall boots recently shined. Little bits of gold winked on his lapels like brass fireflies.

"Evening. You folks lost?"

Normally, Nettie would've said something both smart and

stupid, but considering that she could almost feel how hard some of those fellers were itching for a fight, she stayed mute.

The silence strung out for a minute. The feller with the sword spit. And then someone on the porch said, "Cap, don't you know that's Coyote Dan?"

Quick as a blink, the sword was unsheathed and pointing at the stark white throat of a feller at the rail. "'Course I know, idjit. Wasn't what I asked, was it?"

"No, Cap."

The sword lowered and pointed at Nettie.

"Who's your friend, Dan?"

Before Dan could say something stupid that she'd be stuck with forever, she said, "Rhett."

"Rhett what?"

"Rhett...Boss?"

The fellers on the porch broke out laughing, and Cap held up a hand. They quieted instantly.

"Now first of all, son, I ain't a boss. I'm a captain of the Durango Rangers, Las Moras Company. Second of all, a feller's only as good as his name, and so far, I only heard half of yours."

Nettie swallowed hard, glad the night hid her red-hot face. "Rhett..."

Not a goddamn thing came to mind. Plenty of first names had. But she couldn't say *Lonesome* in case she was wanted for Monty's and Chuck's murders. She knew of only one other last name she'd taken a shine to, so she just went on and said it out loud. Not like anybody in the Rangers would've known the young, sunshine-smiling, hot-shot wrangler who'd stopped in at the Double TK for one all-too-short summer.

"Rhett Hennessy."

A queer quiet descended, broken by a familiar voice.

"You any relation to the Tanasi Hennessies?"

She knew it was him before the lanky shape detached from the porch and hopped down beside the Captain.

"No relation," she muttered, shoving her hat down before Samuel Hennessy could get a good look at Rhett Hennessy, who looked an awful lot like the girl who'd watched Sam, quiet and big-eyed, in the bronc pens a few summers ago.

It had only been a few short months, but Nettie had taken a fancy to the young cowpoke. To his golden warmth, his kind blue eyes, his puppy-dog smile, his open gladness and a sweetness so unusual among the hard-as-nails men who managed to defeat death in the grueling Durango territory. Samuel Hennessy of Tanasi had maybe been the first feller besides Monty who hadn't reviled Nettie in the slightest.

But he'd always been a curious, friendly sort of feller, so he looked to the Captain for permission before walking up to her horse and patting Ragdoll on the neck. "You sure you ain't got no people from back east? Maybe..." He stared up into her face, and her eyebrows drew down in defense of her nose. "Maybe your folks...worked there?"

Her back stiffened. "My people ain't slaves, and we ain't from Tanasi."

With the pup-dog grace she recalled, he shrugged it off good-naturedly and stuck out a hand. "Well, I'm Samuel Hennessy, and folks around here already call me Hennessy, so I hope you won't mind if I call you Rhett."

"Rhett's fine."

She grabbed his hand, surprised that lightning didn't shoot from his palm to hers like the prickles on a metal latch in winter. He just felt like a person, any person, the handshake swift and vaguely punishing. She squeezed his fingers, gave him a bone grinder of a shake in return. He hadn't seemed to care that she was a girl back then, and she didn't want him to notice now.

"Nice to meet you, Rhett. Good to see you again, Dan."

When the Captain cleared his throat, Hennessy nodded and returned to his place in line on the porch, although he was the only one who didn't see fit to keep a hand on his weapon. But Nettie could feel his eyes roaming over her from across the indigo night. He was still smiling, but he knew there was something funny about Rhett Hennessy, and she half-hoped he would persist in trying to figure out what it was just so he'd keep looking at her. But mostly she hoped he wouldn't.

Hellfire stupid of her, to use his name like that.

Durango was a big country, but damned if it didn't seem smaller all the time.

"Dan, Rhett. We got supper to finish, if Qualls ain't et it all. What can we do you for?"

Coyote Dan didn't get off his horse, which Nettie took to mean things might still go south. She kept her hand on her gun and her heels off her mare, hoping there wouldn't soon be a dozen hardened men aiming for her back.

"Rhett here's killed before, and now he's hunting the Cannibal Owl. Ever heard of it?"

The Captain shrugged and spit tobacco as if they were discussing the weather. "Monster's a monster. One's better than a passel. If we see it, we'll kill it."

"This monster is stealing children and destroying good tribes across your sector of Durango."

The Captain hung his sword on his belt and unholstered his pistol, inspecting it in the dark.

"When it hits a town, you just let us know. Men?"

The older man spun his gun and stuck it home in its holster before turning his back to Nettie and Dan. As he moseyed toward the warm rectangle of light, his men faced out. Somebody cocked a pistol, and Nettie felt the first spider legs of doubt tap up her spine. She'd only had a gun for a few days, and although her aim was decent, her mettle was still in question. At least Coyote Dan would probably live, provided no one hit him direct in the heart, if she understood monsters correctly. But if a fight started, Nettie would die like a dog out here, and that wasn't the welcome she'd hoped for.

"Wait."

The Captain stopped. A stocky man with a full black beard hopped to the ground and stumped over to where Nettie sat. When he looked up at her, he was the closest thing she'd seen to a live bear: black beetle eyes in a round face, all surrounded by dark hair and a beard like an eagle's nest.

"What are you, boy?"

Dan chuckled. "Strange, isn't it, Jiddy?"

"Ain't one of us. But ain't one of them. Not quite."

"Jiddy?" The Captain had turned back around, but the grim set of his jaw said he wasn't feeling patient.

With a savage grunt, the man put a hand on Nettie's boot, pressed his nose almost against her britches, and took a deep breath as he dragged his face up. She very nearly kicked him, but she knew a test well enough when she saw one.

"It's like..." Up close now, she could see Jiddy's face working like a cat about to sneeze and felt a brief surge of smugness at consternating him. "Like how a chair's shadow ain't a chair but looks like one? Feller'd have to be pretty sensitive to pick it up. I never seen anything like it. It's like he ain't even there."

At that, the Captain snatched a lantern off the porch and walked toward them, and Nettie's heart ratcheted up into her throat. "Jiddy, are you saying...he's like a shadow?"

Jiddy stepped away and nodded, looking right disturbed. "Maybe a little. Hard to say. Feels human, but not like a human who's killed a monster. Different."

"So if a vampire wasn't being real careful, he wouldn't notice Rhett? But Rhett would notice him?"

Backing away, Jiddy nodded, all slow and thoughtful. "Maybe so."

The Captain strolled up, a little too close, held his lantern high, and used his sheathed sword to knock Nettie's hat back off her head. "What the hellfire are you, boy?"

"Wrangler," she answered, making it a manly grunt. "Bronc breaker."

Up close, she could see how wind-chapped his tanned face was, the gauntness of his cheeks under his whiskers. Their eyes met, and Nettie matched her scowl to his and pulled her hat back on.

"You didn't bring him here to break broncs, Dan. Said he needed to hunt a monster. So you figure we'll, what? Teach him? Help him? Shit, Dan. This ain't no charity house."

"It's not charity if you put him to work. He's good with horses. Killed two monsters before he even knew what they were. Should've died five times this week but didn't. He belongs with the Rangers."

The Captain spit a long stream of tobacco juice into the dirt; it appeared to be his main form of punctuation. "Maybe you haven't noticed, but he's the wrong damn color."

Softly but firmly, Dan said, "If a man can do his job, it shouldn't matter what color he is."

"That's right philosophical for a Injun. And more than a little self-serving. You know, if you're looking to come back and scout for us, you'll have to fight Jiddy first."

Jiddy stepped forward, arms crossed over a barrel chest sprouting thick hair through his shirt.

Dan chuckled, which only made Jiddy angrier. "No thanks, Captain. My path leads elsewhere. But you should take Rhett on like you took me on. His skills are unusual, and you always need more unusual men."

At that, the Captain laughed, a loud bark that startled the stars. "You heard we got hit hard at the Battle of Bandera Pass, huh? Well, yeah, and we're doing poorly in numbers, you nosy bastard. Jiddy, what do you reckon? Should we take him on?"

Jiddy stepped close. "Can you shoot?"

"Yep."

"Can you fight?"

Nettie shrugged. "I can stab a monster in the heart. Probably stab a man, too."

"You look like you eat a lot."

She looked down at herself. Another shrug. "I don't know where you think I'm putting it. But I can cook beans and eggs, kill and roast a rabbit, or fry up biscuits. I ain't above eatin' snake."

The Captain aimed a finger at her chest and stepped closer, so close that she could see the spots on his nose in the moonlight.

"What makes you think you're worthy of being a Durango Ranger, Rhett?"

"Didn't say I thought I was. But I'm bound to hunt the Cannibal Owl, and if it kills me because you wouldn't help, I'll haunt you until you're cold in the ground." She looked to Dan. "I can do that, right?"

Coyote Dan shrugged.

Far off, a woman screamed, and the men went on point like hounds, guns out of holsters. Dan whipped his horse around, ears twitching.

"What the Hades was that?" the Captain shouted.

Jiddy pointed far off, to the butte where Winifred had been hiding in her coyote form, last time Nettie had seen her. Looking now, her blood went cold. A stark black silhouette against the moonlit clouds showed the Injun woman pointing west, seated on the back of the black mare. Something lumpy lay over the ghostly horse's rump. An animal. Or a body.

Dan muttered, "Not again," kicked his horse, and galloped for the butte, screaming a war cry as he readied his bow and knocked an arrow at a full run. It was the most Injun-like Nettie'd seen him act so far, and she spun Ragdoll and took off after him, whipping the horse with her reins as she pulled out her pistol. She'd never forced the mare to run so hard, but it felt like they were moving in water, slow and cold. Far ahead, the dark horse turned, dripping water, and disappeared over the side of the butte. Dan launched an arrow right where they'd been seconds before and threw his bow to the ground.

A few strides ahead of her, Dan hit the mesquite thicket and leaped off his horse. Before Nettie had pulled up, he was on the ground on his knees, keening. He stood and turned, a large bundle in his arms.

It was a limp body. A woman with long hair, dripping water, smelling like salt.

Winifred.

CHAPTER
14

There was, of course, no way Winifred could've drowned in the middle of the desert. Dan laid her on the ground, nekkid as a jaybird, and pressed her stomach until no more water streamed out of her lips. Nettie was cold all over, her knees soaked in the little river flowing off the coyote girl's skin. Dan ran his hands over her body, put his ear to her heart. About that time, the Captain moseyed up with his fellers and tapped Dan on the shoulder.

"May I?"

Dan looked like he might grow out his coyote teeth and bite the older man, but instead he flared his nostrils, nodded once, and stood. Nettie watched closely as the Captain kneeled, folded his hands over the beautiful girl's nekkid chest, and started pressing down hard enough to make her ribs creak in a rhythmic sort of way that reminded Nettie of the sounds of the whores' beds upstairs at the Leaping Lizard. Much to her surprise, he next spit out a big wad of tobacco and leaned over to kiss the girl, his mouth wide over hers. Nettie went for her holstered gun, but Dan's hand on her shoulder stopped her.

"I trust him. So should you."

It was downright unsettling, watching an old white man kiss an Injun girl, especially considering she was nekkid and dead.

Something brushed Nettie's elbow, and she jumped. The anxiety didn't go away when she realized it was Hennessy squatting beside her. He gave her a reassuring smile that only made her more nervous.

"Don't worry. Captain knows what he's doing," he said.

All she could do was nod.

After a few long moments, the Captain went back to pressing Winifred's chest, and Nettie scanned the butte for the Injun woman and the wet black horse, but of course they were long gone. That meant she wasn't watching when Winifred sucked in a whooping breath and upchucked water, raw rabbit, and roasted snake meat all over the Captain's lap.

Nettie stood as the Captain helped Winifred sit up, graciously offering her a blanket one of his fellers had brought, probably to cover up what had looked like a dead body. The girl wrapped herself in the blanket and bent her head to Dan's. The language they spoke was low and liquid, and Winifred had to stop several times and cough up more water.

Finally, Coyote Dan turned to the Captain, one arm still around his sister. "That ghost will haunt Rhett until the Cannibal Owl is destroyed. If you don't help him on this quest, I suspect it'll haunt you, as well. Might be one of your boys, next time, and yours don't come back to life so easy."

"Bullshit," the Captain muttered, but Jiddy nudged him and inclined his head toward their ranch house. Just beside it was a familiar black shadow, a woman on horseback, that danged ghostly finger pointing, as ever to the west.

The Captain pulled a tobacco pouch from his belt and lumbered toward the house. "Damn monsters. No sense of a man's privacy. Come on then, boy. Make yourself useful. Best get back to the bunks before Delgado drowns in his beans, not that I reckon it's possible to drown in something so blasted hard and dry."

"You don't need to be wet to drown," Winifred called, one hand to her throat. "But being human would certainly make it more final."

"Evening, miss." The Captain stopped, tipped his hat, wiped his mouth off, and kept walking.

Nettie looked uncertainly from Dan and Winifred to the men following their leader back to what was left of dinner and what was probably a better place to sleep than the ground by a mesquite thicket full of snake-flecked yark and salty mud.

"Go." Dan tightened his sorrel's saddle and held the horse so his sister could mount. She'd slipped on her leather top and bottoms and maneuvered herself so that she was sitting on the Captain's old blanket but also mostly wrapped in it.

"She gonna be all right?"

Dan gave the strangest smile. "She always is."

Nettie gave him the side eye. "You mean she's died before?"

He shrugged. "Yes, and she'll die again. A panther shaman put a curse on her. Nine deaths, the last one final. Damn cats. That's why I keep begging her to go back to town with the white men, where it's relatively safe. It's easier to die alone, out here. She needs someone around to bring her back."

"What's a panther shaman? And why did it curse her?"

"That's my business and mine alone," Winifred snapped. She kicked Dan's horse and didn't look back as the gelding walked away.

"Are you just gonna leave me here?" Nettie's voice sounded smaller than she would have liked.

Dan whistled, and his sorrel turned and trotted obediently back to him, despite Winifred's yanking on the reins. He hopped up behind his sister, settling on the horse's rump. "It was my job to bring you. I brought you. And now I have my own problems to deal with."

A peculiar wash of anger, shame, and disappointment flooded through Nettie and dug into her chest, right where the Captain had punched with the heels of his hands to bring Winifred back to life. It wasn't that she had expected Coyote Dan to stick around forever, nor that she wanted him to. She just hadn't expected him to dump her off in the night, tossed out like a chicken bone.

"Fine, then. Go on." She mounted her horse, and headed for the nearest corral by the ranch house.

"Good fortune," Winifred called.

"I'll be watching," Dan added, but Nettie just flapped a tired hand.

She didn't need an audience. She needed a friend.

By the time Nettie had Ragdoll fed and rubbed down and had found a place for her saddle, the lights were out in the bunkhouse. No one ever came out to greet her or help her, not even Sam. She took it as a test because that was the only way to keep it from feeling like a slight. At least she didn't have to rush herself in the outhouse, where she savored a rare sit-down piss and the good fortune of a scrap of old newspaper to wipe with. Compared to where she'd come from, the Ranger camp was right fancy.

Staring up at the bunkhouse, bone tired, she couldn't help missing her narrow bunk at the Double TK, surrounded by the deep snores of dangerous men. She started to open the bunkhouse door but nudged it back shut when it let out a squeak of protest. Better to sleep outside and brave the elements than piss off a surly top hand and get sent to break the hellbitches or be the first to scout out a camp of hungry vampires. With her saddle blanket over her arm, she dusted off a spot on the porch and settled down, her eyes focused on the butte.

At least the Injun woman and the water horse had gone to pester and half-kill someone else tonight. Maybe having the hunt settled with the Rangers would be enough to calm the ghost's damn bones.

Lying there, she rubbed the place where Dan had doctored the mesquite thorn. Damned if it didn't feel better, not hot or hard at all. When she unwrapped Monty's bandanna, she found barely a bump. Whatever medicine Dan had used had most likely saved her life. Which only meant she owed him more.

That night, Nettie dreamed that she was dressed in hoop skirts and silk, her long blonde hair tong-curled and braided intricately around her milk-white face and her satin slippers slightly too small. In the dream, she was escorted into the town hall, where she danced a waltz with Samuel Hennessy and made small talk with other white ladies about the price of white sugar.

It was the worst nightmare of her life.

The next few days were about the same as her days at the Double TK. Well, aside from the hours they spent rolling around and stabbing broke-off chair legs into sandbag dummies with painted-on hearts. And when they practiced shooting pistols backward over their shoulders using mirrors, in case they had to face another nest of gorgons or a cockatrice. Or when Nettie was sent in to break a bronc that had a snapped-off horn and a lion's tail.

"Unicorns make damn fine mounts, if you cut off their horns first. Almost nobody can shoot a unicorn out from under you, that's for damn sure," Jiddy said as he handed her a rope and a halter. "Unless they take a shot to the heart, they'll keep running and fighting forever. Damn hard to break, though. Go on in, new boy. Let's see what you got."

What he neglected to mention was that the goddamn beast could use its tail as a whip. Nettie took it as a personal triumph when the critter finally gentled and trotted around under her, lifting dirty white knees like it was dancing in a town parade. Turned out unicorns were just prouder than the usual horses, and as soon as she started whispering praise into its daintily curved ears, it perked right up.

Another day, Jiddy used a heavy key to unlock a weathered building Nettie had taken for a storage shed or a secondary bunkhouse. The room had no windows and was full of trunks, odd weapons, and collections of strange beasts that weren't human but weren't normal, either. One cage had rabbits with fangs, one had overlarge roosters with burlap sacks tightly tied over their heads, and a large jar with holes in the top had butterflies with skulls for heads and huge stingers. Nettie learned so much by the light of Jiddy's lantern that her head ached. Cockatrices, Death's Head moths, pixies, bloodbunnies, bugbears, fiery salamanders. Since she couldn't read, she had to memorize each creature's name, habitat, and defenses, and how to kill it before it killed her. Every day she spent with the Rangers left her exhausted and bruised, but since she never took off her clothes, she didn't have cause to notice.

Most of the men were official Durango Rangers and kept their little brass badges clean and shiny. The few younger ones, those who hadn't seen battle, all but worshipped the ones who had and whispered about how each man had earned his badge with feats of ridiculous valor. A few of the more grizzled veterans wore necklaces strung with teeth and talons too big and strange to have come from normal animals, which they were always finding an excuse to pull out and expose for praise and awe.

At first, Nettie reckoned they were lying, considering Dan had told her that a monster dissolved all to dust when it was killed. But then she remembered the vampire fangs in the bag hanging at her waist and figured maybe some creatures left something behind, if you took the time to sift through the sand. For once, she was glad her time with Pap had trained her to keep her mouth shut, as it didn't pay to question a man about his skills, even if you figured him for a goddamn braggart.

In this case, he was still a braggart, but one who'd killed far more dangerous things than Nettie Lonesome. Or Rhett Hennessy, as she had to constantly remind herself. She didn't speak much at all among the Rangers, in fact. Just nodded along, did as she was told, and tried her damnedest to learn whatever they took the time to teach her. It was hard going, but she'd expected that. She missed the hell out of Monty, though, and the easy way she'd sat with him and Poke and Jar, joshing as they worked.

Although breakfast and dinner were provided, the Rangers had to find their own lunch. The Captain believed it kept them sharp on foraging, a skill a man could use out on the plains. As Nettie—goddammit, Rhett—had finally run out of Dan's jerky and hadn't brought anything with her but the spare weapons and stained clothes in her saddlebags, she set off toward a mesquite clutch to look for some sort of eatin' varmint. On the way, she was overtaken by the long legs and sure smile of Samuel Hennessy. He made her feel right strange, which meant she'd been avoiding him... but which also meant she was glad to see him. Matching her stride, he held out a strip of jerky.

"Figured you might be hungry, other Hennessy. Takes most folks a while to get used to finding their own supper on a ranch that's already been stripped of critters."

Their fingertips brushed as she took the meat and nodded. "Thanks kindly, other Hennessy."

He pointed at the bushes ahead. "You won't find any rabbits this way. We cleaned 'em all out."

Nettie stopped and stared at the little green smudge in the large prairie, calculating. "Any fish in the creek?"

"Too muddy."

"Prairie chickens? Snakes?"

"Ugh. Who eats snakes?"

She snorted. Hennessy had likely never been hungry a second in his life. If a feller who looked like him got hungry, folks would probably line up to cut off a chunk of muscle and drop it in his bowl.

"Plenty of starving folks who can't find rabbits or hens will eat a snake, I reckon. I'll show you how to cook one, if you want."

He scratched the blond stubble on his throat. The sound did peculiar, fluttery things to Nettie's belly, things she didn't quite understand. And it made her a mite jealous, as she'd like to've had some manly stubble to scratch in a thoughtful manner herself.

"What do they taste like?"

"Like meat. Better than starving."

Hennessy took a deep breath and shrugged wide shoulders. He couldn't have been even nineteen, but he seemed so much older and more experienced than Nettie felt. And yet there was something innocent about him, too. "Guess it'd be a good skill to know. How do we start?"

Nettie's life, until that point, had been missing out on fun.

But with Hennessy cracking jokes and lending a hand, even catching a six-foot-long fanged viper was pretty entertaining. She showed him how to skin it inside out and skewer it on a twig, like Dan did, and he showed her how to build a better fire and light it with a bit of flint. Most comical of all was the face he made the first time he held a chunk of steaming snake meat up, glaring at it like it could still bite, even without a mouth and fangs.

"You're sure this ain't poison?"

Nettie held up her chunk and bit in, juice running down her chin.

"If it is, bury me under a shady tree, will you?"

Hennessy shivered. "We don't bury nobody. Always burn 'em."

"Why's that?"

He looked past the ranch house to a blackened stain on the prairie that Nettie had noticed but not remarked upon. "Because sometimes, fellers come back. And they're a damn sight harder to kill the second time around." He went oddly silent, staring at that black splotch, and it made Nettie feel downright twitchy.

"How'd you end up with the Rangers? Weren't you..." She almost slipped and asked him about where he'd gone after the Double TK, but seeing as how he hadn't recognized her yet, she wasn't about to mention it. "Weren't you pretty young to join up?"

He speared another piece of snake on his knife. "I was with a ranch over in Arteaga. We got in a fight with some nasty vaqueros over some stolen horses one night. They shot most of our mounts out from under us and kept shooting. Our bullets didn't stop 'em, though. Got down to four of us fellers holed up behind dead mounts, and I figured we were goners. I was out of bullets, and they quit shooting, so I played dead with my hand on my knife. Soon as one of them bastards came to rootle me, I stabbed him in the heart. Just before he turned to sand, I saw what was really there. Chupacabra. You seen one?"

Nettie's memory served up a flash of Chuck as a scaly reptile monster with bug-eyes and acid spit, his teeth snapping for her. "Yep. I seen one."

"He went sandy and blew away, as they do, and I had no idea what-all had just happened. Didn't know what to do, as I could hear his crew rifling my dead friends and then...eating 'em. So I laid back down and kept playing dead. Guess they took whatever they wanted and got full bellies. Pretty soon, they rounded up the herd of horses and left. Captain and the Rangers found me a few hours later at sun-up, trying to dig six graves with a Bowie knife. They'd heard tell of the chupa gang, but they were too late."

"So the Rangers just took you on?"

A bitter laugh. Sam picked his teeth with his knife and ended with a grin. "'Course not. Rangers ain't a hotel. They told me what had happened, told me my best bet was to head east or north, away from the chupas and rogue werewolves. Said to either find some civilized place full of white people and lawmen or be a mountain man, where all I'd have to worry about was Sasquatches and the occasional bored skinwalker. Instead, I followed 'em on foot, all the way here. Figured I'd rather fight them things than run away and pretend they don't exist." He tossed his knife, and it sunk into the ground. "What about you?"

"Accidentally killed a vampire."

"Well, sure. But why were you with Dan? And what's this thing you got to kill?"

Talking about her past made Nettie downright uncomfortable. It was hard enough to pretend to be a boy named Rhett, but now she also had to pretend she'd never seen Hennessy before, that she wasn't from Gloomy Bluebird, and that she hadn't worked for a few blissful days at the Double TK with Hennessy's old friends, one of whom was now dead by her own hand. Standing, she yanked Hennessy's knife out of the dirt and wiped it on her pants, then held it out, hilt first. He took it, giving her a probing look that made her yank her hat down over her eyes and scratch the itchy scruff at the back of her neck where her hair had been inexpertly slashed by her old jackknife.

"If I knew what it was or why I got to kill it, I wouldn't need the Rangers at all. Now don't we got business to do?" Without thinking, she held out a hand to help pull Hennessy up. He clasped her palm warmly, popped to his feet, and gave her a good-natured shrug.

"There's always business to do, other Hennessy. But I want you to know I'll help you if I can. You remind me of somebody I used to know, I reckon."

Nettie went stone-cold all the way down to her feet. Did he recognize her? If he did, that meant trouble, because no way would the Rangers let a girl live among 'em. But it also meant he'd noticed her the first time around, which felt damn good for someone who'd always figured she might as well be invisible to anyone that mattered. It was nice, too, the way he looked full at her, smiled at her, asked her real questions...even if she blushed fiercely and he made her all rough and tongue-tied.

"Do I remind you of...somebody from home?" she asked, as he picked up the arm's length of snake still steaming on the skewer and kicked dirt over the fire.

He shook his head, took the snake, and dumped the meat in a leather bag at his waist before he started walking. "Feller I lost to the chupas. Ricky. Plucky little half-Aztecan sumbitch. He helped me out when I was first on the trail."

Nettie's heart dove and resurfaced before sinking again. So she was safe, probably. For now. And she reminded him of a dead half-breed boy who'd been his friend, which he could admit without spitting in the dirt. Accustomed as she was to wanting more things than there were stars in the sky, it galled a bit, both needing to be assumed a boy and hating to be seen as anything other than exactly what she was. What was so horrible about being a girl that everyone felt the need to force them into skirts and tether them to ovens and children? Who had decided that women couldn't ride astride and proud and still be women?

Probably fellers who were scared of competition, far as she could reckon.

Nettie didn't feel much like a girl, but she didn't feel much like a boy, either. She just...was.

A hand landed on her wrist. "You need bullets, Rhett?"

"What?" She'd been imagining riding double with Hennessy on a unicorn, and shook the silly fancy from her head.

"Bullets. We carry regular and a couple of silver, each." When she stared at his hand a beat longer, he pulled it away and added, "For werewolves. Damn, that sounds right stupid. But it's the only thing that'll slow 'em down."

By the end of the day, Nettie knew how to mold her own silver bullets, how to turn just about anything into a stake, and that she should never try to eat any part of a monster, no matter how hungry she was or how dead she figured it was. The damn things weren't gone until they were sand, and whatever was left of 'em until that point would try right hard to keep going. The fanged rabbits were dangerous while alive but not actually magical monsters, just predators, according to what Sam knew—and they tasted mighty fine, as Nettie had learned herself. But anything that could walk on two legs or talk was bad news. Fortunately, most of the monsters looked like predators, scavengers, or creatures white folks didn't want to eat even if they could find 'em, like the Javelina. "And remember," Sam said sternly, "don't ever eat a rooster, just hens."

"Begging your pardon, but what's wrong with roosters?"

"Go on, Rench. Show 'im."

A red-headed feller lifted up his shirt to show a scar on his belly. "Ate a bad batch of rooster-foot soup in a train camp. Chunk of cockatrice burrowed its way right out of my gut. I nearly died."

That story, of course, came right before dinner, as they all lined up for beans on the porch steps where she'd first seen them last week. They'd been angry shapes then, shadows with guns. Now she knew their names, their horses, what each man's specialty in killing monsters was. Nettie stood beside Hennessy, her head down, feeling jittery. She could sense at least one other monster feller in the area, and although she was pretty sure it was Jiddy, there was this sort of constant buzz that grated on her nerves and made her stomach flop over. Not that she could ask about it without sounding like a goddamn fool. It wasn't until she was sitting at the table with a dented tin plate of beans and goat that she finally discovered the source of her unease.

The Captain came in, and the fellers stood up and nodded, all deferential-like. He went straight for the beans, and Delgado scraped up the last big chunks of goat meat as if he'd been saving them for the boss. It was clear the big chair with arms was reserved for the Captain, but instead, he sat down his plate and came over to where Nettie stood next to Hennessy.

"You gettin' on, Rhett?"

"Yes, Captain."

The Captain nodded and pulled a pocket watch from his

beat-up vest. Nettie's stomach rippled, and she coughed up a couple of half-chewed beans and swallowed them back where they belonged. She caught a flash of movement in the Captain's hands and looked down in time to see a snake-like eyeball blink at her from tarnished silver, set into the curved watch case opposite the clock face. She nearly dropped her plate as the Captain wound the watch and poked it back into his pocket as if it wasn't half alive.

"That's one of Juan de Blanco's eyes," he said, taking up his plate. "He don't shoot so good, now." He took a few bites, gulping his food down like it was serious work. "Reckon we'll set out at dawn for this Cannibal Owl of yours. You said it's west?" Nettie nodded but couldn't speak. "Fine. The boys teach you enough to kill whatever you find?" She nodded. "Good. Whatever else you need to know, you'll learn on the road. From what Dan said, you can hold your own, and we got to find it before the new moon. So we need to hurry. That right?"

Nettie swallowed down her revolting beans and stuck out her chin. "Yes, Captain."

"You helping him along, Hennessy?"

Hennessy smiled like a loyal dog. "Yes, Captain. Rhett's doing right good. Taught me how to skin a snake today."

The Captain swallowed a mouthful of meat without chewing. "I ain't impressed with skinning snakes unless they're attached to a gorgon's head, boy. You all better focus on killing things that are as smart as you are. Not that a snake ain't close."

Hennessy's head didn't fall, but Nettie felt him deflate a bit as he said, "Yes, Captain."

When the Captain tucked a napkin into his collar and went for seconds, the men were free to eat again, although Nettie had lost much of her appetite. Delgado's cooking was inferior to the Double TK's offerings and what Nettie could scavenge for herself on the prairie. And the cook didn't seem to like her, either, judging by the sloppy way he tossed mostly beans and not much goat on her plate. She still had a few gritty beans left when the Captain belched and stood.

As the older man moved around the room from man to man, giving orders about the days to come, Nettie watched him, sly-like. The Captain knew how to speak to each Ranger, how to reach him. Some fellers, he put a hand on their shoulder and looked 'em in the eye. Some, like Jiddy, he just nodded at and muttered something too low for anyone else to hear. Some fellers, he laughed with and grinned at. But in the end, he'd spoken to every man at the table, given him a job. Best Nettie could tell, of the two dozen fellers, most of 'em were coming along on the hunt for the Cannibal Owl, leaving only the oldest and most infirm behind to guard the outfit. On one hand, it was awful comforting, knowing she wasn't alone. But on the other hand, it was her hunt, and she didn't care to share it with a bunch of strange fellers. Would the Injun woman be satisfied if Hennessy or Jiddy took down the monster? Or did it have to be Nettie herself?

There had to be some way to make sure the Cannibal Owl fell only to her. And that she had some quiet time, before it died, to question it at gunpoint about her past.

After dinner, the bunkhouse was lively and rife with talk as the men packed up their things and cleaned their guns. Nettie learned that since they weren't paid well, regular-like, their only hope of making any money was to plunder. Whatever monsters they killed, they got to keep that creature's things. And if the monster they killed was an old or a rich one, that meant a man could make his fortune with one well-placed stake. Much was said about a Ranger named Bloomfield who'd personally taken down a vampire mayor who'd stuffed his mattress full of gold.

Bloomfield had moved to New York City to buy a newspaper and had a personal bodyguard with a crossbow that shot stakes, just in case the ex-mayor's vamp friends wanted revenge. All the young rangers wanted to be the next Bloomfield.

Nettie didn't have much to pack, but she opened up her saddlebags and laid out all her things just the same. One set of clothes, stained with blood and worse, but that was normal for the Rangers, from what she'd seen. The men wore bloodstains like medals of honor.

Two holsters, three pistols. The one she currently wore on her hip was the most reliable, but the other two might be the difference between life and death in a fight. One Bowie knife, considerably sharper after Dan had whetted it, and two she hadn't yet had cause to test. A few silver bullets and enough regular shot to take down a herd of buffalo. A lariat and an old bullwhip they'd given her, once she'd shown her skill with it, as she'd lost her old one in the desert. Add in her water skins, saddle, blanket, headstall, treasure pouch, more money than she should've had, and Ragdoll, and that was the sum total of her belongings.

Not bad for two weeks on her own, and much better than a one-eyed mule...that she still missed.

With all the bunks taken, Nettie had claimed a space by the door on her second night with the Rangers. At least the ranch house was up off the dirt, which mean the bugs would favor the dark, cool space under the wood boards. She unrolled her blanket and flopped down on her back, keeping her boots on just in case. What with all the excitement of tomorrow's trip and the musical snores of two dozen fellers, she was pretty sure she'd never get to sleep before dawn.

She was wrong.

Sleep claimed her, and with it came the Injun woman.

CHAPTER
15

The whistle came from outside, long and low. No one else stirred, but Nettie felt the ripple deep in her belly. She rolled on her side and squinted out the open door and into the starlight. It was brighter out there than it was inside, and she could see a shadowy shape waiting just beyond the main corral. A seated figure, wrapped in a blanket, atop a dark horse.

A dark horse that smelled of salt and dripped water, even in the middle of the plains.

The whistle came again, and the figure turned and began to ride away, a slow and stately walk. Nettie scrambled to her knees, strapped on her gun, checked her knife, and crept out.

She walked, then trotted, then jogged, but she couldn't quite catch up. The black horse never changed speed, and yet it moved ahead with slow grace as if gliding, always just too far away. When the horse finally stopped, a fire sprang up, red and wild with spiraling, white smoke in exactly the place where Winifred had lain as the Captain brought her back to life. The figure was already off the horse, fingers outstretched to warm before the fire.

Nettie sat across from her, noting that the Injun woman's hands were normal hands, not what she expected from a ghost or a drowned corpse. Nettie held out her hands, too, but the fire gave no warmth. Something soft and hairy brushed the back of her neck, but when she startled and turned around nothing was there. All she heard was the ghost of a laughing whinny. Wet hoofprints marked the dirt, inches from where she sat.

"Moon ain't new yet," Nettie observed.

A low chuckle. "That's why you're still alive, Nettie Lonesome. Best hurry."

"Then why are you here now? What do you-all want?" she said carefully.

"Revenge."

The Injun woman's blanket was wrapped up over her head, her face hidden from the light. Deep within, two white stars shined.

"What are you?" Nettie asked.

"Revenge."

"And why does the Cannibal Owl take children?"

Nettie wasn't surprised when the disembodied voice answered, "Hunger. And revenge."

Standing, Nettie kicked dirt over the red fire, but the flames didn't so much as flicker. Deep within the blaze, she saw, crystal clear, a leather pouch very much like her own but tied with long, gray feathers, so familiar that her heart hurt. When she stretched out a hand to grab it, she felt no warmth. She reached deep into the fire and felt nothing, nothing but the cold suck of starlight and emptiness. No matter how hard she clutched it, she couldn't grasp the leather bag or its long, worn ties.

Withdrawing her hand, she stared at the callused fingers and pink palms that had served others all her life. They weren't burned. They were shriveled with water, and as she watched, the skin dripped off, leaving stark white bones. Holding her bone-hand up to the starlight, she asked the bundled figure one last question, one she was too scared to ask in waking life.

"What am I?"

The fire went out, and the voice said one last word.

"Revenge."

Nettie woke up the next morning with a dry mouth rimmed in scratchy salt. She went straight for her water skin and gulped half the tepid liquid down as the first of the men began to stir.

"Time to head out, boys!" Hennessy called, hopping to his feet and dusting off his britches, all bright-eyed and bushy-tailed. Nettie hurried to be the first to the outhouse. So far, nobody had questioned the fact that she hadn't joined them to piss off the back of the cookhouse after dinner. They probably figured Delgado's food wasn't sitting right, and she didn't care what they thought so long as nobody tried to compare himself to a pizzle she didn't have.

The morning went by fast, but not fast enough. After last night's warning, Nettie was ready to be on the road. She blinked, and she was gulping down her beans. She blinked again, and Hennessy was giving her another water skin and a greasy handful of jerky for the ride—not that she entirely trusted Delgado's jerky, but Sam swore none of the fellers had died from it. Yet.

One more blink, and she was picking out a second mount from the small herd. Rangers rode fast, often without stopping to eat or sleep, and always ponied a spare horse. She went for the smallest, hardiest, steadiest-looking pony, figuring the little paint would hold up well in the heat, eat less than the bigger horses, and not require much work if she had to remount on the run. As most of the men were too proud to ride a short horse with a bald cow face, no one seemed to mind, even when she named him Puddin'. Once they were all ponied up and mounted, the Captain whistled high and raised a hand, and they struck west, the new-risen sun at their backs and Delgado's cook wagon trundling along in the rear.

"Are we headed the right way?" Hennessy asked, riding up behind her on a showy dappled palomino with a leggy black dancing on the end of his rope, the fool.

She could only shrug and recall the brush of cold, whiskered lips on the back of her neck. "If not, I'll let you know." He rode beside her for a minute, and she added, "That palomino's hooves are gonna crack, you mark my words."

Sam's smile didn't waver. "You just watch, Rhett. I've got the devil's own luck."

And, Lord, but if she didn't believe him.

A couple of times as they rode, the Injun woman appeared in the corner of Nettie's vision, a wavering figure pointing and then disappearing much like the mirages she'd heard about that affected men left in the desert too long. Whenever it happened, Nettie trotted up to the Captain to correct his route, then allowed her mount to drop back with Hennessy and the younger hands. Far as she could tell, the order in which the men rode corresponded to their experience and importance, or at least their number of scars and the comparative bushiness of their facial hair. The fellers who rode near the Captain looked like they were carved of old logs and raccoon pelts and got mighty twitchy and proud-looking when Ragdoll and Puddin' approached their larger, handsomer mounts. As if ugly was catching. Lord, what would they say if they knew Nettie was a girl? She pulled her bandanna up and her hat down, hoping she wouldn't have to find out.

A few hours in, Nettie's behind started to ache, her thighs screaming from the hard trot. Monty had always said a cheap saddle was worse than no saddle at all, but she wouldn't let the Rangers see her consternation. There'd been no chance to rest, really, since she'd left Pap's farm. She wanted to ride faster and get it over with, but she didn't dare talk back to the Captain or urge him to hurry. Even her tough life with Pap and Mam hadn't prepared her for two weeks spent entirely in the saddle. Hellfire, but breaking broncs at least allowed a person a few minutes on the ground between horses while something else ached. She began to see the value in a broad-backed horse and a well-cushioned saddle and daydreamed that they'd come upon a town, and she would slip the dead vampire's roll of bills into Sam's hand and tell him to pick out a saddle with lots of silver conchos and plenty of padding for her. And fetch some penny candy for himself, too. In the dream, he grinned, and his breath smelled like peppermint.

Just when she was about to scoot over behind a group of boulders to relieve herself, mainly her legs, the entire company stopped. The Captain and Jiddy had their heads together, whispering excitedly. Nettie closed her eyes and focused on her belly. Sure enough, she felt a tiny ripple like an angry nut doing somersaults.

That meant there was a monster nearby.

Staring the way Jiddy was pointing, Nettie could just barely make out something jutting from the prairie over a rise. If she hadn't felt that ripple, she would've reckoned it was just a group of especially pokey rock formations. Heck, maybe it still was, and one of them ugly harpy-things was sitting on top of a branch, waiting to yank out somebody's eyeballs. Hard to tell, from way back here.

"Jiddy, Virgil, Hennessy, and Rhett. You boys go on down

and investigate if that creature's toeing the line or waiting to kill. You need us, you shoot twice."

Nettie looked to Hennessy to see what to do, and he was untying his ponied horse and handing it off to the next youngest feller. She did the same, tossing her rope to a skinny wrangler named Boyd Chickamauga who'd developed the unfortunate nickname of Chicken, thanks to his bright red shirt and worrisome nature.

"You reckon it's a chupacabra, Rhett?" he said.

She shrugged. "If so, I reckon it'll be dead soon."

Hennessy trotted around the company to meet Jiddy and one of the most respected fellers in the bunch, Virgil Scarsdale. Virgil was second in command and had been at the Captain's side through countless skirmishes, from the stories Nettie had heard. He was a man of few words, mainly because his brother Milo fought with him and would never shut up. Nettie was right uncomfortable around Virgil, as she suspected the gray-maned, hatchet-faced older man could see straight through her disguise and would one day gather up enough words to tell the Captain who and what she really was. For now, he just stared at her like she was a corn on a sore toe that he was too busy to scrape off. Shaking his grizzled head, he kicked his bay and led their foursome toward the shimmering something-or-other on the horizon.

"Can you feel it, Rhett?" Hennessy asked.

Before Nettie could answer, Jiddy spit in the dirt and said, "Don't matter what Rhett feels. I feel it, and that's enough for you, squirt."

"Shut yer trap and come on," Virgil said, and Nettie breathed a sigh of relief that he wouldn't speak again for at least two weeks after using up so many words.

Virgil kicked his horse to a lope, and Jiddy and Hennessy

fanned out to leave Nettie and Ragdoll taking up the rear, which suited them both fine. The ground was rocky and rumpled, which meant she couldn't check her gun so easily, and the jagged shape ahead soon quit wavering and turned into a little town, not even as big as Gloomy Bluebird. There were three tall, false-fronted buildings on each side of a tidy street, their signs lettered in a fancy, curly hand that Nettie admired but couldn't read. The wood was mostly new and honey gold instead of the misty blue-gray of an old town, and a wagon still sat out front, filled with barrels of nails and boards brought in from far off. A little creek to the side explained why some fool had chosen to make his last stand out here in the middle of nowhere. A dozen penned horses bugled their welcome, and Nettie's stomach flopped around like a fish on the ground.

They dropped down to a walk as they entered the lone street. Nettie felt like she was about to get shot, but Jiddy aimed his horse for the building that had the distinctive swinging doors of a saloon. It was downright eerie, how quiet the town was. The only movement came from the flap of washing hanging from a few lines, and not a single dog or person was visible. Nettie waited for Virgil and Jiddy to dismount, not sure if she needed permission to follow the older men or if they wanted her outside, on horseback and ready, gun in hand.

"Reckon I'll have me a drink," Jiddy said.

Virgil looked up and smiled like a slit throat. "Fine idea. Boys, you stay out here and keep watch."

When Nettie followed Virgil's line of sight to the upstairs of the saloon, she saw an open window with a fine pink curtain rustled by someone just gone. So tight-lipped Virgil was a whoremonger. Figured. And if the whores here were vampires, that would make sense for the flopping in her belly, although she did wonder at what an upstanding Ranger like Virgil would get from a woman he considered a monster. Still, vampire whores didn't seem to bother anybody, which meant there might not be trouble.

"I guess we sit?" she asked.

Hennessy looked at the door and sighed with longing. "Guess we do. I can't wait to get my badge and actually do something besides wait."

Nettie grinned. "Look at it this way: If somebody's gonna get gobbled up by a monster, it's gonna be them."

Hennessy swallowed hard, stared longingly at the saloon doors, and gave Nettie a mischievous, secretive sort of smile that made her stomach flip in a different way. "There's ways to be gobbled up I wouldn't mind so much."

She looked away and blushed. It was one thing when Poke said it, but she hated to think of sweet Sam as anything less than perfect. Two pairs of spurs clinked in the dust as Virgil and Jiddy swung through the saloon's double doors. The town was altogether too quiet, and Nettie's stomach kept on cartwheeling like a tumbleweed.

"I got a bad feeling about this," she said.

Hennessy shrugged. "Feel whatever you want, so long as you do what you're told. Last feller who went against the Captain's orders ended up in four separate chunks that wouldn't quite fit together."

Cheerful voices called out inside the saloon, and a piano started up, too jolly for the middle of nowhere. With a sigh of annoyance, Nettie walked Ragdoll over to a water trough and let the mare drink. Hennessy followed, his gelding gulping down the water. A peculiar sound started up, and Hennessy's head snapped to attention, his eyes swiveling back to the saloon door.

"What the Sam Hill is that racket?" Nettie asked, a pinky shoved deep in her ear, as it felt like all the little hairs in there were quivering.

"I reckon that's opry."

Hennessy swung off his horse, clumsy as all get-out, and walked toward the saloon door like he was half-asleep. He didn't even bother to tie up the gelding, which was about the worst thing a smart wrangler could do in the middle of nowhere.

"Hennessy!" He didn't answer. "Samuel!" Nothing. He kept walking. "Sam!"

He'd always been a friendly feller, but he didn't so much as twitch an ear in response. Yanking her lariat off her saddle, Nettie kicked Ragdoll across the street, swung the loop overhead, and lassoed Samuel Hennessy around the shoulders just as his hand was about to push through the double doors of the saloon. Even then, he didn't turn around, just tried to shrug out of the rope. With her stomach erupting and her heart trying to flop out of her chest, Nettie wrapped her lariat around her saddle horn and spurred her mare in the opposite direction, yanking Hennessy off his feet and away from the saloon.

As soon as the feller was on the ground, Nettie turned and hollered, "Dangit, Hennessy! What's wrong with you?"

But Hennessy just stood like a dumb dog and tried to plow back toward the saloon without even bothering to remove the rope. Whatever he was heading for, so far as Nettie could tell, was very bad news. So she walked her mare away slowly, tugging Hennessy step by reluctant step out of the empty town. He fought the rope all the way, but it was clear his brain wasn't working, as he never tried to duck out of the loop. When she'd pulled him to the far end of the buildings, she hopped off her horse and waved a hand in his face.

"Hennessy?"

He shoved her aside and took another step toward town. And that's when she decided the only way to keep the boy safe was to rope him to a hitching pole, which she did, using the mare as an anchor. When he was secured, she stepped away and dusted off her hands.

"You in there, Sam?"

He shook his head like a fly was on his nose. "Quiet. There's purty singing. I wanna go."

Nettie'd heard singing coming from the one-room church in Gloomy Bluebird, but it hadn't been anything that would make her behave like Hennessy was right now. The way his head was cocked toward the saloon and the uneven warbling within convinced her that there was something monster-y going on, something dastardly. Whatever it was Sam claimed to hear, all Nettie heard was a peculiar, fish-strangling sound that made her want to plug her ears with her fingers. It definitely wasn't opry. She raised her gun to the sky and was just about to shoot twice when she saw the entire company of twenty men and twice as many horses heading right for the town, their faces as slack and dumb as Hennessy's.

Whatever was in that saloon was calling the men. And for some reason, it wasn't calling Nettie. And that meant she was the only one who could kill it.

Fast as she could, Nettie unpacked her whip and took up her gun and hot-footed it for the saloon. As she shoved the doors open, the music smacked her in the face, unbearably loud. She crashed through, and no one so much as turned their head, in part because so many of the saloon occupants were dead and half-eaten, sitting in the spindly chairs and staring at the stage with what was left of their eyeballs. The only living men in the saloon were Virgil, Jiddy, and a scrawny, scared-looking bartender polishing a dirty glass behind the bar with tufts of cotton stuck in his ears. Like all the dead folks, the Rangers were staring at a tiny stage and the moon-faced, dark-haired woman standing on it in a faded dinner dress. She was singing, but it wasn't normal singing. It was too high and too low all at once, scraping up against Nettie's teeth and backbone like sandpaper against an open wound. And if she knew anything about men and women, she knew it wasn't the woman's looks and figure that held the men so captivated.

Nettie looked at that woman and saw nothing out of the ordinary, save for a face that even she recognized as plain and lumpy. But she knew it wasn't human. And she knew it had to die.

With her gun drawn, it was easy enough to shoot the woman in the chest from across the half-built saloon. Well, fine. It took her three shots, but nobody complained. For just a second, Nettie felt pretty good about her shooting lessons—until the bullet pinged right back out of the woman's chest and fell to the ground. It had barely dented her dress, hadn't even left a hole, as if the woman's body were made of rock. The broad face jerked to Nettie like a hawk catching sight of a rabbit, and the voice got louder and louder and even louder, so loud that Nettie figured shooting herself in the head was the only way to make enough room for all the sounds inside. It wasn't until she felt the cool kiss of steel against her temple that she realized that was a very bad idea and definitely not something she would've come up with herself.

So she shot the woman-thing again, this time in the face. The bullet bounced off the pale skin between mud-brown eyes, and the singing mouth curved up in a haughty smile. The woman stretched out a hand and curled a finger at Nettie, all welcoming-like. Nettie took one step forward, then reached for the bandanna around her neck, ripped it in half, wadded up each side, and stuck the rags into her ears. It helped drown out the goddamn noise, at least a little. Shoving her gun back in her holster, Nettie took up her knife instead and uncoiled the whip in her left hand.

The saloon door burst in, just then, the Captain leading his entire regiment of Durango Rangers with the dumbest look imaginable on his face. Jiddy hadn't budged in all this time, just stood in the middle of the saloon, staring at the woman with a rapt sort of slackness on his bearlike face. So much for the head scout. Far as Nettie could see, she had to act now or watch the woman's plans unfold, which was doubtless going to be horrible for the Rangers.

Knife in one hand, whip in the other, Nettie stalked around the tables, her eyes never leaving the woman and the woman's eyes never leaving her. Since feeling a gun in her hand for the first time, Nettie hadn't faced a creature like this, something smart that knew it was being hunted as it was, itself, hunting. The Captain's men sleepwalked toward the stage, a bright red shirt leading the pack. Of course Chicken would want to be the first to reach the woman. Nettie was fast, but she wasn't fast enough, and Chick hit the stage before she could stop him. Still singing, the woman grabbed the front of his shirt and pulled him up to join her. His eyes were wide, his weak chin wagging, and his mouth goggled open. The woman pulled him close, brought her lips to his, and wrapped her fingers carefully around his throat as she kissed him.

Seconds later, Chick hit the ground and didn't move again. Also, he didn't have a face.

And Nettie ran.

When she was right up near the stage, the woman's arm stretched out toward Nettie, the fingers joining together into something that looked like a snake's tail as the arm went rubbery and elongated. Caught by surprise, Nettie slashed down with her knife and cut the thing off in a burst of black blood.

Fast as lightning, the woman quit singing and her snake-arm recoiled, her mouth opening up the wrong way, top to bottom, and her other arm shooting out for Nettie's neck. Nettie leaped back, away from the blood spray, and flung her whip like she was going for a calf's leg. The braided leather caught the woman's long arm and wrapped around four times, and Nettie gave a mighty yank. Most of the woman got tugged off the stage, except for the six sticky snake-tail legs that sprouted under her dress and kept reaching to stay up there.

The woman quit singing for one second as she struggled to stand, and the Captain had the good sense to pull his pistol and shout, "What in Hades—?" but then the singing started up again and his face went slack.

In the moment that the woman refocused on the men and opened her mouth, Nettie pulled her lasso taut, stepped on it to pin the woman to the ground, and stabbed her Bowie knife deep into the place where the creature's heart should've been.

But it wasn't there, or at the very least, the skin was too hard in that spot to allow a knife access. The blade skittered off, just like the bullet had. One of the snake-tail legs wrapped around Nettie's boot, and another went for the wrist holding the lasso. Nettie's eyes met the woman's brown ones and found only otherness and hunger and disbelief. So Nettie yanked out the knife and stabbed her again, higher up. The blade sunk in like the critter was made of ripe cheese, and finally, with one deep gasp, the song stopped and the body exploded into wet black sand.

Nettie's knife fell to the floor, and she flopped onto her back on the shiny-gold boards beside the sliding hills of sand. Killing monsters was damn near exhausting.

A second later, the Captain and Jiddy were staring down at her. The Captain yanked the rags out of her ears and said, "I believe I asked you what the hell that thing was."

"Reckon I don't know, Captain. But now it's a pile of sand."

All around the saloon, fellers were blinking awake and being horrified by the scene surrounding them. Three of the Rangers had the bartender backed into a corner, but all he could do was cry and mutter in French. Again and again, he kept saying a word that sounded like *sea wren*, and something else that sounded like *eh-poose*, but nobody had any French, so nobody knew what he was talking about. The more guns they stuck in his face and the more they hollered at him, the more he blubbered. Finally, he just pointed to the back door and passed out, which was a vast improvement.

Through that door, they found a room filled with piles of treasure, or what passed for treasure in the wilds of Durango. Scraggly little gold nuggets and silver dollars were sorted neatly into barrels and chests, along with a few bits and bobs of ladies' jewelry. The next door led to a peculiar sort of general store stocked with neat piles of used clothes, bolts of new cloth, dozens of pocket watches, shelves of worn boots, and saddles stacked up around the walls. Out back, an arroyo was filled with stripped, nekkid bodies that had been mostly picked to bones by the fat vultures waiting expectantly on the fence posts.

"I ain't never seen nothing like this," Jiddy said. "Best I can figure, she lured in men with her singing and ate their soft parts."

Virgil's brother Milo took one look at the pile out back and nodded. "Siren. Just like Odysseus. Don't any of you fellers have your letters? Old Greek monster, used to sit on an island and lure fellers in with singing, then steal their goods and eat 'em. This ain't no island, but it looks like men'll go pretty far out of their way if they think there's a whore and a glass of whisky." He gave his brother a significant sort of look.

Hennessy wandered up, rubbing the raw places on his shoulders where Nettie's rope had held him and looking peaky when he spotted the pile of carcasses. "Somebody tied me to a post, Captain. Now I got the strangest song stuck in my head," he muttered, sticking a finger in his ear. "Won't go away. And what happened to Chicken? What's going on?"

"We're gonna find out, by God." The Captain spit on the ground to seal the deal.

Back inside the saloon, the men had laid out the bodies on the tables. It was common knowledge that almost all the flat wood in any popular business would be whittled down by the knives of cowpokes losing at poker, or at the very least stained and gouged from bar fights and spilled liquor and tobacco juice and blood. But these tables looked like they'd just been rolled off the wagon. Lying atop the smooth wood were four relatively fresh strangers with strange, round bites taken out of 'em at peculiar intervals, and then there was Chicken. Most of his face and lips were gone, an acid-edged circle showing his gums and teeth. Nettie wanted to throw up, but she figured she'd just swallow it down before letting the Captain think she was weaker than any of his other fellers. It was damned inconvenient, wanting to yark all the damn time.

"Poor Chicken always was the first one through the whore's door," Milo said.

Virgil shook his head. "Women is always trouble."

Nettie's temper flared.

"That thing wasn't no woman," she said, making her voice husky and low.

The Captain looked up as if seeing her for the first time, his eyes narrowing. He looked her up and down, and she managed to stick out her chin without letting her chest push out.

"You done good, Rhett. Reckon we'd still be listening to that octopus woman, if you hadn't killed her." Gentler than Nettie would've expected from him, the Captain reached down and undid the Durango Rangers badge pinned to Chicken's shirt. When he'd affixed it to Nettie's collar, he said, "Welcome to the Rangers, Rhett. The spoils belong to you."

With that, he turned and walked out of the saloon.

"Well, go on." Milo jerked his chin at the door behind the bar. "You'd better start with a vest and a decent saddle. Looks like you're the next Bloomfield."

"Don't the Captain take his spoils first?" Nettie asked.

Virgil snorted a laugh, and Milo answered for him. "Captain only takes horses. He'll keep whatever's sound, add 'em to the herd."

"Why?"

"Everything else just weighs a man down, he says."

In the back room, Nettie looked at the riches laid out, unsure of where to start and how much to take. The other men milled around, waiting and watching. With more goods than she'd ever seen in her life laid out before her, Nettie itched to run fingers through the gold and hang the watches around her neck like pearls and pinch silver dollars between her teeth just to feel the soft metal dent.

But she knew a test when she saw one, and Milo had said "Bloomfield" like it was a slur. She wanted the Rangers to think her a good man, so she passed by the barrels of gold and silver and went to where the clothes were neatly stacked. Testing for quality between callused fingers, she picked out a leather vest and a wool serape, selected a few bright bandannas, hunted for a good pair of socks, and claimed a dented silver pocket watch that wasn't too fancy. She took a well-padded saddle, too, but not the nicest one that really caught her eye.

"That all you taking?" Hennessy asked, and Nettie nodded.

"A man don't need to be weighed down," she said. "Y'all can have the rest."

Before they left, and after each of the men had taken a share of Nettie's spoils, they set fire to the town. Nettie'd never seen so much fancy wood go up in smoke, and she wondered what story would reach the fine folk of Durango about another massacre by the Rangers.

Seemed like there would always be a certain dishonesty to Nettie Lonesome's life, but it was better than being eaten by a damn octopus or serving as a drunk man's slave. She kicked her horse and followed Hennessy out of town with a smile on her face.

As she was settling into her cushy new saddle and enjoying the spoils of war, she was pretty sure she heard a woman scream.

CHAPTER

16

She was the last in line, and when she turned in the saddle, she saw nothing but fire.

"Captain, you hear that?" she shouted, but none of the men turned around.

"I don't hear nothin'," Hennessy said by her side, but... she did.

With a final rub of her brand-new Rangers badge, she cussed under her breath, turned her horse, and galloped back toward the blaze.

"Rhett? That's against orders, man! Come back!" Hennessy hollered, but Nettie refused.

She was sure she heard it now, a woman shredding her throat with screaming above the crackling of the fire. It was coming from the building she'd taken for a jail, considering the door had a shiny new lock on it and there were bars on the window. Small hands were wrapped around the iron.

"Help! Please! I'm locked in. Help!"

Even knowing the Captain might draw and quarter her, even knowing it was probably another one of them siren things, still she couldn't just turn her back on a person crying for help.

Yanking Ragdoll to a halt, she jumped off the mare and didn't bother tying her to a post.

The door was locked, but the latch wasn't hot, and the flames were just spreading from the building next door. Nettie tried kicking the door open, but unlike the ramshackle wood of Pap's farm, this new construction wouldn't budge with just a boot.

"Aw, hellfire," she muttered as she pulled out her pistol and fired a round into the lock.

Damn thing didn't budge.

"Stand back, Rhett."

She'd never been so glad to see Samuel Hennessy, which was saying a lot. He moved her gently by the shoulder and stuck a shiny spade into the door's edge, prying it open. The room inside was smoky but not ablaze, thank goodness, and the screaming turned to relief as soon as they stepped inside.

"Help! Please. He locked me in here. I can't..." The woman broke down coughing, and Nettie hurried to the cell, where a woman lay on the floor, ragged and oddly shaped.

"You a monster?" Nettie asked.

The woman shook her head. "I'm in a family way. The smoke...please..."

Sam was already there with his shovel, moving Nettie aside again to work on the lock. After banging on it like a damn blacksmith, he finally got the hasp snapped in half. Nettie pulled it off and wrenched the door open. The woman on the floor inside was unmoving, and Nettie and Sam each took an arm to drag her out. They coughed and ducked low as they dragged her from the building, its walls already catching flame.

Lord, she was more than in a family way—the woman was enormous. Nettie'd never seen a woman in this stage, carrying a belly that had to be bigger than the rest of her combined. Once they'd tugged her out into the street, Nettie leaned down and put her ear to the woman's mouth to see if she was still breathing, which she was.

"Lady, you got to get up. Can you walk?"

The woman shook her head like she was dreaming. "My husband. Tell me. Is he—?" She fell into a violent coughing fit, gasped, and went limp. Fire was licking through the cracks between the boards, the smoke thickening. Sam pulled his bandanna up over his nose, but Nettie had left her new ones in her saddlebag. Best she could do was pull up her shirt and squeeze her eyes shut as they drug the still form out toward their waiting horses.

The Captain and his Rangers were mounted at the edge of town, watching. Nettie ignored them, turning the woman onto her back and checking for worse injuries once they were far out of range of the fire. Sam put an arm behind the woman's shoulders and pulled her to sitting.

"Go get your water, Rhett." When Nettie paused too long, he pulled down his bandanna and added, "Ain't you ever seen a woman with child? Get her some water!"

Nettie fetched her skin from Ragdoll's saddle, glad the mare hadn't taken it into her fool head to run away. Hurrying back, she kneeled at Sam's side and squeezed water onto the woman's lips. Her eyes popped open, and she drank gratefully, one hand rubbing the taut fabric stretched over her belly. As Nettie watched, dumbfounded, the woman's belly heaved and rumpled.

"Is it a monster?" she whispered.

Sam laughed. "Naw, it's always like that, near the end. I was the second of eight, so I seen it plenty of times."

Nettie closed her eyes and felt around inside but sensed no

flip in her belly. Well, until Sam put a hand on her arm, at least. "Go get your second pony, will you? My black's too anxious."

"Can she ride astride like that?"

Sam shook his head and chuckled. "If her other choice is to stay here, I reckon she'll find a way."

"My husband," the woman murmured, eyes closed and face ashen. "Trent. Went in the saloon. You seen him?"

Nettie's eyes met Sam's, and she felt a pang of loss for the woman.

"I ain't seen him, no," Sam said, and Nettie hurried toward the Rangers for Puddin'.

She and Sam both knew what had happened to Trent, but the woman was half dead and didn't need to know about the pile of bodies yet.

"This ain't no charity," Milo said as Nettie took Puddin's rope from one of the Rangers.

The Captain, she noticed, was silent and watchful.

"Well it ain't a hangman's noose for two, neither," she muttered, jogging back with the horse.

The woman was sitting up now, coughing, and Nettie took a moment to switch her new saddle from Ragdoll to the stocky paint pony, cussing to herself all the while. She'd been enjoying that cushy seat, dammit, and now she'd be bareback on the rangy appy, leading along a woman that the Captain, or at least his chief men, didn't care to save.

Well, and what right did she have to call herself a Ranger if she was going to let humans die?

"Can you ride?" she asked.

The woman looked up, eyes red and cheeks gaunt.

"I need to find my husband."

"We'll try to help you," Sam said. "But we can't do that unless you get on this horse."

When the woman held a trembling hand out, Nettie had no choice but to help Sam pull her to her feet, which seemed far too small compared to her huge stomach. Her flowered dress was faded and bare, almost bursting over her shape, and she clearly hadn't been eating well. But when Sam bent over and held out both hands as a step, the woman took the saddle horn in one hand like any good prairie wife and obligingly let the two wranglers heave her mass up onto the fat pony, who grunted but didn't falter, to his credit.

"Trent taught me to ride," she said, all dreamy. "We're going to San Anton. I'll be a rancher's wife, and we'll raise Trent Jr. to be the pride of Durango."

Sam took the rope and swung up onto his palomino, and Nettie grabbed a handful of mane and launched herself onto Ragdoll's bare back. As they turned away from the encroaching fire, it occurred to her to ask, "There ain't any other folks locked up in this shitshow town, are there?"

"I don't think so," the woman said, swaying with the pony's stride. "I didn't see nobody but the man with the mustache and his wife. She said they were keeping me safe for when the Cannibal Owl came to visit. I do wonder what that is, don't you?"

Nettie's eyes met Sam's.

"I do wonder," she said.

That night, they made camp on a butte, starting up two fires and setting guard rotations. None of the men wanted anything to do with the rescued woman.

All the Captain said was "You all want a pet, you all take care of your damn pet."

"But, Captain. She was gonna die," Sam said, the picture of pup-dog innocence.

The Captain looked at him, all sharp. "Hennessy, a man-eating monster took the time to lock that woman up. What makes you think there wasn't a good reason?"

But Nettie knew there was nothing monstrous in the woman's belly—at least, she couldn't sense anything inhuman. The wobbly feeling inside her was solely from hunger and breathing in smoke, and as soon as she'd eaten two bowls of Delgado's swamp beans and some goat, it settled down just fine. The woman ate two bowls, too, and Delgado seemed to favor her with extra meat, an unusual kindness.

Nettie had just settled down to sleep when Jiddy walked by and grunted at her from across the fire. She shook her head. He'd done that, from time to time, since the saloon. The mule-stubborn man was too proud to ask her out loud if she sensed anything dangerous, so grunting and nodding like animals had to be enough. They both knew she was the better, more sensitive scout. For now, there were no new monsters in the area.

The woman was mostly silent, although Sam tried to draw her out into conversation. She allowed that her name was Regina, she was from Fort Leavenworth, and she was fairly certain that Trent would show up in their covered wagon to collect her at any moment. Nettie repeatedly asked her about the Cannibal Owl, but all Regina knew was that it was coming soon and would want to meet her baby.

She beamed with grease all around her lips. "The lady from the saloon called me a fitting tribute. I reckon that means something nice, don't it?"

Then she murmured a few things about hoe-cake recipes and fell asleep with her bird's-nest brown hair flopped over Nettie's new saddle. All Nettie had to pillow her head was a rock.

She settled down and wrapped herself up in her new serape,

which smelled comfortingly of horse. Hennessy had laid down his bedroll next to hers, which made her pulse quicken for just a moment before she recalled that he didn't know she was a girl. Of course the newest and youngest fellers among the Rangers would be close, and Sam was the only other feller willing to sleep near Regina and her great, heaving belly. It was peaceful, bedding down as the fire crackled and the growing herd of horses nickered softly, surrounded by fighting men and overhung by stars. Hennessy got up and came back with a third plate of beans and sat down, shucking off his boots. Nettie was already lying on her back, opting to sleep fully dressed with boots on. She couldn't imagine much worse than facing a calamity on the prairie at night while barefoot.

Some of the fellers were already asleep and snoring through their whiskers when Hennessy finished his plate, belched, and cozied down just a few feet away.

"A siren. Who'd have guessed? The longer I'm with the Rangers, the more I reckon I don't know about the world." His voice was soft as he turned on his side to face her, his blue eyes keen with firelight. Nettie had never felt a moment so intimate with another person, and she instinctively turned on her side to face him.

Damn, he was close.

She swallowed hard. "Yeah."

Hennessy's voice dropped. "Were you scared today, Rhett?"

"Hadn't really thought much about it. A little, I guess. Wasn't much time to feel anything."

"But why'd it take us all so queer and not you? I just remember there being something so purty I couldn't stand it, opry-type music. Voice like an angel. And then I woke up, lassoed to a pole."

"Monsters don't affect me as much, I reckon."

"But why?"

Nettie snorted and rolled onto her other side, but she saw a glimmering black shadow on the edge of the butte, pointing west. As if she could just get on her horse and keep riding on the Injun woman's timetable. Like she was a damn train with a schedule to follow. In more of a huff, she rolled onto her back, but the stars held no answers.

"I don't know, Sam. I don't know anything. All I know is I got to do this or I'll never be free."

"Were you—" Hennessy shifted like there was a spider in his britches "—a slave? Before?"

Rage burned through her, but she measured her answer. She liked Hennessy and wanted him to like her. Normally, she'd say something sharp to a man who asked her such a personal and painful question, but this was Samuel Hennessy, the noon sun to her personal midnight, so she rolled back to face him even though tears threatened. "I was raised by folks who used me like a slave but called me their child. At least with a ghost on my tail, I get to choose how most of my hours are spent. Sitting horseback's better than what I was doing, I reckon."

"Where are you from?"

"G—" She caught herself. Hennessy knew Gloomy Bluebird. "Galvez."

He sighed. "I always wanted to see Galvez. But I keep ending up further west. Figure one day I'll fetch up in Calafia, at this rate. Ever feel like you're not in charge of your destiny, Rhett?"

Considering he'd just assumed she was a slave, Nettie reckoned the question was more about him than it was about her. So she tried to comfort him, a piece of work that was new to her. "I reckon every person on this earth was meant to do something. The hard part's figuring out what exactly it is. And making sure you're up to it."

Hennessy's smile could've lit the moon. "That's right wise, Rhett. Thank you kindly."

A little chunk of something in Nettie's chest melted.

"Welcome," she said. And after a long pause, "And thanks for following me today. I figured the Captain would just keep riding."

"Well, he did," Sam said. "But I turned around, anyway. Once you said you heard screaming, I heard it, too. Poor woman. Should we tell her what happened to her man?"

Nettie shook her head. "I don't see the point. Give her some hope. A body needs hope, sometimes, more than it needs the truth."

Hennessy's hand landed on her shoulder, wide and soft, and her entire body burned up like a cedar on fire. Then he squeezed her, let go, rolled on his back, and started snoring, easy as pie.

Nettie laid awake for most of the night, remembering that touch.

Was it possible Sam could see exactly who she was? And was his destiny all twined up with hers like she hoped it might be?

She let her fingers almost graze his where they lay on the ground. It wasn't enough. Nothing ever was.

The next morning, Milo led over a half-draft horse capable of carrying Regina's considerable weight without wobbling at the knees like the paint did.

"Captain took a dozen mounts from her town," he muttered. "Says she might as well not lame your pony."

Nettie knew better than to thank either of the old coots. Her new saddle barely fit the wide horse, but the big feller took on the weight without protest, and Regina didn't seem to know the difference as Sam ponied her along at the end of a long rope. Riding bareback as she was, Nettie's rump grew calluses and went numb. Every time she jumped down off Ragdoll's back, she nearly fell over on aching legs. Taking her cue from the other fellers, she switched off to ride Puddin' every other day to give Ragdoll a rest, her boots hanging to the gelding's knees. As she'd never ridden bareback for long periods before, it was one hell of a lesson for her, and she swore next time they were plundering, she'd choose two saddles, just in case. At least the paint was short and agreeable, and she could soon hop on and off the little horse at a walk or a trot.

"You must have plenty of Injun blood," Jiddy said with a sneer. "Trick riding that way."

Nettie kept riding, swaying back and forth with the barrel-bellied pony as if the dig hadn't hit home. "You never told me, Jiddy. How was it you didn't see that siren woman coming?"

In response, he spit in the dirt, narrowly missing her new boot, and trotted back up to his place behind Virgil and Milo. The Captain hadn't given him a bit of the spoils from the saloon and had, in fact, burned it to the ground with booty still inside just to prove a point. Nettie looked down at her badge, licked her thumb, and put a little shine to the metal. She wasn't a monster, and she sure as shit wasn't incompetent. Whether or not she was an Injun remained to be seen, but she was starting to figure she'd rather be any sort of mixed breed than a pedigreed man full of hatred.

The land was pretty in West Durango, long swaths of green speckled with purple flowers, all of it watched over by jagged mountains and the occasional herd of buffalo. The horses took every chance to graze, and agreeable creeks and placid lakes seemed to pop up whenever they needed one. Whenever they saw evidence of a ranch, they stopped to feel for monsters before giving the claimed land wide berth. Rabbits were plentiful, and the men took turns shooting at quail and grouse that rose, flapping, from the fields. For the first time in her life, Nettie wasn't hungry most of the time, nor was she lonely, what with Sam riding by her side. If she hadn't been marching toward the monster of all monsters, Nettie would've considered it the best stretch of her life.

Late one night, Hennessy woke her, a hand on her shoulder. She was round-bellied and dreaming deep, thanks to a lost, unbranded beef some of the boys had ridden down and carved up for supper. Regina was a softly snoring mound across the fire, and Hennessy sat back on his heels and smiled at her as she rolled up to sitting and checked the time on her new watch. The moon was as high and nearly as full as it could get, which meant it was practically daylight on the plain. A little after two in the morning, but Hennessy wouldn't know that, as he hadn't yet earned his watch or his badge. Quick as a snake's blink, he snatched her timepiece from her hands, stood, and dangled it out in front of her.

"Time to wake up, other Hennessy," he whispered. "Your turn for night watch. Come and get it."

Nettie leaped to her feet and ran after him before quickly checking herself. Cowpokes did not skip and giggle, and up until just that moment, neither did Nettie Lonesome. Hennessy was behind a screen of scrubby trees, and Nettie hurried back there, trying to appear dignified, should any of the other wranglers be awake.

"Give me back my watch, other Hennessy. I've got guardin' to do."

Hennessy stopped jogging backward and held out the watch,

letting it dangle by its chain. When Nettie snatched it, he grabbed her wrist and pulled her close, his hands hot on her biceps. They were of a same height, although she was whip-thin and he was built of golden muscles held together with sugar frosting, far as she could figure. But the way he was looking into her eyes made her feel like Sam was taller, and stronger, and altogether more real than she was. The light blue of his eyes matched the moon, and the little golden hairs on his cheeks sparked like glass in sand.

"Howdy, pardner," he said, voice mellow and deep, and Nettie realized, all of a sudden, that he meant to kiss her. So she did the only thing available:

Nettie Lonesome turned on her boot heel and bolted.

CHAPTER
17

Hennessy didn't call after her, and she didn't hear his footsteps giving chase, so she slowed to a walk and returned to the fire like her heart wasn't about to beat out of her chest. Trying to catch her breath, she stuck her watch back in her vest pocket, snatched her holster off the ground, and took off for the little valley where the sixty-or-so horses were asleep, tails twitching. The herd had swollen with the sound horses from the siren's town, but they'd blended into the group with little fuss. There was a flattish boulder in just the right sort of place to watch over the area, and when Nettie sat, she sighed deeply. Had Samuel Hennessy's rump recently warmed the same rock? Or was that just what was left of a day under the hot, desert sun? Didn't matter. Nettie lay back, letting the heat soak up into her every crevice, unstiffening her back and thighs from a long day riding bareback.

For a long time, Nettie lay there, trying to make sense of the stars. And of Sam. Horses she could understand, and men a little, too, but the stars were too far away. She'd heard somewhere that there were pictures among the stars telling stories from worlds long toppled, but all she saw were shiny bits of nothing, holes poked in an old, black sheet. And yet they seemed to move, to dance, to slowly twirl. It made her dizzy, watching the stars, but then again, so had Hennessy. What had he meant, looking at her like that? Moving his face so close, his eyes begging her to understand something that made no more sense than the stars? Why had her belly swooped and swirled when he was the opposite thing of a monster?

And why had she run away instead of sticking around to see what happened next?

She knew how horses mated, and she knew how to geld stallions who didn't know their place. As she'd assured Dan, she knew how a herd would behave as each horse found its place. Hell, she even had a good idea of how men and women joined, as it couldn't be much different from what horses or dogs did in broad daylight. But the only man and woman she'd ever watched together were Pap and Mam, and they didn't behave in the logical fashion of animals. During the day, they barely spoke, and at night, if Pap caught Mam, it was as good as two cats fighting and ended with Mam facedown on the old cornhusk mattress, snuffling like a pig. Sometimes Mam cried out, but mostly she just cried, and those were the nights Nettie had slept in the broken rig in the barn with a blanket over her head.

She'd never seen folks kiss outside of the saloon, and even that seemed to produce feeling in only one of the partners—the human one that paid for the privilege. Kissing and bed sport for their own sake had never been anything Nettie had considered as a possibility. Until Hennessy went trying to match his lips to hers.

Suddenly, Nettie had wanted to find out exactly what those lips would feel like.

And that scared the shit out of her.

So she'd bolted.

She could face down any number of monsters, but she couldn't let a feller she liked just fine get two inches closer without turning tail and running away like her hat was on fire. She'd followed him around at a distance, the one summer he'd been with the Double TK, but she hadn't really understood why.

Now she did.

Maybe there was something to being a girl, after all, if Hennessy liked having her around.

"Hellfire," she muttered to herself.

In answer, a coyote yipped, and Nettie realized too late that the pleasant flip-flop continuing in her belly had been caused by more than just thoughts of what a completed kiss with Hennessy might've felt like. When she sat up, she found a brown coyote sitting politely at the base of the rock, a tidy package of sticks and leather at its paws.

"That you, Dan?"

The coyote yipped. Nettie looked back toward the sleeping camp, expecting to see the shine on a gun barrel and the sound of a certain bearded grouch spitting in the dust.

"Can't Jiddy feel you?"

The coyote shook its head, tongue lolling comically.

"Then go put on that little skirt of yours and tell me what you want in people words. I don't speak yip."

With an all-too-human shrug, the critter picked up the leather packet and trotted off behind some scrub. Five minutes later, Coyote Dan moseyed around the corner wearing nothing but his leather flap, his bow and quiver strung over his shoulder.

"Jiddy knows my scent. And if he weren't drunk and full of spite, he might be vexed to feel me nearby. Poor bastard knows I'm a better scout, and he would love to shoot me. But I have the Captain's permission to come and go. And after all, Durango is a free country."

Pulling her knees up to her chin, Nettie couldn't help staring at Coyote Dan, considering most of him was exposed under the peculiar blue-white light of the moon. He seemed entirely at ease in his skin—in both of his skins. Relaxed and yet ready for anything. It was peaceful around him, mostly, just because he seemed like he was exactly where he wanted to be, not rushing or balking or worrying as most fellers did.

"Why are you here, Dan? The Injun woman's been pointing me this-a-way, so I reckon we're on the right track."

He nodded, gave the ghost of a grim grin. "Your passage has not gone unnoticed. The smoking ashes of Reveille and a large herd of stolen horses led me right to you."

Nettie's eyebrows drew down in irritation. "You saying we shouldn't have kilt that siren lady who was luring folks in, stealing their belongings, and eating their goddamn faces off?"

The real grin arrived, wry and wide. "If she was a siren, killing her was necessary. A siren's hunger is unstoppable. Burning her captive husband alive with a well-built town that could have sheltered others was a tragedy."

Nettie went cold, right down to her toes.

"I didn't know about that. Never asked what happened to that feller."

"Most people don't. The Captain takes no chances, which means many innocents suffer in his path. What do you think he would do to the tribe of Javelina we met?"

Nettie just stared through him as it played out behind her eyes. The Captain's men would draw their guns, and the Javelina leader would stand to proclaim their mission. Sure as shit, one of the Javelina would shift or grunt or do something innocent and foolish, and some Ranger idiot dumber than Chicken had been would shoot off a wild bullet, and then there'd be two less Rangers and an entire tribe of well-meaning folk murdered. Just another hill of sand in a prairie of endless sand.

"What the Sam Hill am I supposed to do about that, Dan? I see you looking at me like I can stop it. I can't. All I can do is hunt down this Cannibal Owl, whatever and wherever it is. And it's danged tiresome. Already saved me one troublesome creature this week."

Dan glanced toward the fire, where Regina slept beside the bulk of Hennessy, wrapped in his blanket with his back to where Nettie sat watch. "If only the rest of the Rangers shared your impulse to save innocents. What will you do with the woman? And her child?"

Nettie fidgeted; she didn't like thinking about that. "Leave 'em in the next town we find, I reckon. Provided it's not just the mouth of another damn monster. Her husband's dead, but I ain't gonna be the one to tell her." She fiddled with the strings of her serape. "She says they were keeping her safe for the Cannibal Owl. As a tribute. Best I can reckon, they meant to give it the baby."

"That's logical. She's very near her time. Did you know that?"

Nettie shuddered and looked toward the fire. "That's what Sam said. We'd best get to a town right quick, I guess."

When she turned back, Dan squinted and stepped closer, looming over her. Long fingers reached out to flick the star over her chest. "So you're one of them now."

Nettie shrugged away, wishing she'd had the good sense to tuck the badge under her vest. "I was the only one the siren couldn't call."

"Because you're the Shadow."

She snorted and kept her voice too low to carry. "Or because I'm a girl."

Dan crossed his arms over his muscled chest and sat beside her on the rock, facing the same direction. "You think the siren's song affects only men?"

Scooting away, she muttered, "I seen how it is. Stallions and mares. Cowpokes and whores."

Dan sighed, his bare shoulder close enough that she could feel the heat through her shirt. "Your heart is not a rock that stands unchanging. It's like water. It flows, it moves, it allows neither boulders nor canyons to stand in its way. It hardens and softens and expands to fill new spaces. You are still becoming yourself. And you have a lot to learn."

"You keep saying that, but you keep on teaching me nothin'."

It only put her in a fouler mood when Dan laughed like she'd just mouthed off a joke. She hopped up and stalked toward the horses. At least they didn't talk gibberish. At least their shit was honest.

Behind her, a certain sound set her teeth on edge: an arrow being drawn from a quiver.

She stopped but didn't turn. "You gonna shoot me, Dan?"

"No, Nettie. The opposite. I want to teach you to shoot a bow. A gun can misfire, get wet, or be taken from you. You can run out of bullets. But once you know how to make a bow and arrows, you'll always have a way to fight. And if your aim is as good as I think it is, you'll be able to end a monster—any monster—with one shot to the heart."

She looked over her shoulder, eyes slitted, remembering how her bullets had bounced off the siren. "What'll it cost me?"

Dan walked up and held out his bow. "Only time. In a tribe, it's considered a man's duty to teach others what he knows. Teaching someone how to protect the tribe is expected. The world needs you. If my time will help you stop the Cannibal Owl, I'll be more than repaid."

"I ain't in a tribe, Dan."

"But you could be."

Nettie snorted. "I'm a little late to be a papoose." She took the offered bow and turned it over in her hands, trying to figure out the ways of it. "But I reckon I can learn. It'll keep me awake during watch, at least. It's always useful, knowing a new way to kill stuff that won't shut up."

Dan took the bow back, but gently, and held it out at arm's length. "A simple piece of wood, hard and flexible. Osage orange, cedar, ash, willow, juniper. The bow is thicker in the middle and notched at each end. A cord, preferably rawhide, but sinew or bark will do. The arrows are hard, straight wood, half the length of the bow, tipped with arrowheads and fletched with feathers. Vulture or turkey. These materials are so important that I carry them with me wherever I go as man or coyote. They're more important than clothing or food or water, because they allow me to obtain clothing, food, and water. Do you understand?"

"What I understand is that I need to know how to shoot that thing before I need to know how to make it."

"You think so?"

"I know so."

Dan's laugh was short and harsh. "Because you were raised by ignorant people. They taught you to use things before you understood them. To kill things before you recognized them. To hate things before you knew them. But you'll appreciate a thing better when you know where it comes from, when your hands know the shape of it." He scanned the prairie. "Take the bow and an arrow. I'll make a target. If you can hit it, I'll give you this bow."

"And if I miss?"

"Then I'll teach you to make the bow and arrows so that

you'll truly understand. You have twelve days and nights until you reach the lair of the Cannibal Owl. Perhaps you'll learn something while the moon still shines so that when the sky is dark, you'll have a better chance of hitting your target."

Nettie looked up at the fat orb and shivered. "Twelve days?"

Dan nodded. "It's fitting that you strike just before the new moon."

"Why's that?"

"Owls don't see as well, then. Perhaps it will help."

Nettie snorted. "That's bullshit, and you know it. If the critter likes to hunt on a new moon, I reckon it's strong as the damn devil then."

"Then you'd best be stronger."

While Dan went to muck around in the dry grass, Nettie inspected his bow and the arrow he'd left with her. The marks of a man's care and use were clear beside the gouges from an animal's sharp teeth. The leather grip knew the shape of his hand, and the arrow's feathers were tied with horsehair and an eye for beauty. The tip itself was a marvel to the girl, who hadn't known before that rock could be mastered and shaped to such sharp perfection. The arrowhead in her bag was a rough thing compared to Dan's work.

That would be a powerful trick, to know how to turn a rock into a cutting weapon. She was testing the tip of it against the pad of her thumb when Dan returned and pointed to a roll of dry grass about the shape and size of a large man's torso set up twenty paces off. Its general shagginess reminded Nettie of Jiddy, and one side of her mouth curved up as she took aim as she'd seen Dan do.

He watched her struggle until the arrow had fallen from her hand three times, then stepped closer, both arms going around her as his chest pressed against her back. When Nettie tried to pull away, he held her close in the cage of his arms, his hands wrapped around hers at the bow's grip and the arrow's feathers.

"Back off, Dan. I can do it myself."

She struggled, but god damn if he wasn't as strong as a mule.

"You need to learn to take instruction, Nettie. Other wranglers seek to dominate a bronc, to beat the sense into a larger animal. But you seem to know that kindness and understanding are the true way to a creature's trust. You can gentle a horse, but can you be gentled yourself? You can't learn if you're this tight in mind and body. The arrow won't fly true if your hands are shaking."

Nettie looked at her fingers. "My hands ain't shaking."

More softly, right by her ear, Dan said, "I can feel them. Your whole body is shaking. Thrumming like the beat of a drum. Relax. Focus. Not every touch means something more. Look to your target."

But her heart wouldn't still. She'd never been this close to another person for this long, and it felt ten kinds of wrong. She'd seen other people hug, mostly at funerals in town, but the hard length of a full-grown man's mostly nekkid body pushing up against hers made all sorts of inside organs flip around like a grasshopper in a skillet, and not in a good way. How could she think about arrows when she was trembling like a new colt? And yet she suspected that if he ran hands all over her like she did to a bronc before applying the saddle, she'd bolt instead of calming down. Heck, she'd already bolted once tonight, and that was from a feller she actually liked, a feller who didn't annoy her something awful, as the one currently touching her did.

"Nettie. Focus. Your hand grips here, palm pushing out. Tight but easy. Fingers loose. Pull the bowstring back until your fingers touch your cheek. Left elbow out. Look at your target, not your arrow. Feel the tension in the cord. And when you're ready, twitch your fingers to let go."

"Let go? Just like that?"

His hands released hers, and he stepped away. The tension was gone, and she very nearly let the arrow fly into the ground as her arms collapsed inward. At the last moment, she straightened and pulled and tensed and gripped and loosened and lost all control of what the hundred thousand parts of her body were supposed to do, and the arrow went flying off into the sky, soaring over the target and into the desert like a falling star.

Dan watched her, his arms crossed. "And what did you learn?"

"Nothing. You messed me up."

He grinned. "Only when I released you."

Nettie shoved the bow at him, her face burning red. "This is bullshit." She wanted to storm off, but it was her duty to watch the herd and protect the camp on this side until sunup, and she danged well wasn't going to get hollered at in front of the Rangers for abandoning her duty, much less get stuck burning their chewed-up carcasses after another siren attack. Instead, she climbed back up on the rock and turned her back on Dan to watch the horses twitch their tails in sleep.

"I'll be back tomorrow night, Nettie Lonesome."

"Good for you, Coyote Dan."

"While you're riding today, be on the lookout for a piece of wood for your bow. Osage orange, cedar, ash, willow, juniper. Strong and hard but flexible. It should be a yard long, higher than your waist. You might wish to bring several possibilities."

"And what if I don't want to learn?"

She now recognized the sound of him unstringing his bow

and wrapping his weapons up in his leather skirt. A small part of her fell. Was he giving up on her that easy?

As if reading her mind, he gave a small laugh. "Oh, you want to learn. More important, you *need* to learn. Tonight, you learned something. And tomorrow night, you'll learn something new."

"What did I learn tonight?"

"Tonight you learned how much you still have to learn. And you learned that someone can touch you without wanting anything from you. And when I leave, I hope you will practice learning to relax."

She spun around on her butt to find him watching her, stark nekkid and holding the packet of leather wrapped around his bow and arrows. She couldn't help looking down before meeting his eyes, and there was no way she could hide how hot her face went. Men's parts made no damn sense. Then again, neither did women's parts. The whole thing was ridiculous.

"I know how to relax."

His eyebrows raised. "I don't think you do."

Before she could rebut, he hunched over, sprouted hair down his backbone, and soon sat on a coyote's haunches, tongue lolling. He gave a small yip, picked up his packet, and trotted away.

"See? I'm relaxed right now," Nettie muttered. She leaned back on her elbows, hunting for the warmth the rock had held just a short while ago. But it was cold and hard and pokey, making her squirm all the more.

A coyote cried, far away, a half-laughing song.

She wondered if he'd found his lost arrow.

Just about dawn, as the sun painted the desert in shades of red and pink, she went looking for it herself in the thicket behind the dummy target. But she didn't find Coyote Dan's arrow.

What she found was a child's foot.

CHAPTER

18

The Captain didn't know what to make of the small brown foot, and Jiddy's nose wrinkled up like he'd stuck his face up a bull's butt.

"Stinks of predator," he finally said, holding it out between thumb and forefinger. "Just reeks of leave-it-the-hell-alone. Did you see anything?"

Nettie shrugged. "Nothing but Coyote Dan."

The Captain's head jerked up. "You think he's capable of this?"

Jiddy shook his head, waggling his beard. "That feller couldn't do this to a side of bacon."

"But what is it?" the Captain asked.

Jiddy shrugged, dropped the foot, and rubbed his nose with a filthy hand. "It ain't human, I know that much. Neither was the thing that cut it off."

The Captain spit on the ground, far from the foot, and Nettie was compelled to pick it up. Poor thing, whoever it belonged to. Seemed wrong to just throw it on the ground like so much dirt. It was small and smooth and warm, as if it were still attached to an invisible child, with skin that almost matched the prairie, a reddish-tan slightly lighter than Nettie's own. It was right pretty, with perfect little toes, right up until a person's eyes got to the place where it'd been hacked off.

Nettie had butchered plenty of animals for Pap, so she knew what the insides of a critter were supposed to look like. But this foot made no sense. It should've been bleeding, or at least bled out, but it looked like the cut was fresh, only a heartbeat old, the meat still a happy pink and the bone dark and wet in the middle. Like the foot didn't even know it had been cut off.

"You get anything more off it, Rhett?"

"Injun," she said. "Smells a little like pig. I don't know what all sorts of monsters there is, though."

The Captain snorted. "Ain't nobody knows that. That's why ol' Jiddy's so angry. He didn't know what that siren woman was, and he don't know what this thing is, either. Monsters are like animals. Just when you think you seen 'em all, something else shows up to bite your ankles from under the bed."

"They ain't animals." The ferocity in her voice surprised her. "They're people, most of 'em. But I reckon the Cannibal Owl did this. I can't remember the last time I saw a child. Cannibal Owl's been taking 'em all."

"But why would it drop a foot?" Hennessy asked, coming up to put a hand on her shoulder. She shrugged it off.

"As a warning, most like." The Captain spit again. Nettie figured he had the wettest gullet of any creature in the territory, or maybe just the biggest wad of tobacco. "Means we're close," he said. "Or on the right track, at least."

Nettie swallowed hard and looked to where she'd last seen the Injun woman. "The foot was on our route, in the direction we're supposed to be headed. So maybe we'll find out what it means if we press on. If we hurry."

The Captain nodded at her, almost as if she were an equal. Lord, what a difference a badge made.

"Have your guns ready and be on your fastest horse today, boys," the Captain hollered over breakfast. "Could be trouble."

They left Nettie standing there with a foot in her hand, a pregnant woman in her saddle, and a good-looking cowboy stepping close enough to make her skitty with his big blue eyes full of worry and something else. She couldn't imagine being any more uncomfortable if there'd been a dang scorpion in her britches, so she wrapped the foot in a bandanna and tucked it into her saddlebag under the blood-splattered clothes. Didn't seem right to bury or burn it, since she figured its owner was still alive, but she wouldn't leave it there for the vultures to eat while the Rangers continued west.

Aside from the moment when something twitched and rustled deep in her bag, the foot didn't seem to mind.

The morning went by at a fast trot. Considering Jiddy was acting a mite jumpy, Nettie rode in back with Hennessy and Regina, cussing herself for not keeping her old saddle instead of leaving it to burn with the siren's loot. She was curious if she'd be able to feel any new monsters, considering the nearness of the foot and the spiteful scout and that senselessly random eyeball in the Captain's watch, but she shouldn't have worried. Just as she was staring at the horizon, trying to grasp why a cactus would glint in the sun between two rocky outcrops, her belly just about fell out of her butt.

There was something there—a lot of somethings. Monsters. They felt different from Dan or the Javelina or the siren, different from anything she'd encountered thus far. When Jiddy whistled and the Captain reined up, she checked her gun and knife, hoping for the chance to prove herself again, maybe earn another saddle. She'd most likely be trying to prove herself every day for the rest of her life.

"Rhett, Hennessy, and Qualls. Y'all pull your guns and come on with me."

Nettie nodded and tossed Puddin's rope to Jiddy, who spit on Ragdoll's hooves.

"Unless you got acid spit, you're just wasting water in the desert," she muttered. But he didn't drop the rope.

Sam handed the rope from Regina's horse off to one of the other fellers and leaned in to speak with her. The woman just nodded and rubbed her belly. Qualls was scared half out of his britches and sweating through his burgundy shirt as Nettie and Ragdoll fell in behind his dun mare. She remembered him dashing tears away as they'd tossed Chicken on the pile of half-eaten bodies and set it afire just a few days back. Hopefully Qualls had better instincts and more stopped-up ears than his dead friend.

According to campfire talk, being chosen to investigate trouble with the Captain himself was considered both an honor and a death sentence. After the upset with the siren, Nettie assumed the Captain wanted young, expendable folks by his side but didn't trust them enough to go on their own. She checked her gun yet again as they trotted up the dusty road into another rotten-tooth town at the edge of nowhere. This one was nestled between two craggy buttes and looked a lot more loved and lived in than Reveille had. Laundry failed to flap in the nonexistent wind, and a few patches of land sported just-abandoned plows and picked-over gardens. Dogs barked from behind closed doors and cats twitched their tails from fences and porch rails decorated with carved curlicues and painted daisies. It was downright pretty, actually. A fancy sign just outside the main street made it look right cheery.

"Welcome to Burlesville," Qualls read out loud, and a sharp ping of jealousy jerked through Nettie when she realized somebody had gone to the enormous trouble of teaching the idiot his letters.

The gunshot that punctuated his statement was loud and high, a warning that set the horses dancing.

"Don't feel very welcome," Hennessy said with a grin, but he drew his gun just the same.

Nettie already had her revolver out and her horse pointed in the direction that was pulling at her gut like a catfish on a line.

"Bunch of folks holed up over that way, Captain." She aimed her gun for the general store, which backed right up into the butte as if it were trying to crawl out of a giant's mouth.

"Yeah, but the gunman's in the church tower," the Captain said, putting his big Henry rifle to his shoulder and firing right back. "Luckily, he can't aim for shit. Everybody fire a shot at him, then we'll race for the cover of the stable by the general store, yonder. Time to figure out what this town's so damn scared of."

But Nettie reckoned she knew why the townfolk might be jumpy, considering how the sun winked off the Captain's Ranger badge. A town filled with monsters, however peaceful, wouldn't welcome their crew. With a sigh, she aimed her gun at the wink of metal in the church's bell tower and pulled the trigger. A chunk of wood blew off, Sam and Qualls shot and missed, the Captain whistled, and the four horses full-out ran for the general store. Nettie's heart was racing as fast as her horse's hooves. Another shot pinged over their heads, but they were soon skidding to a halt under the lean-to of a tidy stable shielded by a tin roof. When the Captain jumped off his horse, Nettie and the others followed suit.

"Hold the horses, Qualls. You two, come along."

Qualls shook like a frightened jackrabbit as Nettie handed over her reins. She wished to hell she still had possession of her saddlebags, as two more guns and a handful of bullets would've been more than welcome. If the folks of Burlesville hadn't been so hell-bent on shooting visitors, Nettie would've been glad to leave Regina there and get on with her life in the saddle.

A few shots whizzed overhead as the Captain, Hennessy, and the Ranger they knew as Rhett crept along the wall to the general store. When the Captain cautiously put a hand out, he found the door latched, and when he shoved it with a shoulder, it barely budged.

"Barricades. Idjits."

"Captain?" Nettie pointed to an open window with a clothesline hanging out of it.

The Captain nodded. "Go on, then."

Nettie promised herself she wouldn't point out any more windows.

"Don't worry, Rhett. I'll cover you. I got your back. " Hennessy's grin said something in a language that Nettie didn't understand, but she spoke the language of his loaded gun and his body blocking her from any more shots, so she climbed on in the window.

The general store was empty of people and filled with nicer goods than she remembered seeing in Gloomy Bluebird, although the shelves were half-empty at best. A barrel of food tins was pushed up against the door as a barricade. She couldn't help picking up a shiny tin can with little dancing fish printed on it, but another shot outside reminded her that she wasn't here to shop.

"It's empty," she shouted, and Hennessy and the Captain joined her inside.

"Nice store." The Captain spit on the clean, waxed board floor, and Nettie winced. "Where's the folks at, Rhett?"

Nettie spun around, waiting to feel the now familiar pull of monsters deep in her gut. But it was coming from every direction, which didn't make a lick of sense.

"Maybe they're invisible?" she muttered.

"Not damn likely," the Captain answered. "Should've brought Jiddy, I reckon."

"Not damn likely," she replied, all fierce, closing her eyes to feel out the connection with the people who had to be nearby. She stretched out her hands and planted her feet.

Suddenly, she realized exactly where they were.

"Underground, Captain. Look for a trap door."

The Captain grunted, and they spread out, hunting for grooves in the freshly swept boards. Hennessy finally found it behind the counter, and they all pointed their guns as he yanked up on the handle. The square black hole below seemed empty, but soft scuffling and a muffled child's cry gave the folks away.

"Come on out, or we shoot," the Captain bellowed.

Ferocious whispering and the slap of a hand on a cheek followed.

The Captain grabbed the other gun out of Hennessy's holster and cocked it.

"Please! I'll come up. Just don't shoot down here. It's all rock. And we have women among us."

Nettie made note of the chilling lack of the words *and children*.

A squat feller with a thicker beard than Jiddy soon appeared in the light below, his empty, callused hands held up in front of him.

"Come on up, then." The Captain stepped back and returned Hennessy's gun, and the feller clambered up the wooden ladder to stand, blinking, before the Rangers. He was short and thick, the top of his head as bald as an egg and his half-moon glasses making him look weaker than his bulging arms proclaimed him to be.

"Are you going to kill us?"

The Captain's mustache twitched as he tapped his badge. "Now why the Sam Hill would we do that?"

"Gotta be honest, Ranger. Town's been in a bad stretch. Tinker ain't been through in a while, and every feller we send up the road never comes back. Banditos been thick. And we... there's something..." He took off his spectacles and pretended to wipe them off on his beard while dashing away tears with his hairy wrist. "Our children disappeared in the night, a few weeks back. All but one who ain't right in the head."

The men looked away, giving him a moment to compose himself, but Nettie watched him subtly, trying to puzzle out his nature. The short, squat feller only came up to Nettie's elbows and smelled nothing like any animal Nettie had ever encountered.

"What are you?" she asked without thinking, even as she knew how rude it was.

"People. Mostly miners and smiths. My name's Jasper."

The Captain cleared his throat and flicked his badge again, and the feller sighed. "I suppose you fellers would call us dwarves. We're mountain folk. Our ancestors came over from Germany a while back. Heard there was gold out this-a-way and found a nice chunk of minerals and iron in this mountain. We're harmless folk, I can tell you that. Even Smitty in the tower couldn't hit the broad side of a butte with his old rifle, and he's the best shot among us." He pointed at his face. "Eyesight ain't good in the sun, you see."

The Captain nodded. "Y'all come on up out of the ground

now. We got questions to ask, and you can tell we're harmless enough."

The feller snorted and rubbed his stubby nose. "To us, maybe," he muttered before calling down into the cellar, "Come on up. It's only the Rangers."

Whispers exploded below, and soon a whole passel of short, round folk clambered up the ladder and spread around the store, staring rudely and openly curious. Nettie was deeply confused until she realized that even the women among them wore beards, long and luxurious. Their eyes were like the stones Nettie had seen on the mayor's wife's fingers in Gloomy Bluebird: glittering leaf green and sky blue, others as clear as the stars and a few the hot red at the center of the fire. Last of all, they handed up a chubby child in baggy overalls who Nettie guessed would've been eight or so and yet still had the placid, sweet smile of a baby.

"Rock fall in the mine," said the woman holding him, both ferocious and sorrowful at the same time. "He'll be my sweet baby forever." Tucking the child under her arm, she stormed from the store, skirts and beard snapping.

"He sleeps between his folks, one foot tied to the bedstead so he can't wander," Jasper said. "So whatever stole our other children either had trouble snatching him or didn't want him." Before the Captain could answer, he added, "Seven. Seven children taken between the ages of two and ten. We're a small town, a hard people to breed, and every child is needed. Tell me you're after whoever did this, Ranger." His thick, hard hand clasped around Nettie's wrist, unyielding as stone. Normally, she would've thrown off anyone who touched her like that, but she sensed he could break her bones with no more than a thought and a light squeeze. "Tell me you're here to help."

Nettie answered before the Captain could, yielding to the

pressure of the man's leaking eyes and broken heart and stone-strong fingers. "We're after the thing that stole 'em. The Cannibal Owl. Two dozen men, chasing it. Did anyone see it? Smell it? Can you tell us anything at all?"

Jasper looked around the room, but no one stepped forward. "We sleep like rocks. No locks were busted, no horses stolen. All we found was a big brown feather. Figured it was Injuns, considering they value children. Smitty managed to shoot the last Injun who came into town, yesterday. Just in case."

Nettie's heart flopped over in an entirely different way than it did when she sensed a monster nearby. If Dan had headed this way, he might be just another pile of sand her boots had scuffled through and tracked into the store. But surely he wasn't the type to just walk into a town in broad daylight, down the middle of the street, mostly nekkid? Then again, how the Sam Hill was Nettie supposed to know what sort of type he was? She'd only known him a few days, and although it irked her to admit he'd helped her more than once, he'd also been annoying as hell. She could at least understand why someone might shoot the man; Lord knows she'd wanted to.

"Where's the body?" she asked, fearing the worst.

Jasper scratched his chin and said, "In the old stable. Dang thing's still warm."

"Show us," the captain said.

Tossing his beard over his shoulder, Jasper led them down the street and into a weatherworn barn with only half a roof that reminded Nettie all too much of Pap's farm. The covered half of the structure was being used as storage for things as needed fixing, and the broken half had only an old blanket on the ground, tossed haphazardly over a lumpy form about the size and shape of a man. Or Coyote Dan.

At least, if it was him, he wasn't sand. Yet.

Without asking, Nettie lurched forward and whipped off the blanket.

It was Winifred.

Goddammit, girl. Not again!" Nettie fell to her knees by Winifred's nekkid body, her fingers prodding the edges of a smooth, round hole just over the girl's heart.

"Didn't I bring this girl back to life?" the Captain muttered.

Nettie slapped the girl's cheeks, but gently. "Something like that."

"You know her?" Jasper asked, and Nettie scanned the shed for anything useful, but all she saw were big, clumsy things, like hoes and plows and men.

"I know her. And she's an idiot who dies a lot. You got a doctor?"

Jasper scratched his beard, which seemed to be what powered his brain. "More of a veterinarian. For the cart ponies."

"Get him. We need... pinchy things. Maybe a sharp knife."

"Sorry, son, but that Injun's dead," Jasper said.

"She really ain't. Now fetch your damn pony doctor." As punctuation, Nettie pointed a gun at Jasper's chest, and he waddled off at a fast pace, scratching away.

Nettie put her face up to Winifred's mouth, listening for breathing. Like the foot in her saddle bag, the girl seemed both dead and alive at the same time, and Nettie tried real hard not to look at the unfamiliar curves of her body, laid out for all to see. Hennessy had his back turned and seemed put out, and the Captain was busy looking bored and picking his teeth with a cedar toothpick as if this sort of thing happened all the time.

"How long's this going to take, Rhett? I already saved that

coyote once, and she hasn't been of use to me yet. Don't know how much we'll need a Ranger who wastes time saving women and useless monsters when he ought to be out hunting one that's stealing children."

"Shit, Captain. If Rangers'll watch a innocent girl die, don't know if I want to be one, anyhow. This girl's a pain, but she's helped me. And Dan's helped us all."

"Damn coyotes," Hennessy muttered at the wall.

Nettie was pressing and pinching the skin around Winifred's wound when another squat feller from the town waddled in, a black leather bag unsnapping between his callused hands.

"Jasper tells me I'm to raise the dead," he said with a funny accent, rolling up his sleeves and pulling out a long tweezer.

"You'd best hope she's raisable," Nettie said.

The feller tucked his long, white beard into his shirt and motioned Nettie out of the way. It was hard for her to see what he was doing, considering he was as broad as a buffalo, but pretty soon, he grunted and dropped a chunk of metal into the dirt by her boots.

"The bullet is out. Lodged in her lung, a finger's width away from her heart. But removing a bullet won't bring her back—"

Winifred sucked in a big breath and sat up, coughing blood.

The doctor-feller leaned closer and frowned. "That is not normal."

Nettie shoved him aside and put the blanket around Winifred's shoulders.

"She's a dang skinwalker," Hennessy said. "Won't stay dead." When he stormed out the door, Nettie couldn't figure out why. He'd never seemed to hate Coyote Dan, but now he hated Winifred? Or was it all skinwalkers? Maybe she could ask him later, when he woke her for her watch.

"Are you okay?" Nettie asked, holding out a hand to help the girl stand.

When Winifred drew her into a hard, sudden hug, all the breath flew out of Nettie. They were all lined up across the front, the girl's long arms around her and her chin over Nettie's shoulder. Nettie swallowed hard and clumsily tried to return the hug, her revolver flopping, forgotten, in her hand.

"Thank you, Nettie," Winifred whispered into her ear, and Nettie's skin shivered all over.

"Welcome," she said, pulling away as her mind spun with peculiar feelings that she tried and failed to shove right back down.

Her belly was flopping like mad, and her whole body went over as hot as her face. Noticing the mysterious peaks and valleys of coppery curves and the warm shine in Winifred's eyes, Nettie turned away and feigned interest in her gun. It was a little like what she felt about Sam, but with Sam, she felt it in her heart, and with Winifred, it seemed to be a function of her body. Confusing as hell, the lot of it. The doctor gave her a knowing look and winked.

"Well, considering I have brought the dead back to life, I think I'll go reward myself with a nap," he said, closing his black bag and waddling away.

"And we'd best get back to the men and keep hunting. Rhett, hurry along."

The Captain left, and Nettie was alone in the sun-dappled, broke-down building with Winifred, who was nekkid under a rat-gnawed horse blanket. The girl was very much like her brother, with the same smug calm, lean build, and long, dark hair. The bullet hole over her chest was already patching itself, and Nettie caught herself looking a little too closely in the window's reflection. When Winifred gave a knowing laugh, Nettie spun around to face her, eyes steadily up.

"What were you thinking, walking into this one-horse town like a idjit?" she asked, all gruff-like.

Winifred shrugged a shoulder like it was a silly question. "I needed clothes and wanted to eat something that wasn't half raw. Figured it was safe enough after dark. Who would've guessed an entire town of anxious dwarves would be sitting on watch with all their guns ready? I'd always heard they were kind folk." She shook her dark, tangled hair and pulled her blanket closer. "Next time, I'll stay a coyote."

"Does Dan know you're out here?"

Winifred pursed full lips. "I'm a grown woman. My choices are my own." She smiled, just a little. "But no, he doesn't. He told me to go back east, toward civilization. Toward the security of white men and their walls and doctors. So like a man, to think there's safety among yet more men."

They shared a small laugh, and Nettie realized she could smell the girl, like flowers and honey. Accustomed as she was to the goat stink of unwashed men, it moved something in her, made her want to be closer, to have that same intimacy she'd known curled beside Hennessy, falling asleep. They were the same in plenty of ways, she and the coyote girl. But at the same time, Winifred was pesky, as annoying as a bad penny that kept showing up when you needed a nickel.

And the girl needed to get dressed right quick.

"I got some spare clothes. Boy's clothes. They ain't in good shape, but..." Nettie shuffled her feet and waved an awkward hand toward the door and the Rangers and her saddlebags, waiting beyond. "They'll keep you hid well enough, I reckon."

Winifred raised her chin and grinned. "I don't have to hide, like you. And I don't like the white man's boy clothes. So confining. I'd rather be in my leathers, or at least a skirt that lets me feel the air. I'm sure one of the women in town will give me an old dress, although it'll probably stop at my knees."

Dang, but Nettie felt funny, her belly flip-flopping all over the place at the thought of Winifred in a dwarf's dress. Her own clothes felt itchy and strange, and she remembered what it felt like to wear a chemise at night, the breeze swirling around her bare legs. As confusing as it had been when Hennessy tried to kiss her and when Dan had pressed up against her holding the bow, it was even more consternating to be talking to a mostly nekkid girl about being a girl when Nettie spent all her goddamn time pretending to be a boy instead.

When she'd lived with Pap and Mam, she hadn't given much thought to the differences between boys and girls. She'd learned early on that she was ugly, for a girl, and that being ugly wasn't necessarily a bad thing, considering the many ways a man could hurt a woman who talked back or didn't move fast enough. She'd seen the whores from the saloon, a-walking down the street at night as the churchwomen said unchurchly things from the safety of their porches. She'd seen the few young women of the town kept indoors, then married at fourteen or thrown out in the street bruised or swelling with child, a door shut forever behind them. She'd heard Pap grunting and Mam crying afterward as she washed herself with brown water from the pitcher. She'd seen Mam bleed the normal way and, a few times, a horrible way that looked about like dying after she ate some plants from Gray Hawk up the street.

In Nettie's eyes, being a woman was nothing but trouble and asking for woe, and so she modeled all her behavior on being a feller, albeit a quiet one that was the complete opposite of Pap. Pants didn't make her feel confined. They made her feel safe. Dresses were part of the problem, and the fact that Winifred favored them brought her up in Nettie's estimation. It was a brave thing, being a woman alone, especially when your choices were to wear the skin of an animal no one trusted, to be nekkid as the day you were born, or to be in a dress that left your nethers open to fellers who only saw you as a vessel for their use instead of a person.

"Nettie? Did you hear me?"

Nettie's eyes jerked up to Winifred's face, which was also peculiar to Nettie. She'd grown up around white folk, aside from Gray Hawk and a couple of quiet, dark-skinned Buffalo Soldiers who'd summered at the Double TK. Winifred's face was a different sort of brown from Nettie's own, and as far as Nettie reckoned, the girl was pretty, with high cheeks and eyes as dark and thick as bacon grease. But Pap had told her brown skin was ugly, that Injuns were ugly, that Nettie herself was ugly. So if Winifred was pretty in Nettie's eyes, what did Winifred see when she looked at Nettie? It was too damn much to undertake, finding the truth among the lies.

"Nope. What'd you say, coyote girl?"

"I asked if you had a spare horse."

Further confusion. "I'm ponying a gelding. All the fellers are."

Winifred nodded regally. "Good. Find me a thicker blanket, and I'll be there after I borrow a dress. I'm going with you."

CHAPTER

19

That finally broke through the twisty fog in Nettie's mind, and she caught Winifred by the slender wrist as the girl turned for the door.

"What? No. You can't travel with the Rangers."

Winifred's glare was withering. "Why not? You are."

Pulling her close, Nettie hissed in her ear, "They think I'm a boy."

Hissing back, Winifred pulled away and looked Nettie up and down. "Then they're fools. And they can't stop me. I go where I will. You want me to get shot again and left for dead, or do you want me with you when you go for the Cannibal Owl?"

Grasping for straws, Nettie muttered, "You got a bad habit of dyin'. It's right inconvenient."

"It's not my fault I'm cursed any more than it's your fault you're cursed. We've all got our burdens to bear. And you're not my master."

Nettie choked on her words. She wanted all the help she could get, but having the girl around would muddle the situation. She'd have to be cared for, she'd attract the attention of the men in a way that would make them duller, and she'd use up Nettie's spare horse, right when water was getting scarce and another unwanted woman was taking up her saddle. Not to mention the fact that Winifred made Nettie feel funny, and she didn't have the time or energy to think about that sort of nonsense. There was only one weird flip in her belly that was any use to anyone, and in between Hennessy, Dan, Winifred, and Delgado's grub, her belly mostly felt like a jackrabbit had taken up residence. All these feelings—she didn't want a damn one of them. It was all too complicated.

Being a person was mighty twisty, and yet she didn't want to go back to being nothing.

Winifred stormed outside and down the street and knocked on the first door she came to. Nettie watched from the barn, stunned and disgusted by Winifred's song and dance. The proud girl was blushing, looking down, shuffling her feet, smiling broadly, acting like she was a bother. And the dwarf woman was buying it, smiling back and chuckling behind her beard. She soon invited Winifred in, and Nettie spit in the dirt and walked toward the stable where her horse was tied. A plume of dust signaled the entrance of the herd and the rest of the Rangers, which most likely meant the Captain had decided to stay the night in the town, for whatever reason. That made her downright jumpy, the thought of being stuck amid a town of nosy people with rock eyes and floor-length beards, feeling the constant wobbles in every direction that reminded her she was surrounded by folks who weren't human. And they needed to get back on the trail toward the Cannibal Owl.

Ragdoll whinnied and rubbed her scraggly forelock against Nettie's chest, and Nettie scratched the mare behind the ears like she liked and led her toward the jigging herd of cowpokes and horses shoving into a rickety corral beside four fat ponies and a pair of mules caterwauling like they'd just struck gold. Hennessy hopped off when he saw her.

"You okay, Rhett?" He clapped her hard on the back, and she nodded in a manly fashion.

"'Course. It's just a town of dwarves and a idjit coyote."

"She sure is an idjit, ain't she?"

"Hellfire, Sam, you can say that again."

Hennessy gave her his brightest grin and squeezed her shoulder like he'd completely forgotten last night's rebuff. "We're lucky you found 'em, the way they were hiding. Every time you pull your gun, I watch your back and worry like a mother hen. When I heard that first shot..."

Nettie flushed a bit, not quite sure how to answer to someone who preferred her alive.

"You were right beside me, Sam. And you know dwarves can't shoot for shit." She cleared her throat and looked away. "What's the Captain's plan? Bedding down in the town?"

"Yep. It'll make the folk feel safer. And we'll get something to eat besides roasted goat and half-starved beef. I hear they got eggs and bread. And we'll be able to bathe and wash our clothes."

Nettie's stomach dropped out. "Bathe?"

Hennessy nodded and pointed to a ribbon of green on the other side of the corral. "Little river goes around the butte, clean and not too cold. Us Rangers have to keep better washed than most, as what we hunt can smell us coming. If we go too long without soapin' off the muck, Jiddy says he can't smell nothing but us." He must've seen the concern on her face, as he rubbed her shoulder again and gave her a curling smile that made her feel all melty, like he had mischief planned and wanted her in. "Don't worry, Rhett. We can go off from the fellers a bit. I know you're shy."

Nettie cleared her throat. "That's me. Right shy. Where are we sleeping?"

Hennessy took his saddle and jerked his chin, and she gave Ragdoll a final pat and followed him. The half-finished building they stepped into must've been on its way to being a school, as it was bigger than a house had any right to be and had a blackboard painted on one white wall. The wood floors were still shiny and bright, and all around the Rangers were spreading their bedrolls with saddles as pillows. Compared to the ground, it was a right treat. Nettie's bags and blanket were already in one corner, and Hennessy set up his belongings alongside with his usual fastidiousness.

"Where's Regina?" she asked to cover the strange sweetness of someone looking out for her.

Hennessy stuck a thumb toward the row of close-set houses. "Pair of old maids took her in, clucking like she was a lost cat. Lord, but I hope they offer to let her stay here. A bunch of bearded ladies and a horse doc's a helluva lot better for a breeding woman than hunting a monster with a crew of rough men."

Nettie just nodded. It would be a treat, having her damn saddle back.

And then they just stared at each other like fools for longer than was necessary or useful.

"Rhett?"

Nettie was so consternated by Hennessy's attention that she was almost grateful when a woman's voice called her name from the door. She looked up to find Winifred in a light blue dress tied with a ribbon at her waist and swirling around her calves. The girl held up a sack and waved.

"Come guard me at the creek, will you?"

After rolling her eyes at Hennessy as she reckoned a feller

would, Nettie shouldered her saddle bags, checked her gun, and followed Winifred out into the sunny afternoon.

"I'll find you when it's our turn," Hennessy called, and she raised a hand in acknowledgment, although that wouldn't do at all.

Outside, Nettie stared at the dirt road to avoid looking at Winifred's stubbornly exposed legs.

"Amethyst gave me some soap and a comb, too. Haven't had a proper wash in weeks. Have you?"

Squirming, Nettie said, "Just water in a leaky pot at Pap's place."

Truth be told, she always felt uncomfortable without a nice coating of earth. It was the same color as her skin, and she'd always felt like if she could look at herself and pretend she was seeing prairie dirt, she didn't have to think about the rich brown color that damned her from ever being anything or anybody in Gloomy Bluebird. And anyway, the last time Pap had caught her washing in the creek, he'd looked at her the same way he looked at Mam when she came in from the rain with her calico all stuck to her like an overstretched frog skin. No, Nettie hadn't taken many baths since she turned twelve.

The creek was more of a shallow river, sparkling a beautiful blue under the wide prairie sky. Some of the fellers were already nekkid as jaybirds and splashing around under the Captain's stern, fully clothed eye as he sat his horse, and several wranglers were beating their wet clothes against rocks. Turned out quite a few of their shirts were actually white, which surprised the Sam Hill out of Nettie. Qualls looked up, saw Winifred, gulped, and turned as red as the shirt he was washing, which he tried to hide behind.

"Hey, pretty Injun girl," one of the Rangers called. "Y'on come take a swim?"

"Red and white makes pink," hollered another one, wagging his twig like a damn flag.

Winifred sped up just a little, walking proud but fast. "They're animals," she muttered.

They followed the creek around a bend, and Winifred broke into a run, her bare feet flying over the smooth river stones like she didn't even feel them. Nettie stumbled every time she looked up at the girl and clumped along behind in her boots. Soon, they'd gotten far enough away so they couldn't hear the Rangers splashing, to a pretty place where the water pooled up, hidden by bushes and greenery. Winifred pulled a lumpy ball of soap out of the bag, along with a wooden comb missing a couple of tines.

"You stand there and make sure none of those disgusting Rangers try to find us. If one of them comes around that bend, you'd best shoot him, or I will."

At first, Nettie nodded. But then she couldn't keep her mouth shut. "They've all seen you nekkid, girl. Or at least, they seen you wrapped in a little bit of leather or under a blanket. Why are you so worried for your skin, all of a sudden?"

Winifred looked up from combing her long hair and cocked her head with a gentle smile.

"You don't know much of what happens between men and women, do you?"

Nettie sputtered like someone had shoved her head under the water.

Winifred nodded knowingly. "That's what I thought. It's not like with horses and cows, all straightforward. There's a dance to it, especially among folks that think they're civilized.

229

When they see me in my leathers, they see a dirty, stupid Injun who can turn into a dirty, stupid coyote. But when they see me in a dress and then nekkid and dripping water, they see a woman. And women are all the same color on the inside."

"Then why do you wear a damn dress at all? Why remind 'em what you are?"

Winifred looked down at the faded blue. "Because I do what I want. I might like wearing a dress, but I don't wear it for them. It's for me. Because I like the feel of it. And I'll not have them taking anything from me that I'm not willing to give." She finished with the comb and twitched her hair behind her shoulder in a black, shiny waterfall. "And I'm not willing to give a single one of those fools anything, much less the satisfaction that they've shamed me."

It was a lot to grasp for Nettie, so she just pulled out her gun, faced away from the pool and toward where the cowpokes were, and tried to look competent.

"I'll guard you fine, then. Go on with your bath and quit with the preachin'."

"My hero," Winifred said, then laughed.

The prairie was pretty out here, the sky wide and blue and streaked with fishbelly-white clouds. The creek glittered like a hair ribbon, disappearing around a corner to where the cowpokes were bathing downstream, nekkid without a care in the world. It was hard for Nettie to see them as the enemy, as anything but fellers she wanted to be with and be like. Surely the famed Durango Rangers wouldn't take advantage of a woman? Well, unless she was a vampire and going for a throat. Or, say, a wolf-woman or a harpy. Then again, what they'd hollered at Winifred was rude as hell and made Nettie angry. And the Captain had heard Regina screaming and left her behind to die. Law, but it was hard enough to puzzle out women from men before they started turning into all sorts of new critters and monsters, good and bad.

Nettie had no idea how she fit into what she was constantly learning of the world.

But she understood her orders well enough: Guard Winifred. That she could do.

Behind her, fabric whispered over skin, and flesh sunk deeper into water that would only come up to the girl's waist, which left a good bit hanging out for all to see. Nettie checked her gun to make sure it didn't need reloading. Then she checked it again and spun the barrel. A deep splash suggested Winifred might've dove down, and the sound of spitting water and paddling confirmed it.

"Ain't that cold?" Nettie called.

Winifred laughed. "You'll see well enough when I'm done. Feels good, though. Makes me feel more alive."

"Well, considering you were dead a few hours ago, I reckon that ain't hard."

After a brief pause, water splattered against Nettie's back, making her suck in a breath. She spun on Winifred and found the girl on her knees and chin-deep, scooping up another armful of water to splash her, a huge grin on her face.

"You take life too seriously, Rhett. Don't you ever play?"

Nettie turned back to face away and shrugged. "Nobody never taught me how."

"We need to work on that."

Shaking the impish tone of the girl's words out of her head, Nettie cleared her throat and wished to hell Winifred would put her clothes back on and leave Nettie to return to a life she wanted and understood. Too much thinking just felt...dangerous. And playing was downright stupid. Durango Rangers, she was quite sure, did not play. Winifred sounded like she was back to business, just light splashes, no more being silly. Until strong arms grabbed Nettie around the waist and tossed her into the water, boots and all.

Nettie screeched, her gun flying out of her hand and onto the bank as she landed on her butt in the ice-cold creek. Winifred stood over her, nekkid and blocking the sun behind a sheet of night-black wet hair.

"See? That was fun."

Scrambling to her feet, her heart beating like a humming-bird, Nettie hunted for her gun. "That ain't fun. You could've ruined my gun, girl. I can't protect you if you're going to go on and do foolish things like that."

A firm hand on her shoulder shoved Nettie right back into the creek. Winifred had no right being as strong as that, as strong as a man. And Nettie was wet now from neck to boots. And even though the water barely came up to her waist, she couldn't swim a lick, which made her skitty.

"I changed my mind," Winifred said, laughing. "Any of those old cowpokes who come around the corner can answer to me. Go on and bathe. You're already halfway there. I'll keep watch. Maybe I'll teach you how to have a water fight, once you're clean."

She was right, too, goddammit. Nettie was soaked, her clothes clinging to her and dirt swirling around her in an oily puddle. The creek was sluggish, and it was cold, but it did feel all tingly-like. She'd never been in so much water at once, and goddamn if it didn't make a body feel more alive.

"Aw, hell."

Nettie went on and took off her boots at least, tossing them onto the pebbles beside Winifred's dress to dry. Her socks came next, and her toes stretched out like baby moles seeing sun for the first time. She hadn't seen her toes in weeks, not since switching over her boots in Pap's barn. She tossed off her bandanna, her hat, her vest, and her empty gun belt. Finally, all that was left was her shirt and britches, and she didn't much want to take those off, not in front of Winifred or in front of anybody. Not even alone, if it was still out in the air where anybody might see. She didn't know what to do with her own nekkid body. She felt soft all over, vulnerable, and she hated that.

"Go on, then. Nothing I haven't seen before. Unless you're scared."

Winifred's teasing tone was a dare, and Nettie wasn't about to back down. The only thing she liked less than being nekkid was having somebody think she was too scared to do something as simple and stupid as taking a bath. There was no sight of the Rangers around the bend, and Winifred had sharp enough coyote senses to warn her in time, should any fellers appear.

Knowing her shirttail went down to her knees, she slipped off her britches first. They were all but crusted in places, and she washed 'em right quick, dipping the thick cloth in the water, twisting the fabric up, and beating them against a nearby rock while trying to ignore the unsettling sensation of air swirling around her nethers under the shirt. Winifred watched her, nekkid and proud, arms crossed over something that Nettie herself was accustomed to keeping wound up tight. Law, did she have to take off her wrapping, too? Damn the Captain and his bathing bullshit.

Finally, she couldn't get the pants any cleaner, so she laid them out flat on the pebbles while the cool air whistled over her rump.

"Ain't you going to wash your dress, Winifred?"

"It was clean when I put it on today, which means it's still clean. Why are you so scared to take off your shirt? The men aren't coming down here. The Captain would skin them alive if they tried."

Nettie had three buttons undone, and she looked daggers at Winifred.

"Then why the Sam Hill'd you ask me to guard you?"

Winifred tossed her hair like a lead mare. "For company. And so you'd have an excuse to bathe without being watched. I was doing you a favor. Best finish your cleaning, or the Captain will dunk you himself, and then your little secret will be out. Honestly, if Jiddy were half the tracker he says he is, he would've already smelled you for what you are."

"What, the Shadow?"

"No, silly. Shadows don't smell. That's the point. Any skin-walker scout should be able to smell a woman."

Nettie flushed red. "Don't call me that."

As Nettie picked back up with the buttons, Winifred used the piddly ball of soap to wash herself, the scent of rose petals filling the air around the creek. Nettie felt an ache in her chest she didn't quite understand, and then the last button was undone, and the shirt hung from the low, wrapped-up bumps of her chest. Before Winifred could call her a coward again, she turned her back and shrugged it off and set to beating her anger and confusion out on wet cloth against rock.

"You trying to murder that shirt?"

Both girls whirled at the man's voice. Winifred relaxed when she saw it was Hennessy standing behind her, but Nettie dropped to a crouch in the water, hoping Hennessy hadn't seen much more than her bare ass, which was boyish enough. He stood in the middle of the creek, carrying his boots. Which explained why neither of them had seen him and Winifred hadn't smelled him. Nettie's skin was frozen and tingling, but inside, she was as hot as a cherry-red branding iron.

"Rhett? What's got you scared, man? It's just me."

Nettie turned around, holding the wet shirt over her front and squatting down in the stream.

"Told you I'm shy."

Wearing his million-dollar smile, Hennessy tossed his vest, boots, and gun belt to the shore and started stripping. His eyes didn't leave Nettie's as he pulled off his hat and bandanna. It was as if he'd plum forgotten that Winifred existed and was standing off to the side, hands on hips and gloriously nekkid as she watched the show. Nettie glanced at Winifred, then back to Hennessy.

But he had no eyes for Winifred. Only for Nettie. Only for Rhett.

Sam's face went a shade darker, chin tucked and eyes hooded as he started unbuttoning his shirt. Nettie swallowed hard. It was as if there were nothing in the entire world but her and him, this feller she'd taken a liking to years ago, when she was still a young little sprig of a nobody with nothing. He hadn't even noticed her then, but he damn well saw her now. Hennessy didn't blink as he folded his shirt and placed it carefully on the rock Nettie squatted beside, passing so close that she could smell an animal musk rising up off his skin. The passing heat of Hennessy and the scent of his skin reminded her of being drunk on whisky at the saloon, so very dizzying and dreamlike and yet so very real.

His fingers went to the buttons on his britches as his mouth curled up.

"Hennessy, you don't got to—"

"Fair's fair, other Hennessy. And the Captain ordered us to bathe. Best get every crevice."

Nettie looked to Winifred. The girl was just watching, bemused, a knowing smile on her face. But Nettie couldn't handle it, Hennessy getting nekkid in front of her, almost *for* her, it felt like. She lurched up, holding the shirt in front of her business as she backed away.

"It's just me, Rhett. Calm down." Hennessy put his hands up, which made the flap on his britches fall down, exposing a curious slice of hipbone and a shadow of blond hair and... something else, sticking straight up.

It was the most interesting and terrifying thing Nettie had ever seen, and she was so goddamn surprised that she dropped her shirt and stood up.

Hennessy's face broke like a thrown plate.

"Rhett? What's...why...are you...?"

Nettie shook her head, frozen in place. Hennessy stomped up to her through the water, stared pointedly at the dark thatch of her, down below.

"What happened to you, man? Where's your..."

When Hennessy's hand reached out as if to see if she was hiding a pizzle somewhere, she slapped it away.

"I'm sorry, Sam. It's just..."

He took her roughly by the shoulders and held her at arm's length, inspecting her from face to neck, pausing over the controlled hills hidden by her wrapping, down over her flat stomach and barely-there hips, all the way down her legs. He was breathing like he'd run a mile, and by the time his gander returned to her face, he looked downright disgusted and like she'd stabbed him in the back.

Thick with desperation, he said, "I don't understand, Rhett. Tell me. Tell me you ain't a girl."

Nettie couldn't meet his eyes for a second longer. She twisted out of his hands, snatched her shirt back up over her body, and wished she was small enough to wrap up in it and never see him again like a little bitty mouse. "I thought you knew, Hennessy. You...you tried to kiss me."

Hennessy shoved her, hard enough to lay her out on her back in the stream.

"Goddammit, Rhett. I thought you were a boy."

He grabbed his belongings, shoved on his boots, and stormed back up the creek toward the Rangers, taking her secret and her half-broken heart along with him.

CHAPTER

20

Nettie scrambled up and watched him go with tears in her eyes and a tornado in her heart. When she turned to Winifred, the girl looked utterly unsurprised and even wryly amused.

"What the hell was that?" Nettie asked her.

Winifred rubbed the soap over the hair tufts under her arms and sighed. "You have a lot to learn about people, Nettie Lonesome."

"But I thought he liked me. I thought he knew. He made sly remarks about being alone with me, and he tried to kiss me once, and..." Memories tumbled through, all the little gestures, the smiles, the shoulder squeezes and back claps, how close he spaced his bedroll at night, and the way Hennessy's new beard had glinted in the moonlight when he'd been about to kiss her.

"He did like you, idjit. But you're right about the sly."

Nettie was so angry and confused she forgot about her embarrassment and just wanted to bid the creek farewell forever. She beat her shirt against the rock, loading each smack with all of her hurt. Then she unwound the wrap around her chest and cleaned that, too, all the while keeping her back to Winifred and the girl's knowing, goddamn silence. When she'd finally beat all the pain out, she laid her things out on a hot rock and flattened herself out beside them like a dare and willed the sun to burn her and them up to a crisp on the spot, or at least to dry 'em out faster than usual so she could get on with her troublesome life.

"Remember how I said people aren't like horses and cows?"

Winifred's voice was gentle, which put Nettie on the defensive. Her nose wrinkled up, and she slitted her eyes to stare at Winifred in a blameful sort of way. "So I'm learning."

The other girl pursed her lips, hunting for the right words. "With horses and cows, mostly, the male takes the female to get young on her. They don't marry or mate for life. They might have a lead bull or stallion, but for the most part, the mares can allow the stallions to mount or kick the hell out of them, correct?"

"I reckon."

"Well, people are different."

"No shit, girl."

Half bored and half fascinated with the discussion, Nettie sat up and fetched the Bowie knife off her belt and took to cleaning out her fingernails and trimming them down. Winifred finished with her soap and offered it to her, and Nettie pulled a face at the thought of smelling like goddamn dwarf flowers. Finally, Winifred just sat on a nearby rock and stared off into space until she found the words she wanted.

"Nettie, imagine what life would be like if some stallions favored stallions and some mares favored mares."

"That don't make a damn bit of sense."

Winifred shook her drying hair. "How much of humanity does? Why is white skin more valuable than brown skin? Why is a drunk, uneducated idjit like your Pap deserving of more respect than a hard-working, talented hunter like my brother,

Dan? Why do the Rangers hunt only nonhumans when humans do even more horrible things to each other every day? If you live every day looking for sense, you'll spend your whole life hunting the horizon."

"So?"

"So not every person fits into the little rooms we build to hold them. There are infinite combinations of human and inhuman, male and female, brown and white."

"What's *infinite* mean?"

"Means so many you can't count. Like the stars. Another thing I learned from the white man's books. A creature is what it is, even if it can't show its true face. And Hennessy did like you. *Does* like you. But Hennessy thought you were a boy, and he likes boys. And now, well...he feels like you lied to him."

Nettie's chest felt like a five-pound pickle barrel packed with ten pounds of nails and a stick of dynamite. Nothing in her life with Pap and Mam had prepared her to understand what Winifred had just told her. Her world had been black and white—or brown and white. Brown is bad; white is good. Women are bad; men are good. Women were supposed to cook and clean and have babies, and men were supposed to do all the fun things, and Nettie Lonesome could do all the fun things if she pretended to be a man. Men and women were attracted to each other for the same reason all other animals joined. Everything had been tidy, if mostly unfair. And now this coyote-Injun girl was telling her that there was no good or bad, there just...was.

"Nettie?"

She flapped a hand at Winifred. "Shush. I can't think with you yapping all the time."

Winifred stood from the rock, blocking out the sun and throwing Nettie into shade that was no less hot for its darkness.

"I'll get dressed and head on back, then. I understand it's a lot to take in, but you have to remember... this is a good thing. What you were told isn't always true. You can be whatever you want. Pap's ranch is such a small part of the world. And in the end, what happened there doesn't matter."

"You sound like your brother," Nettie grumbled.

Winifred smiled. "Thank you."

And then she was gone.

To a person unaccustomed to choices, the truths that Winifred had laid down were boggling. But Nettie wasn't so consternated that she sat around nekkid, waiting for some other cowpoke to show up and pitch a hissy fit. As soon as her clothes were getting close to dry, she wound her chest back under the wrap, tight as she could, and tucked her shirt deep into her britches. Everything felt crisp and hot and warm, and although she had always preferred a second coating of dust, she felt oddly free.

Pulling back her sleeve, she inspected the exact color of her clean body. Without the lens of Pap and Mam, just looking at the color, it was right pretty, like the bottom of a burned biscuit. She'd always liked horses this color, a warm and melty blood bay tipped with black, or maybe a dark chestnut with flaxen mane, a right cozy hue. She didn't have to see the tips of her hair to know it was growing out dark and thick, but she didn't so much mind the wind on her neck. Guess that made her a bay.

Standing up, she tried to catch her reflection in the clear

water of the stream, but all she could get was a rough, wavering outline. In a town like Gloomy Bluebird, it was rare to find a patch of clean window and rarer still to see a mirror. Nettie might've had trouble picking her own face out of a lineup, unless all the other fellers were white, like it was in the Rangers. She could see that her limbs were long and lanky without too much hair, which might've bothered a boy her age. Her lips were fuller than she preferred, and her nose was wide at the bottom and sharp at the top, as if it couldn't quite decide which way to go. Her cheeks were high and her chin jutted out just enough to make her look stubborn. Basically, she looked like she was trying hard as hell to not look white, and it was working.

But she didn't walk like a girl, a-swinging her narrow hips. And she didn't talk or act or sit like a lady. She stared too long and hit too hard and rarely gave thought to her looks, which seemed awful unladylike.

If Hennessy had liked her as a boy, did that mean she *looked* like a boy? And what made a boy handsome or a girl pretty, anyway? She rubbed her eyes with her fists. Life had been a lot easier when she was breaking broncs.

When she finally turned to walk back up the creek to the town, she felt as if she'd left some old bit of herself in the water, like the old Nettie had sloughed off and floated away. Her steps were a little lighter, her chin still held high, but this time with more than stubbornness. When she thought back to what Pap and Mam were like, it was hard to believe that anyone had ever given them a sweet goddamn bit of respect. Dirty, mean, lazy, drunk, dishonest. Everyone in Gloomy Bluebird thought they were bad neighbors, and Nettie could recall that many of the folks who'd given her scraps when she'd gone begging on their behalf had carried a particular sadness in their eyes.

Had they felt sorry for her, maybe? She'd always assumed they looked down on her, but maybe what she'd seen was hate for Pap and Mam and not herself.

Her skull hurt like she'd been mule-kicked, and she couldn't wait to lay her head on her saddle and sleep. Of course, Hennessy would've moved his bedroll. A faint pang of regret in her stomach told her she owed him an apology. She had truly thought he knew her secret and hadn't meant to betray him by being born a girl. It hurt, to know that he wouldn't like her anymore, wouldn't give her that grin and squeeze her shoulder. That he'd carried a candle for a boy named Rhett who didn't actually exist.

Which brought a new truth to mind: Life wasn't fair, no matter how handsome and blue-eyed you were. If Samuel Hennessy couldn't get what he wanted, what hope did the rest of the world have?

But of course, that left her with the question: Where did she fall on the spectrum of stallions and mares? She'd been drawn to Hennessy ever since she'd known him, but her skin had tingled and flopped when Dan had held the bow around her, even though she didn't take a shine to him. And when Winifred had stood, all wet and nekkid, in the creek, Nettie couldn't stop herself staring. Could a mare only like mares or stallions, or could a mare like whatever she damn pleased? Maybe she just didn't know enough yet to understand what she was or what she wanted. Or maybe she was lots of things, just as her skin was a mixture of browns. Maybe she didn't have to like anything.

It was too damn much, is what it was.

Sleep would be welcome, so long as she could stop thinking.

Back in the bunk room, fellers were passing around hunks of bread and scooping beans and unusually fragrant meat from

Delgado's pot. Hennessy had moved his bedroll to the other side and was crouched down in grim, forced friendliness with Qualls and a couple of the other young fellers, rolling bone dice. When she looked at him, giving him the most apologetic glance she could muster, he just spit and looked away. As if she could help being a girl.

She ate alone, checked her gear, and settled down while the other fellers moseyed over to the dwarves' saloon to drink, a rare treat on the plains. When Hennessy left, Nettie could finally breathe again. Her head hit her saddle, and she willed herself angrily to sleep. For once, no one woke her. There was no watch, no Coyote Dan, no sign of Winifred's return. She had no dreams of fires and the Injun woman, no promise of the future or painful remembrance of the past. She barely noted the brightness of the night sky, hardly counted down the days to the new moon and whatever threat the Cannibal Owl planned. It was right peaceful, actually.

She woke up to a rooster's call both a completely different person and the exact same as she'd ever been, but more so. When she went outside to piss in the outhouse, she saw a far-off figure on a dark horse, pointing west.

"You see that?" she called to Hennessy as he strode past.

"I don't see nothin', you girl," Sam muttered.

Somehow, it was even more insulting than it used to be.

Nettie didn't see Winifred again until the Rangers were saddling up in the corral to leave. The girl walked among the horses with calm purpose and ease, touching rumps and necks as she went. She was wearing the same light blue dress from yesterday, but with a boy's britches beneath it and covering most of her legs down to bare, slender ankles and dusty feet.

"You can take the saddle," Nettie said, tossing her head at Ragdoll.

Winifred rubbed the mare's nose and subtly inspected her, which raised Nettie's hackles. "Are you sure? I can ride bareback, you know."

Nettie looked around, made sure none of the fellers were nearby. "Wouldn't be gentlemanly, making a woman ride with no saddle."

Winifred hid a laugh behind her hand. "Thanks anyway, Rhett. What a gentleman. But I'll take your paint, if you don't mind." She said it loud enough that a few of the cowpokes looked over, curious, and Nettie growled at her.

Just then, the saddlebag twitched under Winifred's hand, which was exactly what Nettie had hoped wouldn't happen. With her usual quickness, Winifred whipped open the leather flap.

"What are you hiding?"

Nettie shrugged. "Ain't hiding nothing. They're my saddlebags. You're doing what's called snooping. Downright impolite, as a matter of fact."

Of course that didn't stop Winifred from digging deep, past the clothes and jerky. She stopped right before she'd pulled out the foot, and Nettie stepped close to block the men from seeing it.

"Why do you have this?" Winifred's voice was low and anxious. And angry.

"Found it when I was on watch the other night, right after Dan left."

Winifred glanced around to be sure no one was paying them any mind. She cradled the tiny foot in her hand, cupping it like a child's cheek. "Do you know what this is?"

"Warning from the Cannibal Owl, I reckon."

A tear dropped on the foot, and Winifred shook her hair and stroked the ankle bone. "That's not what I mean. This is... it's a skinwalker's foot. A Javelina. And the child still lives, so long as it's whole. But the pain is constant, the leg bleeding from an open wound that can't heal without help. It's torture." Then, softer, "The Cannibal Owl is torturing her."

The foot twitched all of a sudden, the toes going wide as if in surprise or pain. As Nettie and Winifred bent their heads over it, the tiny foot turned to warm, beige sand and ran out through clutching fingers to spill over Nettie's boots. Bile rose in her throat, and she bent to try to scrape up the light sand where it had fallen over the darker prairie earth, mixed with horse manure and hoof prints.

Overhead, Winifred sang a low song, all consonants and liquid and pain. She ended on a high, ululating note and threw her hands into the air, letting the wind whisk the remaining sand from her fingers. In a fit of understanding, Nettie threw the sand she'd managed to scrape up, too. Some of it flew back to stick in the tears on her cheeks.

"Shut yer hole, Injun," Jiddy called, and a few of the fellers nodded along. "That ki-yay song's setting the horses off."

Sure enough, the horses were dancing uneasily, ears pricked and nostrils flaring.

"It's not the song that troubles them," Winifred said.

Nettie's stomach twisted inside out, and she put a hand up to shield her vision as she scanned the prairie. Something moved, far off, in the direction the horses faced as they snorted. She could almost see it—a wrapped figure, tall and dark and balanced all wrong, not on a horse. It disappeared in the wavering sunrise, to the west, far too quick. A cloud passed, and it was just a flock of vultures, all bunched together like they were headed to find something good and dead. Nettie's gorge rose; the shine on their feathers revealed them as harpies.

All around her, the Rangers saddled up, unaware of what had just passed. But Nettie's eyes met Winifred's, and what she saw there was fear.

"Where's Dan?" Nettie asked.

Winifred swallowed hard and shook her head.

"I haven't seen him in days."

They made good time, and Winifred was a savvy enough rider that Nettie couldn't complain, which was vexful. Nettie felt more lonesome than ever without Hennessy by her side, trotting on his palomino or flashy black and cracking jokes. Winifred was a far more somber companion, and Nettie was still shook up from watching the child's foot collapse into sand and learning that Coyote Dan might be in trouble himself. Seeing what had to be the Cannibal Owl, as if the danged thing was taunting her—well, now she had to wonder who exactly was the hunter and who was being hunted. And the presence of the harpies in the monster's wake suggested that Pia Mupitsi didn't hunt alone.

For hours, they trotted across the green-brushed plains, picked their way down arroyos, and sidestepped dusty skeletons where various creatures had just flopped down and decided to die. In this wild, forgotten corner of Durango, there were no towns, no fences, and after a while, no water and nothing alive and bigger than a thumb. The mountains loomed ahead, stark and heavy as the bones of gods left to rot. Time came to mean nothing, and Nettie forgot the hour mere seconds after tucking her new watch back in her pocket. They didn't stop for lunch and barely to sleep, just pulled out their jerky and chewed like a herd of cows as the wind punished them with stinging sand. When the trails grew narrow and treacherous, they had to abandon the cook wagon, and Delgado rode one of his mules and ponied the other with panniers of food and pots heavy on its back. Even Winifred ran out of things to say. Nettie just focused on Hennessy, trying to will him to understand by staring at his back.

For days, she couldn't find a way to approach him. He always turned away, moved his horse to a different place in line. When she finally saw him turn off to check his limping gelding's hoof for stones, she saw her chance and loped away from Winifred and to his side. Feller couldn't run away if he was off his mount.

"Hennessy."

He looked up and flinched like she'd slapped him. "Go away, Rhett, or whatever your name is. We're done."

Nettie's chest ached as she watched him move around his gelding, his fingers light and his every move gentle as he inspected the horse's hooves and extracted a stone from the left rear foot.

"Fool horse," he muttered.

Before he could remount, Nettie pushed Ragdoll toward his palomino, making the horse dance back and preventing Hennessy from getting his foot in the stirrup.

"Goddammit, girl. Why won't you leave me in peace?"

"Because you're acting like I shot you in the foot, and I didn't do nothin' wrong. I just want to be your friend. I..." She looked down, wishing to hell she didn't have a lady's chest burning with sobs. "I miss you. I'm sorry."

He caught her reins and stepped close, hurt written in every line on his young, handsome face. "I can't miss you, because

248

you're not who I thought you were. You led me on. And now, if you tell any of the fellers about me, they'll string me up. And if I tell 'em about you, you're gone. So the best thing you can do is stay away from me." He jerked her reins, making Ragdoll dance as he watched the other Rangers trot on ahead. "Far away."

When he released the rains, Nettie got desperate.

"Dammit, Hennessy!"

Without thinking too much, she yanked out her whip and snapped his horse on the flank, and the palomino took off, galloping across the prairie with the ponied horse in tow. Hennessy cussed and ran a few steps before rounding on her, finally showing his anger in clenched fists.

"Why'd you do that, fool? You want me to hate you more?"

She shook her head. "No. I want you to listen. Nobody ever listens to me, and you're dang well going to."

Hennessy stared at his horses, now cropping scrub grass a good five minutes' walk away.

"You got until I reach my horses, and then I'm galloping the hell away from you. For good."

When he started walking, she swung Ragdoll's head to keep pace. "Look, Sam."

"Don't call me that."

"Fine. Hennessy. I'm a girl. I always been a girl. And I don't like being a girl, I don't feel like a girl, and that's why I pretend to be a boy. I didn't know you were...like that. And I don't care. I reckon a person can be whatever they want to be. But you can't blame me for being what I am, and I can't blame you for being you. I don't. I thought you knew I was a girl. Figured you might feel about me the way I felt about you. And I still don't see why you can't, if you used to. I'm the same person. Just got different parts. But my head and heart are the same, and I'd..." He didn't look back, and she felt all desperate, like her heart was going to climb out and throw itself at his feet like a hungry cur. She kicked her mare to a lope and spun in front of Hennessy, the mare's side blocking him. "I'd take a bullet for you, Sam. I would. And I don't care about boys and girls and all that bullshit. I love you."

He stopped and looked up at her, hands on his hips.

"You love me."

She nodded. "That's got to be what this feeling is, like my stomach's in knots and my heart's about to flop out. I think about you all the time. I feel safe when you're riding next to me or bedded down beside me. And when you tried to kiss me, I got scared. Never kissed nobody before. And I don't need to. I don't expect you to change for me or... or want me, that way. I just want to go on being your friend."

"How can I?" His shout scared Ragdoll, and the mare nearly dumped Nettie on the ground. "The person I thought I might love don't exist, and now the person who killed him wants to be my friend? That's horseshit, and you know it!"

Quick as a crow's blink, Nettie slid off her horse, dropped her reins, and threw herself into Hennessy's chest, pushing him onto the ground. He was heavier, but she'd surprised him. Little as she'd tangled with people, she'd wrestled many a calf or hog to the dirt, and she used his befuddlement and unwillingness to hurt a girl to get him on his back, where she straddled his chest and pinned his hands to the ground. It was right unsettling, her legs split over a body, but she had to make him listen.

"It ain't horseshit, fool. Now listen. This is where we are. You're you, and I'm me, and neither one of us is gonna change. Neither of us *can* change. So we might as well stay friends."

All the struggle went out of Hennessy, and he stared up

at her like she was an armadillo walking on its hind legs and swinging a bumbershoot.

Finally, all quiet-like and blinking back tears, he said, "Hellfire, Rhett. I don't know if I can. I look at you, and I see two different people, and it tears me up inside."

She shook her head in consternation. "I'm lots of different people. But I'm your friend, and I'm a Ranger, and I got your back. I'll keep your secrets to my grave. Can you live with that?"

His jaw worked for a minute, and his head fell back. Nettie figured she'd see hurt in his bright blue eyes for the rest of her days.

"Will you let go of my arms, at least?" Hennessy asked.

Nettie released him and sat back on his chest, hoping she'd managed to convince him.

All in one swift motion, Hennessy sat up and clocked her in the jaw with a brawny fist. Nettie fell over on her back, seeing stars, and he climbed to his feet to stare down at her, hands on his hips.

"What the Sam Hill was that for?" she asked, sitting up slowly and rubbing her aching jaw.

"Because if you're going to play at being a boy, I'm damn well going to treat you like a man. A feller causes me this much trouble, I find that punching him in the face makes me feel a lot better."

He held out a hand to pull her up, and when she stood, they eyed each other warily.

"I can live with that," Nettie said with a nod.

"Can't believe I'm saying this, but come on, other Hennessy, or whatever your name is. We got two flighty horses to catch if we don't want to be left behind by the Rangers. I still got to earn my badge." He flicked the metal star on her chest. "A girl Ranger. I'll be damned."

She shoved him in a friendly-type way. "I ain't no girl. You keep my secret, I'll keep yours."

Hennessy spit in his hand and held it out, a look of grudging respect on his face. Nettie spit in her hand and grabbed his, hard, the cords on her wrist standing out. He looked down with a shadow of his old grin, and she reared back and threw a wild left punch directly into his cheek. As she'd never hit anybody before she'd clocked Winifred the other day, she must've done something wrong again, as it apparently hurt her more than it hurt Hennessy. She'd busted up a knuckle, and probably broke her thumb, and her whole arm was burning. Hennessy watched her hop around, shaking her hand and cussing, and his regular smile finally broke out as he rubbed his cheek thoughtfully.

"You can't punch worth a damn, Rhett. What was that for, anyway?"

She stood up straight, met his glare.

"That was for calling me a liar."

He put his arm around her shoulder, making her stomach bounce like hail on a roof as they staggered off to their horses.

They'd just mounted up when they heard the Captain's Henry crack over the prairie, followed by a dozen more shots and the bloodcurdling screams of Injuns on the warpath.

CHAPTER

21

Nettie's eyes met Hennessy's, and they wheeled their horses and headed off for the Rangers at a gallop. Hennessy was slower, since he was ponying another horse, and Nettie slapped Ragdoll's rump with her hat and drew her gun as they climbed a small hill that hid the flatland beyond. When they hit the top, she pulled the mare to a stop, lay low on her neck, and scanned the scene. The Rangers had circled their horses and dismounted, taking shelter within the ring of their well-trained but panicking mounts. A couple of the fellers lay on the prairie, still and dead, stuck full of arrows like porcupines.

A shot zinged past Nettie's ear, and she rolled off Ragdoll and tugged the little Appaloosa behind a column of rock to figure out the best way to help. Hennessy pulled up beside her, gun likewise drawn and his horses dancing like silly little fools.

"Captain still up?" he asked.

The crack of the Henry and a death scream answered the question, and Nettie squinted.

"Captain's up and shooting. Jiddy's up but bleeding from the arm. Winifred's in there, too. Looks like we lost Lee and Qualls and someone else."

Hennessy peeped around the rock. "Moran. Had a danged fine mustache. Good feller." He spit and aimed his revolver but lowered it before shooting. "Too far to aim true. Goddammit, I hate werewolves."

"Me, too—" Nettie stared at him. "Hold on. What'd you say?"

Hennessy jerked his chin at the nine braves galloping their ponies bareback around the tight wheel of Rangers. They rode flashy horses decorated with dabs of red in the shapes of handprints and paw prints. The men wore strips of leather, and their cloaks were made of gray and black fur stuck through with feathers. As Nettie watched, the biggest feller tipped his head back, and it rippled into a wolf's snout. When he let out a bloodcurdling howl, all the skin rose up on the back of her neck.

She shook it off. "So they're skinwalkers. Why're they attacking?"

Hennessy rolled his eyes like she was dumb as a possum. "Skinwalkers and werewolves ain't the same thing. Not even close. Folks like Jiddy and Winny and Dan, they're pretty decent. They change into critters when they need to. But werewolves are nasty. Turn into giant killer wolves whenever there's a full moon and cause trouble in between times. They ain't even tribes, just the curs that got kicked out for being no good or got turned into wolves by the bad sort in jail. Any time you hear about a massacre, about scalping, it ain't the Injuns. It's Lobos."

Nettie added that to her mental map of all the peculiar things in the world that weren't what she'd been told.

"But why? What good's killing do?"

Hennessy's head swiveled over at her, and she was gladder than anything that he could look at her without wincing again.

"For werewolves, killing means you get to eat your favorite food. In this case, white men. Why do you think the Durango Rangers are known for slaughtering 'em?"

"But why didn't I feel 'em?"

"I don't rightly, Rhett." Hennessy grinned and shrugged, and her stomach flopped.

And just like that, all the pieces fell into place. Nettie realized that as long as she was near Hennessy, she couldn't trust her gut or her senses. All that monster-caused stomach flopping and lovelorn heart-busting: It felt the same. Even if she'd never be more to him than a friend, and the sort of friend you punched in the face when one of you got riled up, she couldn't tell her feelings for him apart from the feeling of nine werewolves murdering her compatriots a mile away.

"Huh" was all she could manage.

"So what we've got to do is figure out a way to kill the Lobos or draw 'em off before night falls and they turn to full-on wolves. They're playing with us now, but soon they'll start shooting down the horses for fun when it gets too easy."

"You saying you done this before?"

He nodded, grim. "Battle of Bandera Pass. Lost a lot of good fellers that day."

The Lobos were trick riding, hopping up and off and around their galloping ponies and taking occasional lazy shots at the Rangers just to make 'em dance. A horse screamed, and Nettie saw that a thick-built dapple gray horse had taken a feathered arrow in the chest. Much to her surprise, the horse reared, pawed the air, and fell away to glittering, sugar-white sand.

"Captain's been riding a unicorn?"

"Finest mounts around. The rest are just normal horses. They'll go down just as easy, though, when the Lobos want 'em to."

Nettie was trying to put it all together, and as if he were well-tuned to her confusion, Hennessy added, "Werewolves won't eat monsters or horses, neither. They're just having fun, now. They only like human flesh." When Hennessy shivered, Nettie did, too. But it gave her an idea.

"And all they got is arrows, right?"

Hennessy squinted. "I don't see any rifles. They can't carry rifles in their mouths, when they're wolves."

"Then all we got to do is split up their attention. I'm going to that ridge over yonder. You go on the other side. We'll try to pick 'em off or draw 'em out. I know only a shot to the heart can kill 'em, but will a shot to another tender place slow 'em down a little?"

Hennessy laughed bitterly and looked down. "Shit, girl. You don't know nothin'. Only thing that'll kill a werewolf is silver to the heart. Bullets do best, although Captain docks what little pay we get if we waste it. Regular bullets anywhere else'll just annoy 'em, and it's right hard to get close enough to hit 'em with a silver knife. That's why the Captain gives every man a handful of silver shot. It ain't just being nice." He was already shaking the shells out of his pistol and reloading it with soft-looking, shiny silver. "You got six, I got six, and each of them fellers in the circle's got six. We keep them braves busy, maybe we'll get a chance to aim."

Nettie rattled her silver bullets in her hand. "Those ain't good odds, and don't call me a girl."

"You are a girl, fool. And nobody ever promised a Ranger good odds."

"That's 'cause most Rangers do their thinking with a trigger finger. I got a better idea. You think they seen me real good, Sam?"

Hennessy snapped his gun barrel shut, cocked it, and stared

at her with a look she hadn't missed since putting on britches. It was the look that said a man was underestimating her because of what was between her legs instead of what was between her ears.

"They just saw two people and three horses, probably. Sun's behind us and you're wearing a hat. Why?"

"I used to hear about how Injuns like to steal women."

With a snort, Hennessy lined up his pistol as if he thought he could hit the broad side of a barn from this far away, which she knew he surely couldn't. "Well, yeah. Women..." Sam cleared his throat. "They can be right useful for men with no family. And they supposedly taste sweeter to werewolves, after."

Nettie shuddered and passed it off by slapping at a bug that wasn't there. "So you give me to 'em. I'll act like a fool, and while they're focusing on me, you and the boys can show up and we'll all take 'em out."

Hennessy's head jerked back, and he looked her up and down. "Hellfire, Rhett. You know what they'll do to you if me and the fellers can't get there in time? Or if we don't aim true?"

"I ain't thinking about that. And I trust you, Sam. Point is, I'm pretty handy with a knife, and we don't got a lot of options if we want to save our men before they all get shot."

As if to punctuate her words, another war cry rent the sky, followed by a horse's scream.

"It don't matter how handy you are with a knife, Rhett. If it ain't silver, you'll just piss 'em off."

Nettie pulled the vampire's knife from her boot and held it up in the desert sun next to one of her silver bullets. "Reckon that'll do?"

Sam took the knife from her, turned it over in scarred hands. "Looks like it's got a heart of silver, I reckon. But are you sure you want to do this? Them Lobos won't care that you style yourself a man. They'll hurt you bad as a girl."

Nettie snatched the knife back and swallowed down her fear as another horse screamed and fell. "I'm sure enough. But we got to hurry."

Before Sam could use his dull brain to argue, Nettie shoved the knife back in her boot, unbuttoned her shirt, and started to unwind the bindings on her chest. Sam gulped and looked away, and she stuffed the fabric into her saddlebag and unbuttoned her shirt to an unforgivable level. Her throat was drier than dry, and she began to understand why there was always whisky where the whores were. She could've used a shot of something hot and wet and burning, something to dull her to the possibilities of what might happen if her plan didn't work. Hennessy tried to pretend she didn't exist as she likewise emptied her gun and packed it with silver. When she held it out, he took it and shoved it into his belt beside his own pistol.

"Get some rope, Hennessy."

He all but dove into his saddlebags as she took off her hat, rumpled her hair, and rubbed dirt into her face. When he turned back around with the softest rope they had, she held out her wrists and looked away.

"Get on the horse first, fool woman."

His black pony was smaller, and Nettie had no interest in losing her new saddle yet again. She patted Ragdoll's fuzzy nose and hobbled her before mounting up bareback on Hennessy's pony. When she held out her wrists again, Sam wound the rope around them and tied a shank knot, giving it a hard tug to make sure it was solid.

"This feels all kinds of wrong, Rhett," he said, all sorrowful-like.

"It'd feel worse to wait until morning and burn what's left of the Rangers, I reckon."

Still, he wouldn't quite look her in the eye. "Fine, then. If you can bruise or scratch yourself around the arms, you'll look like you been fighting," he said, voice husky and blue eyes as sad as a rainy day. "Make you look like my captive."

With a grim nod, she worked her hands back and forth, nose wrinkling at the lack of give in a rope that had seemed pretty soft for tying calves but was damn hard on her own skin. With her shirt flapping open over a front accustomed to being bound up tight, she felt like there was a target on her chest and a chunk of silver sitting heavy at the bottom of her heart. Was she as fast as she thought she was? What if they didn't untie her first? What if they searched her and found the knife in her boot? Would the Rangers catch on in time? And would they snatch back her badge for being a girl, provided they all lived through the night?

"My badge," she muttered. Hennessy just stared at a point over her shoulder. "You got to take it, Sam. Them Lobos can't know."

"We don't usually take these off a feller unless he's dead on the ground." Hennessy's hands were gentle and awkward as he unpinned the star. She couldn't help noticing that he put it in his own saddlebag instead of hers, and that helped her turn fear into anger. Damn if she was going to die and let him have sloppy seconds at her badge. It didn't matter that it was what he wanted most and she cared for him, it was *hers*, by God. She sucked in a hard breath of dusty air and raised her chin.

"Let's go, Sam."

He mounted up without looking back at her and held up a white handkerchief on a stick—he must've fashioned it while she was lost in thought and turning herself into a goddamn damsel. Chin up, back straight, she let her hips roll with the pony's jigging and steeled herself for the worst. As they topped the ridge, a single arrow flew overhead, but Nettie didn't flinch.

"If they wanted to hit us, they would've," Sam muttered. "Act like you weren't born on a horse, fool. Try for once not to look so proud and angry."

There was no challenge in riding a ponied horse bareback, even with her hands tied, but Nettie remembered how silly and unsettled most women looked astride in the saddle and leaned forward, wrapping numb fingers into the gelding's black mane. She'd learned early on that most of riding was knowing where your hips were and settling into your rump, but now she tried to pinch her legs together like she had to piss. The horse snorted and skipped like he didn't approve of the ruse.

"I have a woman," Sam hollered, and the Lobos answered with joyous, echoing screeches that froze her blood everywhere but the place on her ankle where the silver knife pressed. That place—it seemed to warm up at the scream as if sensing a challenge.

"What you want for her?" one of the Lobos called, riding out to meet them with an arrow nocked.

"I want the Rangers."

The other Lobos laughed and hollered and shook their bows.

"One skinny woman for all the Rangers? Good joke. Maybe we kill you, too." The feller riding toward them turned his horse right when he got into pistol range and aimed the arrow at Sam's chest.

"She's a virgin," Hennessy shouted. "I checked."

"But she ain't white."

"She's young and beautiful. Exotic."

Nettie barely stopped herself from laughing along with the Lobos.

"I will check the goods. If you are lying, we shoot you, too."

The Lobo jerked his chin, and Sam looked back and muttered, "Hellfire."

Nettie heard hooves on scree and swallowed down the belly-flop of a werewolf sneaking up behind her. The leader trotted up easy as pie and swung off his black-and-white pony. His smile was wolfish, his lap astir as he walked to her and put a hand on her calf, just above where the knife nestled in her boot. She didn't have to feign clumsy fear anymore; her spine was rigid as a mesquite thorn, her throat dry and her middle as wild as a herd of cornered horses with no place to run.

The Lobo man was kind of fascinating up close, if you didn't mind being face to face with a feller who wanted to kill and eat you. His skin was a color just a shade more yellow than hers, his hair black and oiled in a topknot, slightly streaked with gray. His human body was as ridged and spare as the desert, his hands dusty and hard as they roved under her shirt, testing and squeezing greedily. His teeth were straight and round as new tombstones, his grin promising that her meatless bones would be under one soon, if he had any say in it.

"You scared of me, woman?"

It was all she could do to nod as greedy fingers pulled at one teat and then the next.

"Good," he said, then turned to Sam. "She ain't worth much. Two scrawny Rangers, maybe. My choice."

Sam closed his eyes and swallowed hard. Nettie knew as well as he did that the two scrawniest Rangers were also the youngest, the least proven in battle, and the worst with a pistol. But she also instinctively understood that once you got this close to a werewolf, you took the deal or you took a throat full of his teeth. Nettie put her chin up and looked over the feller's shoulder as he reached down her britches and prodded her like half a pig he was thinking of stringing up to smoke. Far away, where the sky was going purple with evening, a dark figure on horseback raised a hand in warning. Nettie exhaled and felt something deep inside her curl up like a dead bug.

"Pure," the man said. "Tight. Maybe not worth two Rangers, though."

"Fine," Sam muttered. "Take her. She's unspoilt, but she's good with her hands, if you know what I mean. Take the horse, too."

As if he wished her dead, Sam untied the pony's rope and tossed it to the Lobo feller, who gave it a hard tug that upset the black pony and nearly unseated Nettie. When he knelt to run hands up the pony's legs with more interest and approval than he'd given her, she had to hold herself back from kicking him in the face. Standing, he nodded in satisfaction, whistled, held up two fingers to his crew, and gabbled at them in a language of grunts and swallows.

"You. You. Go that way, fast," said the Lobo closest to the Rangers. He pointed into the crowd, at two of the most useless fellers. They mounted up right quick and galloped off in the direction the Lobo had pointed. Knowing them, Nettie was amazed that they managed to stay on horseback, riding that fast.

As for Nettie, she kept her head down. Not only so the Rangers maybe wouldn't recognize her, but also to keep her disappointment from showing. The Captain and his best men were still trapped in an ever-smaller circle of panicked horses, surrounded by Injuns who clearly enjoyed messing with their captives like a kitten playing with a half-dead mouse. So far, her cunning idea was not going according to plan, and she still felt the sick burn of the man's hands on her skin. It was only going to get worse. Sam couldn't help her now; she was on her own.

"You go that way," the Lobo said to Sam, and Sam obligingly took off at breakneck speed without another word. It would've been easy for Nettie to believe he was well and truly glad to get rid of her if she hadn't seen the sweat dripping off his nose just before he'd turned to go.

The Lobo leader pulled her pony's rope, and the black stepped so close to his paint that Nettie's leg was nearly touching his chest. No chance of escape there. He untied the knot around her wrists easily and retied it in a tight, complicated knot that required far less rope. With the remaining bit of the lead, he tied a loop around Sam's pony's neck, effectively tethering her to the damn thing. When he was satisfied that she couldn't roll off and run, he mounted up and pulled her pony near. The two horses touched noses and squealed their dislike, and he laughed as the other feller came up behind Nettie's horse, trapping her. The men spoke in their language and laughed, and the satisfied grunt of the feller behind her told her maybe he'd just been given the privilege of second in line.

For the first time, Nettie wished she'd taken the whores up on their offer. A set of fangs would be mighty fine, right now. At least she'd be facing these monsters as equals, or something like it, instead of as a piece of soft meat to be toyed with and devoured.

"You should not trust white men," the Lobo said to her, as if they'd been having a regular conversation and she'd trade two horse turds for his thoughts.

"Never said I did."

He laughed and gave her a sharper glance, and she cursed herself for not holding her tongue.

"I am Scorpion," he said, watching her like a hawk for some

response, which she didn't offer. "Behind you, that is Black Fang. You know what we are?"

She nodded.

"You know what we gonna do to you?"

She swallowed, shivered, and shook her head. "Don't want to know," she muttered.

He laughed again and kicked his pony to a trot. Uneasy as she felt and leggy as Sam's pony was, Nettie now had a hard time sitting the jig without use of her hands. The other Lobos rode out to meet them, the men circling their ponies around her and whooping and shaking their lances and bows.

One of them was reaching for her open shirt when another screeched an alarm, and they both wheeled and took off for the Rangers. One of the Ranger fellers had broken free of the circle and was riding hellbent for the west. Three of the werewolves took off after him, and as they passed the circle of horses, the Captain's Henry barked and took one down to a puff of black sand. Scorpion's head rippled to a wolf's muzzle, and he growled and bared his teeth at Nettie. She didn't have to pretend to be scared shitless, staring into those utterly alien yellow eyes. When his fur rippled back into skin, he reached out with a huge knife and took Sam's black pony down with one nasty slice across the throat.

"Stay here or die, woman."

Hennessy's pony collapsed under her, and Nettie hit the ground in a roll, barely missing having her leg crushed by the thrashing gelding. As if the Lobo had planned it, the horse had fallen on the rope that bound her wrists, and she did her damn best to loosen any of the knots and failed. Tethered this close to a dying beast, she couldn't even get to the knife in her boot. And she couldn't stop crying. No matter how hard she tried to play a man, she had a soft heart for horses and a dire hatred of any creature who killed so easily and uselessly.

As she worked her hands back and forth, trying to get some play and rubbing bloody welts into her wrists, she tried to track what was happening between the Rangers and the Lobos. She couldn't tell which feller had started the break, but now two more fellers were riding at a full run in opposite directions, away from the circle of Rangers and toward the scrub and mountains. Far as she could tell, that made Hennessy, the two green fellers, and three more, including Virgil and Milo Scarsdale, as the brothers were missing. Fourteen Rangers and a coyote girl against eight werewolves, and the Captain still stuck behind a line of horses, his trusted mount a pile of sand. Nettie spit into the dirt. Stupid Rangers. Couldn't they give her an hour to make her plan work before the fools started running around like chickens with chopped-off heads?

The air was thick with arrows and bullets and screams, and Nettie ached to shoot somebody and see sand spray the desert. Her ropes were no looser, despite the slickness of her blood, and none of the damn Rangers had come to save her; any who ran headed in the opposite direction as fast as he could go. Two more of the werewolves dissolved into black blots of sand, their horses standing over the piles as they blew away as if lost without their riders. Another Ranger took off and immediately fell with an arrow through the neck, and his horse ran even faster without him. Nettie turned to scan the direction Hennessy had taken, but he was nowhere to be seen. Even the Injun woman and her dark mount had disappeared from the horizon. Nettie was well and truly alone.

Well, until a paint pony skidded to a stop, inches from her arm.

Scorpion looked down at her, blood painting his shoulder as a bullet popped right out, his skin healing before her eyes.

"Come," he said, and she held up her wrists and gave an experimental tug to show him that no, she damn well couldn't come.

He grunted and slid bonelessly to the ground, snapping the rope with one swipe of his long, wicked knife. Nettie rolled to her knees and stood, and he tossed her leg over the pony like she was a sack of corn. And then he leaped up behind her, his body tight against hers, his man-parts pressing into her back as he settled her closer to the mare's neck.

"Hold the mane," he said near her ear. "You fall off, I just pick you back up. No time to set broken bones."

Nettie barely had time to grasp a handful of mane before the pony leaped into a run. She didn't dare look back at the circled Rangers as Scorpion steered his horse toward the mountains, hard on the heels of his remaining five men. Did that mean the Lobos were giving up on the Rangers? Or chasing someone who'd run off? Not that it mattered—she was going wherever they took her whether she liked it or not.

Straight to hell.

As if following her line of thoughts, Scorpion leaned forward. "For what I will do to you, I want darkness. And privacy." His corded arm slipped around her waist. "And screams."

CHAPTER
22

The Lobos rode hard for what felt like hours but probably wasn't. The land was rumpled and hard as it got closer to the Aspero mountains, as full of nooks and crannies as a chunk of stale bread. Under a cloudy sky as dark as ink, they skipped down arroyos, wound up tight trails, and skittered through scree as they clopped through canyons following a trail Nettie couldn't see. Around every corner, she expected the Rangers to pop up from a clutch of mesquites, but...they never did.

Nettie was grateful when they dropped down to a walk and disappointed when they stopped and dismounted. Well, *dismounted* was a kind word for the way Scorpion shoved her off his pony's back and to the ground. She'd barely gotten to her knees when they'd finished hobbling their horses in a thicket and began climbing up into the buttes on foot. The heavily scarred feller they left guarding the horses pulled a cudgel from behind a rock and set it across his knees with grim determination and a cold smile, and Nettie didn't envy anyone who faced the brute. Scorpion prodded her in the back with the butt of his knife and laughed when she stumbled, forcing her to walk ahead of him up the jagged path. She focused on the flabby buttocks of the feller in front of her, but he quickly hurried out of view, making it all the harder to stay upright without use of her hands as she fought past scrub bushes and mesquite trees.

The rest of the men made it up the butte first and set up camp on a ledge that had seen use before. A blackened fire pit still held chunks of burned wood and bone, while rocks were arrayed in a sort of circle, as if folks like the Lobos had been sitting on them for centuries as they tortured innocent womenfolk. The ledge was hidden from the valley below by boulders and scrappy trees, and Nettie understood that these fellers would gladly rain arrows on anyone who dared venture up the path.

Scorpion pushed her toward a semicircle of rocks that would've made a pleasant place to sleep, had she been camping here with the Rangers. But now, she saw it for what it was: a private little hole that would be impossible to escape if a big feller was blocking the opening.

"Don't move," he said, shoving her down and pointing his knife at her face.

God damn her, she just shook her head and looked down.

For a while, the Lobos went about their business while Nettie tried not to fret and hated herself for failing. All the while, she was working at the knot that bound her wrists, but the danged thing refused to budge. Her heart leaped up when she heard footsteps scrabbling on the rocks, but she should've known nobody would get past that feller with the cudgel. One of the Lobos appeared on the path, half wolf and all covered in blood, carrying the corpse of a Ranger named Tim. He tossed what was left of Tim down near the fire pit and fell onto all fours before the man's torn belly. Nettie turned away at his wolf snout's first wet rip.

For a few golden moments, it seemed as if the werewolves

had forgotten her, thanks to the application of liquor and tender, white flesh. But how could a monster with a strong nose and a pizzle forget a girl waiting, tied up on the ground? As they laughed and ate on Tim and passed around a bottle of whisky they'd pulled from behind some rocks, the fellers each took a moment to hover near her, sniffing and grinning and crawling over her with their eyes. She huddled against the rock, knees to her chin, tied wrists held tight against her chest. It seemed like what a scared woman would do, as Nettie was a scared woman and was doing it.

"Pretty mouth," one man said, running a wide thumb over her trembling lips.

"Little, like a boy," another one grunted. "Gonna hurt."

"You shouldn't have left town, honey," said the next one, and she noticed that under his deep tan and the blood painting his face, he was white. When he grinned, his teeth flashed bits of gold.

The fourth one just grinned and cackled like a coyote as he rubbed himself and licked Tim's blood off his lips. That scared her the most of all.

"Away," Scorpion said, shoving the feller hard enough to make him stumble. Nettie almost thanked him, but then he gave her a similar grin and tossed Tim's bloody saddle blanket at her. "You ready?"

"I . . . I want to wash first," she said.

That just made him laugh harder.

"We all want water in the desert, woman. Don't mean you get it." He had a whisky bottle in his other hand, and he drank deeply, eyes on hers.

"Can I at least have a drink first? I'm right parched."

He sighed in annoyance, his eyes darting from her mouth to the ground she sat on as if she meant more than she was saying.

Without a word, he yanked her up by the rope, tossed Tim's blanket on the ground, spread it out with his foot, and shoved her back down. She fell hard on hands and knees and scuttled back and away. On his knees before her, he pushed the bottle against her lips and tipped it back, forcing her to swallow more of the smoke-hot liquor than she wanted. It blazed a trail to her belly and settled there like fire, an answering, angry heat igniting behind her eyes. The knife all but burned against her leg, and her fingers ached to wrap around the hilt.

No wonder men drank before a fight. The fear was gone, replaced by ferocity.

Nettie had hated Pap and Mam, hated all sorts of nice folks who'd looked at her like she was trash. But she'd never hated anything like she now hated these werewolves.

When Scorpion pulled the bottle away, she spit the last mouthful of liquor in his face.

"Cur-bitch!" With a howl, he dashed the whisky from his eyes and backhanded her in an explosion of pain that made her ears ring. "You been with white men too long. Forgot your manners." Face still wet, he took a long drink and reached for her hands. "I'll teach you better."

Nettie let him pull her hands to his crotch and tried not to make a face as he adjusted the leather flap across his lap. Confused and naïve as she was, the rope bindings made her clumsier still, and she made a great play at not being able to accommodate him, drawing out the time as he drank whisky and wiggled and grunted. No matter how he moved her hands, how he tried to show her what it was he wanted, she acted dumb, and he eventually reached for her face, intending to use a part of her that was thus far unencumbered.

And the whisky's foolhardy bravery ran dry.

She couldn't breathe, and everything in her rebelled and

pulled away and ran hotter than the sun. It was the last straw for a girl who wanted to be a boy, who'd always feared this exact moment but had put herself here for the sake of her friends. Her friends who should've damn well showed up by now—at least Hennessy. Waiting for salvation had never done her a damn lick of good. So she wasn't waiting anymore.

Nettie looked up, checking that the other Lobos were still muzzle-deep in Tim's belly, all wolf and hunger. Swallowing down a mouthful of whisky-tinged spittle and bile, she finally let her shaking hands do exactly what he wanted, hating herself and fate and menfolk in general. Scorpion leaned against the rock, his eyes closed and his head back. Nettie pretended she was—well, shit. There was nothing in life to compare it to. But she kept it up for a few minutes, right up until Scorpion settled further back and groaned. In one swift move, she yanked the knife out of his belt with both hands and cut off the tall, proud thing he'd been so interested in her holding.

Scorpion screamed like he was dying and scrabbled on the ground for the damn thing, but Nettie tossed it over the ledge into the pass below. Fast as a snake, she stuck the knife between her boots and snicked it through the rope between her wrists. Feller's blade was so sharp it only took one hitch, and then she had her silver knife in her right hand and his bloody one in her left, crouched and waiting with her back to the boulder for whatever came at her next.

The head Lobo was a mess of blood under his loincloth, his head gone to wolf and his hands in clawed fists covered in blood that couldn't stop grabbing for what was now gone. Nettie was pretty sure he was going to kill her, but he was too busy watching his business seal over as if he'd never been cut, as if there'd never even been a pizzle there to begin with, just a sad little stump. For just a second, she thought of the child's foot, and how Winifred said it never healed, and she had to figure that maybe the bone was the important part. She tried to laugh, but it came out a sob.

The other fellers charged over at their leader's screams and began stalking her, hackles up and teeth bared in growls, but they had wolf faces and were doing that fool thing dogs do where they attack real slow instead of just leaping. As the first one launched himself at her, a shot rang out, and the beast burst into a cloud of black sand that stung Nettie's eyes.

"Run, fool!" Hennessy shouted.

More gunshots punched the sky, and Nettie scrambled over the boulder and toward the trail down off the butte. Everything went too quiet and easy for a second, and then heavy paws landed on her back, forcing her to the ground. She let loose Scorpion's knife but not her silver one and twisted around under the claws, struggling onto her back as the werewolf snapped at her face and missed. One punch from the silver knife, and the monster writhed around and howled but didn't turn to sand. Heart hammering and flipping like a fish, Nettie yanked out the blade and tried again and again as he snapped at the air, finally rewarded with a face full of black sand that tasted like ash in her mouth.

A wolf squeal and another puff of sand told her one more Lobo was gone, somewhere in the camp. A feller who wasn't Sam whooped, while another feller screamed. Nettie scraped black sand off her mouth and tried to understand what was happening around the fire. Keeping her head low, she peeked out from the jumble of boulders. One wolf was muzzle down in a feller named Blackmoore, who was still mostly alive and dancing around. Nettie reached for where her gun should've been, wishing to hell she had a way to kill one of them damn dogs without getting close enough to smell Tim's blood on its breath. At the very least, Blackmoore deserved an end to his suffering.

"Rhett?"

Sam had her pistol in hand, a few yards off and crouched, spinning in place as he waited for the next attack. But something told Nettie not to answer him. Scorpion was still on the loose, so far as she knew, and the feller had more reason than most to want her dead.

A twig cracked to her left. She pivoted, knife out.

A flash of yellow eyes in the dark made her stomach tighten and writhe. The stalking wolf was big and bloody and had a lot more revenge in its eyes than any wolf had a right to possess.

Nettie swallowed hard, the knife slippery in her hand.

"What's wrong, Scorpion? Did I not learn my manners?" she spit.

In response, he growled, long and low.

"I could try again. Just let me run back down the trail and find your little pizzle."

She wanted to glance over her shoulder and see if Sam had heard her goading the monster, but she knew better than to turn away from an angry dog. Edging back, she fetched up against the boulder, her boots tangled in Tim's blanket. There was no sound in the world but the wolf's growl, no smell but the hot meat breath hissing between huge teeth as it cornered her.

If she died here, would she join the Injun woman?

Hell no. Nettie had no interest in riding double on a wet black mare.

"Come on, monster. Take what you want. If you can."

As if he'd been waiting for her permission, the wolf that was Scorpion leaped, and Nettie jabbed for him with her knife. It sunk in, but the creature's heart must've been smaller than she'd guessed, as the goddamn thing didn't have the good sense to bust into sand. Her fist pressed into a wet spot in his furry chest, her boots fighting for purchase against his blood-soaked belly as she tried her damnedest to keep his teeth from scoring her flesh.

"You need to end this yourself?" Sam asked, but Nettie was fighting too hard to hunt around for him. All she saw was wolf.

"Hell no, Sam! Just shoot him!"

A gun went off, way too close, and the werewolf's nose exploded in a cloud of foul meat. Nettie spit and rolled away as it clawed at its face, and Sam shot again, this time sending Scorpion to black dust that blew away on the desert night, leaving behind a set of fangs, a silver knife, and a bloodied scrap of leather.

Sam was in her face in a heartbeat, firm hands on her shoulder. "Are you hurt? Are you bit?"

Nettie shrank from his touch, still rattled. "Just deaf from your goddamn gun," she muttered.

Acting fussy as an old woman, Sam dusted hands over her hair as if checking for head wounds she hadn't noticed. Another Ranger wandered up, speckled with blood and fur and looking rattled as he rubbed his arm.

"Last one's gone, I guess," he said.

Sam looked him up and down with the same sharp concern. "Are you bit?"

The feller shrugged and showed a gory wound on his arm. "Just a little tooth scrape. Didn't take a big chunk or nothing."

"How long you been riding with the Rangers, Ty?"

"Couple of months." Ty shifted like he'd been eating too many hard beans. "Fights still take me funny, I guess."

A cloud shifted, letting the moon shine down. As Nettie stared at Ty, she could see the wiry gray hairs poke out where his whiskers should've been, altogether more slowly than it had taken the Lobos to transform. Ty scratched and shrugged his shoulders, licking his lips as his teeth started to extend.

"What do we do?" Nettie whispered.

Sam sniffled and dashed at his face. "Same thing a Ranger always does, what a Ranger's sworn to do. We kill what needs to die."

And as Ty stared down, perplexed at the black claws growing out of his nibbled fingertips, Sam shot him right in the chest. A puff of gray sand fell with the boy's clothes, hat, and gun belt, and Nettie shook with a sob.

It was just too much to bear.

Since that first night in the barn, too many people had died in front of her, good men killed by or turned into monsters, monsters turned into sand. As long as she'd dreamed of life off Pap's farm, life among strong men and fast horses, she'd never known how much blood got spilled beyond the badly kept fence. Maybe there was good reason to seek a lazy life, after all.

"Rhett? You're shaking."

Nettie snatched up Ty's sandy hat and smashed it onto her head and down over her face before standing to button her shirt, ignoring how her hands were indeed twitching like a mare vexed with flies.

"Well, it's cold. And I ain't had food in forever. I need your saddlebags, Sam. I need my things. I need..." She ended in a sob.

Hennessy held out the bottle of whisky, then thought better and pulled it back to wipe the blood on the lip off on his pants. Nettie took it and drank, her eyes not leaving his. This is how she figured Monty would've dealt with such a night: Do what needs to be done, wipe off the blood, and drink until the pain burned away for a while. Hennessy nodded once and disappeared in the dark. For a moment there, on top of the butte, Nettie felt like maybe she was the only person left in the whole world, and damned if it wasn't lonesome, as if they'd named her that on purpose, so long ago, when she was just a little thing dreaming of saddles and reckoning Pap was the worst monster in the world.

How wrong she'd been.

Looking over the camp, she saw a puzzle of black and orange, desert sand and black sand mixing with blood and bodies that had been cracked open and left gaping. The whisky came back up in a rush, and she fell to her knees behind the rock as wave after wave of fire gushed out. Her gut felt like it had been scooped raw with a spoon, and she was so desperate to dull it that she stood and drank another gulp of whisky, swishing it around her mouth first.

When she heard the scrabble of footsteps on rock, she froze. Casting around, she found the silver knife and picked it back up. Her hand knew the hilt well, and she moved into the shadow and waited. Had Hennessy had the good sense to kill the scout with the cudgel, down below? And would she ever feel safe again?

The sound that followed was so peculiar and foreign that for a moment, she didn't place it.

Oh.

It was laughter.

A hand slapped on a back, men talking easy as they walked in boots, spurs jingling. The Captain's voice was a bellow in the silent night, Sam's answering, mellow tones a blessing. But still Nettie stayed in her shadowy crevice. Men and monsters, monsters and men. Once you'd seen 'em both in the same pair of eyes, it was awful hard to step out into the light again.

"Rhett?" The thump-clank of a saddlebag hitting the

ground spurred her out of playing at being prey. If she wanted to be a man again, she'd damn well better act like one.

"Here," she hollered, voice gruff.

Footsteps hunted her, and she waved one hand, the one with the knife. The saddlebags clanked again, this time at her feet. She pulled the hard leather into her hidey-hole and turned her back on the men and the fire they were rekindling before unbuttoning her shirt and rewrapping her chest. By the time she'd tidied herself up and pulled Ty's hat lower, the fellers had a good bonfire going, and Delgado was trying to make yesterday's beans edible with strips of meat that smelled far too similar to human flesh.

Nettie's stomach turned. Whisky was the devil.

"You coming out, Rhett?" the Captain called.

Nettie hefted the saddlebags over her shoulder and put on the sort of grim grin she reckoned a hero should wear after fighting a pack of werewolves.

"Reportin' for duty," she said.

The camp was entirely different from when the Lobos had claimed it. The fire was big and cracking, the rocks around it covered by tired Rangers sharing water skins. Jiddy had biscuits dug down among the cherry hot logs, and one of the younger fellers had found another half-full bottle of whisky and was passing it around. The splotches of red had been cleaned off the bottle's green glass, but the sight of the damn thing made Nettie near to yarking again. The spot where Tim's body had lain showed black and tan sand mixed and piled over a bloodstain. Far off, another fire sent white smoke into the sky, and Nettie watched it curl up, hoping wherever Tim and Moran and the other fellers had gone on to, there weren't any werewolves in the afterlife. When a pair of vultures took to circling over the smoke, she had to look away.

"Hennessy here says you took down half the Lobos on your lone," the Captain said, looking her up and down.

Nettie shook her head, fighting the flush creeping up her neck. "I took down a couple, Captain, but if Hennessy and Ty hadn't showed up with pistols, I'd be howling at the moon, close as I can reckon."

"Where is Ty?"

"Bit," Sam mumbled.

The Captain swept off his hat and held it to his chest. "Goddammit. Ty was coming along right fine. We lost five men tonight. But it could've been worse." Smashing his hat back over his gray hair, he narrowed his eyes at Nettie, then at Sam. "What happened to the woman?"

Sam was just about to open his fool mouth when Nettie jumped in and said the craziest thing she could think of: the truth.

"There weren't no woman, Captain. I just covered up and acted like a fool. Sam wouldn't send a woman into a werewolf camp."

The Captain tugged at his mustache, his eyes dead as stone as he looked her up and down. "Them werewolves must've been blind and dumb then, son. I can't believe you boys got away with it."

"Rhett's a damn brave feller." Sam's voice was strained, but the truth could do that just as easily as a lie.

With a solemn nod at Nettie, the Captain turned his measuring gaze on Sam. "By my reckon, you took down at least four Lobo wolves tonight, Hennessy." Sam nodded once, his jaw wound tighter than a watch. Reaching into his pocket, the Captain pinned a shiny badge to Sam's collar. "It's about damn time. You did good, Ranger."

"Thank you, Captain."

The older man took a step back, pulled a rolled cigarette from behind his ear, and stuck it on his lip. "We kill what needs to die, boys. Don't mean we like it. Get some sleep, if you can. We'll have a service for the lost boys in the morning."

"Then what, Captain?" Nettie asked.

A high whinny carried on the wind, wavering like it was underwater. The Captain shook his head and stuck a finger in his white-haired ear.

"You know what, son. We keep on after the Cannibal Owl, fast as the horses can carry us. We do what needs to be done."

With a nod, the Captain moseyed to the fire and squatted to light his smoke. Sam's eyes met Nettie's, and he seemed a foot taller and a good deal harder, now that he had his badge.

"Congratulations, Hennessy."

Sam held up his collar to admire the flash of firelight on brass, his mouth twisted up funny.

"Thanks. I guess. Speaking of which..." Sam made as if to shake her hand, and she felt cool metal in her palm. Her badge. She gave him a nod of respect and pinned it back on.

"Where you bedding down, Rhett?"

Nettie scouted around the camp and jerked a thumb at an empty place near the fire and away from Tim's blood and Scorpion's pile of sand.

Without a word, Sam laid out his bedroll just beside the spot she'd indicated and went to fetch his saddle. Nettie dragged Tim's saddle blanket over and curled up beside Sam's blanket but not too close. He was gone for a while, so long that she began to worry and imagine him ripped apart by wolves, and she wondered if she would ever relax again, now that she cared about somebody. But eventually, as he always seemed to, Sam showed up smiling, dropped her saddle and blanket on the ground, and muttered, "Your dang mare misses you something awful."

Nettie's heart wrenched so hard she could only look away and nod. She tossed Tim's blanket on the fire and settled down with her own kit, glad to breathe in Ragdoll's good, sweet scent. "They killed your black pony, Sam."

"Could've been worse. He was a good feller, though, and I'll miss him."

It was as close as they could come to apologies.

When he handed her a bowl of beans and a biscuit, she shoveled it into her mouth as if filling in a hole, right up until her spoon scraped on tin, then quickly lay on her back, hoping it would all stay down where it belonged. Long after Sam was asleep with his hand on his new badge and his hat over his eyes, Nettie watched the stars and listened for the far-off whinny of a wet black mare. Soon the Rangers were nothing but snores and farts as Delgado slunk around the campfire, fetching the bowls and scouring out what was left with sand.

"I know what you are."

Nettie jerked up at the hissed whisper, but Delgado was focused on his bowls, mouth closed and frowning. Surely the cook hadn't spoken to her? Surely he didn't know? She watched him for a minute, and when he looked up, held his gaze.

"You say somethin', Delgado?"

He only shook his head.

Which figured, as somebody had told her, long ago, that the feller was missing his tongue.

Soon the fire was just a smudge, and Delgado was gone, and Nettie couldn't keep her tired, sand-burned eyes open for another damn minute. When she fell asleep, she imagined forever being the scared woman she'd been for just a few hours, her hands tied and her head bent. She rode pillion behind the

Injun woman on the wet black mare, leading the Rangers to vengeance with her tongue cut out.

The next morning, she looked around the waking camp and realized that something was deeply wrong. Someone was missing, and Nettie hadn't seen the familiar and annoying figure since Sam had pulled away to check his horse's hooves for stones, long before the werewolves had attacked.

Winifred was gone.

CHAPTER 23

Winifred was gone, and no one seemed to notice. Or care.

Nettie sat up, her head stuffy and her belly aching. Hennessy had already tidied up his bedroll and gone off to do whatever fellers did in the morning. He'd left her some jerky and a biscuit, and at first, she was angry as a one-eyed mule that he thought she needed his protection and help just because she was a girl. Then she bit off a hunk of the jerky and felt her mouth pool up with spit and realized how hungry she'd been.

Maybe he would've left breakfast for a boy.

Maybe she wouldn't punch him again. Today.

But now she wasn't sure who to ask about Winifred. She didn't see Jiddy or the Captain or any of the Rangers she knew by name and could approach without being too skittish. And after last night, she was still mighty skittish of men.

One of the fellers had coffee boiling in a pot, and the smell was highly seductive. Pap had had coffee, now and then, whenever he'd managed to fleece some fool into paying too much for a nag Nettie had gentled. Mam had always done it up thick with a few squirts of fresh cow's milk, and when it was gone, Nettie had had a fondness for sticking her nose in the cup and swishing the dark brown grains around her mouth. If it was that rare, it had to be pretty good, she reckoned. So she didn't so much like it as admire it, and the smell made her mightily crave as much as she could swallow down.

After packing up her things, she shuffled over to the feller with the coffee and stood a polite distance away.

"You want a cup?" he asked.

"How much?"

The feller snorted and handed her a dented tin cup with blue speckles. "You're a Ranger now, Rhett. Ain't nobody gonna charge you for trail food."

Nettie gave him a nod and accepted the mug.

"That's mighty fine," she said after an appreciate slurp. The man grunted and poked some eggs, but at least he wasn't looking at her, which made her feel a bit bolder. "Say, you know what happened to Winifred?"

The feller looked up, squinted, and scratched his parts. "Is that one of the horses?"

Nettie hid her sneer behind her cup. "Never mind. Many thanks for the coffee."

Winifred, a horse?

These fellers really didn't see the coyote girl at all, did they?

Nettie was still mighty tempted to goad the man, so she went a little ways away to enjoy the coffee on her own terms before she said something foolish that meant she'd never get to drink it again. The Ranger feller made it different from Pap and Mam, and there wasn't any cow's milk for it, nor even any cows nearby. It tasted a bit like ashes and dirt, but the warmth set up camp on top of the jerky and biscuits in her stomach in a right friendlier way than the whisky had. At least she hadn't kept enough of the damn firewater down to make her sick this morning.

Considering she wasn't about to ask another stranger about

the coyote-girl, she might as well take her goddamn time enjoying life for five minutes, at least until the Captain or Sam showed up. Nettie found a convenient rock and pulled her knees up to enjoy the sun rising on the prairie. Far below, half hid by mesquite, the Rangers' horses milled with the siren's horses and a couple of Lobo paints in friendly competition for a little grain. Nettie hoped to see Winifred there, among the creatures who wouldn't judge her, but all she saw was Sam. The boy walked among the horses with fond pats and gentle admonitions. He'd always been good with horses. Nettie couldn't help smiling. Things would be different between them—hell, how could it be the same, after all they'd been through? But whatever they'd be from here on out, at least one person knew her secret and would still run into a camp of angry werewolves to save her skin.

Winifred would probably do that, too, but Nettie still hadn't seen hide nor hair of the girl, and it made her twitchy.

"This seat taken?"

Nettie just about jumped out of her boots and ended up spilling half her remaining coffee. The Captain had appeared from nowhere to sit beside her, his eyes crinkling up as if to say that even old dogs had their tricks.

"I reckon you can sit anywhere you goddamn please, Captain." She took a sip of the coffee, just to show him she could, and he settled back and spit a stream of tobacco juice at a fractious grasshopper.

Just when Nettie thought maybe they were going to sit and enjoy the sunrise together as men, the Captain said the last thing she'd ever expected him to say:

"I'm sorry, Rhett."

Nettie coughed up some coffee, and he whacked her helpfully

on the back until she had enough breath to say, "What the Sam Hill for, Captain?"

The Captain exhaled, a long and sad sound. "You did something brave last night, son. You sacrificed yourself for the Rangers, and I'm just damned sorry at what almost happened to you." He paused and cocked his head sideways. "It was *almost*, wasn't it? Boy?"

After clearing her throat and pitching her voice lower, she nodded. "Yessir. I reckon that was about as almost as you can get."

"The Rangers—well, it ain't easy to be one of us. Plenty of people think we're the bad guys, just because they don't know which war we're truly fighting. Durango territory is a place wilder still than most, and by the time news reaches a town, all that's left of the monsters is sand and ashes. We keep folks safe, and they villainize us for it. That's a word, ain't it, Rhett? *Villainize*?"

"I don't rightly, Captain."

"Well, it is now, I reckon. Thing is, most folks don't know what we give up, much less what we lose with every fight. And nobody but me and Sam know precisely what you almost sacrificed for us last night. If them werewolves had got what they wanted before Hennessy and the boys showed up..." He trailed off, shook his head. "I'd just feel mighty bad. I had a daughter once, you know. Got stole away by chupacabras while I was waging the wrong war. Maybe that's why I fight so hard. Never know who you might be able to save, if you just kick your horse a little harder and have enough bullets in your pocket."

His worn hand reached out, patted her knee so quick she was almost sure she'd missed it.

Nettie's heart was beating like a rabbit in a snare, sure he was gonna send her home and trap her in petticoats, maybe even pack her back to Pap's house. Because he'd all but admitted he knew what she was, hadn't he?

"Captain?"

The old man stood and looked her up and down. His eyes didn't linger over her lips, her chest, nor even her watering eyes. Flicking her badge, he said, "Don't you ever try that play again, boy. Might get more than a mouthful of sand. But on behalf of the Rangers, I thank you kindly. Never did want to die at the hands of a wolf, myself."

The sun chose that exact moment to escape the horizon, spilling cherry-red light over the prairie like a river of blood and throwing the old man's bones into sharp relief. Nettie could barely breathe, recognizing that she was about to say something that couldn't be unsaid. "So I'm still a Ranger?"

The Captain snorted and spit a stream of brown juice at the sun. "Why the hellfire wouldn't you be? You do your duty, you'll always be welcome with us." He took a few steps, spurs clinking, then turned around to wink at her. "Unless you break Hennessy's heart. That would be a right damn shame."

Hardly believing that he would let a girl mess up his company, Nettie almost forget the most important question she'd wanted to ask him.

"What about Winifred?" she asked. "I haven't seen her since the shoot-out."

"She ran off last night on your paint pony. Ain't seen her since. But her brother's down there with the horses, and he's waiting for you. Don't break his heart, neither."

Nettie hopped up and put the empty coffee cup in the Captain's hands before walking down the trail.

"I ain't here to break hearts, Captain. I'm a Durango Ranger. And I'm here to kill what needs to die."

Ragdoll's whinny was a welcome distraction from dealing with the tangled-up trouble of a confused cowpoke named Hennessy who still wore her knuckle prints on his jaw. At least her skin hid her bruises. He gave her something like his old smile and kept at his work, and she blushed and went to her mare.

Nettie didn't know how to go about apologizing to a horse, but she scratched Ragdoll in all the places she figured a creature without fingers might itch and fetched an extra handful of grain from Delgado's packs. Dan sat on a rock, doing nothing in particular as he stared into the sky. Sam was half ignoring her and half being anxious on her behalf, hovering just out of her range and staring with his eyebrows all rumpled up. That was what finally made her talk—the way he was looking at her like she might suddenly shatter like a tea cup.

"Lord, Hennessy. You look like a church woman watching fellers jingle into the saloon on Saturday night, like my soul might fall out and roll down the street if you don't pray hard enough. If you're so concerned, you might as well wish me good morning."

Sam shook his head and tugged on his bandanna. "Morning, Rhett."

"Morning, other Hennessy. You and Dan been jawin', I reckon."

Sam snorted, a welcome sound, as it wasn't focused on her. "Shit, no. Can't get two words out of the fool. Just sits there, muttering." He flapped a hand at Dan and headed up the path toward what Nettie suspected was whatever was left of the beans. "Good luck not shooting him."

As soon as Hennessy was out of range, Dan rose from where he sat, his face solemn and his body tense. Without a word, he picked up his bundle, turned his back, and walked right past Nettie, close enough to stir the air on her sleeve.

"Come. There's something you need to see."

Nettie looked at the horses, then watched Dan head toward a gathering of tall rock formations. She'd noticed the hard line of his mouth and the fact that his eyes weren't dancing like usual, not one damn bit. Dan's back was straight, his feet dusty, his hair desperately tangled. And she knew that even if it was against the Captain's orders and even if she didn't want to go, she had to follow the damn fool.

Coyote Dan moved like a cloud, brushing through the land like he could dissolve and re-form and disappear, if he needed to. Obstacles didn't seem like obstacles to him, and the underbrush bowed to let him pass. When he started up a deer path into a rock face that had looked mostly solid, Nettie tied on her bandanna and did her best to keep up, although it took her a lot more damn effort. Little lizards startled out of her way where they waited for the sun's morning breath, and a few sleepy snakes still curled in dark crevices, enjoying the last of the night's cool caress. The slivered moon hung like a cat's claw caught in the clouds. Nettie felt tangled between the real world and dreaming, between night and dawn, between yesterday and tomorrow. And most definitely between a rock and a hard place, as she had to clamber up and over all sorts of deadfalls and stones and clattering scorpions. It was not, by any stretch of the imagination, a pleasant walk.

And still Dan didn't speak.

Finally, he disappeared behind a scrub-covered outcrop, and Nettie followed him through and pushed out onto the top of a butte, higher up than she'd ever been in her life. The whole thing was about the size of Gloomy Bluebird, almost long enough across to get in four beats of a canter before the horse would fall to its death, if it was stupid enough to oblige. Strangely, she didn't feel a bit of fear at the height; it felt right homey. There was something sweet about being so far up, above the petty misdeeds of the world. Satisfying, that's what it was.

Dan didn't look back at her, didn't say a goddamn thing. He just walked over to a pile of rocks, sat down on a weathered piece of cowhide, and started banging stones together like a goddamn fool.

Nettie took her time, enjoying the butte. She peered over the eastern edge, hunted for the Injun woman, picked Ragdoll out of the herd, and found a jackrabbit in the clouds before moseying over to the place where Coyote Dan sat, cross-legged, knocking rocks together. She almost started joshing him, but then she realized what he was doing. With each careful, sharp smack, a sliver of rock sheared off, leaving a pile of cleverly shaped shards. Danged if the feller wasn't making himself a mess of arrowheads and other blade-looking chunks. And danged if the area around him didn't show that the butte had a history of such use. Neat piles of shards, bigger chunks, broken pieces, and ready, round stones suggested that it was a popular place to bang rocks, if a feller had the knack.

"You planning for war, Dan?" Nettie pulled down Monty's bandanna, settled down on her haunches, and reached out a hand like she might touch one of the arrowheads, then realized he might take offense and jerked her arm back, all casual-like.

"A wise man doesn't plan war. He spends every day of his life preparing for the war that he knows will find him."

"Looks like you're plannin' harder than usual," she observed.

With a hard snort, Dan sorted through the slivers of stone

and held up a serrated triangle that looked like a giant cat's tooth. "I like to know the monster I'm hunting. I like to study it, know how hard I'll have to cut to find its heart. This time I don't." A ghost of his old smile flittered across his face like the last butterfly of summer. "Means I need lots of sharp things, just in case."

"You worried about the Cannibal Owl?"

Dan looked up, his usual calm utterly departed. "Pia Mupitsi took my sister last night, Nettie. At the very least, Winifred went after it herself and was captured. So, yes, you could say I'm worried."

A chill skittered down Nettie's spine.

"How do you know the Cannibal Owl's got Winifred? Maybe she's lost. Maybe she went to the next town over for a bath with rose-stinkin' soap. Maybe she's hunting down another dress off some old lady's clothesline."

Without a word, Dan reached behind him, to the bundle he always carried. Long fingers shook as he unwrapped the coyote-tooth-marked, water-stained, beat-all-to-hell leather. The object revealed was almost the same warm brown as the tanned doeskin but smoother, softer, altogether more familiar.

It was a foot.

Winifred's foot.

CHAPTER 24

Nettie flat out didn't know what to say. *Sorry your sister's foot got cut off* didn't really cover the depth of terror she was feeling and that his face was showing. She couldn't help thinking about the child's foot she'd once held, once watched dissolve into so much shifting sand, or what it'd felt like to watch the light fade from Monty's eyes. As if sensing her sudden fear and sharing the same concern, Dan twitched the leather back over the foot and placed it gently on the ground. Maybe, so long as they weren't looking at it, it wouldn't dissolve.

"And the woman you left in Burlesville..." He sighed and shook his head.

"Regina?"

"She had her baby. And it was taken from her arms in the night. She was alone when the Cannibal Owl came. She was distraught. Hanged herself the next morning."

Nettie waited for more, but Dan simply picked up his stones and made more blades.

"At least Winifred's still alive" was all Nettie could manage, and it left her so dry-mouthed that she would've chewed a chunk of cactus just to swallow again. "She has to be."

"For now."

"But we're close, right? Don't that mean we're awful close?"

Dan stood, slow as an old man with aching bones, walked to the butte's dark edge, and gestured to the shadowy west, where the peaks left long swaths of purple prairie untouched by the rising sun. "Look for yourself. This is why I brought you up here: to see what lies in your path."

Nettie held up a hand to shield her eyes and squinted. The area got right strange, on the other side of the butte. The stacked rocks made hallways of stone leading up to the mountains, jagged and dark. In a thicket of gray thorns, a familiar shadowed figure sat on a wet, black horse, finger pointing up and still farther west. Following the Injun woman's bone claw, Nettie saw only stark trees clustered around caves carved into the mountainside. One big tree sprawled menacingly like the mountains' gate, skeletal and sharp. At first, Nettie thought the lumpy shapes among the branches were dead leaves gone brittle and gray. But when they shifted unnaturally and sparked, she recoiled with a hiss.

"More goddamn harpies."

Dan's laugh was short and sharp. "Did you know a group of vultures is called a wake? As if they waited for a funeral instead of causing one. A normal person walking past would see only useful scavengers waiting to pick off the weak and old or to feast after a battle."

But Nettie saw cruel, blue-eyed bird-women with hanging dugs, sharpening their beaks against the bark and preening. As the sun topped the rise, their razor-sharp feathers shone like blades and screeched like steel as they shifted and stretched.

Like they were getting ready for war.

Like they were hungry.

"Do the buzzard-women work for the Cannibal Owl?"

"I already told you. They are scavengers. They go where blood and meat are easy to find. Don't you see the valley below their perch? They've been here a long time. Feeding."

When Nettie looked down, she almost lost her coffee.

It was bones.

All bones.

Small bones.

Piled under the trees, scattered among the rocks, lining the little creek like they were barreling up to the bar for a drink. Years and years of bones, some washed clean by sun and rain and others still mucky with patches of skin that the harpies hadn't yet picked away. All the size of children, their skulls heaped under the trees and tangled in the roots.

"Dan?"

"Yes?"

"Why hasn't anybody killed this goddamn Cannibal Owl yet?"

They stood, side by side, staring down at the valley of death.

"Because no one could find it. Or catch it."

Nettie took a deep breath, felt her stomach wobble as she honed in on a cave half hidden by the rocks. "That's a lie, ain't it?"

"Yes."

"What's the truth?"

"You know the truth, Nettie. You know why the Ghost Mother draws you here."

On any other day, she would've laid into him for being shifty, but today, she just nodded. "Because nobody knows how to kill it, do they? Because nobody else can."

Dan nodded. "People fear monsters. Monsters fear the Cannibal Owl."

Nettie reached for Dan's hand and took the arrow point from him.

"And the Cannibal Owl's going to fear me," she said.

They spent the morning practicing different ways to kill the unkillable.

Nettie took to it like a possum to water.

It was too late for her to master arrows, so Dan taught her the ways to hold a knife, the ways to strike. Overhand, underhand, slashing for the eyes, plunging deep for the heart. He showed her where even the sharpest blade would skitter over ribs, where it would sink into soft spots like a broom straw into biscuits. Again and again, she rose from a crouch with a sparkling blade of quartz or the silver knife yanked from her boot. Again and again, she slashed for the man's tender parts, pulling back at the last second, knowing that the Cannibal Owl would be in no way tender.

No one had ever seen it, not really.

Pia Mupitsi was a nightmare, a hole in the starlight holding a silver spike.

Pia Mupitsi was the absence of the wind, the sound of no sound, a feather left in an empty cradle, nothing like an apology.

Pia Mupitsi, Nettie Lonesome told herself, would be dead by the next day's dawn.

She didn't know what it was that made her special, made her the Shadow, but she could feel the rightness of it in her bones, lighting her from within like the spark of a fire catching tinder.

She had a crystal point to Dan's neck now, her knife tip pressing over his heart. He shoved her arm aside and stood as if she weighed nothing, holding out his hand to help her up.

"Again," she muttered, muscles aching.

"No. You need rest and food."

"What about Winifred? What about the Javelina children?"

"You can't save them if you can't fight."

"I want to fight now, Dan."

He shook his head and reached for Nettie's hand, unclench-ing her fingers from the white quartz blade he'd wrapped in leather when her blood had rendered it too slippery for her to hold. Her knuckles were grazed, her palms laced with weeping blisters that kept reopening.

"Pia Mupitsi is a creature of the night. Enjoy this day, for it might be your last."

Nettie stretched her fingers and laughed, a sad sound stolen by the wind.

"Bullshit, Dan. Either I kill the owl, or I die and join the Injun woman on the back of a black horse and watch it steal more children. I got plenty of folks to haunt. Whatever hap-pens tonight, I ain't done. And tomorrow's the new moon. So it has to be tonight."

The smile Dan gave her made it clear a fanged trickster lurked always under his skin. "I didn't say anything about enjoying the night. I said to enjoy the day. If you fail, you'll never see sunlight again, but you'll get more than enough moon."

She slid the knife back into her boot and wiped her hands off on her pants. "Remind me again of why this is my fight. Ain't you and the Rangers gonna be there, too? With two dozen guns and every chunk of sharp stone you can muster?"

Dan wagged his head at her like she was a dumb dog that just wouldn't learn, but she still followed him as he gathered up his blades and leather bundle and took off for the trail. Vexed as she was, she knew goddamn well that she'd never find her way off the high butte without him. And she also figured he had an answer that would be equal parts truth and fury. She forgot, sometimes, that they were little more than children. She, Dan, Winifred, Sam—none of them were even twenty-five, and yet Dan acted like he was wiser than the Captain himself, the uppity son of a bitch.

Halfway down the ragged path, he finally answered.

"We'll be there. But I suspect it won't matter. All fights, all battles, lead to the moment where two beings test their tenacity, their will to live. One will die, one will prevail. No matter how many bodies clog the river, the last man standing is the only man that counts. And all the signs point to you."

"I'm the last man standing?"

He looked her up and down. "Hopefully not. I'd like to stand, as well."

She wouldn't let herself think about Winifred's foot and whether the girl would ever stand on it again. Could it be reattached, if Nettie managed to kill the Cannibal Owl before it ate Winifred?

"That's another question I got, Dan. How can this monster eat monsters? Didn't the Rangers tell me that monsters would burrow back out of you? And when you kill them, don't they turn to sand? So how can that valley be full of little baby bones?"

Dan shook his head. "Magic doesn't care for logic. Maybe that's why it only eats children, because they stay put in its belly. Maybe because they have small teeth and can't chew their way out. Maybe all the bones are from human children. There is plenty of sand in that valley, too. No, I don't wish to know what laws let the Cannibal Owl rule over death. I just want to know the laws that will let death finally rule over the Owl."

Nettie had to concentrate on every step down the butte, as the path was invisible until Dan had trod it. By the end, she could barely walk, and her hands stung like hell. With a final hop, they landed on the prairie. Nettie felt smaller down here, tiny and useless and altogether too squishy and easily killed. On top of the butte, she was an eagle; down here, she was a rabbit—and not the kind with fangs. She didn't know where the Cannibal Owl's heart might lie, but the creature knew exactly how easily her own life could be snuffed. They might call it an owl, but whatever it truly was, it was clever enough to avoid detection, to send pointed messages in the form of body parts.

And to swoop down and take its tribute from a new mother, snatching its prey from the middle of a carefully guarded, civilized town. Poor Regina.

Nettie couldn't help wondering what exactly it was that separated man from monster. Vultures with blue eyes, wolves that could walk as men. Was evil only evil if you did it on purpose? She'd always figured predators were predators and prey were prey. But then again, she'd always figured men were men and women were women and men wanted to be with women, and…

Hellfire.

The world was not a place of black and white, night and day. It was shades of gray and shadows, dusk and dawn, in-between moments and shifting sands. And somehow, knowing that nothing was permanent or real made it easier for Nettie to slip into her own skin. For the first time, she stopped trying to be something else and accepted that what she was was as real and fine as what anybody else was.

Her hand caught the small leather bag tapping against her hip and holding all the bits and bobs that had outlined her life, right down to one of Scorpion's wolf teeth, added just last night. The vampire's fangs, her first nickel from Monty, a chunk of arrowhead, even the tip of the mesquite thorn Dan had pulled from her shoulder—he'd added it while she was unconscious, that night, along with a smaller pouch that he told her not to open.

"Guard your magic," he'd said. "Even from yourself. Until you need it most."

She liked that—carrying her magic with her. Everything she'd been through, good and bad, had brought her to this moment, to this task.

They wanted her to be the Shadow?

Fine. She was the Shadow.

Because a shadow was a thing that defined itself, and Nettie didn't have to fit anyone else's shape. From the knife in her boot to the gun hanging low on her hip, she didn't mind shooting anybody or anything that disagreed.

She stepped into the camp a man of her own making, a Ranger and the Shadow, unstoppable.

"You look different, Rhett. What the Sam Hill did y'all do up there?"

Nettie's gaze swiveled over to Hennessy, who seemed somehow shorter than he'd been. She couldn't explain everything that had happened on the butte, couldn't quite put it into words in a way a feller as simple and pure as Sam could understand. Seeing Winifred's foot, watching the harpies play among the skulls, absorbing her destiny like parched land sucking up the long-awaited rain. Instead of answering, she looked up at the butte, to where she'd stood and looked down. The harsh red rock was impossibly tall now, with no visible path to the summit. Shielding her eyes, she thought she saw a figure there, looking back down, a little girl with long pigtails and a patched nightdress staring back at her. When she blinked, the figure was gone.

Once, she'd answered whenever a white man had spoken to her.

Now she understood that silence was sometimes the only answer.

When Nettie didn't respond, Sam cocked his head and wrinkled up his nose. "Did Dan work his Injun magic? Did you find your spirit animal or something?"

Dan snorted, and Nettie raised her chin. "I'm my own spirit animal," she said.

And walked on.

In the valley beyond the horses, the Rangers were practicing with their guns, shooting cacti full of holes while training the newer horses not to care about the sound of bullets.

"Care to fire off a few rounds?" the Captain called.

Nettie shook her head. "Reckon this fight'll be more personal," she answered.

When she walked on, he didn't protest. Just turned back to shooting the world full of holes.

She went to the horses next, said sweet, earnest things to the ugliest mare in the valley. Ragdoll forgave her, at least enough to use Nettie's butt as a scratching post for her nose. Fat little Puddin' was back, too, all scratched-up and skitty and wearing a sweat stain in the shape of Winifred. Nettie rubbed him over and fed him a handful of grain, sorry he hadn't been fast enough to keep Winifred safe. She wondered who would ride her ponies if she died. And because they were quiet and didn't care who she was or ask anything of her, she stayed among the horses until the sky went soft and purple-gray, the clouds roiling low and dark and the hangnail moon rising.

At some point in time, Dan disappeared to his own devices, and that was fine. For once, it felt good to be lonesome.

By the time she found the Rangers and dinner, Delgado's pot was as empty as his smile.

He showed her both.

Nettie realized Delgado did not like her.

And she realized she did not like Delgado.

Coyote Dan sat a little away from the Rangers, wearing her old clothes and squinting at his newly made blades. When she jerked her chin at him, he rose. Together, they walked away from the camp, away from the river and the bones and the harpies. Without speaking, companionable as wild things, they aimed for a green muddle of scrub and mesquite. Nettie pulled one of Dan's stone knives from her boot, pricked a finger, let her blood drip down on the prairie.

When the rabbits came near to lick up the red drops, she caught two by the ears.

Dan made the fire. Nettie stripped the skins and tossed the fangs into the flames. They roasted the meat in silence. This time, Nettie took as much as she wanted. The leather bundle twitched beside Dan's knee but did not deflate into sand. As Nettie sucked the hot bones clean and looked into the small fire, the sun curved downward and lit the sky in reds and violets, blood and bruises.

"Soon?" she asked.

"Midnight," Dan answered.

"Can I ask you a question?"

As if sensing it was a bigger question than usual, Dan put down his rabbit and stared at her, really stared at her. He nodded once.

"The Injun woman...she told me in a dream that the Cannibal Owl knew my past. Knew my...my tribe. Do you think that might actually be true, or was the ghost just trying to give me another reason to go do her revenge?"

Dan shook the rabbit bones off his roasting stick and used it to draw figures in the sand. Since Nettie didn't have any school, she didn't know if they were letters in English or some other language, or if maybe he was just giving himself some time to think.

"The ghost has no reason to lie. And if she did, how would she know the one thing you most long to know? The workings of gods and monsters is beyond what most of us can reckon."

"So you think it might actually give me answers?"

"They call Pia Mupitsi the Ghost Mother. Maybe sometime, long ago, it had a heart."

"That don't make me feel any better."

He cracked the stick in half and tossed it in the fire. "I can't imagine what would."

The moon was as tiny and thin as it could get before it was nothing, and Nettie held her thumb over it for a moment, wishing she could shove it back down like a fishbone and lure the sun back up in its stead. "I reckon this is how a feller feels waiting for the noose."

"Then you're looking at it wrong."

"How you figure that?"

Dan's grin was a feral, sharp thing, his eyes coyote green. "Don't you see? You're the one holding the noose."

Nettie went back to settle with Hennessy and the Rangers for a bit, as Dan said he wanted to be a coyote for a while. He figured he'd be more useful if he could sniff around for more clues that the nose of a sensitive critter might pick up more readily with no men around to mess things up. Nettie still didn't know how she was supposed to get to the Cannibal Owl, and she knew Dan was her best goddamn chance to find its trail, so she gave him his space, and welcome.

The last thing he said to her was "Don't leave without me." And then hair was sprouting up his back like pea shoots in spring, and he curled over and yipped as he ran away.

Nettie had nudged his leather bundle with a toe and watched him go, her pockets heavy with his stone blades. Funny, how a feller could tell you not to leave without him while he turned his back on you and ran. And where had he left his bow? She understood that he thought it would be a close fight, but she'd enjoyed knowing that Coyote Dan would be waiting somewhere out of sight with his arrow nocked and ready. Destiny was fine and all, but she'd rather have the deck stacked in her goddamn favor when it came to killing unkillable monsters.

"Take a seat, Rhett. You got to be plum tuckered out, after a day in the sun." Hennessy scooted over in a puff of sand, patting the ground beside him.

"Reckon I'm too jumpy, other Hennessy, although I thank you kindly."

Right that moment, Nettie wished for nothing more than to be alone with Sam Hennessy. Not for any untoward reason— just because there was a comfort in a friendship where a feller knew exactly who she was and didn't want much from her, other than companionship. But as Nettie watched, Hennessy gave a great, jaw-cracking yawn and nodded, staring dreamily off into space.

"Care for some whisky, Rhett?"

The Captain held up the bottle, but Nettie noticed he didn't drink from it himself. Come to think of it, she'd never seen his whiskers moist with liquor. The rest of the Rangers had surely had a sip or more. They sat around the fire, some flopped back against saddles and some squatting and others perched on rocks they'd rolled over from nearer the buttes. It was right comforting, being among the men again. Their empty, dented bowls were stacked and tossed beside gooey spoons that Delgado should've already been scouring off with sand.

The Rangers were doing their level best to give off an air of relaxation and ease, but any feller with sense could see that underneath the calm they were jittery as junebugs at a jaybird party. Jiddy's flat stare would've made Nettie's skin crawl just a few short days ago, but now she knew it for what it was: fear.

"No thanks, Captain. I had enough the other night to last me awhile."

The Captain nodded and handed the bottle to the next feller. "Reckon you did. You eaten your fill? Ready for what's coming? We took down a little mountain goat earlier and got Delgado to cook up a second round of stew. Better by half than the beans we had earlier." He inclined his leonine head slightly, inviting her to sit, and Nettie squatted down by his side. She'd never felt the equal of such a grand man and might've fallen over, if she'd stayed standing. Her belly was flip-flopping all over, thanks to sitting between the Captain's pocket watch and Jiddy. "Delgado. Get Rhett a bowl. Best supper the bastard's ever served up."

The scrappy little cook hurried over with a blue bowl brimming with steaming hot stew, but the smell turned Nettie's already wiggly stomach. She shook her head and held up a hand.

"I already ate some rabbit, thank you kindly. If I'm to die tonight, I'd rather it not be from Delgado's cooking."

With a strained grunt, Delgado pushed the bowl at her more forcefully, slopping meat and gravy onto her boots.

Nettie stood and knocked the bowl to the ground. Half the contents spilled into the fire, and Delgado jumped back, his hands in fists.

"Don't push me, Delgado."

She'd have punched him right there if the Captain hadn't hollered, "Stop, boys!"

Nobody could move a muscle when he spoke in that voice. Nettie and Delgado were squared up, hands in fists, fire flickering over their faces. She was taller than him, but he was a wiry feller, in his forties at least and built like a handful of stiff rope, covered in the scars of past fights. Had they been in a fair tussle, she didn't know if she could win. And as it was, she had no rightly idea why the rest of the cowpokes were just flopping around like sleepy cows instead of jumping up at the prospect of a brawl. Even the Captain was still sitting, for all his shout had rent the night. And then, slow as you please, the bowl slipped from his hands and clanked against his spurs.

Nettie looked down to find him blinking, all sleepy-like. Jiddy let out a rip-roaring snore, and Sam snuggled deeper down against his saddle. All the men were slopping over, breathing deeply, mouths open.

Asleep.

"Captain?"

"He can't hear you no more. Only Pia Mupitsi hears you now."

She looked up at Delgado in confusion, lips drawing back in disgust when she saw a long, black snake's tongue flicker out of his mouth.

"You can talk, Delgado? What the hell are you?"

And that was when he shot her.

CHAPTER 25

It hurt like a sumbitch, first of all.

The bullet slammed into her shoulder and sent her left arm numb.

Nettie grunted and staggered back, tripping over Hennessy's feet. That was what saved her, considering Delgado shot again and missed, the second bullet hissing off the rocks.

But the first bullet—sweet hellfire, that bullet.

It hit harder than Pap's whip or Mam's hand, sharper than a wasp and hotter than a mesquite thorn in full fever. But like all those pains she knew so well, it pissed her off beyond all reason, and she managed to pull her own gun as she scrambled away, squint around the rock, and fire for Delgado's grinning, snake-tongued mouth, fueled by the pain shooting through her veins.

The bullet hit Delgado in the stomach, and he staggered back and doubled over, arms curled around his faded blue shirt, howling. Nettie fired off another round, right into his chest, and he fell to the ground. Not a single cowboy stirred, but Nettie figured that in between a gut shot and a lung shot, she could probably afford to hiss and poke a finger into the wound in her shoulder, right above her armpit.

She expected the pain. She expected blood and the feeling of bone scraping on bone.

What she found was a flat piece of steel, pushing its way out of her body.

Just as it plopped out like a worm oozing out of an apple, she caught it in one hand and held it up. Nettie had never seen a bullet pulled out of a body before her time with the Rangers, and she'd never seen one covered in her own blood. She took the time to dump the dang thing in the pouch at her waist before running blood-wet fingers over the hole in her shirt.

The skin there was unbroken, save for a tiny, raised scar.

The hole was gone.

Which meant...

Aw, shit. It meant she was...something.

She looked at her hands. Just a few hours ago, they'd been ripped, torn, bleeding, blistered. Now they were smooth. Completely healed. She hadn't even noticed.

Quick as a snake, she crawled to the Captain, just behind him, and shook his shoulder.

"Captain? Captain, you in there? I'm something, Captain. I'm one of them. I need..."

"You need to die."

She felt the bang before she heard it, and half her world went out in a flash. The punch of the bullet was wet and hot, a thousand fireworks in the dark.

In her eye.

Delgado had shot her in the hellfire goddamn son-of-a-bitching eye, and...and the bullet wasn't popping out like it should have been.

And Delgado wasn't dying like he should have been, neither.

But, then again, a feller with a snake tongue had only one sure spot to aim for, didn't he?

One-eyed and covered in blood, Nettie aimed her pistol at the crouching man and emptied it, four shots in quick succession that sent him barreling back into the fire as she screamed herself raw. He tripped in the flames and went up like a pile of tinder, his scream higher and more frantic than hers. Still half blind and rage full, Nettie slipped the Henry from the Captain's side, aimed it at the burning form of the crappiest cook in Durango, and pulled the trigger sixteen times. At some point, she must've hit the bastard's heart, as he exploded in sand that sent the fire crackling into the sky. But she kept pulling the trigger and screaming because she wanted the son of a bitch who took her right eye to die and be gone forever.

When the trigger finally clicked without kicking, she dropped the Henry and put fingers to her eye socket. It was a mess of gunk and blood and burning hurt, and she felt the bile rise up her throat as she reached around, hunting past the bone for the bullet. She was crying, but it hurt so bad, and no matter how many times she called out to the Captain and Hennessy and even, desperately, Virgil and Milo and Jiddy, nobody stirred from their sleep.

When her stomach flipped, she struggled for Sam's pistol, but firm hands landed on hers, pulling them away.

"Stop, Nettie. If you shoot me, you'll be alone."

The world spun when she looked up into the solemn face of Coyote Dan. Try as she might, she couldn't stop shaking. She couldn't quite see as much of him as she should've, and he was stark and flat and strange when seen through only one eye.

"It wasn't supposed to happen like this, Dan. I was..." She swallowed hard, tasting tears and blood. "I should be whole, Dan. Hunting the Cannibal Owl. Ending all this bullshit. What happened?"

Dan let her hands loose to gently hold her head, which

normally would've made her twitchy as hell. As it was, she let him pull her to the fire and lay her back, one eye open to the stars and the black spot where the moon should've been.

"Looks like you got shot."

"Delgado. Delgado shot me. What the sweet goddamn was he? Why didn't I feel him?"

"Shh."

Dan held her face down with one hand, fingers gentle as moth wings. With his other hand, he suddenly dug into her eye socket, making her scream at the explosion of pain. His knee hit her belly, pinning her down as she struggled against him. All of a sudden, he grunted and pulled something free with a sick, wet suck. She felt the healing start, soft parts and skin knitting together in her skull like a darned sock. It hurt, but in a reverse sort of way. Waiting for her sight to return, she closed her other eye, more aware than ever of the darkness and trying to remember that first vampire, the stranger she'd caught in the eye with a sickle. Had his eye healed before she turned him to sand?

She couldn't remember. It was like a nightmare, then and now.

Dan released her gently to the ground. "He shot you with a silver bullet. What was he?"

"Hellfire, Dan. How should I know? He had a snake tongue, but his eyes weren't all buggy like a chupa. He said something about Pia Mupitsi. I didn't even feel him. In between you and Jiddy and Cap's watch, I just thought his food made my gut squirm. Aw, hell."

"There are things that I don't know. I didn't know. I'm sorry. I shouldn't have left you."

"That's your problem, Coyote Dan. You always think you know everything. And you don't know shit."

"That's what my mother told me, before she died in my arms. She was human. It happened so fast. I was out hunting that night, too, when Pia Mupitsi struck my tribe. Did I tell you that?" She couldn't see his face, but she could hear him fighting tears. The world was in a strange place, if Dan was admitting that he was lost.

Nettie swallowed hard and tried opening her eye, but it wasn't done doing what it was doing, and all she saw was black. She probed it gently with a finger, tried to close her eyelid. Nothing happened.

"But how the Sam Hill did we all miss that? You, me, Jiddy? Nobody noticed Delgado?"

Dan cleared his throat, and when she blinked, she saw that he was back to normal, jaw set and tears gone. "Things that want to stay hidden often do. Coiled snakes especially. Perhaps he was a halfbreed, more human than monster in body if not in deed. When many voices are talking, it's hard to hear an individual's song, especially if they sing it softly." He exhaled in annoyance, his fingers pressing the taut skin around her shot eye. "Which is just me acting wise because I never thought that horrible cook might be more than what he seemed. Maybe he was poisoning you all along, maybe there was magic in his food. But you. Nettie, tell me. What are you?"

His finger probed her eye, and she moaned and thrashed. He put a firm hand to her shoulder to hold her down, and Nettie curled her hands into fists and pounded the dirt. "I don't know what I am, goddammit! I thought I was the Shadow you kept talking about. You told me I was human. But now a bullet popped out of my shoulder, and your hand's on the wound, and it don't even hurt anymore. My hands are all healed, but my eye ain't. I'm something, but I don't know what. What the hell am I?"

"I don't know. I don't understand. What happened here?"

"Here?"

"The Rangers are asleep. What did Delgado give them?"

"I don't care. My eye, Dan! What about my eye?"

"It's not growing back. The lid is gone, but the skin is knitting over the wound. I'm going to wipe away the weeping. I'm sorry for the pain this will cause." He untied the bandanna around her neck, and her stomach roiled at the feeling of wet, wadded cloth dabbing in her eye socket. It was peculiar, how it didn't feel like a wound anymore, didn't sting and burn, but she still couldn't see. And it smelled like Monty, goddamn it. The sweat on his bandana was just another reminder of her failure to save something fine for the second time.

She clutched at it, pulled it free. "No! No. Just give it time. It'll come back. It has to."

Dan sighed sadly and tugged her hands away. "There's no time to waste on mourning what's gone. Keep moving or perish. Don't you hear that sound?"

Nettie swallowed, tried to hear around the pounding of her heart. Her ears were sharper now, as if the world had always been full of tiny rustles that she couldn't quite catch.

And what she heard was the harsh sound of air, of metal, of feathers, of...

"Wings," she rasped. Her good eye winked open, and she sat up. "What's coming?"

Dan scrambled to collect the guns of the nearest sleeping Rangers and pile them on the ground beside Nettie. As the flapping grew louder, she checked the pistols, making sure they were loaded. One of the other fellers—Virgil—had a Henry like the Captain's, and she scrambled over to grab it from his limp arms. Coyote Dan was stark nekkid, lacking even his little skirt, but Nettie didn't care about anything but her missing eye and whatever was blotting out the stars and screeching like hell's own demons. She had a new appreciation for Dan—a feller had to be right brave to go into a monster fight without his clothes, considering how terrified she was even while wearing all her clothes and surrounded by guns. Putting the Henry to her shoulder, Nettie tried and failed to squeeze her eye shut and realized she'd never aim that way again.

That didn't matter now. All that mattered was killing what needed to die.

CHAPTER
26

The first of the harpies punched through the night, claws outstretched, and Nettie's Henry popped off the filthy critter's head, sending her crashing to the ground.

"You knock them down. I'll go for their hearts," Dan shouted, and Nettie focused on the rain of buzzard-women streaking toward her, their feathers glinting like thousands of tiny swords in the firelight.

She had sixteen more shots from the Henry, and she didn't pause between bullets. The rifle was hotter than Hades, and her shoulder was beyond bruised, but each shot knocked one of the vultures out of the sky and onto the ground, where Dan pounded her between the dugs with a quartz knife. And, hell, Nettie's bruises would just disappear now, wouldn't they? She was a monster.

But the goddamn harpies kept coming, and no matter how many shots she fired, no matter how many pistols she picked up fully loaded and discarded hot and empty, no matter how many bodies Dan punched into dirty sand, still the tide didn't slow down. Arms aching, ears ringing, one eye weeping, Nettie Lonesome learned what eternity was that night.

Eternity was stars blotted out with heavy bodies and sharp feathers.

Eternity was clever talons clutching the back of her shirt, ripping into her back, tightening around her arms, heaving her up into the sky, screaming.

Eternity was the time it took Dan to turn to her and reach into the air, nekkid and sweating and covered with bloody sand, shouting her name until he was hoarse, his hands clutching nothing but wind.

Eternity was a wake of vultures, a harem of harpies, a brigade of bragging bitch-buzzards carrying her through the night, flying her toward the gaping mouth of a cave at the top of a mountain that nothing on two legs could ever reach.

Eternity was the time she fell through space before landing roughly on stone.

Eternity was the hollow laugh from the darkness, followed by six barked words:

"Been a long time, my child."

CHAPTER 27

Nettie was on hands and knees on the floor of a cave. Her good eye saw as much as her bad one, which is to say: not a goddamn thing beyond the starlight kissing the rock ledge.

"Gonna be a lot longer when I kill your ass," she shouted, figuring that bravado beat honesty at least half the time.

A dark chuckle wiggled up the cavern. "Come closer. Let me see you."

With a groan, Nettie stood, rubbing a hand over her face. She'd been all cut to ribbons and bruised to lumps by the harpies' rough treatment, but she could already feel things healing up, as if her body had no truck with the wounds of such nasty critters. She'd always healed fast, but never this fast.

She could just barely stand without scraping her head, and she looked around real quick to see if she was alone. The front of the cave felt tidy, swept clean, yet somehow carried the scent of death. One tiny moccasin curled by the ledge, and Nettie picked it up, running a finger over the intricate beadwork. Her heart wrenched, and she tried to throw it out of the cave but failed. Instead, she tucked it into her shirt and let the tips of her boots hang into space as she played with the idea of jumping. Suicide was a pleasure she couldn't afford.

Instead, she looked away.

Far below, in the valley of bones, the harpies roosted in their trees, whispering together and smoothing the metallic feathers mussed by their passage. From up here, they looked right personable and homey, like silver chickens with highly wringable necks. Across the river, in the shadows, a dark figure sat a wet, black horse—not pointing, this time. Just standing. Waiting. Even farther away, across an infinite gulf of space and sky, a nekkid man moved around a fire on top of a tableland, stabbing silvery bodies and brushing away clouds of clinging sand. She wanted to call to Coyote Dan, but she didn't see what good it would do. He had plenty of work to do, taking care of the half-dead harpies.

She had to do this alone. And she'd always known it, hadn't she?

Nodding to herself, Nettie checked for what she had left. A stone knife in one boot, a silver knife in the other, and a sharpened Bowie knife in the sheath on her belt. A hand-stitched leather bag containing coins, various fangs, and a crushed, bloody bullet that matched the hole in her shirt. One old red bandanna that smelled like an old man's kindness and was still wet with blood and fluid from her destroyed eye. One last sliver of a bone knife, squirreled away between her breasts under the tight wrap of muslin. Twisting away from a peculiar pain in her back, she felt around inside her shirt until she found the offending object: a harpy's feather, sharp as a man's straight razor. Taking it out, she held it up to the moonlight and reasoned that although it looked much like a vulture's flight feather, the quill was made of bone, the end pricked with black blood from where it'd been pulled off a monster's wing.

Well, fine, then. She hoped the harpy suffered from the loss. She tucked the feather into her hat for luck.

Deep within the cave, something clicked with a worrisome rhythm that made Nettie's skin crawl.

"Don't make me wait, child."

The voice was strange, alien and gritted and high.

"You waited this long, Pia Mupitsi. I reckon you can wait a little longer."

The chittering laugh that reached her set Nettie's teeth on edge, and she figured she might as well find the Cannibal Owl before the goddamn thing annoyed her to death. Unsheathing her Bowie knife, she put one hand in front of her and edged into the darkness. She slid forward, light in her boots and wary of the many ways she might be attacked. The only sounds were the rock scree sliding under her heels and the beating of her heart, which she swore she could feel in her gone eye. Dead black was the tunnel, and it angled ever so gently upward. With every inch she moved, Nettie expected to fall endlessly into a hole, to run into a wall or the roof, to be attacked by a thousand deadly monsters she'd never even heard of. She expected bats and bears and harpies and chupacabra, vampires and scorpions and unforgiving men with snake tongues. But all she found was darkness and cold.

"Almost here. The fire is waiting."

The voice was still forever away, and Nettie was tired to her very bones. The day had lasted years, and it took every-thing Nettie had not to turn around and run for the ledge and launch herself out into the night and be done with it. But every time she thought about giving up, deep in the bowels of the mountain, she'd feel the weight of the moccasin in her shirt, the fangs rattling in her bag, Monty's bandanna around her neck. She carried revenge in her heart, and it drove her relent-lessly forward more surely than any ghostly finger pointing ever west.

For Monty, she kept walking.

For the tiny foot that might've fit this moccasin before it'd turned to sand, she kept going.

For every hurt she'd ever received, every bit of warmth she'd never known, every beating she'd ever taking with closed lips, she inched forward.

And then she heard a familiar whimper and broke into a run.

So Winifred was still alive, but the terrified sound that had just echoed down the cave made it clear that the girl's future was hanging in the balance. The chittering laugh came again, almost covered up by the pounding of Nettie's hobnailed boots and the desperate beating of her heart.

She smelled the fire before she saw its light dancing with nightmare shadows against the widening walls of the tunnel. Knife still outstretched, she skidded to a stop and looked, for the first time, on the Cannibal Owl.

CHAPTER
28

"Greetings, girl," said the monster.

"Go to hell, monster," said the girl.

Winifred just whimpered.

As Nettie edged around the fire, the monster tracked her with eyes as big as dinner plates and as yellow as a dead man's teeth, blinking with terrifying infrequency. The sharp, black owl's beak clicked like a thousand insect legs, sometimes opening to show all-too-human teeth. It was everything she'd never hoped to see, a collection of wrong parts put together as if by an angry child with a hammer and a box of bent nails. It crouched behind the fire in something like a human's form with a raptor's silent wings arching overhead, wearing a black suit that reminded Nettie of the town preacher, like it wanted to be fine but wasn't quite sure how to go about it.

The arms and legs of the suit were too short for the overly thin beast, the knees shiny and shabby where they were drawn up under the creature's chin. Long, clawed fingers like dying stick bugs clicked and curled and uncurled, that strange snicking sound that had been so vexful, all along. The noise was oddly familiar, oddly painful. To one side of the creature sat a large, woven basket, and inside the basket was Winifred, on her back and pierced through the belly by a long, silver spike. The girl was alive and hating every second of it, her blood pooled and soaking the basket, and Nettie put out a hand and edged toward her friend.

"Business first," the Cannibal Owl said, reaching out to smack Nettie's hand with a claw. "Sit."

"What if I don't want to sit?"

With an awkward shrug, the creature stretched out a long arm, placed its claws on Winifred's chest, and pushed her down farther on the spike, causing her to cry out something awful.

Nettie sat.

"You ain't my long-lost mother or something dumb like that, are you?" she asked.

The Cannibal Owl just laughed, high and mad. "Your Comanche call me Owl Mother and Ghost Mother, but I am neither. I have no children. I eat children." It paused, tapped fingers against its beak. "And only the softest bits of those fully grown. I ate your mother's guts."

All the air rushed out of Nettie's body; she hadn't known the long-dead truth could break her heart like that. "Fine. You ate my mother. What do you want?"

The Cannibal Owl twitched its head sideways and clicked its beak, its giant eyes boring into Nettie's soul.

"Same thing I've wanted since the first time I lost you: to eat you. Nothing more."

Nettie's fingers ached for the knife in her boot, but she didn't make a move for it.

"If you want to eat me, why'd you have to go to so much goddamn trouble? You could've knocked me over with one finger in the desert a few weeks ago. You could've snatched me from the porch of the hellhole where I spent the last fourteen damn years of my life. Your goddamn harpy almost took me down with one bite."

The Cannibal Owl leaned forward, fingers lacing together arounds its knees. "Not my harpy. Took a long time to find you. Wanted to study you. Wanted to understand the only creature that ever escaped me. What are you?"

Nettie's one-eyed glare was flat, her patience gone. "I'm the feller that's going to kill you."

"You're not a feller."

"That's not yours to decide."

And as punctuation, she whipped out her Bowie knife and leaped across the fire to plunge the blade into the creature's chest. It sunk in like butter, but the critter didn't dissolve into sand. Its beak clicked, and the long fingers laced around Nettie's shoulders and pulled her away, the knife with her. Lifting her as if she didn't weigh a goddamn thing, the Cannibal Owl flipped her onto her back, spun her around, and ever so gently draped her over the basket, the long, silver spike digging into Nettie's back, right under the ribs.

Nettie shrieked and scrabbled to get hands and feet onto the edges of the basket, to hold herself away, but the material flopped under her hands.

"Will you talk now?" the creature asked, as if they were chatting about the weather.

"I don't got the answers you want, but if you'll take me up off this spike, I'll try."

"Tsk, tsk. No. Talk now. Where have you been?"

The spidery hands lowered her enough to let the spike just pierce her skin through her shirt, and Nettie yelped, "Here. Durango. Border town called Gloomy Bluebird."

With an irritable snap of its beak, the creature muttered, "Among the white men. Perhaps that's why."

"Yeah, with the white man!" Nettie shouted, skin crawling away from the spike. "And it was goddamn miserable, so don't feel too bad about it. Might as well have let you eat me for all the good it did me. Bought myself years of bullshit. What did you expect?"

The huge eyes were suddenly right up in Nettie's face, the long fingers pressing into her flesh like drills. "Expected to find you with your tribe, with any tribe. Been looking. Wanted to know how you escaped. Can't have it happen again."

Nettie stared, unblinking, breathing through her nose. Below her, Winifred whimpered and reached a hand up to barely touch Nettie's shoulder.

"Don't know how I escaped. I was too small. Nobody ever told me where I came from."

The creature clicked at her, its fingers tightening around her sides. With sudden force, it shoved her down onto the spike, and Nettie screamed as the silver metal pierced straight through her back and punched out to the side of her belly button. The world became a hell of fire and pain and snakes and white explosions behind her one good eye.

"I killed your village. I took the children. All stacked up on the spike, nice and juicy. But you escaped. You were different. Different color, different meat. I know your scent. I know the taste of your fear." One long finger reached out to swipe a tear from Nettie's cheek and deliver the dab of wetness to the creature's beak, a slender black tongue poking out to test it. "I ask again. What are you?"

"I don't...I don't know." Nettie moaned and put hands to her belly, to the wet place around the spike. As much pain as she'd known, she'd never known pain like this. And she remembered feeling it once before, long ago and far away like a dream, but she couldn't for the life of her remember how she'd gotten there or how she'd escaped from it.

"You were a baby. Too young to walk. Cradleboard and clean moccasins." The long fingers left Nettie's sides, and she slipped down the spike another inch. One by one, the claws curled around her face, thoughtfully probing the soft parts, up into her nose, deep into her ruined eye. "You're something different."

"Well, no shit!" Nettie shouted, driving the bone knife from her boot deep into one of the giant, yellow eyes and slashing sideways. The Cannibal Owl reared back, screaming, as its eye slit open like an egg over easy and gushed white and red gunk. The knife clattered to the ground.

Without its claws holding her up, Nettie had nothing to support her, nothing to keep her from slipping farther down the spike toward Winifred's body. The hole in her gut—it was the size of her own arm, the red-smeared silver poking up as high as her face. She could feel her guts trying to knit—and failing. Poor Winifred, below her, was pierced even more deeply and moaning. With nothing to hold on to, there was no way to slide off the spike, and she figured she'd just keep cutting on the Cannibal Owl every time it got close. It was across the fire now, clicking and clucking and smoothing bony fingers over its own ruined eye.

Nettie smiled, a tiny thing. *Eye for an eye*, the preacher feller always said.

Or maybe that was the sheriff. The past had a way of running together.

She slid down the spike a little farther and closed her good eye, trying to get beyond the pain. She'd heard one of the Ranger fellers say that when you were dying, your life flashed before your eyes, and that had to be what was happening. She saw Hennessy's face, grinning in the firelight. Dan's hands breaking stones and holding an arrow's feathered tips to her cheek. Punching Winifred and seeing her dead twice and touching her long, brown foot. Killing the harpy, killing the vampire. The Captain and Monty and Chuck and years and years of ducking away from Pap's fists and Mam's broom and days spent breaking horses she'd never be able to afford and feeding brown grass to an old mule. That first, fine moment of pride as Boss Kimble offered her a job, a way out, that moment when anything had been possible.

And then things got right peculiar, a fuzzy riot of flashes both familiar and strange.

The rump of a paint horse, swinging back and forth below her. Bodies dancing by a fire, high up on a mountain. Laughing at birds, clutching at feathers. Fear and darkness and a promised monster. Freedom and the feeling of floating. A hawk's sure talons and the world spinning. The ground rising, hard and brown, and a dirty white face grinning at something that looked like luck.

Nettie swallowed hard and forced her eye to stay shut. She was so, so close.

Claws dug under her eyelid, forcing her good eye open.

"Tell me," the creature said, one eye weeping as it loomed over her, face to face.

"I don't owe you nothing." Nettie spit in the Cannibal Owl's remaining eye, and when the great orb blinked closed, she whipped the silver knife out of her other boot and slashed it across, too.

She was still stuck on the spike, but it felt damn good to blind the monster whose minion had taken one of her eyes first. It sat back against the cave wall to yank out the knife and throw it in the fire, keening with its knees clutched to its chest.

"You will pay for that," it said, unfolding to stand.

The Cannibal Owl's head was unnaturally big, even with

the eyes destroyed, and now it came at her gushing blood with claws curled and crowned in sticky feathers, beak opening to show a row of human teeth, and inside that, another row of fangs.

Nettie ripped her shirt open and dug around inside her bindings for the last shard of rock she'd hidden there. The spike's piercing pain in her belly never lessened, never calmed, but she reckoned it would hurt about the same whether she fought or gave up, and Nettie Lonesome wasn't one to give up. If the Cannibal Owl was dead, she could figure out a way off the spike, even if it was just hollering her fool head off until Dan found a way up the mountain. She was a monster, somehow. She could survive that much.

The Cannibal Owl kicked the basket, jarring Winifred and making her groan as Nettie clutched the bone knife hard enough to draw her own hand's blood. It was her last shot, and the creature was completely blind and utterly bloodthirsty and all the nightmares her mother had ever warned her about but she'd never had a mother but oh yes she had and she sucked in a deep breath and felt long fingers scrabble for her tear-wet face as the beak rose over her, sharp as glass and full of teeth and hungry for what it had been denied.

Just as Nettie was pulling back her knife and aiming for where the critter's heart should've been, Winifred shifted below her. Warm hands found Nettie's shoulders, one foot curled against her rump. A wet, hot stump of bone dug into her hip—Winifred's sheared ankle. Nettie gritted her teeth in understanding and waited.

"Fly," Winifred said, and with one mighty push, she shoved Nettie right off the spike and into the air.

CHAPTER
29

In the air, everything felt good. For a long moment, Nettie floated, the pain of the spike already disappearing as her body healed itself. And then bony fingers scraped against her arm, and she twisted away and landed hard on the cold, stone floor of the Cannibal Owl's cave with a sliver of white quartz cutting into her palm.

The Cannibal Owl dove for her, and she rolled away, right into the fire. It was not like the ghost woman's fire—it was real and hotter than hell. Her clothes caught, but so did the monster chasing her, and she rolled through to the other side and smothered herself against the stone. The blind beast staggered toward her, lit up like a goddamn torch and shrieking like a dying rabbit, and Nettie stood and stabbed it smack in the throat with the stone shard.

"Nettie..."

Winifred's whisper pulled her attention away long enough to let the Cannibal Owl grab her wrist and snap its beak around her forearm, clamping down like a goddamn river turtle. Nettie screeched and tried to shove it off, but it wouldn't let go, and the layers of teeth inside tested her, chewed through her with a strange delicacy. The knife in its throat didn't slow it down one dang bit, and Nettie was all out of weapons. Across the fire, the silver knife glinted, pretty as a creek to a dying man in the desert and just as far out of reach.

"Please..."

Nettie spun around to face the basket and the spike and the girl sunk down deep in a puddle of blood. When Winifred had pushed Nettie off the silver blade, that meant Winifred herself had been pushed farther down on it, the hole in her gut as big as a mule's hoof now. But the Cannibal Owl wouldn't let go of her arm, and Nettie didn't have a knife, and Winifred took up crooning to herself in her own language.

Fed up and numb and alive and done beyond all reason, Nettie yanked the Cannibal Owl along with her, dragging it step by aching step across the cave, feeling it swallow a chunk of her arm meat and open its mouth for another bite. When the blind, hungry thing tripped on its small feet, she shoved it right on top of its own goddamn spike.

CHAPTER
30

The silver spike slipped into the Cannibal Owl like a fish sliding into a river, smooth and slick and sure. As the creature had fallen sideways, the blade lodged under its armpit, in that soft place above the ribs, and stuck. Its beak snapped open to scream, and Nettie backed away, rubbing her chewed-up arm and full of hate and white-hot fire.

"Who were my people?"

The Cannibal Owl's beak clicked, its teeth gnashing, its suit on fire, but it said nothing.

Nettie put her hands on its shoulder, pushed just a little bit, just as it had done to her.

"I said who? Who was my father? What village did you steal me from, you goddamn bastard?"

With a squeak, the Cannibal Owl's screams turned to laughter.

But still it didn't answer.

Teeth bared and expression full of flame, Nettie put two hands on top of its shoulder and shoved as hard as she could. The spike scraped against something hard, and Nettie pushed harder.

And then the Cannibal Owl exploded into sand.

CHAPTER

31

Nettie nearly lost her other eye as the monster disappeared suddenly under her pressing hands. Pulling her face back from the bloody spike at the last possible second, she coughed and staggered away from the basket. Her mouth was full of sand.

"Please, Nettie."

She shook her head and reached into the basket, pulling the flaming black suit off the spike and tossing it into the fire. The silver was smeared with black as her fingers found Winifred's shoulders. The girl had the good sense to put her foot down on the bottom of the woven reeds and press up as Nettie pulled her, gently and slowly, off the spike. At the end, Nettie had to slip a hand under Winifred's knees and shoulders and lift her, nekkid and shivering, off the silver tip. It was all she could do to stay standing, and she staggered sideways into the wall. Her shoulder hit hard, and she slid down the cold rock, cradling Winifred like a baby. The girl grunted when her stump dragged on the floor, a painful reminder of the Cannibal Owl's legacy.

"Can Dan put your foot back on?" Nettie asked.

Winifred shook her head, breathed deeply, and let her head fall against Nettie's shoulder.

"I don't know. Just hold me. Get me out of here. Please."

Without meaning to, Nettie's hand was stroking Winifred like a spooked colt, and it seemed to work a little. The skin of her belly twitched as it knitted back together, and when the hole was finally sealed over, Winifred sighed deeply and relaxed back against Nettie's chest. Nettie was suddenly aware that all of her senses were full of a beautiful, blood-smeared nekkid girl, and she wasn't sure how she felt about that, so she cleared her throat and gently slid Winifred away, hoping the girl was decent off enough to stand on her own. Because that was what Nettie needed to do: Stand up and get on with life.

The cave held nothing new: just a handwoven basket with a deadly silver spike firmly attached to the bottom. The goddamn thing looked like an elephant's tusk Nettie had once seen in a fancy leather book that Mam and Pap had received in payment and quickly traded away, but it was shining and silvery and taller than her waist. The only thing she knew for sure was that she never wanted to see it again. So she threw the basket in the goddamn fire, which seemed like a good idea. Until thick smoke filled the cave.

"Idjit," Winifred muttered. "Now we're going to asphyxiate."

"Or choke to death, either one," Nettie said. "Can't you turn into a coyote and sniff a way out of here?"

"I was already on my way," Winifred snapped, curling over and sprouting tan fur.

The coyote limped around the cave on three legs, sniffing every bit of stone and coughing from the smoke before hurrying back to Nettie and whimpering.

"No other way out, huh?"

The coyote yipped, pointed her nose at a single small smoke hole in the rock overhead, shook her head, and limped toward the tunnel. Nettie got on her hands and knees, where the smoke was thinner, and scrabbled on the floor for her silver knife before following the sound of the coyote's panting down the pitch-black tunnel.

It took as long to go out as it had to go in, and Nettie figured this had to be what the preacher's Hell was like, just endless smoky darkness with nightmares at either end. For hours and hours, it seemed, she crawled toward the daylight. The first shred of sunlight was a blessing, the weak lavender light nearly blinding to her one good eye. Soon she saw the coyote standing at the lip of the cave, whining.

"Quit bellyaching, you girl," she muttered, sitting down beside the coyote and letting her legs hang off the edge.

For now, being out of the Cannibal Owl's lair and in the sunshine was good enough.

Far below, tiny skulls sparkled with dew. Across the river and even farther away, the dark figures of the Rangers moved around the butte in some confusion. The harpies were gone from the trees, whether because their leader was gone or there wouldn't be any more leftovers for them to crunch on. Coyote Dan was noticeably absent, but when Winifred tipped back her muzzle and howled a mournful tune, another coyote voice answered, somewhere in the distance.

"Turn back, would you? A nekkid woman's better than a crying dog."

The coyote stuck its tongue out and sat back on its haunches. Moments later, Winifred was a girl again, all warm, brown skin and tangled black hair. And Nettie went prickly all over and kind of wished the girl had stayed a coyote.

"We can't get down, Nettie. The cliff face has no handholds."

"The Rangers will figure it out."

Winifred snorted and tossed her hair. "I doubt it. The best we can hope for is that Dan can find a long rope or maybe sweet-talk some nicer harpies." The girl couldn't seem to get comfortable, what with being nekkid in a stone cave and missing a foot, and all her shifting around and grunting was making Nettie feel like jumping might be a good alternative.

"Did the Cannibal Owl ever say anything to you about my people?" Nettie asked.

Winifred shook her head. "The Cannibal Owl wasn't one for words. Mostly skittered around, muttering about *the one that got away* and *sweet babies* and *the time is soon*, and...ugh."

"Are there lots of monsters like that?"

Leaning back against the stone, Winifred watched the men scurrying below and tried to comb the snarls out of her hair with dirty fingers. "There's a reason animals live in groups and people live in tribes and cities. When we get off alone, we start to go a bit crazy. People need to be touched and talked to, they need to know somebody else in the world cares. You take that away, and you have a monster. Not a shifter or a vampire. A real monster. You get something like the Cannibal Owl. A thing apart."

"I didn't have a tribe," Nettie muttered.

Winifred stilled her with a hand on her arm. "You did. Once. You were loved. And you lost it. But surely you had kindness, somewhere along the line?"

Nettie smiled and stared into the clouds. "Wrangler named Monty was nice to me. Put me on a horse when I was just a little thing. All I ever wanted was to be like him. I reckon everything else I ever loved was an animal of one kind or another."

"Then you found a tribe. Who knows what the Cannibal Owl used to be, or might've been? Point is, it doesn't matter what tribe you came from. You can make your own."

A shout down below had them both leaning over the edge, staring at Dan's dark hair and waving arms. The ground was so far away that he was just a brown blot among the skulls.

"We're looking for rope!" he shouted.

"No good. Nothing to tie it to," Nettie shouted back.

"Well, you need to get down somehow!"

"No shit, Dan!"

Even from a mile away, she heard him chuckle.

Nettie settled back down against the wall to wait it out, as exhausted as she'd ever been. Winifred leaned up against her, more for support than anything else, her head on Nettie's shoulder and her legs sticking out in front of her. Nettie wished to hell she had some kind of clothing to offer the girl, but the only spare piece of cloth she possessed was a bandanna covered in dried eyeball. She gingerly poked a finger around the wound, but it had sealed over smooth. No eyelid, no eyeball. Just flat skin.

"Goddammit."

"What happened?" Winifred asked.

"Delgado surprised me. Shot me in the eye. Reckon it must've been silver, probably laced with acid spit or poison. Dan took out the bullet, but it was too late."

Winifred reached out, taking Nettie's face in gentle hands and turning her this way and that in the sun. Her scrutiny was so intense that Nettie closed her other eye.

"I'm sorry, Nettie. That's horrible."

"Could've been worse. Can't somebody patch up your foot? Maybe not Dan, but...somebody?"

Winifred shrugged. "I don't know. I figure I'll try that dwarf sawbones in Burlesville. At the very least, I'll get a fake leg. Maybe Dan can carve a chunk of whalebone with pretty designs."

Gently probing her own eye, or what was left of it, she tried to get used to what was bound to be permanent. "Seems like you don't mind so much."

The other girl's head flopped up to glare at Nettie. "I spent a couple of days in a dark cave, impaled on a spike by the monster my mother taught me to fear most. I can live with a limp." She snorted in sad, sick laughter and added, "And thank you for killing it. Pia Mupitsi."

"I'm a Durango Ranger. I kill what needs to die. And you helped, so thanks back."

And then before she could stop herself, Nettie Lonesome was crying.

She only had one good eye, but it boiled up tears. She cried for the loss of her other eye and the loss of her history. She cried for the maybe Comanche mother she couldn't remember and the tribe she'd never know. She cried for Monty and Chuck and Chicken and Ty and Moran and Tim and all the fellers who'd been stuck full of arrows, thanks to the werewolves. She cried for Sam Hennessy and Winifred, who'd each lost something dear. She cried for herself, as she would rather be almost anywhere else but trapped in a cave on a mountain without food or water or a decent place to piss. But most of all, she cried because she was glad to finally be free.

That was one thing she hadn't seen when she'd looked out on the valley. No matter how hard she'd looked and how many shadows she'd hunted, she didn't see that old Injun woman on her wet black steed.

At first, Winifred just patted her as she bawled, but then the coyote girl pulled Nettie Lonesome into her lap and held her face and stroked her cheek, muttering singsong nonsense to her in another language.

"What's that you're singing?" Nettie asked, as there was something strangely familiar about it that made her skin prickle all over.

"It's a lullaby. What the mothers in my tribe sing to their

babies, hoping they'll turn out to be shifters. It's the story of skinwalkers. Tells the babies how to change. *Little one that I love, you are two creatures with one spirit. Reach down inside, deep inside, and find the golden core of you, connecting you to the earth and sky, the trail the moon leaves on water. Pull it like a rope, inside out, and know that you are perfect in either skin.*"

Nettie was shaking, memories flashing behind her ruined eye. The paint horse, the cradleboard swinging, shadow puppets on walls of leather, laughing brown faces and one dark black with white, white teeth, a high fire against the starlight, holes in the red cliffs with wide windows to deep blue, gray feathers and tiny talons and wind and falling and landing. A face, glowing with love, singing that song. Shrugging out of Winifred's arms, she looked out into the morning sky, past the clouds glittering with sunlight. A breeze brushed her cheek like a mother's caress, and it felt right.

"Nettie? What's wrong?"

Twitching her shoulders, Nettie pulled the harpy's feather out of her hat and ran a finger down the quill.

"Nettie?"

Stepping to the ledge, letting her toes hang over, Nettie clutched the stone wall with one hand and the feather in the other and leaned out. The wind blew sweet against her face, and she let the feather go, watching it twirl down gently until it caught a breeze.

"Nothing's wrong. I finally understand."

Taking a deep breath, Nettie stepped out of her boots, stripped off her socks, shrugged out of her shirt. She untied the leather pouch around her waist and held it in one palm, memorizing the weight of it, of the memories she carried. Those strings she tied tightly around her ankle, hoping it was enough. She unwound the linen around her chest and kicked off her britches until she stood, nekkid and unafraid in the morning sun.

"If this don't work, give my stuff to Hennessy."

"What?" Winifred struggled to stand on her good foot, one hand on the wall and one reaching for Nettie.

But she was too late. Nettie took a step back and launched herself into the sky, arms spread wide and smiling.

AUTHOR'S NOTE

I would like to hereby call out my failings as a historian and remind you that this book is in the Fantasy section for a reason. As Dr. Terry could've told you in my AP U.S. History class in high school, I'm here for the story, not the facts.

The journey outlined in *Wake of Vultures* is loosely based on the terrain I internalized from watching *Lonesome Dove* on repeat from the moment I saw it on live television in 1989. I did my best to piece together maps from late 1800s Texas and pinpoint where the Cannibal Owl's lair would be and how Nettie would journey from Gloomy Bluebird to her final destination, but much of the actual route is imaginary, as is Durango Territory. Nettie's world is a work of my imagination, so if at any time you wish to e-mail me regarding misrepresentation of facts or flaws on the map or time line, please recall that it's chock-full of monsters and meant to be an alternate world, not the real world. It's only going to get weirder in Book 2. The time line here is roughly analogous to our 1870s, and most of the place names (Tanasi, Azteca, etc.) are based on historical names given to lands by their original people.

My Durango Rangers, likewise, are a pastiche of reality and fiction. Many historians agree that the Texas Rangers of the 1800s, although glorified by today's media, were the

orchestrators of multiple atrocities against nonwhites. I recognize that there are two sides to every story, and that there
were good men and not-so-good men among them. I will tell
you that the Texas Rangers were founded by Stephen F. Austin
in 1823 to protect pioneer families in Texas after the Mexi-
can War of Independence. And you know what happens when
heavily armed white folks set out to protect white folks.

Look deeper, and you'll find more fantasy. Can a girl gentle
three wild mustangs in one day? Probably not. Can a spirit quest
range 150 miles without food or water? I doubt it. Did dwarves
venture west during the Gold Rush? Maybe. Again, Fantasy.

As for Nettie, she's written as a Black Indian, with her tribe
most likely Comanche. The terms *Injun* and *Indian* have been
used throughout the book not as a slur but as a reflection of
the language of the time. *Native American* wasn't in common
parlance until the 1960s and felt out of place in this context,
and it is my understanding that the best term to use is whatever
the person in question damn well prefers. Raised the way she
was, Nettie would've known no other way to refer to these people. If you want a truly enlightening read, check your library
for *Black Indians: A Hidden Heritage* by William Loren Katz.
Their history has been all but erased, but Nettie had a people,
and they were integral to America's history. She's not as alone
as she thinks she is.

Last, I'd like to ask your forgiveness. You can't please all
of the people all of the time, and chances are, some of the
themes and terms in *Wake of Vultures* will cause outrage.
When I committed to respecting diversity in my books, I knew
that I would sometimes mess it up. When Nettie arrived in
my imagination, fully formed and thoroughly, unapologeti-
cally herself, I was intimidated by the thought of writing a
half-black, half-Comanche heroine raised in unspoken slavery

who self-identifies as a man and is attracted to both men and women. Surely people like Nettie have existed at every point of the world's history and in every place, and many of them have been sadly forced to hide their true selves and play along with the laws and morality of their times. Among many of America's native people, there is a gender variance called two-spirit that is and was highly respected; the Comanche did not recognize this identity. Dan and Winifred, however, are based on the Chiricahua, so Nettie's nature would've been familiar and welcome to them.

I hope I have done justice to Nettie's struggle and inner strength and made it clear that I believe a person can be whoever and whatever they choose to be.

Happy trails, and thanks for reading!

ACKNOWLEDGMENTS

Nettie can't always say her thanks, but I can.

Thanks, as always, to my husband, Craig, whose support, belief, and gifts of fine coffee keep me going. Thanks to my kids, parents, and family, especially to my folks for introducing me to *Lonesome Dove* at a very young age. Dad, can you find Gus in here?

Thanks to my amazing agent, Kate McKean, whose skills are nothing short of magic. Thanks to my editor, Devi Pillai— I should've known we'd make a great team when you bought me a drink in New Orleans and we bemoaned the bartender's lack of creativity. Thanks to Lindsey, Lauren, and everyone at Orbit.

Thanks to Chris from Jax on Twitter and Sean Patrick Kelly for playlist recommendations, to Mike Sheldon for a caffeine infusion when I needed it most, to Anamuk for chocolate hippos from far-off places, and to Julie and the Phoenix Comicon folks for my favorite cookies when I broke my back on my birthday. As always, thanks to Cherie Priest, Kevin Hearne, Chuck Wendig, Janice Hardy, the Holy Taco Church, and the Council for encouragement and a kick in the pants when needed. Thanks to all my author heroes who blurbed the book and to Matt Stover, in addition, for writing the fight scenes that

ACKNOWLEDGMENTS

have always informed my written brawls. If you haven't read *Heroes Die*, please do.

Thanks to Von Tuck for the rad author photo that makes me look like a spy.

Thanks to Beth Hickman, who helped me get back in the saddle after Polly bucked me off. You learn a lot of lessons with a broken spine, and I'm glad we're back on the trails.

Thanks to David Hale of Love Hawk Tattoo Studio, whose artwork helped inspire the book. I do believe the vulture quill on my forearm was part of the serendipity that brought Nettie to life.

This book was written to the music of Gangstagrass, the masterminds behind the *Justified* theme song and a fine bunch of folks who put on an amazing live show. See, Rench? I told you I'd put y'all in!

And remember: You don't have to be what they tell you to be.